PRAISE FOR

CHLOE LIESE

"Chloe Liese's writing is soulful, honest, and steamy in that swoon-worthy way that made me fall in love with romance novels in the first place! Her work is breathtaking, and I constantly look forward to more from her!"

—Ali Hazelwood, *New York Times* bestselling author of
Love on the Brain

"Quirky and delicious romance. I could curl up in Liese's writing for days, I love it so."

—Helen Hoang, *New York Times* bestselling author of
The Heart Principle

"There's no warmer hug than a Chloe Liese book."

—Rachel Lynn Solomon, *New York Times* bestselling author of
Weather Girl

"No one pairs sweet and steamy quite like Chloe Liese!"

—Alison Cochrun, author of *The Charm Offensive*

"Chloe Liese consistently writes strong casts brimming with people I want to hang out with in real life, and I'll happily gobble up anything she writes."

—Sarah Hogle, author of *You Deserve Each Other*

"Chloe Liese continues to reign as the master of steamy romance!"

—Sarah Adams, author of *The Cheat Sheet*

Always Only You

A BERGMAN BROTHERS NOVEL

CHLOE LIESE

BERKLEY ROMANCE
NEW YORK

BERKLEY ROMANCE
Published by Berkley
An imprint of Penguin Random House LLC
penguinrandomhouse.com

Library of Congress Cataloging-in-Publication Data

Names: Liese, Chloe, author.
Title: Always only you / Chloe Liese.
Description: First Berkley Romance edition. | New York: Berkley Romance, 2023. |
Series: The Bergman Brothers Identifiers: LCCN 2023026684 (print) |
LCCN 2023026685 (ebook) | ISBN 9780593642375 (trade paperback) |
ISBN 9780593642382 (ebook)
Subjects: LCGFT: Romance fiction. | Novels.
Classification: LCC PS3612.I3357 A79 2023 (print) | LCC PS3612.I3357 (ebook) |
DDC 813/.6—dc23/eng/20230622
LC record available at https://lccn.loc.gov/2023026684
LC ebook record available at https://lccn.loc.gov/2023026685

Always Only You was originally self-published, in different form, in 2020.

First Berkley Romance Edition: December 2023

Printed in the United States of America
1st Printing

Book design by Kristin del Rosario

For the misfits.
You are wonderfully made. You belong.
Always.

Dear Reader,

This story features characters with human realities who I
believe deserve to be seen more prominently in romance
through positive, authentic representation. As a neurodivergent
person living with chronic conditions, I am passionate about
writing feel-good romances affirming my belief that every
one of us is worthy and capable of happily ever after, if that's
what our heart desires.

Specifically, this story portrays a character who is autistic,
has rheumatoid arthritis, and lives with chronic pain. No
two people's experience of any condition will be the same,
but through my own experience and the insight of
authenticity readers, I have strived to create a character who
honors the nuances of those identities. This story also touches
on the loss of a parent in the past. Lastly, this story includes a
number of references to the wizarding world that was once
beloved by many but now is sullied by its creator's capacity
for harm against the trans community. That harm is
vehemently condemned by me and in this narrative, and
since this story's original publication in 2020, I no longer use
any wizarding world references in any of my books.

If any of these are sensitive topics for you, I hope you feel
comforted in knowing that loving, accepting relationships,
which make space for all of who we are and celebrate those
beautiful idiosyncrasies, are championed in this story.

XO,
Chloe

You want nothing but patience; or give it a
more fascinating name: call it hope.

—Jane Austen,
Sense and Sensibility

ONE

Frankie

Playlist: "Better By Myself," Hey Violet

Ren Bergman is too damn happy.

In the three years I've known him, I've seen him not smiling *twice*. Once, when he was unconscious on the ice, so I hardly think that counts, and the other time, when an extreme fan shoved her way through a crowd, yelling that she'd had his face tattooed on her lady bits because, and I quote, "a girl can dream."

But for those two uncharacteristically grim moments, Ren has been nothing but a ray of sunshine since the moment I met him. And whereas I myself am a little storm cloud, I recognize that Ren's Santa-on-uppers capacity for kindness makes my job easy.

As in-game social media coordinator for the Los Angeles Kings, I have my work cut out for me. Hockey players, you may have heard, are not always the most well-behaved humans. It inflates the ego, getting paid millions of dollars to play a game they love while tapping into their inner toddler. *Hit. Smash. Shove.*

With fortune comes fame and fawning females at their fingertips—those don't help matters, either. Yes, I'm aware that's a lot of *f* words. So sue me, I like alliteration.

While the PR department has the delightful privilege of putting out public-image fires, I do the day-to-day groundwork of cultivating our team's social media presence. Glued to the team, iPhone in hand, I make the guys accessible to fans by implementing

PR-sanctioned hype—informal interviews, jokes, tame pranks, photo ops, gifs, even the occasional viral meme.

I also document informal charitable outings geared toward our most underrepresented fans.

It's not in my exact job description, but I'm a big believer in breaking down stigma around differences we tend to ostracize, so I wormed my way into the process. I don't just want to make our hockey team more accessible to its fans; I want us to be a team that leads its fans in advancing accessibility itself.

That makes me sound sweet, doesn't it? But the truth is nobody on the team would call me that. In fact, my reputation is quite the opposite: Frank the Crank. And while this bad rap is formed on partial truths and ample misunderstandings, I've taken the moniker and run with it. In the end, it makes everyone's lives easier.

I do my job with resting bitch face. I'm blunt, all business. I like my routines, I focus on my work, and I sure as shit don't get close with the players. Yes, we get along for the most part. But you have to have boundaries when you're a woman in the near-constant company of two dozen testosterone-soaked male athletes—athletes who know I'm in their corner but who also know Frankie is a thundercloud you don't get too close to, unless you want to get zapped.

Just like rain clouds and sunshine share the sky, Ren and I work well together. Whenever PR has a killer concept and I come up with a social media home run—pardon my mixing sports metaphors—Ren is my man.

Campy skit in the locker room to raise money for the inner-city sports programs? There's Ren and his megawatt smile, delivering lines with effortless charm. Photo shoot for the local animal shelter's fundraiser? Ren's laughing as kitties claw up his massive shoulders and puppies whine for his attention, lapping his chin while he lavishes them with that wide, sunny grin.

Sometimes it's practically stomach turning. I still get queasy when I remember the time Ren sat with a young cancer patient. Turning white as a sheet, given his fear of needles, he told her the world's lamest knock-knock jokes while he donated blood and she had her bloodwork done. So they could be brave together.

Cue the collective female swoon.

I shouldn't complain. I shouldn't. Because, truly, the guy's a nonstop-scoring, smiling, six-foot-three hunk of happy who makes my job much easier than it otherwise would be. But there's only so much sunshine that a grump like me can take. And for three years, Ren has been pushing my limit.

In the locker room, I scowl down at my phone, handling an asshole troll on the team's Twitter page, while I weave through the maze of half-naked men. I've seen it all a thousand times, and I could care less—

"*Oof*," I grunt as my face connects with a bare, solid chest.

"Sorry, Frankie." Strong hands steady me by my shoulders. It's the happy man himself, Ren Bergman. But this time, he's shirtless, which Ren never is. He's the most modest of the bunch.

I'm tallish, which places my gaze squarely in line with Ren's chiseled-from-stone pectoral muscles. And flat, dusky nipples, which tighten as the air chills his damp skin. I try to avert my eyes, but they have a mind of their own, drifting lower and lower to his six-, no, eight-, no—dammit, his *a-lot-of*-pack.

My swallow is so loud it practically echoes in the room. "I-it's okay."

Well, hello there, husky, sexed-up escort voice.

I clear my throat and tear my eyes away from his body. "No worries," I tell him. "My fault." Lifting my phone, I wiggle it from side to side. "Serves me right for traipsing around, nose-deep in Twitter."

Ren smiles, which just spirals my mood even farther south. The amount of dopamine that this guy's brain makes daily is probably my annual sum total.

Smoothing a hand over his play-off beard, he then brings it to the back of his neck and scratches, which I've learned over the past few years is his nervous tic. His bicep bunches, one rounded shoulder flexes, and I try not to stare at his massive lats, which give his upper body a powerful V shape, knitting themselves to his ribs, and a long, trim waist.

The visual feast results in a temporary short circuit, wiping my thoughts clean but for a two-word refrain.

Wowy. Muscles.

It must be because whereas the rest of the team are practically nudists, Ren always disappears for a shower and comes back rocking a fresh suit, crisp shirt, and tie. I've never seen this much Ren Bergman nakedness. Ever.

And I'm riveted.

"You're rather unclothed," I blurt.

He blushes and drops his hand to his side. "True." Leaning in, he lifts one eyebrow and says conspiratorially, "This *is* the locker room, you know."

I resist the fierce urge to tweak his nipple. "Don't sass me, Bergman. I wasn't finished." I take a step back because, holy hell, does that man smell good. Fresh soap and a warm spiciness chasing it. Something enticingly male. "You don't *normally* waltz around naked like—"

Kris streaks by bare-assed on a high-pitched shriek, whipping his towel playfully at Ren as he passes. I lift a hand in the doofus's direction. "Schar makes my point for me."

Ren's blush deepens as he glances away. "You're right. I don't normally traipse around like this. I just forgot something I needed."

"What did you forget? Your suit's right back there." I can see it from here, hanging near the showers. Smart man. Steamy air takes out the wrinkles.

Dammit, now I'm thinking about Ren taking steamy showers. "Well, uh . . ." he says. "I forgot what goes *underneath* the suit."

"Oh."

My cheeks heat. Good grief. Of course. The guy forgot his boxers—*ooh, or maybe briefs?* I need to stop thinking about this—and here I am holding him up like it's the Spanish Inquisition.

As if he can read my dirty thoughts, Ren pins me with those unnaturally intense eyes—catlike and pale as the ice he skates on. "I'll just go get them, then. . . ."

"Great idea." I step to one side as Ren goes the same way. We both laugh awkwardly. Then Ren tries for the other side, just as I do, too. "Jesus," I mumble. So mortifying. Were the earth to open up and swallow me whole, this moment would be significantly improved.

"Here." Ren's hands land warm on my shoulders again, his touch gentle, unlike that of most of the guys on the team, who seem incapable of not knocking into me like they're the Hulk. While I flinch before incoming contact with them, there's something graceful and controlled about Ren.

"I'll go this way," he says. "You go that way."

Like a revolving door, we finally manage to move past each other. Once Ren's strolling away, I'd like to say I don't glance over my shoulder to ogle the guy's backside from the revealing contours of a locker room towel, but I'm not in the habit of lying.

"Fraaaaankie," an obnoxious voice yells.

That's Matt Maddox. Evil yin to Ren's pure-goodness yang.

"Jesus, keep me strong," I mutter.

In our little nature metaphor, in which I'm the thundercloud and Ren's the sun, Matt's the reeking sulfurous geyser that everyone runs away from. While Ren is warm and always gentlemanly, Matt is, in short, a natural disaster of Grade A douchery.

Matt crosses the locker room and closes in on me, not for the first time. Not by a long stretch.

Bracing myself for impact, I pocket my phone and prepare to mouth-breathe. I'm used to the stank of our locker room, but post-game, the guys smell extra ripe, and I have a sensitive sniffer. I gag in here regularly.

Slinging a stinky arm around me, Matt jars my whole body. I clench my jaw and try not to wince. "Where's your phone?" he says. "I think we need a selfie, Frank."

I duck and shuffle backward, out of his reach. "And *I* think you need a shower. You do your job, Maddox. I'll do mine."

He rakes his sweat-soaked dark hair back from his face and sighs. "One of these days, I'm gonna crack you."

"I'm a tough nut, champ." Turning, I unearth my phone, swipe open to the camera, and angle it over my head so it cuts out Matt and catches the guys behind me. Nobody's in a state of extensive un-dress anymore—a few bare chests, most everyone almost done put-ting on their suits. Fans eat that shit for breakfast. "Smile, boys!"

They all whip their heads my way, plastering on dutiful grins as they say, "Cheese!"

I have them so well trained.

"Thank you." Pocketing my phone, I head toward the exit. "Don't forget, drinks—not in excess—and burgers at Louie's. Uber if you plan on getting shit-faced anyway."

On a chorus of *"Yes, Frankie"* echoing behind me, I shove open the door, buoyed by the satisfied purpose of a woman whose life is ordered and predictable. Just how I like it.

———

At Louie's, I throw off my blazer and push up my sleeves in prepa-ration for the meal I ordered. Suits and greasy bar food aren't the best combination, but there's never time to change after my postgame duties before we head out, so I'm stuck sporting my usual work outfit.

Like the rest of the staff and players, on game day, I wear a suit. The same one, every game. Black peplum blazer, matching ankle-cut dress slacks, and a white dress shirt with black buttons. My cropped slacks show off my Nike Cortez sneakers in our signature black and silver, and my nails are of course painted their usual glossy black with silver shimmer on the middle finger, because it makes flipping people off extra festive. The whole look is very Wednesday Addams, with a similar and intended repelling effect. People leave me alone. Which is how I like it.

"Double cheeseburger," Joe, our bartender, says.

"Thanks." I nod and pull the plate my way.

Nice thing about Louie's is they give our orders first preference— bunch of hungry jocks need food *stat* after a game—so not ten minutes after arriving, sleeves rolled up, grease drips down my wrists as I bite into my burger. I hold it over my plate and lean to trap my drink's straw with my mouth, taking a long pull of root beer.

Louie's is one of those hole-in-the-wall gems of an LA burger joint that feel fewer and farther between with each passing, granola-crunching year. I swear, even just four years ago when I moved here, LA was still the land of the greasy burger and the world's best street food. Now it's all juice bars and whatever shit Goop says will flatten your stomach.

As root beer fizzes happily in my belly, I extract a pickle from my sandwich and crunch on it.

"Life's too short to give up burgers."

Willa grunts in agreement from her seat next to me. She's dating Ren's brother Ryder, and they try to come down for a handful of games each season, so this isn't the first time Willa and I have talked, but it is the first time we've bonded over the sad turn for the healthier that Southern Californian food has taken. Or more accurately, I've been monologuing about it for five minutes straight while she grunts and eats and seems to agree with me. I tend to fixate on something, then talk longer than most people about it, which I've learned annoys people sometimes, bores them others, and every once in a while manages to interest them similarly.

Unfortunately, I usually only recognize in retrospect when I've monologued. I swear, I'm not making that up. I cannot tell when it's happening. Everyone knows the saying "time flies when you're having fun," and that's the only way I can explain how my awareness works when I'm in a groove, talking about something that I like—I have no sense of how long it's been.

Because this isn't my first time around Willa, though, I know she and I are comfortable enough with each other that she'd shut me up or change the subject if she wanted to. We've only hung out a few times, since, as a professional soccer player, she's pretty busy, but we've clicked at the handful of games she and Ryder have attended.

"Glorious burgers," she says thickly around a bite. "I could never let them go. I mean, Coach would kill me for eating this, but goddamn, there is nothing better than a double cheeseburger after a long day. I don't care what my carbon footprint is. Kill that cow and get it in my belly."

Ryder leans away from his conversation adjacent to us and says to her, "I'll overlook that environmentally insensitive comment because you're a good kisser, Sunshine, and I cook plant-based for us eighty percent of the time."

Sheepishly, Willa smiles up at him. "Sometimes I wish those doodads around your ears didn't work *quite* so well, Ry."

Ryder wears hearing aids, which I can barely see amid his thick blond hair. Like Ren, Ryder is a handsome guy. Short beard, bright green eyes, and Ren's cheekbones.

Willa and Ryder live up in Washington State, where Willa plays for Reign FC, and their place is nestled in the middle of the woods. To look at them, you can totally picture it. Ryder gives off an outdoorsy vibe with his plaid flannel shirt, faded jeans, and boots. Willa fits with him in her warm, practical clothes—a UCLA hoodie and ripped-up jeans, no makeup in sight to accentuate her big amber eyes and pouty lips. She has an incredible head of hair that's untamed waves and curls, no product, no styling. Just wilderness beauty.

Willa's as au naturel on the inside as she is on the outside, and that is my kind of person. The people I get along with typify a "what you see is what you get" mindset, and in that way, Willa's very like my two good friends in LA, Annie and Lo. Making friends doesn't come easily to me, but I feel like I'm becoming friends with down-to-earth, cheeseburger-loving Willa Sutter.

Ryder grins at her, making Willa's smile widen. I drop my burger to my plate with a splat and drag a fry through ketchup. "Good grief. Just kiss already."

Ryder laughs. Planting his lips softly on Willa's temple, he then turns back to his conversation, a half circle of men made up of Ren; Rob, our captain; François, our goalie; and Lin, a promising rookie defender.

"Sorry about that." Willa's cheeks turn bright pink as she sips her lemonade. "We're still in that 'I really like you and always want to jump your bones' phase."

I wave it away, fry in hand. "I'm the one who should apologize. My brain's an unfiltered place. Most of what it thinks tends to come barreling out of my mouth. I didn't mean to be rude. You're in love and happy. Nothing to be sorry for."

Willa smiles as she picks up her burger. "Thanks. I mean, I used to find it gross when I saw people in public looking so in love. I always thought, 'Is it *that* hard to keep that kind of hanky-panky for home?'" She takes a big bite of burger and says around it, "Then I met Ryder and realized, yeah, with the right person, it's that hard."

My burger catches in my throat. What a terrifying possibility, to find yourself so attracted to someone you can't *help* but love them. I try to smile to show her I'm okay, but I'm incapable of an involuntarily grin. Every time I try, I end up giving the impression that I'm about to throw up.

Willa laughs. "You look like I just told you that's dog shit between your hamburger bun."

Bingo.

I finally clear my throat and stare down at my food. "I, uh . . ." My stance on relationships is hard to explain. And while I like Willa, it's not something I'm ready to get into with her.

She nudges me. "Hey, I'm just teasing you." Tipping her head, she stares at me for a long minute. "You're not a relationship gal?"

I shake my head, then take a bite of food. "No, I'm not. No knocks against them. They're just not a good fit for me."

"Yeah. I was very against them myself when I met the lumberjack." She throws a thumb over her shoulder to the group of men where Ryder stands. Ren laughs at something he says, making Ryder laugh, too.

They're nearly twins in profile, except that everything about Ren just screams at me to look at him. Unruly russet waves, long nose, and sharp cheekbones. That play-off beard he somehow keeps neat, so I can still see the hint of full lips that twist in wry amusement. His eyes crinkle when he laughs, and he has this habit of clutching his chest and bending over slightly, like someone's capacity to amuse him goes straight to his heart.

So happy. So carefree. What's it like to live like that? To be so unburdened?

I have no clue. In past relationships, *I've* been the burden. A set of issues to be handled, complications to be managed. Back home, people treated me like a problem, not a person. And so I came to two conclusions. First, it was time to move away, and second, for the sake of protecting myself from repeating that humiliation, my heart is best left alone, safe under lock and key.

So I wear black. I don't smile. I hide behind a heavy curtain of dark hair and a mile-long to-do list. I welcome the witch metaphors, walk around with a frown, and grunt in response whenever possible. I don't make friends with the neighbors or attend team picnics. I stay safe in my solitude, cold and untouchable.

For damn good reason. I will not be treated how I was ever again.

Willa pats my hand gently, then pops a fry in her mouth. "Want to know what made me change my mind?"

I glance up at her. "No."

That makes her laugh again. "Ah, Frankie. You're a keeper. Rooney's going to love you."

"Rooney?"

"My best friend from college. She's at Stanford now. Biomedical law."

A rare feat for me, I manage to bite my tongue and not mention my own plans for law school.

Yes, I sent my application to UCLA months ago. Yes, I obsessed and slaved over my application, and I'm practically positive it's perfect. But I haven't received my acceptance letter.

I keep my mouth shut and suck down some root beer.

"One of the Bergman brood will inevitably have a birthday soon," Willa says. From what I can remember of what he's said about his family, Ren has a daunting number of siblings, most of whom live nearby. He's one of those rare athletes who got drafted by his hometown and never wants to leave it. Which, to this ex–New Yorker who deliberately moved cross-country, is mind-blowing.

"Ziggy, is it?" Willa stares up at the ceiling, going through some sort of mental calendar. "Yeah, I think Ziggy's next. Once Ry and I got together, especially once we moved to Tacoma, Rooney started coming to all the Bergman family parties to have the most time to see me and catch up. She's an extroverted only child, so she fell in love with the big family, and now she's an honorary Bergman. Come to Ziggy's party, and you'll meet Rooney then."

I choke on my soda. "Uh, I don't know why I'd be there."

Willa pats my back gently. "Because I just invited you. I need solidarity at these things, Frankie. All these Bergmans, Rooney, too—none of them are surly or maladapted enough. Not like you and me."

"Thanks?"

"I need a kindred cantankerous spirit. Seriously, come next time. You and Ren are friends. His mom's always nagging him to bring a lady. I bet he'd love to have you come along."

There are so many stupefying components to what she just said, I'm coming up short of words. I blink away, shuffling my fries around my plate.

Willa picks up her food but pauses before she takes a bite. "Also, from one crotchety soul to another, should you ever find someone who makes you want to reconsider your stance on relationships, I'm here for you, okay? Just say the word."

TWO

Frankie

Playlist: "How to Be a Heartbreaker," MARINA

Before I have a chance to respond to Willa's unsettling offer, Matt, the Master of Douchical Mischief, drops next to me at the bar. I can smell beer on him.

Reaching right over me, Matt offers Willa his hand. "You're the soccer star. Renford's sister-in-law," he slurs.

"Not quite. Just Willa." Shaking his hand, she quickly releases it, then wipes her palm on her jeans beneath the bar.

Matt's arm lands with a hard thud around my shoulders, nearly knocking me into my food. "Frank. Frank, Frank, Frank." He sighs. "When are you gonna stop with the ice-queen act?"

I straighten and try to shrug off his arm, but he just locks it tighter. "Frank," he says. "We both know there's something here—"

"Matt. Get your arm off of me before I crush your nuts with the Elder Wand."

The Elder Wand is what I named my cane.

Yeah, I'm twenty-six, and I use a cane. It looks like smoked glass, but instead it's acrylic and totally badass. It's also great for smacking dweebs like Maddox in the nuts.

Matt drops his arm and frowns. "I don't get you. You're so hot and cold."

"No, I'm not, Matt. I run as consistently frigid as a high-end freezer. Don't put this on me. Just because I'm a female who's regularly in your vicinity and not fangirling over you like the many troubled souls who buy your jockstraps on eBay does not mean I secretly desire to screw you into next week."

Matt frowns. "You don't?"

"I don't."

"What the hell, Frank?" he yells. Loud enough that everyone in the private room we're in stops talking for a second and glances over at us.

"Matt, I think you should order an Uber now."

"I drove," he growls, signaling Joe.

Seeing Matt call him, Joe walks toward us. When I catch his eye and gently shake my head, Joe stops, pivots, then turns back to continue washing glasses.

Matt curses under his breath. "Did you just shut me off, Frank?"

"Yes." I turn and smile apologetically at Willa as I otherwise ignore Matt. Tipping my cup, I take a drink of root beer.

"Frank." He grabs my wrist, which sends the root beer flying from my hand and landing with an ice-cold splatter all over my shirt.

I hiss at the shock of it. "Jesus, Maddox."

Suddenly a large hand grabs the back of Matt's shirt and wrenches him off the barstool so violently, he tumbles to the floor. Ren bends, sweeping up my blazer, which fell, too, and immediately throws it over my shoulders. When he straightens, my mouth falls open.

Ren Bergman is *really* not smiling.

And not-smiling Ren Bergman is a whole new animal. No, *man*.

Move aside, Erik the Red. There's a new enraged ginger Viking come to slay, and Lord help me, cinnamon sexpots are my weakness. I've been relying on the fluorescents we work under to dull Ren's hair to burnished bronze. I tell myself every time I see him that he's not actually a *ginger* god of ice hockey glory. He's a brassy blond god of ice hockey glory. It helped.

Marginally.

But now I have to face the facts: Ren's hair is the gorgeous copper of a fading sunset, and the anger radiating off of him is equally breathtaking.

I gape at him, Ren the Red, vengefully sexy, and command my jaws to snap shut. It's time to find my inner feminist. To bolster my walls. Ren throwing down on my behalf should not be affecting me like this. Especially given my history.

Archaic male demonstrations of protectiveness are not sexy. Archaic male demonstrations of protectiveness are not sexy. Archaic—

Dammit, this is sexy, and my body knows it. I can't deny it any more than I can deny my Harry Potter panties are now as wet as a rainy day at Hogwarts. Ren swivels his pale eyes, a stunning wintry blue-gray, right on Maddox. They're cold fury as they glare at him, then return to me.

"Joey, a towel, please." His voice holds a tone of command I've heard Ren use on the ice countless times before, but never in any conversation involving me. My belly does a somersault as I watch a towel fly his way, before Ren immediately sets it in my hands. "Here."

"Th-thanks," I mutter stupidly, dabbing my shirtfront. I'm already shivering from this cold-as-balls wet shirt plastered to my skin.

Abruptly, Ren lurches toward the bar. I glance up and realize it's Matt who slammed into him.

"Maddox," I snap. "Stop!"

Ren shoves him off, spins, and deftly grabs Matt by the throat. "You fucking *torture* her. It's enough. Leave her alone."

Wow. Ren never swears. Well, not like that, at least not in public or with the team.

Elizabethan oaths are more his speed. *Hugger-mugger. Malignancy. Canker-blossom.* He's subtle about it, muttering them under his breath, but I have exceptionally good hearing, and since I caught the first one, I'm always craning to listen when I'm around him, hoping I'll overhear another.

The worst part? He's good at it. Like, I have to feign a coughing jag every time he uses them, or I'd run the risk of laughing, maybe even smiling, and then my reputation as resident ice-queen hardass would be shot.

Ren's still throttling Matt. Perhaps it's time to intervene before our most valuable player gets himself benched for misconduct.

"The chivalry's unnecessary, Bergman," I tell him. Standing slowly off the stool, I swallow a groan as my hips scream in disapproval.

We don't like barstools, Frankie, my joints holler. *You know this.*

I wrap my hand around Ren's forearm and try to ignore the soft fiery hairs beneath, the powerful tendon and muscle flexing under my grip. "Please, Ren. He's drunk. It's pointless."

"Oh, there would be a point." Ren glares at Matt and shakes him by the windpipe. "He'd learn a lesson if I beat his ass."

"Hey now." Rob slides in.

I sigh in relief. "Where've you been?"

"I had to take a leak." Rob manages to pull Ren's hand away from Matt's throat. "Can't a guy piss and not come back to the kids trying to kill each other? Ren Bergman, resorting to violence. Never thought I'd see the day. I'm sure Maddox deserves whatever you were about to do, but let's handle this like adults."

Matt leers at him. "Bergman's just jealous."

I rub the pounding spot between my eyes. "*Jealous* would imply he has something to envy between us, Maddox." Or that Ren even cares who does or doesn't hit on me. Why would he?

"Now, Matthew." Rob cups his hand around Matt's neck and pulls him aside. "You're catching an Uber home. You're going to sober up. Then, tomorrow, at practice, you're going to apologize to Frankie."

Rob catches my eye and furrows his brow. The first few times he did it after I started working for the team, I thought he was angry at me. That's because I suck at reading facial expressions.

How, you ask, does someone with that kind of interpersonal hang-up work in social media? She watches lots of sports interviews and sitcoms to memorize the context and meaning for as much human behavior as possible, that's how. But sometimes even that's not enough, and I find myself in the dark. That's when I simply have to ask. Which is what I had to do with Rob. Now I know that this particular expression is a nonverbal check-in.

"I'm okay," I tell him.

He nods and yanks Matt away. Ren's still glaring in their direction as they disappear down the back hall. When he turns and looks at me, pinning me with those icy eyes, a shiver rolls up my spine.

"Are you all right?" he asks quietly. His voice is deep, warm.

"I'm fine, Ren." Except for my soaked Harry Potter panties. And my shredded emotional boundaries, after seeing his pissed-off, fiery alter ego that's made forgotten corners of me blaze to life.

Leaning against the stool, I reach for my purse and signal to Joe that I want to square up.

Ren's still watching me. I feel his gaze like sunshine, heating my skin. "You're staring at me."

Ren blinks away. "Sorry. I'm just . . . concerned."

"Concerned?"

"He grabbed you, spilled your drink all over you."

"Thanks." I sweep a hand down my drenched front. "I hadn't noticed."

Raking a hand through his hair in frustration, Ren tugs at the wavy ends. "He could have hurt you."

I slide my card across the bar toward Joe and stare at Ren. People normally assume that I'm helpless, let alone when a handsy, over-sized drunk athlete throws himself my way. Here's Ren, referencing that physical vulnerability. This is when the usual embarrassment and anger should arrive.

But it doesn't come.

Because as Ren looks at me, as I process his words, I can't recall a single moment Ren's ever acted or spoken like he thinks I can't take care of myself. He's never hovered behind me like I'm going to take a tumble. He doesn't talk to me like I'm an invalid. Saying that Maddox could have hurt me isn't a reflection on my weakness. It's an indictment on Matt's misuse of his strength.

Ren's eyes lock on mine. My heart pounds against my ribs, and my throat dries up.

It's too much. I blink away, and when I glance back, Ren's gaze has finally shifted to my mouth. A jolt of heat sears my lips, slides down my throat, and lands warm in my belly.

Someone's hand rests on my back, breaking the moment. I don't know Willa well enough to read her face, but thankfully she speaks before I'm left wondering any longer. "I was hoping you'd get to use the Elder Wand," she says. "You okay?"

"You're not the only one who's disappointed. That guy's overdue for a dick smacking." I thank Joe when he returns my card and receipt, which I sign with a flourish. "But, yeah, I'm okay. Just tired. I should head home."

Not that I'm sure how that's happening. Normally, I drive myself everywhere and burn through audiobooks to pass the staggering amount of time I spend in LA traffic. But my car's check-engine light was on yesterday, so it's in the shop. Rob drove me to Louie's and would, I'm sure, gladly drive me home as well, but he's still handling Maddox, meaning I have to wait or catch a ride with someone else. I don't do late-night taxi rides alone.

"Frankie," Ren says. "Let me drive you."

I glance up at Ren and commence a Frankie stare for the books. His eyes are luminous, gray as fog, the kind that blots out your world but for a few feet in front of you, that makes you question what's up or down. So many times, I've had the unsettling feeling I could get just as lost in them.

"Let him drive you," Willa says. She smiles while threading her arms through her jacket.

Ryder steps behind her and helps her get it up over her shoulders, giving her arms an affectionate squeeze as he plants a kiss on top of her head. A small, intimate gesture brimming with so much love, I feel like I just saw something I shouldn't have.

"I may be a little rusty on my LA geography," she says, "but Hawthorne's on the way. We're staying at Ren's for the night, and he's driving us, too. It'll be a dance party in the new van."

My attention snaps to Ren. "You bought a van?"

Ren's cheeks redden, but he stands tall. "Heck yes, I bought a van. There's no shame in owning a Honda Odyssey."

Willa clears her throat and grins, while Ryder's shoulders shake with what sounds like laughter. He hides it behind a cough into his fist.

I recognize Ren's posture as signifying defensiveness and immediately feel bad for opening my mouth. This happens sometimes. I ask a question, and people hear . . . *more* than a question. They hear criticism or judgment or teasing. I've given up trying to explain that my brain isn't wired for that subtlety, that I couldn't imply those kinds of layers of meaning if I wanted to, because one too many times, people haven't believed me. They hear excuses rather than context. So I stopped trying and told myself to quit caring when I'm misunderstood.

Now only those closest to me are trusted with knowing the real reason Frankie has dubious success with sarcasm and picking up on jokes. Why she works resting bitch face and deadpan delivery, wears earplugs at the games, and is obsessively fascinated with Harry Potter, root beer gummies, NHL statistics, linguistics, knee socks, and only wearing gray-scale clothing, among many other things . . .

Autism.

"Ooh!" Willa says. "I call dibs on the music."

Ryder's laugh-cough abruptly becomes a groan. "When Willa DJs, I wish my ear doodads didn't work so well either—*oof.*"

Willa slugs him playfully in the stomach, then grasps his jaw and plants a firm kiss right on his mouth. "Asshole lumberjack. You're just looking for a fight."

He grins and wraps an arm around Willa as she drops back on her heels. "Maybe I am."

They walk out ahead of us, waving good night to the rest of the team and their families. A balmy night breeze slips through the door as they head outside, and Ren steps close to me.

Carefully, he unhooks my cane off the bar ledge and, bowing with a flourish, tips it toward me.

"Your scepter, my liege."

I feel a rare smile lift my cheeks. "I have heard rumors that you're a closeted Shakespeare dork, Bergman."

"They got it all wrong." He straightens and smiles. "There's nothing closeted about it."

A surprised laugh spills out of me, and Ren's grin widens, brighter than the California noontime sun. But for once, that sunshine smile doesn't bother this grump one bit.

THREE

Ren

Playlist: "For the Time Being," Erlend Øye & La Comitiva

After walking Frankie to her door—complete with a reminder, in her deadpan delivery, that she's a big girl who can make it from the car to her house—I hop back into the van. She locks herself into her canary-yellow bungalow on 133rd, and I see lights flicker on in the front room before her silhouette shortens as she walks deeper into the house.

Enjoying my super-fancy rear-drive cameras, I pull out of Frankie's driveway.

"Soooo." Willa grins at me, batting her eyelashes. After Frankie vacated the shotgun seat of the van, Willa hugged her goodbye, hopped into it, and is now curled up, staring at me expectantly.

I hope this isn't going where I think it is.

"Renny Roo." Willa leans closer. "We need to talk about Frankie."

My hands death-grip the steering wheel. "What about her?"

"Uh, about how I *like* her. I want to keep her. I love her bone-dry humor, she knows *everything* possible about Harry Potter, including the latest horror that is its author's Twitter drivel—"

"What did she do now?" Ryder asks from the back seat.

"Just showed that you can write a magical world brimming with complex, label-defying characters and still be a trans-exclusionary feminist disappointment."

I sigh. "What's wrong with people?"

Willa shrugs. "Who the fuck knows. Power corrupts. You'd think writing about it would have given her a little awareness."

Ryder and I grunt in agreement.

"Back to Frankie," Willa says. "Did you see how she demolished that burger at Louie's? I want a woman in the family who destroys bar food like me. Freya's too health-conscious, and Ziggy eats like a bird. So go back to that front door, find your inner Viking, throw her over your shoulder, and tell her she's stuck with us."

Willa and Ryder aren't engaged, but it's only a matter of time. She's family now and is clearly making plans for in-laws down the line. Wiggling into a new position, she sets her feet on the dashboard and gives me a saucy grin.

I can't afford to even indirectly acknowledge my interest in Frankie, because if I tell Willa, it's telling the world, which is the last thing I want to do. I change the radio station so we don't miss bluegrass hour. "I don't care how well-insured those feet are, Winifred. Get them off my dash."

Willa sighs and drops her feet. "Focus. Talk about Frankie."

"I'm focusing. On the road." Clicking on my right-turn signal, I check my mirrors and turn off of Frankie's street onto Hawthorne Boulevard.

"Dude," Ryder huffs. "*Left* onto Hawthorne, then right onto Inglewood. It's so much faster."

I glare at him through the rearview mirror for a microsecond. "Will you ever not back-seat drive?"

"Nope." Willa grins over her shoulder at him. "When we first moved to Tacoma, we had so many fights because he was telling me my business from shotgun. Now I just let him drive and pretend he's my chauffeur. It was that or dismember him."

Ryder smirks. "I didn't mind fighting in the car with you. It generally led to consequences I was more than happy to suffer."

"Okay." I throw up a hand. "This van is a G-rated space."

That makes Willa snort-laugh. "I still can't get over the fact that you bought a van." She sighs happily. "It's so you."

"Between the guys on the team and Shakespeare Club, I'm always driving a handful of people somewhere. Plus, it has tons of room for my equipment—"

"And those babies you and Frankie are going to make."

If I weren't a freakishly coordinated athlete, I would have crashed the car.

"Willa," Ryder says from the back seat. "Go easy on him."

"*Easy?* I don't know what that word means." Poking my shoulder, Willa leans in. "So, tell me, how far do you two go back?"

"She started working for the Kings one year before me."

"So you've known her your entire professional career. Hmm." Willa narrows her eyes and strokes an invisible goatee. "Interesting."

"Willa," Ryder says warningly.

She makes a shooing motion at Ryder, as if he's an annoying gnat, not a guy built like a linebacker who has no problem tickling her until she pees herself. "And have you or have you not refrained from dating since you signed with the Kings?" she prods me.

I studiously focus on the road. "Like most rookies, I've spent virtually every moment since I signed focused on my career."

"But you're not a rookie anymore."

"Doesn't mean I suddenly have time for romance."

She scowls. "I don't buy that. You got your kicks in college, didn't you? You balanced the demands of Division I hockey, academics, and romance *then*."

"I didn't have a girlfriend in college." Pressing a bunch of buttons without breaking my focus on the road, I finally find the one that lowers my window. Willa's interrogation is making me sweat.

"That's an evasion if I ever heard one. The point is you made time to date. Or, shall I say, for the benefit of your Renaissance romanticism, thou didst woo and court."

I roll my eyes. "Forsooth, Wilhelmina, sometimes 'I desire that we be better strangers.'"

Willa scrunches her nose. "Huh?" She works it out and smacks my chest. "Hey, that's rude. And untrue. You love me. I'm your favorite almost sister-in-law."

"You're my *only* almost sister-in-law."

"Renny Roo, I will not be distracted. You like her, don't you? It's why you haven't dated anyone since you joined the team."

I stare at the road. Why does it take this long to drive a few miles to Manhattan Beach?

Willa sighs dreamily. "Gah. It's romantic as hell. You're pining for her."

Ryder pats my shoulder sympathetically from the back seat. I don't expect him to chime in.

He's the quietest of all of us, and when Willa's on a roll, there's no stopping her, anyway. "Willis." I glance over at her as we wait at the red light on Sepulveda. "Frankie is incredibly serious about her work. I've known her for three years, and in that entire time, it's been clear that I'm just one of the guys to her, a part of the job. A job with clear rules discouraging staff-player dating, at that."

Willa stares at me as the light turns green, which saves me from meeting those intense amber eyes. "Interesting answer." She sits back and opens her window, letting in a new gust of warm spring air.

"Why was that interesting?" Ryder asks.

Willa grins. "Because it really wasn't an answer at all."

———

Unlike most of my peers—and trust me, they hate me for this—I didn't grow up dreaming of playing professional hockey. I come from a big Swedish American family of footballers, as Mom's side of the family says in Europe, or here in the US, soccer players.

Ryder, who's next in birth order after me, was playing for UCLA with deserved confidence he'd go pro after, but bacterial meningitis damaged his hearing and equilibrium so severely his freshman year, his career ended there. Freya played at UCLA, too, but hung up her cleats afterward, got her doctorate, and began practicing physical therapy. She didn't love soccer enough to make it her life, she said. Axel, my older brother, kept up with it through high school and still enjoys playing in a competitive co-ed league.

My two younger brothers Viggo and Oliver are both excellent, but only Oliver is playing college level, while Viggo decided not to go to college and now plays competitive rec like Axel. The baby in our family, Ziggy, is eons beyond her high school peers' skill level and plays for the U-20 Women's National Team. She's determined to be on the women's Olympic team one day, and if I doubted her ability—which I don't—just her persevering nature would convince me that she'll get there.

As for me, I played and liked soccer. I was good at it. But I never *loved* it. When I hit high school, I wasn't close with anyone on the soccer team, and while I excelled at goalie, my heart wasn't in it. I was a recent transplant from Washington State. I didn't fit in with the Cali boys, this gangly, dorky, six-foot ginger who liked poetry and live theater, who didn't feel comfortable talking about girls the way the other guys did, who hated the petty power games and awful way guys treated each other in the locker room and hallways.

During my sophomore year, at some party my parents were hosting, my dad's colleague took a look at me, apparently saw potential, and asked if I was interested in trying hockey. In his downtime, Dr. Evans coached a league of guys my age and said he'd give me personal lessons, see if I liked it.

There was grace and fluidity to hockey that I'd been missing in soccer that unfurled inside me the moment I laced up a pair of skates and took to the ice. When I got that stick in my hand, the cool silence of a rink to myself, the puck in front of me, it was like

I'd finally found my natural habitat. I came *alive* skating, playing hockey. I still do.

Every day I pinch myself that this is my job. That I get paid to play a game I love, to be a role model to little kids, and to contribute to my community. I also pinch myself that I get to see Frankie every day I work.

She's one of the first people I met when I signed. After meetings running through legalese and expectations and schedule and logistics, there was Frankie in the doorway, strutting in with a smoke-colored cane and fresh Nikes in the team's colors. Looking at her, I felt something slam inside my chest as air rushed out of me, more brutal than any check against the boards.

She sat down across from me, explaining what I'd need to do to cultivate my social media presence, how to tweet and post on Instagram, how to engage, how to complement what she did during practices and games.

My favorite moment was when she gave me a critical once-over and said, "I apologize in advance that I have to say this, but if you post a dick pic on any social media platform or send one to any woman's inbox, when I'm through with you, you won't have a dick to *pic* anymore. Get my meaning?"

She was courteous and entirely professional after that, like she hadn't just threatened to castrate me, albeit for good reason. I remember trying to listen to what she was saying while struggling not to stare at her mouth. I still struggle with that.

The door to the treatment room swings open, followed by a familiar "Ren Zenzero."

ZENzehrro is how Frankie says it.

My head snaps up from the massage table. I have no idea why she calls me that. I know it sounds Italian, and I've almost googled it a dozen times, but I'm kind of scared to find out what it means. I just know when she uses the word, it rolls off her tongue in a way that makes my whole body tighten, the hair on my neck and arms stand on end. It sounds effortless and emphatic, only further evidence that Frankie is very much Italian, as if her name wasn't a dead giveaway.

Francesca Zeferino. Though if you call her anything other than Frank or Frankie, she'll twist your nipple until you burst into tears. Her hair is a sheet of coffee-colored silk that falls halfway down her back. She has forever-golden skin that glows like she's lit from within, big hazel eyes, thick dark lashes, rosy lips, and a ridiculously deep dimple in her left cheek.

Frankie stops at the side of the massage table, lifts her cane, and smacks my ass with it.

"Ow!" I yelp.

John, one of our trainers, is used to Frankie's authoritarian approach with players. He lifts his hands and backs away. "Just holler when she's done beating you."

I stare up at Frankie. "What the heck was that for?"

She scowls. "Your Shakespeare reading club is attending en masse tomorrow. I did not know about this."

My stomach drops. That was not supposed to get out. A furious blush crawls up my throat to my cheeks. This is one of the disadvantages of having reddish hair. Dad and Ziggy, as the fellow gingers in the family, empathize. You can't hide your emotions to save your life—you wear them on your skin.

I swallow nervously and slowly sit up. "Who told you that?"

"That is irrelevant." Frankie leans on her cane and gives me a stern glare. "This was almost a *huge* missed opportunity. What were you thinking, keeping it from me? Do you know how many ideas I have? In the five minutes since I've known, I already—"

"Frankie." I lean forward, elbows on my knees. With her height, and because she's right next to the bench, we're eye to eye, our noses nearly touching.

For just a second, her eyes lock with mine, slivers of bronze and emerald disappearing as her pupils expand. She blinks, takes a step back, and clears her throat. "What?"

"Frankie, that part of my world . . . it's private."

"Why?" She tips her head like I'm genuinely confusing her. Like she doesn't understand the discrepancy most people would see between who I am here—former Rookie of the Year, alternate captain, Viking on ice—and the part of me that still nerds out on Shakespeare and poetry readings.

"I'm not ashamed of them or my interests, but some of those guys, they're not into the camera and the spotlight. They're dorks like me, who find any kind of undue attention too reminiscent of the kind of attention they got in the past."

Frankie steps closer. "Zenzero, are you telling me that *you* were a nerd in high school? That you had dorky friends?"

"Yes."

She gives me a rare smile, and the dimple pops out. God help me, not the dimple right now.

"Are you saying . . ." Her eyes search mine. "Are you serious? *You?* You were teased in high school? You were—"

"A misfit. Yeah. And not all of my Shakespeare Club necessarily moved out of that demographic. I don't want to make them uncomfortable, okay?"

Frankie covers her mouth. "Okay." It comes out muffled.

"Are you laughing at me?"

She shakes her head. "I'm dying of adorkableness."

At least that's what I think she mumbles. I don't know whether to be offended or amused. "Frankie, how long have you known me? Do I not have *weirdsmobile* written across my forehead?"

She snorts behind her hand. Another shake of her head.

"Wow. For your job relying entirely on social astuteness, you missed the signs big-time."

That makes her stop laughing. Her hand falls away. "Sometimes . . ." She swallows and twists her fingers around a necklace she nearly always wears. It has metal shapes and charms on it that she slips her fingers through, twists and rolls and spins. She does it often, like it soothes her.

"Sometimes I misread people," she says quietly. "I'm sorry. I wasn't laughing at you. It was a pleasant surprise. I thought the Shakespeare stuff was . . . an eccentricity. You telling me that this runs much deeper, I'll respect that it's private."

She avoids my eyes, focuses on a piece of lint on her sleeve, and brushes it away.

There's incongruence between her words and her appearance right now. She sounds fine, but she looks like I just yanked the rug out from underneath her. I feel simultaneously guilty and curious. What is she hiding?

I make to stand, but Frankie sets her hand on my chest and pushes me back with surprising strength. "Back to Shakespeare Club," she says. "The dork years. I need details. I need so many details—"

"Frank the Crank." Matt strolls into the treatment room and walks up to her, blatantly interrupting us and ignoring me. He sticks out his hand. "I've come to kiss ass and say sorry."

Rage rolls through me. I still want to throttle him until his creepy brown eyes pop out of his head for what a jerk he was to her at Louie's.

"Water under the bridge," she tells him. Frankie takes his hand and flinches as he squeezes too hard.

Andy and Kris stroll in, breaking the tension of the moment. Matt releases her hand just as Kris pulls the elastic on Matt's shorts and releases it with a snap.

"Asshole!" Matt barks.

Kris ignores that and offers Frankie a gentle fist pound, which she meets. "Hey, Frankie."

"Frank the Taaaank," Andy calls.

Frankie smiles as they both race for the same massage table, like the overcompetitive dweebs that they are. Kris trips Andy, but Andy brings him down with him. They both flip over each other across the stretching mat and land on twin groans.

Lifting her phone, Frankie snaps a picture, then grins down at it and sighs. "You guys really do make my job easy."

"Frankie." The door into the trainers' room bangs open again, revealing Millie, one of the admins who works part-time in the corporate office, part-time here at the front desk. She's a spry seventy-five, a voracious reader, and she officially joined Shakespeare Club last year. "You gotta move your car, toots. They're paving."

"What?" Frankie groans. And that sound . . . It goes straight to my groin.

I clear my throat and have to recall a particularly traumatizing memory involving Viggo, Oliver, and a Costco-sized jar of mayonnaise to stop my body from further responding. "I'll move it for you, Frankie."

"Nah." She's halfway to the door when she turns and points her cane at me in the air. "I'm not done with you, Bergman. I want answers."

I give her an innocent smile. "Sure thing."

Grumbling, she leaves, passing Millie, who holds open the door and crooks a finger at me. I follow in Frankie's wake, stopping when Frankie turns the corner and I'm close enough for Millie to whisper, "Club meeting is still on for next week?"

"No, the following week. Two weeks from now."

She smiles and adjusts her glasses. "Oh, okay. Good thing I asked. Now, I'll admit, this is my first time reading *As You Like It*, and I'm a little confused. Everybody's in love, but nobody's together, and they're all hiding something."

"That's Shakespeare's version of romantic comedy. It will all be clear in the end."

Her laugh is soft and wispy. "Fair enough. But—" She pulls out a few pages and unfolds them. "Can you help me break down this dialogue? I'm worried I'm going to read it wrong. . . ."

I take a few minutes to help Millie find the subtext in her lines, but we're interrupted when Tyler comes strolling our way. She pockets her script and is halfway out the door before she stops and spins to face me. "Say, maybe you should make sure Frankie's not having trouble with her car."

I frown. "Why would she have—" Suspicion dawns. "Mildred Sawyer. You did not tamper with Frankie's car."

"Who, me?" She grins and wiggles her eyebrows. "'Love goes by haps; Some Cupid kills with arrows, some with traps.'"

"You're getting Second Yeoman next script," I hiss as I breeze by her and jog toward the parking lot.

Mildred's cackle echoes down the hallway. Maybe I'll cast her as a witch instead.

I stumble outside, then freeze as I see Frankie sweating over her car. The hood is thrown open, her hair's up in a haphazard bun, and she has car grease on her cheek. I stand there stupidly, committing the image to memory.

"What?" She straightens and wipes her hands with a rag that's draped over the headlight. "Never seen a woman fix her car?"

I swallow. "Sorry. I was . . . That is . . ." Walking closer, I peer down at the crazy puzzle of wires and parts. "What's wrong?"

"Loose spark plug. Easy fix. Just making sure nothing else is off. First my check-engine light, now this. Some punk is enjoying fucking with my car."

I'm going to throttle a seventy-five-year-old. Mildred obviously doesn't know Frankie very well. I could have told her tampering this trivially was a waste. Frankie's the most fiercely independent person I know—of course she can troubleshoot her car's basic issues.

A loud noise from nearby makes both of us glance up. The asphalt machine rattles, a slew of construction workers waiting at the edge of the parking lot.

"Well," Frankie says as she drops the hood, "thanks for coming to the rescue, but I managed to save myself."

"I never doubted it, Frankie."

She squints up at me, shielding her eyes from the sun. "Here." I grunt as her fist connects with my stomach, her blazer balled up in her grip. "Take this inside for me, will you? I've got to move the car already, and I'm sweating my ass off."

Throwing open her car door, Frankie flicks off the pavers when they whistle at her and peels away toward the alternate parking lot.

FOUR

Frankie

Playlist: "The Love Club," Lorde

My whole life, I've been either a puzzle or a predicament. As a girl, I was obsessed with routines, anxious, and prone to emotional outbursts. I screamed when clothes were put on me and slept terribly. I had one best friend, and I wanted her all to myself. I hated noisy spaces and cried every week at Mass when they used incense.

As a tween, I'd get so absorbed in reading stories that I forgot to eat all day, talked about books I loved incessantly, cried when they ended, and exhaustively read all fanfic there was. I flipped my shit when my older sister, Gabby, chewed too loudly, when my pants had static cling, when Ma deviated from the meal plan, and when something I left in one place wasn't there when I went to find it.

Sometimes, I drove my family nuts. Confused Ma, irritated Nonna, and frustrated Gabby. But Daddy always got me. He'd hold me tight and rock me in his arms. He gave me warm baths and asked Nonna to sew me loose, swingy dresses to wear over the only kind of leggings I could tolerate. Under Nonna's firm matriarchal power, I was drilled to sit still, focus, listen, be polite. Social clues and unspoken messages whispered around me, too slippery and evasive to catch, so I turned to my peers, watching and mimicking their movements, gestures, sayings, and facial expressions. I played sports, was a good student. I did my best to pass as one of them.

And for a while, I did. I seemed like a typical kid—whatever the fuck that is—until depression and anxiety after my dad's death threw me into a tailspin, obliterating the emotional reserves it took to fake normality.

I was thirteen when I was diagnosed with autism. The psychologist said I'd have been diagnosed sooner if not for my fantastic ability to follow rules, copy behaviors, and pretend I was "normal." Everyone hits a breaking point, the shrink said. It was only a matter of time before I'd have to stop pretending and get honest about my neurological difference.

In our traditional Italian Catholic household, dominated by Nonna's skepticism for anything but prayer as a solution to all problems, it was a wonder I'd been brought for an evaluation at all. It's a testament to how worn-out my mother was that she defied Nonna's insistence I was just a normal, albeit stubborn, handful. But my mom trusted her intuition, sneaking me to a number of appointments with the pediatric psychologist who eventually diagnosed me. I probably haven't thanked her enough for that.

After diagnosis, I started therapy for managing my anxiety, dealing with deviations from my compulsions and obsession through emotional regulation, and coping with that sometimes depressing outside-looking-in feeling most autistics experience.

Then, as I hit puberty, a growing presence of aches and stiffness creeped into my life. For my seventeenth birthday, I got another diagnosis: rheumatoid arthritis. Over the span of one summer, I went from being a daily runner and highly active person to someone whose knees and hips were so stiff, I couldn't get out of bed. A teenager whose hands couldn't open water bottles or use can openers.

And that's when I became a problem, not a person. Perhaps if it had just been autism *or* arthritis, I'd have been allowed to be an independent, empowered young woman. But with my mother's fear and anxiety after my dad's death, she easily tipped into oppressive, infantilizing hovering. Frankie was fragile, broken, and weak. It was suffocating.

No noisy places, Frankie doesn't like them.

Not that ball game, those seats are too hard for her to walk to.

Frankie can't be left alone. Who knows what would happen?

I was an impediment to fun activities and locations, a source of worry and exhaustion, a burden. Wet blanket. Party pooper. Eeyore.

Until I moved away. My family got to have fun again. And I got a shot at proving to myself I was capable of living on my own, strong and safe and independent.

And I have proven myself, and then some. Even so, I can admit there are days my life is hard. Autism is a lifelong reality that you'll never quite catch the cues, follow the timing, see the world like a lot of people do. And sometimes that has isolating, frustrating, depressing reverberations.

And then there's rheumatoid arthritis, a bitch of an autoimmune disease for which there's no cure, only damage control. The sooner you slow chronic inflammation created by the body attacking itself, the better. Because I was quickly diagnosed, medication largely spared my joints permanent damage. But even with good medication and care, flare-ups happen.

Each time, each flare, my left hip hurts the worst, a favorite hub for my immune system's overenthusiasm. Three years ago, I developed enough chronic pain and weakness in the joint that a cane was necessary. My family fretted—shocker—that it was a sign of my frailty, being twenty-three and needing a cane.

But I embraced it. Perhaps because of my autistic brain and its analytical practicality, I didn't have *feelings* about the cane. I simply saw its functional advantage. It helped. I was steadier with it. My leg didn't give out. I didn't fall on my face. What the hell was bad about that?

Didn't hurt that I found a cane that made me feel like a badass Hogwarts witch, either. Do you know how much mileage you can get out of owning an ersatz wand and a stunning memory of charms and hexes? A lot, that's your answer.

No, life isn't always easy or pain-free, but I have a few friends who know and love the real me, and I've found comfort and stability with the Elder Wand. I also go to counseling, do physical therapy, ride my stationary bike, practice yoga, swim. I take my meds and find my discomfort and challenges survivable most of the time.

In short, I have my life managed for the most part. And when it feels less managed, when my immune system and autistic brain sabotage me, I have my trump card: cannabis, which provides a much-needed break from chronic pain and anxiety.

That's right. Sometimes, to cope with this wild ride that is my life, I get high. Sometimes, my guy Carter at the medical marijuana dispensary convinces me to try this new "perfect strain," and after I smoke up, I fly so high, I'm in the stratosphere, and that's when I know it's time for Frankie to go to bed. But first she must order Chinese. After sticking a pizza in the oven.

I'm so hungry. I just polished off the pizza and have moved on to inhaling gummies while I wait for my moo shu pork, egg rolls, and wonton soup, when the doorbell rings. Pretty fast turnaround for the Chinese, but I'm not complaining. Slowly, I shuffle over to answer it.

Struggling with the bolt, I eventually manage to unlock the door. After I throw it open, I extend a hand to receive my Chinese feast when I realize who I'm seeing.

I knew I shouldn't have had that last hit on the doobie. I'm imagining things.

A mirage of Ren Bergman stands on my stoop, smiling as always, with a blazer thrown over his arm and a small paper-wrapped package in his hands. Tousled, half-wet hair. A sky-blue long-sleeved shirt that makes his eyes pop. Worn jeans and a pair of beat-up Nikes. Goddamn, the man can wear clothes.

His gaze quickly travels my body as a tomato-red blush stains his cheeks.

Ah, yes. There's reality, punching me in the face: *Attention, Frankie, you're in only a pair of boy-short undies emblazoned with the Deathly Hallows, barely covered by an oversized Kings hoodie.*

I tug down the sweatshirt, wishing it was long enough to reach the tops of my neon-green compression socks, which stop just above my kneecaps. I wear them because they give my joints a sensory-friendly, pain-relieving squeeze.

My cheeks burn as heat more intense than any flare roars from my toes to the crown of my head. Just staring at Phantom Ren stirs a heavy ache low in my belly.

As I take stock of my raging-to-life libido and the less sexually appealing aspects of my outfit—which would be all of them—I begin to have a crisis of sorts. I am aroused by the sight of Ren Bergman. Again. First in the locker room, then at Louie's, then in the training room today. And now, here, at my front door. I've always thought him striking—because, duh, he is—but I just tried to ignore it. And now it seems I can't anymore. I saw an enticing side of him when he threw down with Matt, and now I can't unsee it. I can't stop thinking about it, honestly.

He's not real. That's what I need to focus on. The real Ren has no reason to be here, looking like sex on a cinnamon stick. Meaning it won't hurt anything if I allow myself to ogle this figment of my high-as-a-kite imagination.

I stare at him, falling headlong into those wintry irises. I stare. And stare. And stare.

But like all fantasies, my indulgence in it has to end. Taking a deep breath, I slam the door on the mirage. Otherwise, I might get imaginatively carried away and invite Fictitious Ren in, then fantasize about undressing him with a ferocious need to know if the carpet matches the gorgeous ginger curtains.

And that, I simply can't afford to do.

I'm not sure how long the door's been closed. How long I've been panting for air, my back against its smooth surface as I wait for my body to cool off from my hallucinations. I am never smoking that weed again, seeing as it's clearly laced with something else. Carter at the dispensary has some answering to do.

But then Ren's voice dashes all hope that this is a drug-induced fantasy. "Frankie?"

I yelp, jumping away from the door as nimbly as I can.

"Y-yes?" I peer through the peephole.

Mary Mother of Jesus Riding on a Donkey, that hair. In moonlight, it's the precise color of a faded copper penny.

I must have been a real asshole in a past life, because karma seems bent on punishing me this round. Namely, my inability to moderate myself with those prohibitively expensive root beer gummies that I can only buy from extortionist third-party sellers, and being a total freak for the ginger man-candy of this world, who are of course the most statistically rare of male species.

In retribution for whatever I did as some remorseless cat in a former life, cosmic forces placed the United States' finest redhead specimen in my sphere and made him entirely off-limits. He's a team member. I'm staff. Ren and I are forbidden. *Verboten. Impossibile. Interdit.* Not. Allowed. I can't be attracted to a player on the team. I can't even *think* about being attracted to him.

"Frankie." Ren's voice is muffled from the other side of the door. "Is everything okay?"

Clearing my throat, I wrench open the door again, quickly tugging down my hoodie in a hopeless effort to look dignified.

"Sorry about that. You surprised me." Stepping back, I motion him in. "I was expecting Chinese food."

His brow furrows. "Sorry to disappoint."

"That's okay. I just ate a whole pizza and pounded a bag of root beer gummies. I'm due for some GI rest."

Leaning his shoulder against my doorjamb, Ren's features shift to something warm, maybe amused. There's that cheery, "ain't nothin' gonna bring me down" smile that drives me up the god-damn wall. Mostly because I wish I could replicate it. Then people might not think I'm such a grump when in reality I just can't vol-untarily make myself smile.

"You're stoned, aren't you?" he says.

"Excuse you." I sniff indignantly. "I'm as sober as a nun." As soon as I say it, I search my extensive memory for that simile and come up empty. There's a good chance I just pulled it out of my ass. Damn.

Ren grins. "The nuns I know are notorious partiers."

There he is, rolling with it, being nice. Curse him, this unrea-sonably nice man.

"Guess you found the cool nuns, then," I tell him. "The ones I knew smacked my hands with rulers in grade school and made me stand in the corner for my *insolence*."

Ren's laugh is soft and warm. "You? Insolent?"

I turn toward the kitchen as I hear my dog, Pazza, start barking from the backyard, just in time to see her throw her paws up to the window.

When I glance over my shoulder, I notice Ren is where I left him, at the threshold. He seems hesitant to advance.

"That's just my dog out back. She's harmless . . . sort of. Well, not really. I was worried she'd maul the delivery guy, so she's outside."

Ren blanches.

"I'll keep her outside," I tell him, dropping onto my giant exercise ball with a groan. "I just need to sit, Zenzero. Come on. If you want to talk, here's where we're doing it."

Ren closes the door behind him and walks slowly through my living room, his eyes roaming the place curiously. His smile stays but he looks . . . Is it shy? Nervous? God, what I'd give to better read faces.

Gently, he sets down his arms' contents. First, a blazer, which I now recognize as mine. Then, the package he was holding. He slides it across the kitchen counter, pushing it my way. "Your jacket that you left behind," he says. "And a gift of thanks for letting the Shakespeare Club angle go."

I frown up at him. "You don't understand how much that hurt. We're the LA *Kings*. I had a skit in my head. Costumes and lines. So much material to work, ya know? *King Lear. Henry IV, Henry V, Richard II, Richard III, Macbeth. Cymbeline. King John.* That's not even all of them. . . ." My voice dies off as I search Ren's enigmatic expression. "What? Have I shocked you with my categorical knowledge of Shakespeare?"

"A little bit." It comes out hoarse.

"Don't get too attached to the idea. I just know all the titles and some lines here and there that I had to memorize for a quiz back in college. I don't know much about most of them otherwise."

Ren clears his throat and shakes his head, snapping himself out of whatever that was. His easy smile is back as he pushes the package closer. "Right. Well, I didn't want to make it weird by giving it to you at work tomorrow, and I thought it would be even weirder if I mailed it to you. Plus, I had your jacket, so . . ."

Yanking the package my way, I tug warily at the string. Knots are the bane of the arthritic's existence. But the string unravels effortlessly.

I glance up at him and feel myself smile. "Thanks for avoiding the double knot."

He smiles bashfully and nods. My smile deepens as an unfamiliar warmth floods my chest. I pull the paper away, tearing it easily. A bundle of soft cotton drops onto the counter and I lift the fabric. "A dress shirt?"

Ren steps closer, flipping it over before he smooths it along the granite counter. I stare at his hands longer than is most likely "appropriate." But they're . . . beautiful. Long and faintly freckled. Upon closer inspection, they're also red at the knuckles, like he recently punched something.

"Maddox ruined your other one," he says. "And I was pretty sure it looked like this. Is it a good match?"

I stare at the shirt, processing what he's saying, my fingers sliding along the buttons. They're different. I can tell that immediately. I have four of the same shirts, pants, and blazers that I wear to all games, and while this shirt looks almost identical, I can feel its difference. I pull at the shirt gently and watch it snap apart.

"The buttons—" His voice cracks, and he clears his throat. "The buttons are adhered to a durable magnet. The panel around them holds the opposite magnetic pull and is reinforced so they can take a good tug."

I normally leave my shirts buttoned but for the top two, so I can slip them over my head and not deal with buttoning them. Buttons are a bit hard for my hands—especially early in the day or late in the evening, when they're at their stiffest. Despite the pains I take to ensure my clothes are comfortable, I never considered clothes could be *easier* while still allowing me to wear what I wanted.

"Ren, where did you . . ." My throat feels weird, thick with an emotion I can't begin to name.

"My sister is a physical therapist, but she's an overachiever who nerds out on adaptive everything, from clothing to kitchen utensils." He shrugs. "She's mentioned them before, said a shop in the Fashion District sold them."

Peering up at Ren, I am so damn confused. Clearly, he's aware of my challenges, to the point he bought something for me out of consideration. Yet there's no trace of that stifling, demeaning claustrophobia I've felt with just about everyone else I know. In this moment with Ren, I just feel . . . seen. And I feel a terrible need to kiss him.

Damn weed. It's all to blame.

Weed never makes you this *horny.*

Shut it, pothead brain. No more wisecracks.

"That's really thoughtful of you." Tentatively, I wrap my hand around his, squeeze it once, then release it before I give in to the impulse to tug him my way and kiss him senseless. "Thank you."

A furious blush crawls up Ren's neck, past the play-off beard. It's beyond sweet but so odd to see this side of him. Because the Ren I've seen the past three years is humble, yes, but confident, assertive, striking. Rookie of the Year. MVP. Thrown on all the magazine covers, voted for hottest this, sexiest that. The guys tease him about it, and he just shakes his head and moves the conversation along. Ren's got it all, and he's always seemed pretty happy about it.

But then there's this other side I glimpse, that I'm seeing right now. When he blushes and does his nervous tic of scratching the back of his neck. Almost like he's uncertain of himself, not the confident guy who's taken the hockey world by storm.

"You're welcome," he says. "I hope it's not . . ." There it is. He scrubs the back of his neck. "I hope it's not crossing a line or anything."

"No, Ren. It's a very thoughtful gesture from a caring friend." Ren's eyes flicker with something I can't read. "I mean, I know we work together. But we're friends, aren't we?"

Aren't we?

"Definitely. Yep. Completely." He nods, shifting his weight.

Silence falls. I've learned how best to try to make small talk. I'm still not great at it, and I definitely don't *like* it, but I've memorized some ways to move through quiet gaps in conversation. I just don't feel like playing normal right now. I feel like being the real Frankie with what I'm starting to suspect is the real Ren. So I let the idle hum of my fridge, the whisper of crickets outside my kitchen window, serve as our soundtrack. I let myself stare at Ren how I probably shouldn't, while he gazes at my mouth with the kind of focus that I've only ever seen him devote to game tape.

The moment bursts like a bubble when the doorbell rings.

Breaking his stare, Ren glances toward the front door. "That's the Chinese?"

"Unless someone else from the team brought me magnetic-snap slacks."

He laughs quietly. "Right. I'll check it, if you want."

"Thanks, that would be great." When he turns away, I scramble for the joint I stubbed out earlier and furiously light up.

FIVE

Frankie

Playlist: "Atlantis," Bridgit Mendler

Watching him walk toward the door, I try really hard not to check out his ass, but you need to understand how hard that is. One, all hockey players have incredible butts. It's a fact. Two, Ren has a *really* fantastic butt. It deserves to be immortalized in sculpture, a marble homage to the glory of the male backside.

I bounce on the exercise ball to lose my jitters, drag on the joint, feeling its acrid sweetness fill my lungs. That long hit mellows my racing thoughts enough to help me stop ogling Ren and get myself together. Jesus, I am a mess. I stub out the last of it and wave the air to clear the smell a little.

"Wow." Ren reenters the kitchen, sets down the massive bag of food on the counter, and peers inside. If he's perturbed by the cloud of secondhand marijuana he's standing in, he doesn't let on. "Feeling extra munchy tonight, are we?"

I tear open the bag and nearly drop the moo shu pork. Ren catches it. Gently setting it down, he lifts the lid and sets it aside, glossing over the moment as he smiles at me.

"Can I get plates?" he asks. "Chopsticks?"

He rounds the counter before I've answered. A rush of self-consciousness pricks me. "Only if you join me."

Ren freezes at the cabinet and looks over his shoulder. "Frankie, I don't want to take your food."

"Please share it with me, Ren." I hold his eyes.

Don't go there. Not you. Please don't make me the poor creature you help and fuss over.

Ren's pale eyes sparkle with his deepening smile. "Well, okay." He pulls out plates and bowls, then shuts the cabinet and makes himself at home, riffling through the drawers until he finds chopsticks and spoons. "But I call first dibs on the wonton soup."

As he serves me first, I realize he was joking about getting first crack at the soup. Ren serves us equally with easy efficiency while chatting about nothing in particular. I hate being served normally, but this is friendly, comfortable. I don't feel one bit coddled. He also sucks at chopsticks worse than I do, which helps my ego.

"You sure you don't have joint problems, too?" I mumble around a mouthful of moo shu.

Ren laughs and covers his mouth. "I beat the hell out of a punching bag before I came. My hands are useless right now."

"Makes two of us." I smile at him, and he smiles back. My focus shifts to his battered knuckles. "Any particular reason the punching bag earned such a beating?"

Ren pauses mid-chew, looking slightly caught off guard. "Um. No, not really. I just hit the bag to help keep my . . . temper in check."

I frown at him. "You? A temper? This coming from the guy who has yet to brawl in his three years playing for the NHL, except for shoving a guy off of him when he tries to start something. The guy who hugs babies like *that's* his job, not hockey. Who signs anything, *anytime* a fan asks. *You* have a temper?"

"I did almost wring Maddox's neck the other night. Give me credit for that."

"Eh." I sip some wonton broth. "He's had it coming. I'd be more worried about you if you *hadn't* throttled him."

"But you get my point. It's not that I don't have a temper, I've just figured out how to manage it. Lots of bag work. 'I must be cruel to be kind.'"

I swallow my bite of moo shu. "*Hamlet.*"

Ren pauses, and a smile makes his eyes crinkle handsomely. "So she does know her Shakespeare."

"I have a good memory. When I hear something, it sticks. But yes, I like *some* of Shakespeare's plays. *Hamlet* is not one of them. That guy likes to hear himself talk way too much."

"So does Maddox," Ren mutters.

"I wouldn't blame you for hating him."

Ren taps his chopsticks against his plate and stares off in thought. "I don't hate him. I hate *playing* with him. He has a terrible energy."

"And here I thought he was just a dick."

Ren laughs loudly—a deep, beautiful belly laugh.

"Wasn't *that* funny," I say self-consciously.

His laughter dies off. "I don't think you realize how witty you are, Frankie."

I glance down at my moo shu and scooch it across my plate. "I think you need to get out a bit more, if you find *me* witty, Zenzero."

He's still looking at me when I peer up. Clearing my throat, I take a long drink of water. "You were saying, about Maddox? Before I made you aspirate a wonton."

Ren blinks away finally. "He frustrates me. He should show you and every other person he crosses paths with a lot more respect. But Maddox is still the asshole jock that I'm sure he was in high school."

"Which you weren't."

"No, I wasn't. I was good at sports, but I was also the kid who got emotional in tenth-grade English when our class read aloud *Romeo and Juliet.*"

I bite my lip so I don't laugh. I think that's insanely endearing and healthy, that Ren's in touch with his soft side, but I know first-hand how hard it is to tell if someone's laughing at you or with you. I don't want to hurt his feelings.

In the past, I wouldn't have thought anything could bring Ren down. I wouldn't have worried about laughing. But in the past few days, Ren's shown me that much more lies beneath his chipper smile. All I ever knew him to be was this effortlessly upbeat, hunky, talented guy. The sun shone out of Ren's ass, the world was at his fingertips, and secretly, that level of happy-go-lucky perfection grated on me.

But what Ren's shown me is that inside this mature exterior of the pristine swan, there's a long-ago ugly duckling. A sweet, awkward dork who never really fit in, who *still* maybe doesn't feel like he fits in anywhere. And that means we have a metric shit ton more in common than I ever thought.

Not that commonality is important. For someone I'm not attracted to. Who I don't want to sleep with. At all. Ever.

I clear my throat and try to straighten my posture on the exercise ball. "So, having to rub shoulders with Maddox bothers you. The punching bag is how you deal with your frustration that the bullies are still at large."

Ren glances up from his food, looking surprised. "Among other things, yeah."

"Well, listen." I snap a fortune cookie in two and give him one half. "If it makes you feel any better, you got the last laugh. Matt's a mean-spirited prick. His reputation is shit, and I think we'll end up having to pay another team to take him. Then look at you, look where you are."

Ren accepts his fortune cookie. "I'm not sure what you mean."

I almost fire back a blunt remark about false modesty, but I'm stopped by this newfound knowledge he's given me: Ren honestly doesn't see himself how everyone else does. He isn't feigning humility or fishing for a compliment. He really means what he says when he expresses self-doubt. If anyone can empathize with seeing yourself one way and being perceived so dissonantly from that, it's this mostly invisibly ill, autistic woman right here.

A new crack forms in my heart. This is a travesty. No one this wonderful should feel so unsure of himself.

I toss the fortune cookie in my mouth and crunch. "Ren the Red. You're a twelve out of ten, inside and out. I bet the queue of women waiting for you is longer than the line for the next Apple product."

"Women I don't know." Focusing his attention on his cookie, Ren slips out the fortune paper and stares at it.

"Well, that's why you get out, buddy. So they become women you *do* know. Problem is, you're a saint. I've never even seen you with a woman. I'm aware puck bunnies aren't your thing, but in the off-season, you let yourself have some fun, right? Now that you're not a rookie anymore, your career's totally on track, maybe you're ready to look for someone who's relationship material."

"There's someone." His eyes dance across the fortune cookie paper. He folds and pockets it.

"And?" I press.

"And she's unavailable for the time being. I'm also not sure she sees me that way."

"Then she's thick as a brick. Move on, dude; that's her problem."

He shakes his head. "It doesn't work right now, but maybe one day it will. That unavailability won't last forever. When it ends, I'll work up the courage to tell her how I feel."

"Does she know you're waiting?" Also, shit. What guy waits for a woman these days? Most men I've known do not have that kind of old-school courtship patience. They can't even wait ten minutes in a Starbucks line for a mediocre latte.

He runs a hand over his beard. "No. And right now if I told

her, it would put her in an awkward position, which isn't fair to her. The timing's just not good."

"Well, welcome to working in professional athletics. The timing is never *good* for a relationship. Not until retirement. But, then again, as you know, some of the guys are blissfully paired off, at least until play-offs, when their partners are over an eighty-game season. I don't mean to sound so cynical. If anyone could make it work, it would be you."

Ren crunches his fortune cookie and stares at me curiously. "I can wait. I've waited this long. A few more years won't kill me."

"But you should have fun, Zenzero. Get your kicks. A guy like you shouldn't be sitting on the shelf."

"A guy like me?" A wry half smile tugs at his mouth. "What's that mean?"

My high is slowly dissipating. I grope frantically on the counter for my root beer gummies and rip open a new bag. Tugging one between my teeth until it snaps, I chew and buy myself a minute. My unfiltered brain still wins out. "You know women drool over you."

He stands, then clears our empty plates and bowls to the sink. "You're not answering the question."

I watch him run water in the double sink and add a splash of soap. The jerk is going to wash my dishes and prove the very point I'm about to make. "Dammit, Bergman, you're the total package. You're thoughtful, talented, handsome, and a true gentleman. You're a prince of a man. Okay?"

Ren stops washing for a moment. Then he starts scrubbing again. I watch him rinse the plates and prop them on the rack to dry without saying a word. Finally, he turns and leans his hip against the counter, arms folded across his broad chest. "Do you think that? Or are you saying what you assume other people think?"

Of course I think that. What woman in her right mind wouldn't? I tear another gummy with my teeth. "Does it matter?"

"Yes." His jaw is set, those pale cat eyes locked with mine intensely.

Dread washes over me. God, I have to be horrifying him. Here I am, half-baked. Barely clothed. And so far past the line of professional behavior.

"Ren, I—" I swallow nervously. "I'm sorry. That was an inappropriate direction I took us. I'm unfiltered to begin with but the cannabis doesn't help. Please ignore everything I said."

Ren walks toward me, stopping at the counter where the gummies sit. Holding my eyes, he plucks one from the bag, sets it between his teeth, and tugs until it breaks clean in half. My eyes shift to his mouth.

Joseph in a Juniper Tree. Watching Ren tear a root beer gummy like a lion ripping open his prey just turned my knees to jelly. Thankfully, I'm already sitting. Well, bouncing, on the exercise ball. I'm one of those people who need to be in perpetual motion.

"You still haven't answered me," he says, unsticking his jaw with a loud *pop*. "Wow, these are chewy. And for the record, we're not at work. It's not inappropriate at all."

I grab a fistful of gummies and shove them in my mouth. Hopefully, I'll choke and black out so we can forget about this mortifying corner I've backed us into.

"Oh, it's inappropriate," I say around my grotesque mouthful. "You're a player, I'm your social media manager, no matter where we are. I'm sitting here in my 'Boy Who Lived' panties, high on hashish, nagging you about your intimate life. It's so far past inappropriate, I almost want to fire myself."

Ren's face tightens with an expression I can't read. "You're not going to fire yourself, Frankie. You'll be at work tomorrow."

"I mean, you're right. But only because I like my insurance and the mild weather. I'll be there, on one condition: no more nice gestures like this, especially when I'm marijuana-ly impaired."

Ren's laugh is warm. It ripples along my skin, making the hairs on my arms and neck stand on end. Pushing off the counter, he sweeps up his keys, then smiles down at me, that easy, sunshiny Ren Bergman smile. "Good night, Frankie. See you tomorrow."

He's halfway down the hallway when I call, "Ren!"

In one smooth turn, he now faces me. "Yes?"

I tell my heart to stop trying to run out of my chest. "Thank you."

Ren's smile changes; his eyes dip to my mouth, like he's waiting for me to say more. But it's all I have. Finally, he says, "Of course."

With one more fluid turn, Ren strolls away and pulls the door closed behind him. It's only when I hear it click shut that I realize how weirdly easy that felt, having him here, and how *un*easy I feel now that he's gone.

This is bad. Very, very bad.

Ren

Playlist: "Neighborhood #2," Arcade Fire

"Bergman!" one of the guys yells from the kitchen. "I can't find the honey mustard!"

I come in from the deck with another tray of grilled chicken. "I'm going to take a wild guess and assume you didn't check the refrigerator."

Lin frowns. "Why would I do that?"

Sliding the tray onto the range, I yank open the fridge and pull out a slew of condiments, including honey mustard, and shove them into his arms.

"Wow," he says.

I pat his arm. "You wear your bachelorhood on your sleeve, my friend."

Lin gives me a look. "Says the guy who doesn't even *look* at women."

"Please. It's called subtlety. Unlike you, I've learned not to drool at them. And when it's time to settle down, I'll even know how to navigate my own kitchen."

Spinning Lin, I shove him toward the table where all the food's laid out and then survey the state of my home. It's currently tipping the scales from quiet beachfront oasis to frat house. I shudder. Like my mom, I'm a neurotically tidy person. It's one of the few things I have in common with most of my siblings, except for Freya and Viggo, who, like Dad, are unrepentant slobs.

The entire team is here at my place after practice. I'm feeding them before we hop a flight later tonight to Minnesota and start our first stretch on the road for play-offs. Virtually all the guys live in Manhattan Beach, so it isn't unusual to get together here, *but* there's a specific reason for this gathering: superstition.

Two years ago, we barely clawed our way to the play-offs. Tensions were high, the guys were a nervous wreck, and Rob, our captain, for the first time turned to *me* for help. I'd recently been named alternate captain, which was a huge honor after just finishing my rookie season.

"I need a distraction for the guys," he said. "Not more pep talks or watching game tape. Help me get them out of their heads."

So, I did what he asked. I invited everyone over to my place for a night of distraction.

It was . . . not what they were expecting. There was no poker. No cornhole. No bro games.

There were twenty-two printouts of the "rude mechanicals" scenes from Shakespeare's *A Midsummer Night's Dream* and a smorgasbord of Swedish food.

I'd been prepared for skepticism and awkward silence, because I'm me and I've encountered that plenty of times in my life. The guys were wary, until they started eating and then devouring food, and Rob asked me to explain what this was all about as he flipped through the pages, a grin tugging at his mouth.

"I know we're under pressure," I told the team. "But there's a reason we got where we are. We've been doing what we're supposed to, and we'll keep doing what we've done well. So tonight, we're just going to get out of our heads. A little distraction. Lightening up, laughing at ourselves."

The guys looked nervous as well as self-conscious when I assigned parts and explained the setting of both scenes in the play—the first scene, in which a half dozen skilled tradesmen—the "rude mechanicals"—decide to enter a theater competition held by the king of Athens, and the second, in which they actually perform the tragedy, which is well beyond their understanding, with entirely comedic results.

I could tell they were apprehensive, but if any bit of Shakespeare was going to work for a newbie, it was this. Not four lines into reading, laughter began. Flubbed language, falsetto voices affected for females, bad English accents, and countless mispronunciations. The undeniably ridiculous physical comedy that unfolded as a bunch of athletes intuitively performed the scenes. The aha moments when they got the humor. It led to grown men crying, we were laughing so hard.

That night, everyone ate well, got their minds off the pressure, and left full and happy.

Maybe even a little more comfortable with each other in a new way. And then we won our way straight to the Stanley Cup.

Thus, a ritual was born. Because hockey players are truly some of the most superstitious athletes you'll meet. If they took a crap backward on a toilet before the night of their first hat trick, you better believe they'll be pulling that stunt before every game without even blinking.

We read Shakespeare before the first away play-off game that led to our first Cup in far too long. So, now this is what we do before we hit the road for our first away play-off game: eat my mom's best Swedish recipes and read the "rude mechanicals" scenes.

"Moreaux." Andy pokes François. "Swap parts with me."

"Get fucked," François tells him. "Do you know how long I've been waiting to play Thisbe?"

Andy pouts. "Besides Halloween, Rude Mechanical Day is the

one day of the year that I get to dress adventurously and not get crap for it."

Rob starts down the line of food, piling up his plate. "Not true. You dress *adventurously* regularly during the off-season, and none of us says a word. That bikini you wear on the beach belongs on a much less hairy ass."

"Hey." Andy glares at him. "It's a Speedo. And it's European. The ladies like it."

François snorts. "Trust me, Andrew. I am European, and both I and these *ladies* you speak of would prefer if you kept to your American swim trunks."

"Okay, let's eat," I call to the stragglers outside and in the living room.

The guys descend on the table like hyenas on a carcass, quickly draining platters of food.

They trickle into my living room, which is a wide-open space with a vaulted ceiling made cozy with built-in bookshelves, pale blue-green walls like the ocean outside, and an expansive dove-gray L-shaped sofa bracketed by mid-century end tables.

Throw in a couple of ivory oversized chairs and a huge wool rug in coordinating colors to absorb sound, and it's my favorite room in the house, besides my bedroom. I had few feelings about the décor, so I let my brother Oliver pick everything out for me. He has a good eye and ended up putting together a space that I really like.

There's plenty of room, and the guys are used to making themselves at home here, so they settle in tight on the couch and chairs, even cross-legged on the floor at the coffee table.

"Damn, you can cook, Bergman," Rob mumbles around a bite of food.

I sit in the last open spot, which is next to him, and dig into my plate. "Thanks. I'm glad you like it."

"Like it?" He chuckles. "I'd eat this over anything they serve at those fancy places Liz likes." After a moment in which he demolishes a shrimp sandwich in three bites, he leans in a bit and drops his voice. "Speaking of Liz. I was wondering, would you mind giving me a cooking lesson or two? Once the season's done, I want to make the wife a nice meal, start pulling my weight a bit more at home. I'm going to have my parents take the kids for a few days once this is over. Just to show her how much I appreciate her putting up with the insanity."

I grin. "Sure. Anything you want to learn in particular?"

"Steak. Maybe mushroom risotto, too? She always gets that when we're out." He glances up at me and catches my smile. "What? You think it's lame, don't you?"

"No way. I think it's exactly what a guy should do for his partner after a long stretch of her shouldering all the home responsibilities. I'd love to help out."

Before Rob can respond, something crashes in the kitchen.

"Shit!" someone yells. "Rennnnn."

I groan. "They're like children."

"They're worse," Rob says. "At least worse than mine."

I stand on a sigh and shove a shrimp sandwich in my mouth. "I'm coming!"

"Hey." I snatch Kris's phone out of his hands and shove it in my pocket. "This is a phone-free zone. We agreed everyone does their best acting when they're not worried about showing up on Twitter in a toga saying, 'O dainty duck! O dear!'"

"It's blackmail gold. No, platinum," Kris whines, lunging unsuccessfully for my pocket that now holds his phone. "I *need* it, Ren."

I fold my arms across my chest. "What are the rules of theater in this house?"

Kris pouts. "Respect the story's intent. Make your fellow actors look good. Foster a safe space for performance."

"Thank you." I gesture to François. "Continue, please."

"*Merci.*" François begins to bow but freezes halfway through and switches to a curtsy. True commitment to character, right there. This is the moment where Pyramus and Thisbe, two lovers meeting in the garden and separated by circumstance—a *Romeo and Juliet* homage, no doubt—meet for a clandestine kiss.

"Right." Tyler clears his throat and adjusts his helmet. He's reading Pyramus this year. "'O grim-look'd night! O night with hue so black! O night, which ever art when day is not! O night, O night! alack, alack, alack, I fear my Thisbe's promise is forgot! And thou, O wall—'" Tyler looks around. "Where's the fucking wall?"

Andy bounds in. "He had to take a piss."

François sighs.

Andy sweeps the blanket off my couch, wraps it around his shoulders so it drapes nicely, and extends his arms. "There. Sorry."

Tyler lifts his script and finds his place. "'O sweet, O lovely wall, That stand'st between her father's ground and mine! Thou wall, O wall, O sweet and lovely wall, Show me thy chink—'"

Andy lifts his hand, joining his thumb and forefinger, then Tyler continues.

"'—to blink through with mine eye! Thanks, courteous wall: Jove shield thee well for this! But what see I? No Thisbe do I see.'"

Tyler rolls up his script and whacks Andy over the head. Andy yelps.

"'O wicked wall,'" Tyler yells, "'through whom I see no bliss! Cursed be thy stones for thus deceiving me!'" he says, whacking Andy a few more times.

A roll of laughter travels the room. Some of the guys whistle and hoot as François saunters to the other side of Andy's blanketed arm.

"Maddox." Kris lobs a pillow at his head. "It's your line, asshole."

Matt slowly glances up from a magazine he's been flipping through. "I'm sorry, where are we?"

Everyone groans.

"Why'd you give him Theseus?" Rob whispers from my right.

I shrug. "Trying to extend an olive branch. Obviously, a wasted effort."

"I hope he gets traded," Rob mutters. I keep my mouth shut, but Rob knows I feel the same way, and I'm not the only one. Nobody likes Maddox. He's made enemies of all of us.

Kris stomps over to Matt. "I'll read it if you won't—"

"I'll. Do it." Matt glares up at him, then delivers in an underwhelming monotone, "'The wall, methinks, being sensible, should curse again.'"

A collective sigh of disappointment. I have to stifle a laugh. The guys get so into it now that we're a few years in, they're beside themselves when someone messes up. Tyler says Pyramus's line, and then it's François's moment.

He delivers his lines in a French-accented, perfectly over-the-top falsetto, before Tyler puckers his lips near Andy's hand, where his thumb and pointer create the chink. "'O kiss me through the hole of this vile wall!'"

François leans to purposefully misplace his kiss—his next line is supposed to be "I kiss the wall's hole, not your lips at all"—but before he can, Andy lowers his hand so that Tyler and François actually smash mouths.

An eruption of entertained *ooooohhh*s echoes in the room. Tyler glares murder at Andy. François grabs Andy by the blanket around his neck, and before I can even step in to avoid disaster, François tackles him to the ground. Tyler jumps in, and soon it's a mosh pit of brawling, hyped-up hockey players.

"Guys!" I yell. Kris hurtles past me, flinging himself on top of the growing pile of bodies. I drop my head and sigh. "This is why we can't have nice things."

The plane ride is uncharacteristically sullen. Rob and I had a hell of a time pulling people apart. Most of them were just cranky after it, but a few of the guys came out the worse for wear.

François hasn't stopped scowling, and Tyler, still horrified by the kiss, keeps rinsing his mouth with water, then spitting into an empty container. Andy has a somewhat-deserved black eye. Kris has a split lip—serves him right for jumping headlong into violence. Thankfully, hockey players don't draw much notice for looking beat-up.

Rob's passed out in the seat next to me, snoring. I have *As You Like It* in hand because that's up next for Shakespeare Club, and it's a good distraction. I'm trying not to be entirely aware of Frankie, who sits across the aisle, flipping through her phone, with her laptop up and running as well.

Her hair's down, dark and smooth as melted bitter chocolate. She's in relatively casual clothes—black, slim pants, a fuzzy gray sweater that looks like a feather duster—Freya has one in ice blue, so I'm guessing they're *in* right now—and her sneakers, black and silver as always. Her cane rests between her legs, and she weaves her fingers through her necklace as she glances between screens.

My already weak resistance evaporates as I drop my book to the lap tray. "Plotting world domination?"

She peers up and locks eyes with me. A slow grin warms her face. "But of course."

I feel a blush heating my cheeks. Thank God for the play-off beard somewhat hiding it. How can I be so calm on the ice, in press rooms, in front of everyone else, but I'm a blushing schoolboy when it comes to her?

"You're staring at me," she says.

I blink rapidly. "Um. I. What?"

Frankie lifts a hand self-consciously to her face. "Do I have powdered sugar on my face or something?"

Earlier on the flight I had to studiously *not* observe Frankie eat a box of powdered mini donuts. I made sure I *didn't* watch her lick every single fingertip. And I definitely didn't put down my lap tray to cover a growing problem crushed against my fly after watching each long finger slip into her mouth, then slide out with an erotic *pop*.

I lean across the aisle, and don't you know, God's looking out for me. There's a smudge of powdery white right on her cheekbone. I wipe it away and fight the urge to lick my thumb clean. "Just there."

Her smile deepens, making the dimple appear. "Thanks. Now, how about you tell me why everyone's acting like we're heading into arctic hell to get our asses handed to us."

"Because we *are* heading into arctic hell, probably to get our asses handed to us." Saint Paul, Minnesota, has a hell of a cold front tearing through it for early April, and the Wild aren't playing around this year. There's a fair chance we'll lose.

She lifts one dark, arched eyebrow. "Seriously, you're all so frowny. What happened? You guys disappeared after dry-land, then you show up like this. Don't think I haven't noticed that the past few years you all drop off the radar right before our first on-the-road play-off game."

She taps her finger against her lips and narrows her eyes. Like always, her nails are painted glossy black. The thought of those claws scraping down my torso tightens everything low in my stomach. Never have I been so grateful for airplane lap trays.

"It's just a little ritual," I finally manage. "It got out of hand this year."

"Let me guess. Kris had something to do with it. Maybe Tyler."

She lowers her voice and leans closer, infusing the air with her perfume. "Definitely Andy."

"Uh." I swallow thickly, trying to think straight. It's hard when I'm this close to her. Just her scent alone scrambles my brain, the clean whisper of evening air and orchid blossoms. For the longest time I couldn't pinpoint what made Frankie smell so good. It drove me nuts. Until last summer, after putting away leftovers, watching the sun set from my parents' kitchen window, when I smelled Frankie. A cool summer breeze blew past the night-scented orchids that my sister Ziggy had taken on in her loneliness as the last kid home. They were full and fragrant, their blossoms open. That was it, her soft perfume exactly. If I closed my eyes, I'd have sworn she was standing beside me.

If only.

Frankie drops her finger from her mouth and leans back. "Hmm. You're good at hiding things, Bergman, I'll give you that. But I'm going to get the truth out of you one of these days."

She has no idea how likely that is. Or how nervous I am to hear what she'll say when the truth finally does come out.

SEVEN

Frankie

Playlist: "New Rush," Gin Wigmore

I didn't always know I wanted to work in professional sports, but I've always loved watching them. Some of my most treasured memories of my dad are sitting on his lap, watching the Mets on our tiny TV. We'd snuggle on the sofa in our Queens apartment, which we shared with Nonna, and squint to try to spot the ball when Carlos Delgado sent it soaring across the field.

Gabby and Ma would watch from the cutout in the cabinetry over the sink as they cooked dinner, and we'd all yell at the screen. Nonna would say bad words in Italian that made Daddy clap his hands over my ears, and Ma would hoot in laughter.

Sports were integral to our family. Gabby and I played softball and basketball. We went to baseball games when we could afford it. But it wasn't until high school that I fell in love with hockey. Gabby's then boyfriend, now husband, Tony, was friends with one of the players' brothers and got us tickets to the Islanders. From that game on, I was obsessed. The game was grace and power, it was a dance of agility and grueling physical discipline.

That's when I knew that in some way, I always wanted hockey to be a part of my life. I went to school, got a degree in digital communication and media relations, went through the school's intern program, and got placed with none other than the Islanders—yeah,

I freaked out, too—then moved on to an entry-level PR assistant position with them after graduation.

But as I adjusted to the realities of life with arthritis, frigid northeastern weather became painful to contend with. When my dream job located in balmy SoCal fell at my feet, I snatched it up and moved cross-country. And even though saying goodbye to Gabby and Tony, Ma and Nonna, hurt like hell, I felt relief. I was no longer a burden or worry. I was a weekly phone call.

A biannual visit to ensure we didn't feel totally estranged and to pester me about getting regular X-rays. A country between us, I became a person to them once more.

Since moving here, I've made two friends in LA, through water aerobics class and book club, Annie and Lorena. Other than that, my Kings family *is* my family. Their victories are my victories, and their losses are my losses.

Which is why before every game, I feel as close to shitting myself with nerves as all the guys probably do.

After another trip to the porcelain throne thanks to my anxious tummy, I head into one of the exercise rooms reserved for the visiting team. Everyone's in various states of physical activity, still in shirts, shorts, and sneakers, warming up their bodies.

"Frank the Tank!" Andy calls.

I salute him, then turn to Tyler, who's doing lateral rotations with a medicine ball. "Johnson. Don't forget you're live on Instagram in half an hour."

Tyler grins. "Yes, ma'am."

"Schar." Kris looks up at me while completing hip circles. "Kindly stop engaging the trolls on Twitter. It accomplishes nothing, and Minnesotans hate you."

He nods.

"Good." I turn, take a step, then freeze because Jumping Jehoshaphat, Ren Bergman is doing T-stab push-ups.

Shirtless.

Let me help you picture this. You'll thank me, I promise. It's a push-up. Until he straightens his arms, and instead of dropping back down for another rep, he swings one arm up to the sky by rotating his waist. It looks like *trikonasana* for the yoga nerds out there. The key takeaway is, every muscle in that man's torso, back, shoulders, and arms ripples and knots as he dips, then swings up, dips, then swings up.

My eyes drag down his body, mesmerized by the rhythm of his hips lowering to hover above the floor before they thrust upward. Thrust up, then down, thrust up, down.

I'm rooted to the floor, hypnotized. As I've said, I've only seen Ren shirtless a few times.

Even while doing dry-land practice, he's always modest, consistently wearing shirts while exercising.

Today is apparently a day for glorious exceptions. "Lose a shirt, Zenzero?"

Ren freezes mid-push-up, which doesn't help the state of affairs in my panties as his ridiculous triceps pop, along with every muscle in his back. Tonight, I'm wearing my lucky Hedwig boy shorts, meaning, as the Ren Effect takes place, this time it's Harry's beloved pet owl that gets caught in the rain.

Finally, Ren straightens and leaps to stand as effortlessly as a big jungle cat. Snatching a towel from nearby, he drags it down his face and chest, then turns and faces me. I startle when I get a look at him. His eyes are glassy, his cheeks pink. Stepping closer, I feel his forehead before he quickly pulls away.

"You look like shit." I put the pieces together. "That's why you're shirtless. You're hot with a fever."

Ren glances over my shoulder at the other guys. I realize too late I wasn't discreet when I should have been. Another something

I'm not stellar at: sensing during conversation when I should be subtle and hush-hush.

"I'm fine," he says quietly.

"You're not." When I reach for him again, he backs away.

"If I'm not, you shouldn't be touching me. I could get you sick."

"You won't get me sick." Concern knots my stomach. I want to cover him in cold washcloths, ply him with Popsicles, and shove his ass into a hotel bed.

"Your meds, Frankie. They weaken your immune system."

"How do you know that?"

He blinks away. "I-it's common knowledge."

"No, it's not."

Ren shifts his weight and folds his arms. "Frankie. My dad's a doctor. My older sister's a physical therapist. One of my brothers is premed. I have to sit at family dinners and listen to them nerd out on anatomy and the latest therapies and pharmacopeia. I know that most RA treatments work by suppressing the immune system, meaning you can get sick easily."

I stare at him, feeling my heart do a backflip in my chest again. Just like the other night when he gave me the shirt.

"Returning to my point." Ren clears his throat and gives me a stern look. "You need to stay back. It's bad enough that we were already in a plane together, you breathing my germs in that god-awful recycled air—"

"I'm okay," I tell him. "I take the world's largest handful of vitamins every morning. I'm an obsessive handwasher. I'll be fine. But you. You look like shit warmed up. Tell Coach you're out."

He laughs dryly, moving even farther away and lowering his voice. "You're funny. I'm not out. Give me six to ten feet, Frankie. I'm serious. If I get you sick, I'm going to get cranky."

"That's not a disincentive, Bergman. I'd pay a lot to see you get cranky."

He narrows those cat eyes at me.

"Fine," I mutter. "But I'm going to sic Howard on you afterward." Dr. Amy Howard is our head physician, who travels with us. She is zero bullshit, and I love her. If she decides Ren's sick, she'll have no problem benching his ass the next game.

"Don't even think about it," he says. "I'll talk to her myself afterward, okay?"

I scowl at him. "Fine."

————

For burning with a fever, Ren's a flipping machine. He already scored in the first period, and he looks poised to score another right as we start the second. I'm wandering my normal haunt near the bench, catching shots with my phone, tweeting, posting on Instagram, engaging in real time with fans and sharing their posts, but my eyes are on Ren, and the rest of the players of course, as much as possible.

Ren streaks after a Wild defender. Right when he could easily crush the guy against the boards, Ren instead deftly swipes the puck free and slips past him with it glued to his stick. That's Ren in a nutshell. Classy. Strategic. Solid. Now, don't get me wrong, I've seen him knock the wind out of a guy against the boards. I've watched him throw a shoulder and shove back. But he never *seeks* violence. He never takes the ice like a man with something to prove. He just plays.

Beautifully.

Of all the guys on the team, Ren's always held my respect the most. He's a good person, a dependable athlete, a natural but unassuming leader. Yes, he's annoyingly cheery and polite, but I now understand that's more a choice to protect his private life, to be a positive presence on the team, than some indicator of a carefree existence.

Since the evening involving one generous adaptive clothing gift and excessive amounts of marijuana, I've been spending a lot of time trying *not* to think about Ren. It's driving me crazy, but that's how I work. Ren showed me a new fascinating side of himself. And when I find something that fascinates me, it's hard for me not to devote inordinate time to it.

Except *it* is a *him*. And that's a problem.

Ren soars across the ice, weaving, dodging, that puck forever anchored to his stick. With his skates on, he's six foot six, his body powerful, but his grace rivals that of a figure skater. Deep in our offensive zone, he works the puck, feinting, teasing, dropping the biscuit, then flying around the net.

Defenders swarm him, their sticks smacking against his, their bodies diving for checks against the boards, but he evades them every time, like a cat slipping through the narrowest opening in a door. It shouldn't be possible. He shouldn't be so graceful. But he is.

Ren maintains possession of the puck even while double-teamed, then slips it central to Tyler. Tyler fakes a slapshot, passes it to Rob. Rob has a shit angle for a shot, but Ren swings back around the net just in time for Rob to pass it to him. Ren connects with the puck and curls it effortlessly inside the net.

"*Goooooaaaaalllll!*" the announcer shouts.

The buzzer sounds, the light glows red, and we're all standing, yelling victoriously. With my earplugs in to dull the roar around us, it's an oddly serene moment, watching fans explode, the swarm of players huddling in celebration. Ren, as always, just lifts his stick, chest bumps his teammates, and skates away. Calm and smiling as ever.

Matt's not far off on the bench, breathing heavily from his

shift, glaring daggers at Ren and Rob. He glances over at me and gives me a stony head-to-toe scan before he refocuses on the game.

After the face-off and in possession of the puck, the Wild sail up the center, but Ren's racing with them, skating backward like it's nothing. My body hasn't moved that effortlessly in so long, but I can almost feel what it would be like, the rhythm as he transfers his weight and cuts across the ice. He's low, his stick swinging, and when he pokes for the puck, Ren manages to steal it off of the Wild's player again and break away into the attacking zone. Rob's trailing right behind him, which of course Ren knows. He pulls right, flicks it to Rob, then slips behind the defender. Rob feints right, then passes it left to Ren, who fires a slap-shot into the net.

The light beams red, the horn blows, and Rob wraps an arm around Ren's neck with a proud-papa smile on his face. I catch it on my phone and immediately tweet it.

My eyes traveling down the bench, I see Coach still isn't smiling, but his usual scowl is nowhere to be seen, which at this point I've learned means he's positively fucking blissed.

Ren crosses the center line and squares up, looking focused and relaxed, like a hat trick in the play-offs is just part of the job. His ruddy red-blond hair curls under his helmet, his beard shines copper beneath his visor, and right before the puck drops, Ren glances over at me with those icy eyes and grins.

A flood of warmth pours through my body, cutting the chill that always seeps into my clothes when I'm in the rink.

None of that, Francesca. Don't make something of this that it isn't. He smiles at everyone.

But does he smile at them like *that*? A tiny, preposterous part of me hopes not.

I distract myself from those unsafe thoughts by tweeting the video of Ren's goal, with a quick caption and the relevant hashtags. When I glance up, Lin's working on clearing the puck and sends it flying up to Tyler. Tyler dumps it to Ren, who charges down the center, dekes, then passes left to Kris. Number 27, who's been up Ren's ass the whole game, is flying toward Ren from behind, and I have to swallow the impulse to yell, *Watch out!*

Lifting his stick, 27 deals a brutal hit to Ren from behind. Ren surges forward and smashes into the boards, his head connecting with the plexi and bouncing back, too loose and unanchored for my comfort. I gasp as he drops to the ice like a felled tree.

A good portion of the crowd boos as the whistle is blown. Coach and half the team are screaming, the noise dulled by my earplugs, as if in a faraway tunnel.

"Illegal hit!"

"Dangerous play!"

"Throw him out!"

Noise fades even further until I hear only my pulse. My nails dig into my palms as I stare at Ren's immobile body. Anxiety, my old familiar friend, creeps up my spine, making my legs weak. I drop onto the end of the bench, my eyes glued to Ren.

My breath echoes in my ears. I use yoga breathing, long, slow inhales and exhales through my nose. The pound of my heart slows marginally, but my hands are shaking badly. I shove them between my knees and focus on my breathing some more.

He's okay. He'll be all right.

Anger chases anxiety, tearing through my system. I squeeze my phone, flagrantly ignoring my job for the moment. I don't want to tweet or reassure fans. I want to run out on that ice and punch 27 right in the face.

The ref's bent over Ren, who's out cold, his body splayed helplessly while his arm juts at an unnatural angle. Amy heads out onto the ice and is soon hovering over him, too. He doesn't move. There's no sigh of relief or consciousness. Just ringing, frightening silence.

Then comes the thing I hate to see. The stretcher on wheels.

EMTs shuffle out, quickly stabilizing Ren's neck while leaving his helmet on, and carefully transferring his massive body to the stretcher. Everyone stands in the arena and claps as he's wheeled out. As Amy passes by with him, I see his eyes are shut, his mouth slack. I wipe my nose and feel wetness on my cheeks. When I lick my lips, I taste salt.

Fucking fish sticks. I'm crying. I don't cry. Well, not often. Never publicly. Andy pats my shoulder gently, and I rip out an earplug. "What?" I say sharply.

He's used to my prickly delivery, so he simply pats my shoulder once again and says, "Don't worry, Frankie. Ren's unbustable. He'll be fine."

I watch Ren's skates disappear from view as he's wheeled away. "I hope so."

I'll be the first one to admit that for the rest of the game, I do a rare shitty job at in-game social media. I'm distracted, my fingers slower than normal. I keep fucking up tweets, and my pictures are shit. I use the wrong hashtags, and I can't stop glancing over my shoulder, hoping Amy comes out and ends my worry before I give myself an ulcer.

She doesn't.

Though I'm worried about Ren, this isn't my first season up close with professional hockey, and I know that in all likelihood, he's going to be okay. If something unthinkable happened, I'd know by now. I comfort myself with that bit of rationality as I focus on the postgame necessities. We won, though only because of the goals Ren gave us.

"Frankie," Rob calls from his side of the locker room.

I weave my way through the guys, careful not to catch my cane on a rogue skate lace or piece of clothing. When I get to Rob, I feel winded with anxiety. This has to be about Ren. At least I hope it is. "Yes?"

"He woke up," Rob says.

"Concussion?"

He sighs. "Seems so, yeah."

"Shit." That means Ren's out for the next few games, at least.

"Hurt his shoulder, too, but he's okay."

"His shoulder? Does he need surgery? Is he—"

"Hey. Take a breath. He's all right." Rob gently squeezes my arm. "See? Behind that grumpy front is a soft heart that cares about us."

I scowl at him. "Don't let word get around."

Rob grins. "Your secret's safe with me." When I make to turn away, Rob stops me. "I actually called you over because he asked for you."

"What?" Ren asked for *me*?

"Just go see him. Humor the guy. He's with Amy, and he's comically disoriented."

"That's not very reassuring."

He chuckles as he yanks off his jersey. "Come on. He's always so well behaved. Ren unfiltered is a rare treat. You should be thanking me."

Grumbling, I stroll down the hall, take a few turns, and find my way. Ren's propped up on an angled mattress, an IV, which I hope is just saline, in his arm. Amy's chatting with Coach. They don't notice when I walk in. But Ren does.

"Francesca." He flashes a big, wide grin. Like a Loony Tunes big, wide grin. Holding up the arm that's not bound in a sling, he waves.

Okay, then. There's clearly something else in that IV drip.

"Francesca," he says again, his eyes tracking me as I walk up to him. Nobody has the balls to call me by my full name. I made it very clear to everyone that my name is Frankie. But if anyone could get away with it, it's concussed, delirious Ren. It helps that I have his full name to wield in retribution, too.

"Søren." God, I love his name. It's more Swedish than IKEA. Rather fun fact, his spelling is actually Danish. Being a bit of a foreign languages and linguistics lover—it's a special interest of mine—I can tell you that ø is not in the Swedish alphabet. On one of our many flights, Ren told me its spelling was debated extensively between his Swedish mother's preference for Sören and his American father's love of the Danish philosopher Søren Kierkegaard.

Obviously, no one's wondering where Ren gets his dorkdom. Ren's naming process involved an existentialist theologian and multilingual debate. Pretty sure my parents just pulled an Italian name out of a hat and threw it at me.

"Got yourself good and banged up, there, huh?" I ask.

His eyes dart over my face. "Uh-huh. But I didn't piss myself, and I know my birthday, so Amy said I'll be okay."

At hearing her name, Amy breaks her conversation with Coach and smiles at Ren. "Oh, he's in rare form right now. Had to give him Percocet for his shoulder."

"No social media!" Coach warns.

I lift my hands, demonstrating my innocence. "Not a camera in sight, I promise." I glance at Ren. "You needed a narcotic for a bruised shoulder?"

"Give him some credit," Amy says gently. "It's slightly separated, and that hurts like hell." She leans in and grins. "He also passed out when I inserted his IV."

"Wow, Judas." He narrows his eyes at her, then turns back toward me. "Redheads have been scientifically proven to need higher doses of pain relief, Francesca. We're sensitive."

"I'm teasing you, Ren the Red. I can't imagine how much it hurts. That check was dangerously late and high."

Coach grunts in agreement as he swigs from his water bottle. "Absolute bullshit. Glad they threw him out." Patting Ren's good shoulder, he tosses his water bottle in the recycling bin. "Time to round up the boys. Take it easy, Bergman. You did good, as always."

"Thanks, Coach."

When the door bangs shut, Ren clasps my hand suddenly, fingers curling around it.

"Francesca, pay attention. This is important."

He's like a kid right now. Wide-eyed and deeply sincere. I let myself stare at his features, knowing he probably won't remember. His hand holding mine feels oddly familiar. It's warm and heavy, the scrape of his calluses soothing my skin.

"You need a masky thingamabob. I have a fever. And I keep touching you. And breathing near you. Dr. Amy!" he hollers.

"Ren." She laughs. "Right here, buddy. What's up?"

"This here Francesca is . . ." He frowns. "Ah, I can't think of the word right now. But it means her medicine makes her body very friendly toward the germs. She needs something so she's safe from my plague."

Amy grins at me, then directs herself to Ren. "While that's very considerate of you, I'm confident your fever isn't due to anything plague related. When I was assessing you, I noticed signs of a sinus infection. Remember, I told you I was going to give you some antibiotics?"

He stares at her. "I do not remember that."

She pats his good arm. "That's because you got your head knocked nicely. You told me you'd had a cold recently, and I told you it seems like you developed a secondary bacterial infection in your sinus cavity from it. That's why you're fevered."

He squints at her one-eyed. "Can you maybe condense that to smaller words? I'm not following."

"What I mean to say is," she says gently, "you aren't contagious. You won't get Frankie sick."

"Oh, good." Ren sighs and lets his eyes fall shut. "So, she can keep holding my hand, then, and I won't give her the plague."

"I should go anyway," I tell him. "Time for you to sleep, Zenzero." Slowly, I start to pull my hand away, but Ren clamps down on it, and his eyes pop open.

"That's it. *That's* what I wanted to ask you." He tries to sit up and falls back, grimacing. "Forgot about that," he groans.

"Easy. You know I'm always around. We can talk tomorrow."

"No." He stares at me seriously. "I need to know this. *What* does *zenzero* mean?"

A hot blush floods my cheeks. I clear my throat self-consciously. Amy's loitering near the door on her phone, and she's entirely within earshot. The last thing I need is her giving me shit for this. "Well, it's silly," I say, lowering my voice. "It's just Italian nonsense."

"Nonsense." He frowns. "You call me *nonsense*?"

"Dammit, Bergman. No," I whisper. "It means *ginger*, okay? Because you're . . ." I wave my hand in the general vicinity of his face. "You're a ginger. It's cute."

Ren's smile is so bright, its voltage could power a city block. He cranes his head toward Amy. "Hear that, Dr. Amy? She thinks I'm cute."

But before I can say a word in my defense, he shuts his eyes on a soft sigh, drifting off, his hand locked tight around mine.

EIGHT

Frankie

Playlist: "Undertow," Lisa Hannigan

If Ren remembered our little narcotic-induced heart-to-heart, he didn't let on. Over breakfast at the hotel the next morning, he flashed me his standard friendly smile, and then he treated me like he always does. Like a woman he works with. *Not* like a woman he called Francesca, whose hand he insisted on holding until he fell into a restless sleep.

Which I'm fine with. Honestly, it's easier that he doesn't remember. If he had remembered it, I could just picture his acute embarrassment, that furious blush, the remorse that would paint his apology, even though I found what he did amusing and oddly endearing.

Back on the plane home after losing game two, unfortunately—but unsurprisingly, since we played without Ren—I stick my nose in work and avoid talking to anyone. If I don't glue my eyes to my phone or laptop, they keep stupidly wandering across the plane to where Ren sits, leafing through a small paperback that I'm 99 percent sure is Shakespeare; the dork.

Dammit. This is why lines can't be blurred, boundaries can't be crossed. Just a few nonstandard encounters with him and now every time I'm near Ren, weird sensations simmer beneath the surface of my skin. When I saw him yesterday at the game in his charcoal-gray suit and noticed it turned his eyes the color of rain-slicked slate—when I watched him talk with his teammates, giving them his entire focus and that wide-mouthed laugh—my stomach knotted furiously.

Just after I got seated on the plane, my breath caught when he strolled past me and left in his wake that familiar clean, spicy scent. It made my mouth water. It wasn't the first time it happened, but previously, I chalked it up to it being an astonishingly nice scent. The guy has good taste in cologne. So what?

So what? So this time, as I breathed him in, my body ached so fiercely in neglected places, I nearly slapped myself. And then I buckled down on work.

The flight hasn't been the smoothest, and it's hard to concentrate on work. Twice, when I glance up, I could swear Ren's eyes had just gone back to his book. And now he busts me watching him. That pale, catlike gaze slides up from the page it's been tracking and locks with mine. My breath catches in my throat.

I blink away.

What *is* this?

Heartburn. That's it. I had that spicy tuna roll for dinner before we left. I rub my chest, trying to coax away this hot, tight, burning *something*. Ugh. No more tuna roll.

Dipping my head back to my computer, even after I'm forced to pack up for descent, I don't look up until our wheels touch down with bone-rattling bumpiness. Until I'm safe once again, grounded to earth and reality.

Player. Employee. And "never the twain shall meet." Yeah. Ren's not the only literature dork around here.

I might not hard-core jam on Shakespeare like Søren, but I like my books. They're one of the most vital tools in my arsenal for navigating human behavior, to explore my feelings about the parts of life that most confuse me. Books help me feel a bit more connected to a world that often is hard to make sense of. Books are patient with me. They don't laugh at me instead of with me. They don't ask why I'm "always" frowning, or why I can't sit still. Books welcome me—weirdness and all—and take me exactly as I am.

After our rough landing, we deplane and head onto the bus back to Toyota Sports Center, our practice facility. Seated alone, I power on my phone, only to see Annie's text:

> Worst timing ever, but I'm at the hospital.
> Can't tell if it's preterm labor or a false alarm.
> I'd tell Tim to leave me here and come get
> you, but I think he'd divorce me for it. I'm SO
> sorry. Can you call me when you land? I feel
> awful. I know you don't like Ubering this late
> at night.

Shit. I'm worried about Annie. And I'm worried about getting home. Because Annie's right.

I find late-night rides alone in a taxi driven by a strange dude nerve-wracking.

Maybe it's the New Yorker in me, but I'm cautious about what situations I place myself in. I have pride, yes, and I don't like to be babied, but I am also a practical woman. I can acknowledge that my ability to defend myself is objectively less than that of a woman whose hands and feet move much more readily.

My car was acting weird before we left for Saint Paul and had to go to the shop *again*, so Annie and Tim offered to pick me up when I got back. My other friend Lorena doesn't have a car, so I can't ask her to come instead. Which means, now that Annie's unable to get me, I'm screwed.

"Everything okay?"

I jump in my seat at the sound of Ren's voice and drop my phone. It lands with a sickening crack on the bus floor.

"*Zounds!*" Ren leans and picks it up.

"Did you just swear in Shakespeare—"

"Let's move on and pretend I didn't do that." Ren's cheeks are bright red. Sighing in relief when he turns it over, Ren hands me my phone, demonstrating the screen somehow survived the drop. "I'm sorry I startled you."

"That's okay." When I take my phone, our fingers brush, and a crack of electricity snaps through my skin. I yelp and pull away, a scowl tightening my mouth. I always look murderous when caught off guard because, while most people startle mildly when surprised, I jump out of my skin, adrenaline floods my system, and all I want to do is curl up into the fetal position. It's unsettling and embarrassing.

"You okay?" Ren asks.

"I'm fine." I make a fist and release it. My hand's trembling. "That didn't hurt you?"

He shrugs. "I felt a jolt. But I was expecting it."

Expecting it. What does that mean?

Ren's eyes are on me, his mouth shifting from an easy grin to a frown of concern. "You don't *look* okay. What's up?"

I glance at my phone, staring at Annie's text. "My ride home fell through. I'm a grouch when it comes to a change in plans, but it's not a big deal. I'll figure it out."

"Let me give you a ride." When he sees my uneasy look, he nudges my thigh gently. "You've already been in the minivan. You know how cool it is. How can you say no?"

His eyes hold mine, that easy, gentle smile in place. Something tells me getting in that van alone with Ren is asking for trouble. But weighed against a late-night Uber ride with a possibly cane-fetishizing murderer—laugh all you want, but it's a statistical possibility and those aren't chances I want to take, even when chances are slim—it's not enough to deter me.

"All right," I tell him. "Thanks."

Ren's smile widens before he schools his expression. "Cool." He picks up his book and doesn't say another word.

When our bus rolls to a stop outside the practice facility, Ren stands and stretches. It sets his hips at my eye level and it's too easy to picture him more than shirtless—pale skin, the shadow of hair arrowing down his stomach. . . .

I glance away furiously as heat floods my cheeks. After fumbling with shoving my phone in my bag, I ease up from my seat, stifling a moan of discomfort. My joints practically creak as I straighten, a process that takes longer than it should. When I hike my bag onto my shoulder and stand fully, I notice Ren's positioned himself slightly behind our row of seats, his arms braced on each side, sealing off the row until I'm clear.

Half the guys stand behind him, eyes on their phones, their small carry-on bags on their shoulders. They're waiting.

"Sorry!" I call. "Granny Frankie's slow moving."

A bunch of variations on *"You're good, Frankie"* travel the bus. Taking my time down those stupid steep steps off the bus, I make it out into the balmy California air waiting for us and draw in a long, deep breath.

Suddenly, weight leaves my shoulder. I gape as I watch Ren fluidly hoist my bag up his arm, as he hauls not only his equipment—yes, the man *insists* on carrying his own equipment and not letting the lowly assistants schlep his stuff—but also both of our suitcases, all with the use of one good arm.

"I'm feeling slightly useless," I yell. "And you're supposed to be careful of your shoulder."

Ren grins back at me. "My shoulder's fine. Besides, I'm antsy. I had to sit on my butt and watch a game. Just getting a little functional fitness in."

Ignoring the option to drop off some of his stuff in the facility,

Ren pulls out his keys, and the van's trunk hatch opens with a chirp. After neatly loading our luggage, Ren steps to my side to open the door for me, waiting as I slide into the seat and buckle up. My laptop bag is set neatly at my feet before he closes my door and jogs over to his side.

Our practice facility is in El Segundo, a ten-minute drive west of my rented bungalow in Hawthorne, which is the opposite direction from Ren's house in Manhattan Beach. I feel bad about making him go out of his way to take me home, but having a safe ride back is worth taking this bite of humble pie.

Before he pulls out, Ren turns on the radio and picks a station that's quiet but strummy.

Guitars, violins, maybe even a ukulele. The man's voice is gentle and soft. It's relaxing. I stifle a sigh as I settle into the soft leather of my seat and crack open my window, hoping it'll wake me up a bit from this dreamy stupor his car's putting me in.

"You can change the music, if you want." Ren watches the road carefully, then crosses traffic.

"I like it. Thanks, though."

He nods and focuses on the road. Ren looks absurdly right driving a minivan. I can just picture him years down the road, behind the wheel, a few more lines at the corners of his eyes, a wedding band claiming his left ring finger. Taking his kids to soccer practice, passing Goldfish bags and juice boxes to the back seat, singing loudly to Disney music on the stereo. And then, stupidly, I see myself in the exact seat I'm in, somehow belonging in that picture.

Honestly, Francesca.

Snapping my glance away, I focus out the window. After a long spate of comfortable quiet, I clear my throat and tell him, "Thanks again for the ride. Sorry to take you out of the way."

"It's no problem, Frankie. I'm always happy to give you a ride home." He takes the right off El Segundo Boulevard onto In-glewood.

Minutes later, we pull up to my house, and Ren unloads my stuff as I fish out my keys from my bag and walk up to the door. I slide my key into the dead bolt first, freezing when I turn and don't feel the bolt slide back. It's unlocked. I test the handle. That's un-locked, too.

"What is it?" Ren sets my suitcase gently between us.

"My door . . ." It comes out hoarse and threadbare. "My door is open."

"Frankie." The urgency in Ren's voice makes my head snap up just in time to realize he's sweeping me up off my feet, holding my entire body easily in one arm—*holy shit*—and carrying my suitcase in the other.

I'm stashed in the van, Ren sprints around to the other side, and he drives quickly down the road, before parking and opening his phone. I watch his fingers dial 911.

"W-what are you doing?" I ask him.

Ren glances up at me as the phone rings. "Calling the police. Most violence related to burglaries happens during break-ins, when the homeowner walks in on the intruders. If someone's still in there— Hi, yes . . ."

I stare at Ren as he speaks calmly with that composed, even voice he uses on the ice, the one that he used after Maddox got drunk and stupid on me.

I always find it fascinating to watch people like Ren in action during a crisis. People whose stress response isn't shutting down their ability to function. Ren's the guy who thinks analytically and keeps his shit together when the world's burning. I'm the one who sinks to the floor and forgets how to breathe.

He tells them my address, explains the situation. I should be helping. Talking. Doing anything to take control of the situation.

But instead, I sit there, staring down the road at my little rented bungalow that I've worked so hard to make feel like home. It's been broken into. Invaded.

A cold numbness sweeps through my body.

Ren's voice rushes over me, a warm breeze that pulls me from my frozen shock. "Frankie. Police are coming. It's going to be okay. Do you have your landlord's number?"

I nod. But I can't seem to move my hands to find my phone. Carefully, Ren bends and extracts my phone from my bag. "What's his name?"

"Mike Williams," I whisper.

Ren dials, slowly opens his door, and stands outside the van, his eyes glued to the bungalow. He leaves the window down so air comes in, so I can hear his conversation, if I were capable of following it. But slowly, a roar louder than the Pacific's waves eclipses my hearing. Tears prick my eyes.

There are these tiny moments when missing my dad is acute and unexpected. He died when I was twelve. I'm twenty-six. I've lived longer without him than with him, so why, so many years fatherless, do I feel like I would give anything right now to feel safe in his strong arms, to hear his gravelly voice comforting me?

Great. Now I'm crying. And I don't cry in front of others. Because since I moved to California and realized I had a chance to rewrite the script on how people saw the autistic girl with a limp, Project Make Frankie Badass consists of an impenetrable, chilly front. Nowadays, I cry *privately*.

I cry into bowls of ice cream on the twenty-fourth through twenty-ninth days of my cycle. I cry watching those TV shows where they build homes for people in crisis. I cry when that humane shelter commercial comes up on the hotel TV every away game, because I miss my dog, who's staying with Aunt Lorena while Mommy travels, and I want a houseful of cats, and my

bungalow, which was affordable-ish, close to both the practice facility and the arena, was perfect but for one small thing—"*no
cats!*"—so I can't be the cat lady I've always wanted to be and now
my house doesn't even feel like it's safe and—

"Frankie." Ren rips open his door, dropping into the driver's
seat while he lunges over the console and wraps me in his arms.
"Hey. *Shh*, it's okay. You're okay. We'll get it figured out."

Now I'm not just crying in public, I'm *sobbing*. In Ren Bergman's arms no less, getting snot and tears all over his nice suit and
fisting that soft blue dress shirt as hard as my aching fingers will
let me.

Have you ever started out crying for one thing and found yourself crying for so much more by the time you really get going?
That's what happens to me sometimes. That's what happens now.

Crying because I miss feeling safe in my home already. Crying
because I'm hurting, and I'm tired of hurting. Crying because
when shit happens, I want my sister, my mom, my grandmother,
and they're an entire country away. Crying because I need my dad,
and he's not here, and he never again will be. Crying because I miss
my dog. Crying because this break-in scares me and makes me feel
vulnerable, and I work very hard not to feel that way.

"Frankie." Ren presses his cheek to the top of my head and
holds me close. "Can you take a deep breath?"

I breathe in, then release a long, shuddering exhale.

"Good," he says softly. "And again?"

I take another slow, calming breath. And another. And another. Until my breathing is even, and my tears are only silent, sliding down my cheeks. At some point in my breakdown he started
rubbing my back in a slow, soothing, circular motion. I sigh and
lean in to him.

"I called your landlord," Ren says. "He's going to talk with the
police, make sure they get the place clear and safe again." Ren's

hand slides up my back, then cups the nape of my neck. "Do you have any pets they need to keep an eye out for? Your dog, right?" he asks gently.

I burst an ugly sob against his chest. "Pazzaaaaa."

Ren pulls back enough to cup my face in both hands and search my eyes. "Frankie, I can't understand you."

"Pazza, my dog." I manage a long, slow breath without crying. "She's with Lo."

"Your friend Lorena?"

I frown. "Y-yes, Lorena. But how did you know?"

"You've mentioned her a bunch of times, Frankie."

Pretty sure I might have mentioned her *once*, but . . . Ren's thumbs stroke my cheeks, making this dazed feeling wash over me. My breathing calms again and tears finally stop blurring my vision. "Pazza," I whisper.

"Do you want to go to Lorena's? You need somewhere to stay until they sort this out and you feel safe to come home."

Lo has a new girlfriend, Mia. A new girlfriend that she's mildly obsessed with, who recently took the cohabitation leap and moved into Lorena's studio. I can't stay at Lo's. There's nowhere to sleep and no privacy.

Then there's Annie. Annie and Tim are expecting their first baby, and their second bedroom is now a nursery, not to mention, they're at the hospital possibly preparing to bring home a premature baby. Sure, they have a couch, but I can't sleep on couches because they're hell for my joints.

Last time I slept on a couch was at a house party in college, and the next morning, I couldn't get out of it. I had to be helped upright by the guy I'd just finally given in to dating. As soon as he got me standing, he made up some excuse about a Saturday study session he'd forgotten about.

He'd never seen me have a bad day, and on my first one, it

scared him off. On my slow walk home, I texted him we were over. Then I sat in the shower until the hot water ran out, soothing the aches in my joints as much as my heart.

"Um." I wipe my nose. "I think I'll just get a hotel tonight."

Ren frowns. "The hell you're sleeping in a hotel, Frankie. You just came home to a ransacked house. You need to be with friends."

"Søren." I scrub my face. He's right, and I don't want to admit it. I don't want to stay somewhere impersonal and be alone. But I don't have any other options. "You're being high-handed."

"Francesca. You're being stubborn."

I drop my hands. "I do not have a wide friendship circle. I have two friends, and neither of them has room for me."

Ren bends so our eyes meet. Holding my gaze, he sets out his hand, facing up. Without thinking, I slide my palm across his, swallowing a sigh at the heat of his skin. His fingers gently wrap around mine.

"You forgot about one more LA friend, and he has more room than he knows what to do with, Frankie." That bright Ren Bergman smile twinkles in the moonlight. "Me."

NINE

Ren

Playlist: "Sisyphus," Andrew Bird

This is fine. It's fine. I'm fine.

If I tell myself this enough, it's going to be fine.

Frankie sits in the back seat, baby talking to her dog, Pazza, a Siberian husky and Alaskan malamute mix. She's not crying anymore, which has significantly improved my ability to breathe properly and drive us safely to my place. Frankie crying made me feel like my heart was being cut out of my chest.

After we talked with the cops, they confirmed a break-in and took inventory of what was stolen—her TV, her computer monitor that she connects to her laptop, emergency meds, most of her clothes, and a lot of pantry items. One small comfort was she kept all sensitive information in a secure safe, so the police were confident her identity wouldn't be stolen.

With nothing left to do at the bungalow, I navigated us, per her request, to the In-N-Out drive-through, prepared to buy the franchise if necessary, whatever it took to put a smile on her face.

Two chocolate shakes, three large fries, and a Double-Double later, Frankie seemed tentatively comforted. But our trip to Lorena's place in Echo Park was the real fix. She hasn't stopped smiling, cuddling Pazza, a massive black-and-white dog with keen gold eyes who stares at me in the rearview mirror, baring her teeth.

"Frankie?"

"Yes?" she singsongs right into the dog's furry neck. "Who's my good girl?"

Pazza finally breaks her glare long enough to turn and lick Frankie's face.

"Your Musky looks like she wants to eat me for dinner."

Frankie laughs softly. "This mix is called an Alusky, Søren."

I try to ignore how much I like hearing Frankie say my full name. I've healed from most wounds sustained in the tough teen years, but the brutal teasing I got for my name is like the last aching scar that just won't fade. *Nobody* calls me Søren, except Axel when he's looking for a fight.

When Frankie says my name, it sounds warm, and when I let my imagination get carried away, I'd even say affectionate.

I pull into my driveway. "An Alusky."

"Yes. And she doesn't eat big, tough hockey players. She eats grain-free."

Throwing the car in park, I peer over my shoulder. "Well, I'm grain-free, too. This isn't comforting, to hear your wolf is paleo."

"She's not a wolf!" Pazza nuzzles Frankie, gently knocking her back on her seat.

Immediately the dog whines and drops her head to her lap. "I'm okay, Pazza."

"Do we have everything she needs for now?"

Frankie smiles at me over the dog's head. "Yeah. Lo made her enough food to last a few days."

"You *make* her food?"

Frankie's eyes narrow. "Yes, Søren."

"Don't 'Søren' me, Francesca. It was a question."

"You repeated what I said."

"I was just surprised, Frankie. I'm not judging."

"Good," she says. "Because feeding your dog fresh food is proven to increase their health and longevity." Frankie kisses Pazza's head. "I want her around for as long as I can have her."

There's tenderness in Frankie's voice that I've never heard before. At work she's brisk and no-nonsense. But just like when I surprised her the other night bringing her that shirt and ended up sharing her takeout, it's another side of Francesca Zeferino that makes me experience even more off-the-table feelings for her.

Which is disastrous. Super disastrous. I might not read romance novels as voraciously as Viggo, but I've picked up enough in my day to know that forbidden love is a messy trope, about as fraught a story line—besides love triangles, and eff those—as it gets.

Exhibit A: *Romeo and Juliet*. Their love is forbidden, the timing is terrible, but they're so infatuated with each other, they throw caution to the wind. Impatient courtship, shotgun wedding, miscommunication, hotheaded tempers, violence, missed connections, it all ends in the star-crossed pair offing themselves.

Yep. Forbidden love is the one to avoid. Which means, of course, that I find myself in the thick of it. Typical life of Søren Bergman.

I step out of my car on a sigh, circle the van, then slide open the back-passenger door. Frankie eases out of it, followed by her dog. "Pazza, sit," Frankie says.

Pazza drops to her haunches, tail wagging.

"Good girl. *Ben fatto. Brava*," Frankie croons, and scratches her ear. Her voice is low and cadent, like when she says *Zenzero*. It's ridiculously hot.

Glancing up at me, she frowns, her eyes tightening with concern as she searches my face.

"Everything okay?" she asks.

"Yep. Everything's okay." *It's so not okay.* "You, uh, speak some Italian?"

"Oh. Pretty much fluent. My dad came over with my grandmother when he was five. So I grew up speaking it with them. And I'm a bit of a polyglot. I love learning new languages."

Great. Just great. The woman who's about to be a guest in my house and for whom I harbor unrequited, inappropriately love-like feelings also speaks a sexy Romance language.

The unbidden image of Frankie whispering Italian in my ear while her touch wanders my body practically blinds me as it soars across my mind, a fantasy with as little chance of a future as the dying star that bolts through the sky overhead.

I blink, shaking myself out of those thoughts. "That's . . . impressive."

"*Pazza* is Italian, too," Frankie says cheerily, bending to kiss the dog's snout. "Well, her name is. Means *crazy*. Because she was absolutely nuts as a puppy—I'm talking psychotic. She was like the Energizer Bunny. . . ." Frankie's eyes dance my way, and she frowns. "You sure you're okay, Ren? I guess this is a bit more than you bargained for when you offered me a ride home, huh?"

"Frankie, I'm glad to be able to have you here. Well, I mean I'm not glad your house was burgled." I sigh and scrub my face.

A smile tips her mouth. "I know what you mean," she says quietly.

"Right. Let's get inside." I take a step toward her, reaching for the heavy messenger bag weighing down her shoulder, but Frankie throws up her hands. "Wait, Ren! Pazza's territorial. . . ." Her voice dies off as the dog approaches me, sniffs my hand, and drags her tongue right along my knuckles.

I stand still, watching Pazza nuzzle me, before she makes a soft whining noise. She glances up and holds my eyes, cocking her head to the side.

"She likes you," Frankie says quietly.

I break my gaze from Pazza and look over at Frankie. "Seems like a friendly dog. Doesn't she like everybody? Besides the delivery guy."

"Nope. She's cautious around everyone except Lo and Annie. She's okay with Tim, warming up to Mia."

"Well, then I'm honored." I scratch Pazza's other ear and smile at her. "That's a nice club to be a part of."

When I glance up, Frankie's watching me curiously, a small smile tugging at her mouth until it morphs into a reluctant yawn.

"Come on, Francesca. Let's get you and Pazza tucked in."

———

I wake up to faint sunlight, early, like always. The house is quiet. No clatter of dog paws, no soft noises I might expect if Frankie was awake. Throwing on a pair of gym shorts and a T-shirt, I walk by the guest bedroom I set up for her. The door's closed.

In the kitchen, I notice my Nespresso machine was used, and a solitary spoon sits by the sink in a small caramel puddle. Milk with coffee. Exactly how Frankie likes it. Cream, if it's available, one sugar.

I sound like a creeper knowing that. But having unrequited feelings for a woman for over three years, with no appropriate opportunity to socialize outside of work without raising suspicion, you soak up every little detail you can when you're together.

The faint noise of a dog barking comes from the shore. I follow the sound, opening the sliding doors onto the deck, and I'm greeted by a sight I wish I'd had the wherewithal to prepare for.

Frankie in yoga pants and another oversized sweatshirt. She stands barefoot down on the shore, tossing a ball for Pazza, who bolts along the packed sand, then scoops it nimbly away from foamy waves curling toward her. Wind sweeps Frankie's dark hair into inky ribbons that glow against the sunrise. The sun creeps over the water's edge, bouncing off her cheekbones, the soft upturn of her nose.

Her smile is small, her thoughts seemingly far away.

There's rarely a smile warming Frankie's face. Most times her mouth is set in a hard line. The guys joke about it—Frank the Crank, they call her. But I've never seen her that way. She's serious. No bullshit. But often women feel they have to be like that to be respected in their work, to ensure men don't get ideas and cross boundaries.

Also, she has arthritis. She doesn't always seem to be uncomfortable, but I can tell when she's in pain, and it's not infrequent. I wouldn't exactly walk around smiling constantly if my body hurt like that.

Not that you'd believe inflammation riddles Frankie's joints as she whips the ball through the air in a fastball pitch. An involuntary whistle of appreciation leaves me, and her head whips my way, the portrait of surprised.

Then the weirdest thing happens. Her eyes crinkle. Her mouth tips into a wide smile. The dimple pops. And my heart nearly tumbles out of my chest. She looks . . . happy to see me.

I soak it up, greedy, starved. A look like that is once in a lifetime. Because Frankie does a lot of grunting hello. Cursory, no-eye-contact waves. Of course, I know she respects me, that she trusts me to be a decent person as it pertains to our work, but this?

This is new. Rare. A knot of nerves tightens my stomach as I lift a hand tentatively.

She raises her thermos of coffee in response and yells, "Come on! I can't throw this ball forever!"

Jogging down across the sand, I take the ball from Pazza when she next bounds back with it.

Then I throw it in a high arc through the air.

Frankie watches with narrowing eyes. "Show-off," she mutters into her thermos before she takes a sip.

"Says the woman with a mean softball pitch."

She glances up at me. "You saw that, did you?"

"I did. You been holding out on me, Zeferino?"

"Hardly." She sips her coffee again. "I haven't thrown a softball since junior year of high school, before . . ." Another sip of coffee. "It's been a long time. And it hurts like hell. How I didn't dislocate my elbow pitching like that, I'll never know."

When she returns, I give Pazza an affectionate pat to her side, then throw the ball for her again. "Well, it looks like you still have it."

Frankie gives me a sidelong glance. Her cheeks pink a little before her eyes dart away.

"Thanks."

Silence falls between us, but I don't mind it. I grew up with chaos—a family of seven siblings and two busy parents—and I know my way around it, how to yell loud enough to be heard, how to shove and tease and vie for attention. But two years into living in my house on the beach, this big house that I hope one day grows as full of lovable chaos as the one I grew up in, I've learned to enjoy quiet. So, I listen to the waves break on the shore. I watch the wind curl Frankie's hair up into the air as sunrise breaks over the water. And it feels inexplicably right.

"Zenzero."

I snap out of it. "I was staring. Sorry. You look good backlit by the sunrise—that is, I mean, that was a strictly platonic statement. . . ." My voice fades as a blush burns my cheeks.

Frankie grins up at me. "Don't worry. You're still cute, even tripping over your words, Mr. Calm, Cool, and Happy."

I frown at her. "*That's* how you see me?" Try Crazed, Hot, and Bothered.

She shrugs and returns her focus to Pazza. "I'm starting to figure out there's more to you than that sunshine smile."

"And what's that?"

Pazza comes barreling our way and skids to a sandy halt at our feet as she drops the ball.

Tipping her head, she glances between the two of us, her tongue lolling happily out of her mouth.

Frankie sweeps up the ball from the sand and tosses it softly into the air, catching it as she walks by me. "A bashful, dorky sweetheart. I pity the women of Los Angeles when this gets out, Ren."

"Wait." I scramble to catch up to Frankie, which isn't hard. She moves slower in the morning. She's also not using her cane, so she favors her left leg and walks carefully. "Frankie, just to be clear, I want my personal life to be just between me and friends."

Frankie stops at the bottom of the steps up to my deck. "So, we're friends, are we?"

"You said so the other night."

She lifts an eyebrow. "True. But if my hazy weed memory serves me correctly, I made you impersonate a tomato when I said it."

I scrub my neck. "You caught me off guard. I didn't know you liked me enough to call me a friend."

Frankie's smile disappears. "What?"

"No, wait." I swallow nervously. "That came out wrong. I—I need coffee. Let's go inside, and I'll try that again."

Frankie leads the way, but Pazza stops, blocking my progress as she looks up and gives me an incredulous look.

"Trust me," I mutter to the dog. "Ryder's told me all about it. I'm the king of sticking my foot in my mouth." Pazza huffs, then trots off ahead of me.

After Frankie hoses off Pazza's paws and her feet, we settle into the kitchen. The sound of a dog lapping up her meal is the only noise in the room as Frankie stands at the island and grins at me over her coffee. I swallow a scalding gulp and try to formulate my thoughts. I'm so infuriatingly clumsy with my words around her.

Setting down my coffee, I narrow my eyes at her amused grin. "Enjoy watching me squirm?"

Frankie's grin deepens and out comes the dimple. "I can't lie, Zenzero, it's entertaining. You're usually so chill."

I turn my coffee mug slowly, clockwise. "I've learned things go better for me when that's what other people see."

"But that's not all there is, is it? What most people see is . . . incomplete."

My eyes lift and find hers. Her irises glitter, forest green dappled with gold, like sunlight peeking through a canopy of leaves. "Yes."

"Well," Frankie says as she sets down her coffee and clears her throat. "I very much empathize with that, Zenzero. Your secret is safe with me."

I tip my head, hoping she'll give me more. Instead she shifts on her feet and says, "While we're on the subject of privacy, I want you to consider how my staying with you looks. I need it to be very clear with the team that extenuating circumstances, and nothing else, led to me staying with you."

"Understood. I'll tell the guys so there are no rumors. Your place was broken into. I live close by. It was late. You crashed here. You'll be staying here until it's safe to move back. That okay?"

"Yes, that works." Slowly, she walks over to the sink and rinses out her mug, whistling to Pazza. "Except . . . do you mean that about staying here until the house is ready? Not that it will be long, just until the landlord fixes the little bit of damage, changes the locks, and insurance gets what they need."

"Of course I mean it. And I imagine it might be a while before you feel comfortable going back home, even after they straighten everything out and it's secure again. So, just know that this place is yours for however long you want."

She seems to hesitate, biting her lip. "Thank you. On my side of things, I'll talk to Darlene, let her know our living situation. Just be open about it so it's not weird." Darlene's her boss. The head honcho for all our media and PR. "I'm going to hop in the shower, then."

Heat rushes through me. It's too easy to picture water sliding down her chest, furrowing between her thighs. I exhale roughly and tug my shirt, trying to cool myself off. "Shower. Sure. Great."

God, I'm hopeless.

Frankie gives me an amused smile. "Okay. I'll be ready at eight?"

"Sounds good." I throw back the remainder of my coffee, hoping its burning path down my throat distracts me. *Don't do it. Not anymore. Don't think about Frankie naked in the shower. Don't. Don't. Don't.*

The hot water kicks on, and I drop my head to the counter with a groan. Too late.

TEN

Frankie

Playlist: "Go Wild," Friedberg

Annie stares at me in disbelief. "Why am I just hearing about this?"

I shift in my seat at the outdoor café that's our usual lunch spot. It's a midway point between the practice facility, Annie's research lab, and the campus where Lorena teaches. Ren and I have an afternoon PR gig at Children's, and he offered to drive me after this lunch date with my friends.

As I hesitate to explain myself to Annie, I glance over at Ren, seated on the other side of the café. He takes a sip of his tea, book in hand. He's hidden at a two-top tucked into a shady corner.

"I didn't want to worry you," I tell her. "You were possibly birthing a human last night. You're in a delicate condition."

Annie snorts. "Listen, I know we read that scintillating historical romance the other month in book club, but that phrase does not hold up. I'm not delicate. I'm pregnant. And it was indigestion, apparently. I can handle bad news without having a fit of the vapors. Call me next time your house gets broken into and ransacked."

I meet Annie's big moss-green eyes. She pushes her nerd glasses up her freckled button nose and frowns at me. "I'm serious," she says.

I grasp her hand and squeeze. "I'm sorry."

"I forgive you." Annie stabs a chunk of chicken, lettuce, and tomato, then shoves it in her mouth. "Provided you come to water aerobics tonight."

"Ugh, fine. I know I've been missing a lot, but play-offs schedule is brutal. I'll be free to watercize my ass off consistently once we're done."

"You two and your water aerobics." Lo shakes her head, then freezes mid-scrolling through her phone. "Hey, Frankie. Have you been on Twitter lately?"

I feel my color drain. I'm social media savvy enough to know that lead never bodes well.

"Not since this morning. We did a live-session Q and A in the locker room this morning after practice, for play-offs hype; then I came here. Why?"

Lo slides her phone toward me. It's a paparazzi shot, taken right outside the practice facility, before Ren and I left to come here. His hand rests low on my back as he reaches for the car door. A tiny gesture as I caught my toe on uneven asphalt that felt so surprisingly *good*. Maybe it was because he didn't say anything. Just gently steadied me with that warm, solid hand as he opened my door.

Annie leans over to see Twitter unfurling with comments that have my stomach rolling. Pushing her glasses up her nose, she glances from Lo's phone to me. "Wow. Lots of women really don't like you already, huh?"

The comments unfold at alarming speed. Some are nice. Many are awful.

> Ooh, I want her shoes. Is that a *cane*?
> Wow. I thought he was gay.

Lorena crunches on an ice cube from her tea and swears under her breath. "That right there is why we need feminism. To exorcise embedded patriarchy from our culture, women have got to stop internalizing toxic male practices like hierarchical aggression and then wielding them against each other."

Annie sits back in her seat and puts her plate on her round belly with a sigh. "While true, Lo, maybe what Frankie needs is less cultural critique and more practical insight right now."

Lo throws up her hands. "I'm in liberal arts academia. I'm the worst person to come to for anything practical."

Both of my friends turn to face me. Their heads tip in twin looks of concern. Sweet and tiny Annie, with her pragmatism and her big heart. Lo with those sharp mocha eyes and badass facial piercings that hide a sensitive, philosophical soul. They're as different on the outside as they are on the inside. And especially right now, I don't know what I'd do without them.

"It's all right." I shrug. "Nothing to be done, really. Just wait for the comments when they call me his pity fuck."

"Oop, one just rolled in," Annie mutters.

Lo and I swivel our gazes at her.

Annie turns bright red and sinks lower in her chair. "Sorry. Pregnancy brain. Can I have a pass for that?"

"One," Lo says sternly. She takes the phone back from Annie, scrolling through the comments. Her expression hardens, and she flips over her phone, setting it on the table so the screen is hidden. "I want to throat-punch those evil trolls."

"But you can't," I remind her. "So, let's move on, shall we?"

Lo stares at me for a long minute. She has a very disturbing ability to intuit my thoughts, so I blink away, avoiding eye contact as I take a long, slow breath to quiet my pounding heart. I have experience with this, maybe not with it being directed so aggressively at *me*, but social media is a beast I handle capably every day.

It's not a big deal. People are assholes. I'm used to being judged for my appearance—the cane *and* my flat expression. What's a few hundred thousand people thinking the worst of me?

"So," Annie says, squeezing my hand affectionately. "When do you get your acceptance letter from UCLA?"

"That's not a sure thing," I remind her. "Who knows if I'll get accepted?"

Annie rolls her eyes. "Please. You'll get accepted. You are made to do sports law. Your admissions documents were perfection."

"It's true," Lo chimes in. "I edited them for you. I made sure of it."

"We'll see," I mutter.

Annie pats my hand. "Let's move on. I can see you getting upset talking about it."

"It makes me anxious to think about it. I'd rather just forget I applied and be pleasantly surprised if I somehow manage to get in."

"Fair enough," Annie says. "How's teaching, Lo?"

As Lo answers, my gaze wanders over to Ren, tucked into his circumspect corner. His book rests flat on a small two-top table, his water and tea neatly side by side.

"Frankie." Lo's voice startles me.

I glance back at her. "What?"

She flicks her lip piercing with her tongue and wiggles her eyebrows, making her brow piercings do a little dance. "See something you like?"

My cheeks heat. I twist my fingers in my necklace. "I was just staring into space." Lo quirks an eyebrow. I've learned this is code for *bullshit*.

Annie groans, oblivious to our exchange. "God. I'm sick of being pregnant."

"Aren't you due soon?" I ask her. "You look like my grandma's bread when she leaves it out too long to proof."

Lo chokes on her water.

Annie stares at me in disbelief. "Frankie. I have another month, at least."

There's one of my "why did you open your mouth and state the obvious?" moments for you. I grimace. "Sorry, Annie. I didn't mean to be insulting. You're just a tiny person with a tall guy's baby in you. And—"

Lo clears her throat loudly and raises her eyebrows. If a stranger did that, I'd lose it on them, but I've built trust with my friends and I don't find a little social direction here and there offensive or condescending. It's helpful, actually, and I've told them as much.

Annie picks up her fork, holding it poised over her salad. "I want to laugh without peeing myself. I want to drink beer again." Staring at the plate on her belly, Annie frowns at her food. "And I want to eat you. But I don't have room."

"Poor Annie." Lo gives Annie an empathic smile before biting into her tofu-and-bean burrito. "So, once you get into law school, Frankie, how much longer do you do this job? You going to take some time off? Because I want to plan something fun with you between this and the start of the semester."

"No, it's okay," Annie says. "I'll just be leaking breast milk, wrecked from birthing Tim's monster baby. But please, plan a Napa trip without me."

Lo *tsk*s. "I'm talking like a day at the spa and a movie in pj's. For *all* of us. New mama included."

Annie perks up and grins. "Okay. Keep planning, then."

I sip my root beer. "Depends on the play-offs. My thought is I'll give my two weeks' notice once we lose. I've saved up a little nest egg. I'd like to do some studying and otherwise take a few months off to just relax a bit until school starts."

"Good." Lo smiles, staring past my shoulder. "Any plans to *relax* with the hockey hottie?"

"Yeah, right," I mutter around a bite of pizza. "Banging Ren would be a high point in my life, if he's any bit as coordinated in bed as he is on the ice, but he's holding out for someone else."

My stomach sours saying that. I rub my belly and drink some water.

"Who is she?" Lo asks.

"Someone who's unavailable right now but who he's hopeful he can eventually pursue. I don't know the details, just that he's willing to wait for her."

Annie tips her head, glancing from Ren to me. "You have no clue who it is? He hasn't told you, not even hinted?"

"Well, if he has, you know I don't pick up on hints," I remind her. "And no, I really have no clue."

"Huh." Lo stares past me, straight at Ren, her brow furrowed in thought.

I peer over my shoulder and look at Ren again as he turns the page in his book, then grins.

My heart squeezes weirdly and I turn around. "What?" I ask the two of them.

"Lord help me," Annie says. "He smiles while reading."

Lo grins. "And he drinks herbal tea."

"He's *adorable*," they say in unison.

"Shh!" I feel my cheeks turning bright red. "Seriously, stop, both of you."

Lorena's eyes scour Ren. "I don't know, Frankie. I say give your two weeks' notice, then jump his fine ass."

Annie sighs wistfully. Her plate of food doesn't even teeter, resting steadily on her round stomach. "Lo's right. Go for it. You like him. You two get along."

"Wow, what a compelling reason to throw myself at him," I say dryly. "By that criterion I should be asking out our waiter."

Annie groans, locks eyes with Lorena, then glances back to me. "Frankie, he's cute. And ridiculously nice."

I give her a look. "You've met him once. He said hi to you and smiled. That's it."

"So?" she fires back. "His greeting was delightful and memorable. And you said you two consider each other friends. I'm just saying that I think Lo's onto something."

"Ladies. He's not into me. He's the epitome of polite and friendly, that's it. Plus, we know Frankie's not going down the love road."

Annie's small hand rests over mine. "We've discussed that guys are a bit of a blind spot for you."

"And *you* say you're not going down the love road," Lo says with a quirk of her pierced eyebrow, "but we say, bullshit."

I scowl at her.

Lo takes my other hand. "The man who is worthy of your love is not going to treat you how your family did. You're a bright woman, Frankie, but you seem to need the reminder that interabled coupledom can be mutually intimate, empowering, and reciprocal—"

"Here we go," I mutter.

"It's time to move past that negative attitude toward it," she continues blithely. "Talk about it with the therapist, please? It's time to suit up for love. Because trust me, when love comes, you're going to want to be ready. You haven't felt those butterflies, that flip of your stomach, the sensation that your heart's about to jump out of your chest. When you feel that, it changes everything."

My pizza churns in my stomach. I've felt most of those things just looking at Ren. I keep that unsettling tidbit to myself.

"And just because a guy isn't jumping your bones doesn't mean he doesn't want to," Annie adds. "In the absence of him seducing you, let's consider the fact that Ren *does* exemplify important prerequisites for a solid boyfriend candidate." She lifts her fingers and starts ticking them off. "He's gentlemanly. He's a ginger."

Lo cackles. "Frankie's such a freak for redheads." I kick her under the table.

"He likes to read," Annie continues. "He cares about his community. After this you're going to go take video of him reading to sick children, for goodness' sake!"

"Your point?" I shove a bite of pizza in my mouth and chew.

Annie blinks at me, owl-like through her glasses. "My point is, he's special. He's sitting in a café, clearly not because he's hungry, but because he'd rather deal with being ogled by an entire restaurant so he can carpool with you than avoid this bullshit and meet you there. I think he's not just a fantastic human. I think you mean something to him."

"That's . . . That's . . . It's a work thing."

"You know in science," Annie says, "the logical principle called Occam's razor."

I eyeball her. "Yes?"

"Well, it says that we must accept, until we have reason otherwise, that the simplest explanation for your data is the most logical and thus likely one. It applies broadly, I think. To life. To feelings."

"Annie. I'm not a scientist. Ren and I aren't an experiment."

"Well, you're right, of course." She steals a slice of my pizza and takes a bite. "But this is the simple truth: you and Ren like each other and feel comfortable around each other. Don't you?"

"Yes," I grumble.

"So, explore it. I mean, if you want to. Which I think you seem to. . . . Am I wrong?"

I stare down at my pizza and sigh. "No. I mean, I do like him."

Like him. Okay, maybe I more than *like* him. But it's just carnal, isn't it? I'm so sexually attracted to that sweet cinnamon roll of a man, it's crazy.

Annie leans in. "And you're attracted to him?"

"Yes," I admit. "But I really don't think he sees me that way, and we work together—"

Lorena claps her hands. "Hallelujah, she's gonna get laid. Then maybe she won't be so salty at book club."

My pizza gets the brunt of my emotions. I bite down viciously and tear off another mouthful.

"I wasn't being salty. That book was trash. Nothing happened for, like, six hundred pages."

Lorena sucks in a breath.

"What?" I follow her glance back toward Ren's table and nearly choke on the pizza making my cheeks chipmunk full.

A woman hovers over him. She's leaning her ass on Ren's table, wrapping her arm around his chair. He leans back all the way in his seat and scratches the back of his neck. He's nervous. Cornered.

Red tints my vision. "That puck-bunny punk—"

"Whoa, lady," Lorena says. "What's this all about, Miss 'I Mean I *Guess* I *Kind* of Like Him'?"

I swallow my painfully massive bite of pizza and stare. "I'm just . . . He's my friend. He's shy. He hates attention like that."

"He's a big boy," Lorena purrs. "He doesn't need you to stick up for him. Unless you *want* to go clear up a few things with the woman who's clearly broadcasting her interest . . ."

I war with myself. Lorena's right. Ren is a grown man. He can take care of himself. But Ren usually doesn't when it comes to fans. He's always polite. *Too* polite.

Standing, I sweep up my cane and stroll across the café. Ren's eyes lift and lock with mine as I cross the room, a thrum of energy and purpose washing through me with each step. His gaze holds mine with a brazen intensity that weakens my knees and makes me glad I have something to lean on.

The woman's voice dies off when I stop at the table. Ren stands, making her release his chair and sit back on the table. His eyes dance between mine, a small smile playing at his lips.

"Hi," I say to the woman on an attempted smile. She rears back slightly, so I'm guessing my fake smile was a brilliant failure like always.

My stomach does a weird tumble as I lean on my cane and turn my attention to Ren. "Hey, Zenzero."

He swallows thickly. "Hi, Frankie."

"You must not have seen me when you came in." I nod toward my table, where Annie and Lorena wave much too enthusiastically. "There's a fourth seat calling your name."

Ren's shoulders relax. He smiles as he sweeps up his book and leaves a fifty on the table. "Excuse me," he says to the woman on a polite nod, while stepping closer to me. "I have to get going."

We turn, and once again, Ren places his hand low on my back to indicate I should go ahead of him. It's just a fraction of a second before it falls away, but I swear my heart ran a marathon in that tiny space of time.

"Thanks," he says quietly. "I should get better at escaping that kind of situation."

I smile at him over my shoulder. "What's your usual tactic?"

"Making up an excuse for why I need to leave."

"Ah. And you didn't leave this time because . . ."

He stops in his tracks. "Because I was waiting for you. Of course I didn't leave."

"You could have waited in your car, Ren." I spin so I can face him. "You didn't have to deal with that for my sake."

Ren's mouth quirks in the faintest grin. "What do you say you let me worry about how and where I wait for you, Francesca?"

"As you wish, Søren." I pinch his bicep teasingly. "Now, help me finish off my pizza so we can make it to Children's, then get home. Before Pazza poops on that fancy couch of yours."

———

"Your friends are great," Ren says.

I scowl as I stare out the car window. "They're in the doghouse."

Next time I'm at water aerobics, I'm going to tell Annie that terrible vegetable joke she can never get over. She'll pee herself in the pool from hysterics—thank you, Annie's advanced pregnancy. Lorena's the worst offender, though. I'm sending a Chippendale dancer to her office hours. That'll teach her.

Ren laughs. "Frankie. You're badass and cool. Your friends telling a few barely embarrassing, entirely hilarious stories only rounds out the picture."

I grumble under my breath and shift in my seat, trying to find a comfortable position. Kind of hard when both of your hips hurt.

Ren grips the steering wheel at exactly ten and two o'clock, leaving two o'clock just long enough to adjust his rearview mirror at a red light. "You weren't serious about Pazza pooping on the couch, were you?"

"No, I wasn't. She's crated for the day. I mean, it's been years since she chewed out of her crate and ripped up my entire living room furniture set."

Ren makes a strangled noise and hazards a glance at me. "You're messing with me, aren't you?"

I grin. "You're fun to tease, Zenzero. I can't help it."

"Trust me, I've heard that one before."

Guilt hits me, settling heavy in my gut. Both because I've borne the brunt of missing a joke or tease too many times to count—happens a lot with a highly literal brain—and because he told me the other day that he was one of those kids for whom high school was pure misery. He's probably been messed with enough for two lifetimes.

"Hey. I'm sorry." I set a hand on his thigh, and Sweet St.

Nicholas Stuck in the Chimney, this man's legs are granite hard. I yank my hand back like I burned it.

Ren clears his throat and accelerates as the light turns green. "You don't need to apologize, Frankie."

I feel like he's holding something back, but I'm terrible at figuring out moments like these. These are the times when being autistic is frustrating and exhausting. Especially when people don't know what you're up against.

I don't talk about autism at work. I mask, which is another way of saying, I do what I need to do in order to seem "normal," which is why Ren and the guys only see Frank the Crank, serious, no-smiles me. But sometimes I wish Ren knew. Because right now he doesn't understand how much I need him not to dance around the truth but give it to me straight. I can't see through those gauzy linguistic layers like so many can.

It nearly comes tumbling out of my mouth, but instead I shift in my seat again and change the subject.

"So . . . I have something to tell you." Might as well lower the boom now. "Paps got a picture of us leaving for lunch together. Twitter blew up. There might be minor conjecture that we're together."

Ren hits the brakes hard, lurching us forward. "I'm sorry, what?"

"It'll blow over, Zenzero." I grip the handle above the car door, just in case I'm in for another jolt.

A furious blush crawls up his neck and darkens his cheeks. "Oh."

"Oh?" I poke his shoulder. "You're going monosyllabic on me." He starts sputtering, his cheeks darkening to raspberry red.

I try to ignore that stab to my pride. Is it *so* terrible to be temporarily linked to me this way?

"Ren. Relax. It'll die down on its own. And if you want it to go away faster, put yourself out there and go on some actual dates. Get yourself seen with another woman—"

"No," he says sharply. Taking a long, slow exhale, Ren grips the steering wheel tight, then relaxes his fingers. "Sorry, that came out harsh. I'm flustered. What I meant to say was, I'm not interested in dating right now."

A weird surge of jealousy pricks me. Who *is* this woman he's waiting for, who has this deep claim on his heart?

"This woman better be worth it, Bergman."

His mouth is tight. He shakes his head. "I'm . . . It's not . . ." Sighing, he turns the van into the hospital parking garage and nabs an accessible parking space. I pull out my parking sticker and hook it around his mirror.

"Will this impact your job?" he asks. "Do you want me to touch base with Darlene?"

I shake my head. "Don't worry. I already emailed her to explain earlier. I'm just sorry you have to deal with people thinking you're with me—"

"Frankie."

I freeze mid-unbuckling. "Yes?"

Ren turns in his seat and locks eyes with me. "I'd be *flattered* if someone thought you were with me."

My ears ring. A dull ache tightens my heart as every alarm goes off inside me.

Danger! Danger! You are catching feelings for Ren Bergman.

While living with him. And trying to keep my professional integrity intact. And keep my heart sealed off.

Shitty shit shitballs. Terrible, terrible timing, Francesca.

I throw open my car door, which I know will end this conversation, at least for now, because Ren is hell-bent on chivalry. He all but sprints to my side, holding open the door and offering me a hand, like he does every time we descend the travel bus and he's ahead of me.

Not because he thinks I'm fragile or I can't do it on my own, but because Ren should have been born two hundred years ago, when men stood as women entered a room, and courtship was stolen kisses in moonlit gardens.

"We're not done with this conversation," he says firmly.

I pat his shoulder reassuringly and stifle my grin. "Whatever you say, dear."

ELEVEN

Ren

Playlist: "Port of Call," Beirut

I will not cry. I will not cry. I will not—

Carbuncles. I'm crying.

I'd ask whose idea it was for me to read *Wherever You Are, My Love Will Find You* to a group of toddler- and preschool-aged patients, but I have no doubt it was Frankie's doing.

She leans against the wall, with a smile that's so dangerously beautiful, I'm worried my heart's going to beat right out of my chest. At least I'm at a hospital. Someone could probably do something about that here.

"You okay, Mr. Ren?" My new little buddy, Arthur, smiles up at me and adjusts his glasses.

He's sitting close and rests his small hand on my arm.

"Yeah, Arthur. I'm okay. Sometimes I feel big feelings and they make me have tears."

Arthur's smile widens. "Me too. I cry when things hurt. And when I miss my family. Daddy told me that's okay. He said mommies and sisters aren't the only ones who cry. Brothers and daddies have tears, too."

"That's what my daddy told me when I was little, too."

Arthur grins and leans in closer, poking the book. "Can you read more now?"

"Right." Picking up the book, I clear my throat and blink away the wetness blurring my vision. "'So hold your head high and don't be afraid to march to the front of your own parade. If you're still my small babe or you're all the way grown, my promise to you is you're never alone.'"

I swallow another lump in my throat. Christ, these books. It doesn't help that half of these kids have parents who can only visit occasionally. California's a huge state, and this is a top hospital for childhood illnesses. A lot of these kids' parents have to work to pay for their child's treatment while living hours away. If anyone needs to be reminded that love doesn't fade when Mommy or Daddy leave for a while, it's these little ones.

I glare up at Frankie, who's holding her phone with the concentration of one filming a video, biting her tongue square between her front teeth. She *always* does that, and it *always* stirs my body.

I'm starting to have a response that is beyond inappropriate for a children's hospital reading time, so I blink away and refocus on the book. After I finish reading, we make a craft and eat some healthy snacks, and I give hugs goodbye, promising Arthur I'll come by soon and say hello again.

Walking down the hallway, I notice Frankie's limp is a bit more pronounced, but I'll be damned if I say anything about it or offer to pull the van right up to the exit. She'll shove that wand of hers up my butt faster than I can open my mouth to say *sorry I asked*.

"Well, that was a home run," she says. "And I won the bet with Nicole in PR."

"What bet was that?"

She grins as we stop in front of the elevators and pushes the down button. "That you couldn't read that book with a dry eye."

"Wow. I made you some money with my soft side, Francesca. How nice to be used for profit."

She shoves me and bounces backward, since my body doesn't budge.

I catch her by the elbow and steady her. "Easy."

Frankie peers up at me. Heat slides through my hand as I hold her arm. She flexes her lean bicep underneath my grip and cocks an eyebrow. "Careful," she says. "Don't hurt yourself."

I give the muscle an experimental squeeze, narrowing my eyes in feigned concentration.

"Impressive."

Her smile fades as her gaze drifts to my mouth. And suddenly it doesn't feel like we're being playful. Not anymore.

The elevator door springs open, I drop my grip, and the moment is gone.

Once we're in the van, making our way down the 110 South toward Manhattan Beach, Frankie disappears into her phone, muttering to herself as she answers emails and checks in on social media platforms. Then she brings her phone to her ear, working her way through voicemails. I steal every possible glance I can safely take and tell myself I can handle this. I can have the woman I'm crazy about in my home and keep myself together. I can—

"Ren!"

I tap the brakes, look around, assuming Frankie's seen something that I'm about to hit. "What? What is it?"

She drops her phone. "Sorry. I wanted to stop you before we pass Hawthorne. I just remembered I was hoping to go grab my mail."

A sigh of relief leaves me. "Sure, Frankie, that's fine."

We were just about to pass her neighborhood, so it's only minutes later that I'm pulling in front of her house. "Can I get it for you?" I ask.

Frankie opens her mouth. Closes it. Blinks rapidly. "Um. I was going to say I'm a big girl who can get her own mail from her recently broken into home, but now I'm feeling a little uneasy."

Throwing open my door, I give her a smile. "I'll be right back."

When I return to the van and set her mail in her lap, Frankie quickly riffles through it, stopping when she gets to one envelope. Her knuckles whiten as she grips it.

I should mind my own business. Peeling away my gaze, I focus on pulling out and heading home. Frankie stares at the envelope until we're so close that my place is in sight.

Abruptly, she rips open the seal and yanks free a small pile of tri-folded papers. She presses them open and her eyes dart frantically across the text, until a squeal erupts in the van.

"I got in!" she yells.

She got into what? I glance at the envelope's return address. UCLA School of Law.

Angels sing "Hallelujah Chorus" in my head. Frankie's going to law school. Which means Frankie isn't going to work for the Kings much longer.

Which means soon . . . Frankie will no longer be off-limits.

Parking the car, I stare ahead in a daze. A wave of belly-dropping fear hits me. Frankie's going to leave. The waiting game's over. Finally, I get to make my move. And suddenly I realize I have no idea what that is.

"Congratulations," I manage hoarsely.

Turning toward me, her eyes glisten with unshed tears. It's the happiest I've ever seen her. "Ren, I'm sorry I'm freaking out. I just didn't think I'd get in."

Finally, I find my voice and shift in my seat to face her. "You didn't think you'd get in? Frankie, of course you were going to get in. Are you doing sports law? You plan to be an agent?"

She smiles up at me, wiping her eyes. "Yeah."

Be mine, I want to say. Except, as much as I'd love to have someone as smart and tough negotiating my every contract, what I want from Frankie is so much more. I want her smiles. Her body. Her humor. Her undivided attention and sharp wit.

When I really let myself dream, I want her love.

I want Francesca Zeferino. She's been the ultimate goal. And now I finally have a clear shot.

"You'll be great, Frankie," I tell her. "You should be proud."

The tiny space in the van grows almost claustrophobic. I'm drowning in her orchid perfume, hearing her soft, steady breaths as she smiles at me, fairly glowing with happiness. Now that our possibility is before me, I'm confronted with the yawning gap between what we are and what I want us to be. I've been one of the guys to her for three years. I've held off, bitten my tongue, waited. And waited. And waited.

But that doesn't mean I can't do this. After all, I've done it in the rink—bided my time, worked toward my goal until the right moment opened up, then acted on that patience with stunning accuracy. If I can do this in hockey, I can do it with Frankie.

Right?

———

"I can't see you, Axel." Tipping my laptop screen, I angle it so that my older brother can at least see *my* face.

"You don't need to see me," he drawls, half off-screen. Something bangs, and he curses under his breath. "I'm listening."

"Wow, thanks. I feel like a really high priority right now, Axelrod."

He freezes, then leans into the screen, a long middle finger right up close. "See that?"

I grin. "Thank you."

He sits on a sigh right in front of the screen and drags his fingers through his hair. "I stopped painting for you. Let the record show. How's that for prioritizing?"

Noise from inside my house makes me glance over my shoulder. Oliver and Viggo traipse through the kitchen and immediately begin to raid my cabinets, yanking food into their arms.

I jerk my thumb toward them and look back to Axel on the screen. "They don't even say hi. Just ransack my pantry."

He shrugs. "They're animals. I think Mom was too tired by the time they were born to bring them to heel."

Viggo and Oliver are as different as night and day but just as inextricably bound. Exactly twelve months apart, they're often mistaken for twins because now, fully grown, they're the same height, the same lean build, the same pale eyes as me. Their only obvious physical difference is Viggo's hair, which is rich brown like Axel's, while Oliver's is blond like Ryder's.

"What's this about?" Ax drums his fingers on his desk. "You okay?"

"I'm fine. Let's wait for Ryder to dial in before I explain."

"I would eventually like to go back to painting, by the way. I don't have all night."

My older brother is a particular and rigid personality. He's not overtly affectionate, avoids being touched, is solitary and incredibly direct. Most of the time, his expression is serious, his delivery terse, but beneath that prickly exterior is a loving, loyal person. You just have to see past the standoffishness.

"I'm aware," I tell him. "I won't keep you. It'll be brief. Once we're all here." Ax laughs dryly. "Us? Brief? It's almost like you don't know your own family."

Viggo drags the sliding door shut behind him and Oliver as they step onto the deck. "Quite the criticism," Viggo says, "coming from the guy who moved to Seattle and visits twice a year."

"Traitor," Oliver grumbles.

Ax scowls. "First of all, I'm down in sunny fucking LA at least ten times a year, okay? And you know how much I hate flying. Second, I'm an adult. I have my own life. It's a foreign concept to you two man-cubs, but one day having a career and fending for yourselves won't be an abstract concept. Then you'll understand."

Viggo sits and rips open a bag of chips, as Oliver pops off the lid to a jar of salsa. "And somehow," Oliver says, "we'll manage to do it without abandoning our family."

Ax's face tightens. I turn and give Viggo and Oliver a look. "That's harsh, and you know it. He didn't abandon anybody. He moved to the place that makes him happiest."

Viggo snorts as he dips a chip into the salsa and crunches. "Axel. Happy. Hah."

Ax opens his mouth, looking both pissed and defensive. This little assembly is getting away from me.

"Okay." I raise my hands. "Let's table this conversation for another time."

Ryder's face flickers to life on the screen. "Sounds like I showed up at the right time."

Oliver stops inhaling food long enough to wave hi to Ryder.

"Hey, Ry!" Viggo calls.

Ax leans in and squints. "Is that my brother or a yeti?"

Ryder flips off Ax. "The beard isn't going anywhere, no matter how much you hate it."

"You were beardless the first twenty years of your life," Ax says. "I just don't see why people have to change things like that. It bothers me."

Ryder snorts a laugh. "I'm so sorry to upset your routine by growing facial hair, but I like it."

"Guys." I clear my throat.

Ax starts arguing with Ryder. Viggo and Oliver are playing tug-of-war with the bag of beef jerky. No one is listening to me.

"Guys!"

Everyone freezes in a tableau titled *Guilty*.

Ryder and Ax both straighten in their seats on-screen. Oliver lets Viggo have the beef jerky.

Viggo rips open the bag and throws a hunk into Oliver's lap.

They both tug the meat between their teeth, the simultaneous snap as it breaks the only other sound besides crashing waves along the shore.

"Thank you for joining the emergency meeting." Clearing my throat again, I glance inside, making sure Frankie hasn't come home early. She's supposedly at water aerobics and said she'd be home late, muttering something about getting out of my hair. It was on the tip of my tongue to tell her just how off the mark that is.

"Okay, so as everyone here knows, I'm a bit of a klutz when it comes to the ladies." A chorus of snorts and suppressed laughter interrupts me but quickly dies away. They all school their faces.

"Proceed," Axel says seriously.

"Right. Well, you guys remember Frankie, who I've mentioned. She's our social media coordinator."

Ryder wiggles his eyebrows. "Willa was riiiight," he singsongs. I give him a look. He only grins wider.

"I'm attracted to her," I tell them. "I'd love to ask her out. I've wanted to since I met her, but Frankie and I can't date right now, not while we work together."

Ax gives the universal sign for *speed it up*.

"She's quitting once we're out of play-offs or after we win the Cup," I press on. "She got into law school, and soon we won't be coworkers. Which means, now's my shot to ask her out. And I . . . I have no clue how to go about this. What do I say? And when? 'Hey, Frankie. I've been pining for you for three years, secretly wishing I could date you, and now I can'? I sound creepy. Stalkerish." I scrub my face. "Why is this so complicated?"

Ryder and Axel steeple their fingers in front of their mouths at the exact same time. Oliver crunches a chip thoughtfully while Viggo swallows his jerky, then finally says, "Do you know if *she's* into *you*?"

"Well, I didn't think so. But something she said the other night made me think maybe? At least maybe she'd be open to it?"

I tell them about our conversation over takeout at her place, and when I finish, they're all staring at me with these wide grins.

"What?" I ask.

Ryder slaps his hands together and rubs them in excitement. "Okay, we've got lots to work with here."

Oliver and Viggo start talking over each other, clamoring to share their two cents.

Axel holds up a hand, silencing everyone. "Before we form a plan of attack, I have to ask. Have you told us everything we need to know?"

"Well, I guess there's one part I forgot to mention. She's living with me temporarily."

Ryder's jaw drops. Axel's eyes widen. Viggo and Oliver blink at me in shock. And then all four of them explode with advice, frantically yelling over each other. I open up my phone's notepad. Make them take turns. Break up six different fights when they disagree on tactic.

As Ax predicted, it's anything but brief, and by the time I'm jotting down Axel's tenth point, while cross-referencing it to Ryder's somewhat conflicting advice, the noise of a car pulling in front of my house makes all of us freeze.

"*Dewberries!*" I hiss.

Oliver snorts. "Did you just say—"

"That's her!"

I slap the computer shut on Ryder and Axel. Oliver and Viggo stand, clumsily bumping fronts as they try to escape their chairs. They stumble over each other, down the stairs to the sand, and around the side of the house just as Frankie walks into the kitchen. Her eyes travel to the deck, taking in the giant pile of food my brothers left on the table. She raises an eyebrow, but before I can so much as wave hello, she's gone, out of sight.

I stare after her, like a dumbstruck idiot, hearing all my brothers' thoughts ricocheting in my head, their voices warring with each other about what I should do next. Anxiety and nerves tighten my stomach. What do I do? Which move is the right one to make?

Frankie tugs open the sliding door, and Pazza bounds out, sprinting toward the shore. She smiles up at me, starlight dancing over her skin.

My brothers' voices die away. The ocean breeze wraps around us. And the answer is crystal clear. "How about a moonlit stroll, Francesca?"

Her smile deepens as she slips her arm through mine without saying a word. But it's all the answer I need.

TWELVE

Ren

Playlist: "Hallelujah," Jake Shimabukuro

"I saw a Subaru out front." Frankie jerks her head toward the house but keeps her eyes on Pazza dashing across the sand. "Neighbor's car?"

I throw the ball for Pazza, then turn to look at Frankie.

So beautiful. No makeup, her hair slicked back in a bun from the pool, those soft lips she tugs between her teeth, dark lashes blinking slowly.

She leans in and drops her voice. "Maybe it's the mystery lady's car. She finally got wise and paid a visit."

I can tell she's mostly joking. She wouldn't be down on the sand with me if she truly thought someone else was waiting for me in my home. But it's so hard to know what to say when Frankie brings herself up without knowing it's Frankie I'm always thinking and talking about.

The wind snaps between us and tugs a dark ribbon of hair across her face. Carefully, I slide my finger along her cheekbone and tuck that loose espresso strand tight behind her ear. I shouldn't, but I can't help myself. She leans, almost imperceptibly, into my touch. I let my fingers trace the shell of her ear, whisper lighter than a breeze down her neck, before I drop my hand.

"It was my brothers," I manage hoarsely.

She frowns. "Your brothers? Where are they?"

"They left. Right when you got here. Trust me, you're not ready to meet them. Not the man-cubs. You saw the carnage they left on the table."

Her soft laugh and smile hit me, a double wave I wasn't braced for. I can count on one hand the times I've made Frankie laugh. It feels like a gift.

"Did you tell your family about UCLA?" I sweep up Pazza's ball, fake her out, then send it flying in the air.

"I did. I called them before water aerobics and told them. They were excited for me." Frankie clears her throat. "Oh, and I had a voicemail from my landlord. He said they're still fixing the damage done to the kitchen and my room, but after that it'll be ready. I should be able to get in by next week, after our games in Minnesota."

"Well . . . that's good."

Verbal brilliance, Bergman.

I'm a nervous wreck. There's so much I want to tell her and none of it will disentangle in my brain. I want to ask her to stay, even when that bungalow is safe to return to. I want to confess that I'm wild about her. I want to ask if she's even a little wild about me, too.

But the one thing all five Bergman brothers agreed on tonight was that I should wait to tell her how I feel.

The *when* was not a unanimous agreement between my brothers. While Axel and Oliver said to wait until she'd left the team, Ryder and Viggo voted not to wait that long, just until she's back in her own space again, at which point, if I told her and she didn't feel the same way, she at least wouldn't be stuck under my roof.

Just stuck working with you.

Frankie stares at me. I've noticed she does it sometimes, like she's not just looking *at* me, but as if she's trying to look *into* me.

"Is everything okay?" she asks.

I balk at that. "What do you mean?"

"I thought maybe you were angry. Your answer was short. And that usually translates to me as anger."

"Frankie, no." I have to restrain myself from hugging her. I want to kiss her forehead and beg to know how I made her feel I was angry with her when I'm so far from it. "Why would you think that?"

Her gaze drifts to the waves breaking on the shore. "Reading people is tricky for me. Usually, I can't tell by someone's face how they're feeling, not until I know them really well and I have lots of time to learn their expressions." She turns and stares at me again, her brow furrowing seriously. "That's because I'm autistic."

Air rushes out of me. Frankie's on the spectrum.

God, I've been thick. While I know it's unique to each person, I'm familiar with autism's complexity, the way it both hides and sneaks out. My youngest sister, Ziggy, whom I'm close to, was diagnosed just a year ago. Axel hasn't been diagnosed, but more and more since Ziggy's diagnosis, I wonder why he hasn't been. The point being, I'm well acquainted with the autism spectrum in people I'm close to. Why didn't I recognize it in Frankie?

Stepping nearer, I tentatively thread my fingers through Frankie's, bracing myself for her to pull away, to reject the gesture. But she doesn't. Instead she slides her fingers tighter with mine. "Thank you for telling me, Frankie. For trusting me."

She tips her head, lifting her eyes to meet mine. "I wish I'd told you sooner. But when I met you, you were just another player on the team. It didn't seem necessary."

One little word—*were*—but it makes hope soar through my body.

"Can I ask why you don't tell others? Why you're telling me now? If that's personal, I understand."

Frankie squeezes my hand, and I have to stifle the rough inhale it causes. Her palm's soft and cool from the night air. It fits perfectly inside mine.

"I have a . . . a mask that I wear for work," she answers. "I hide a lot of myself to do my job. Why tell people I'm autistic when I act like I'm not?"

"Isn't that exhausting?" I remember that being Ziggy's refrain: *I'm so tired. So tired of pretending and still feeling like I suck at it. I feel invisible. Even to myself.*

"Yes." She smiles. "Thus, law school. Studying and negotiating the law, it's a strength to be fastidiously observant and detail oriented, methodical, hyperfocused, literal, direct. Sometimes I worry what I'll do when I miss things interpersonally. I know law can get dirty and people can twist their words, but I'm not battling it out in a courtroom. I'll be reading fine print, negotiating contracts for clients I get to know well, so I think I'll do okay. I'll get to truly be myself."

"I'm happy for you, Frankie. You deserve to be yourself. At work. With friends. Anywhere."

She peers up at me, another one of her incisive stares. "Thank you."

Pazza barks and spins, chasing her tail. We glance over at her as quiet settles between us but for the incessant pound of the ocean nearby.

"You remember I have a small country's worth of siblings, right?"

Frankie wrinkles her nose, clearly confused. "Yes?"

"My little sister is on the spectrum. So, while everyone's unique, and I'm no expert, I love someone who's autistic. And I hope you know I'm a safe place for you to be you."

Frankie sniffs and wipes her nose. Blinks a few times and dabs her eyes with the heel of her hand, gripping her sweatshirt.

"You okay?"

"I'm not crying," she says immediately.

I squeeze her hand, rubbing my thumb in a gentle circle across her palm. "Of course not."

"It's windy," she says.

"Very windy."

When she glances up at me, she's smiling. And it's an arrow to the heart. I want to kiss Frankie. Badly.

Not while she's your guest, with nowhere to go. Be patient. You've waited this long. Wait a little longer.

"You're staring at my mouth," she whispers.

"S-sorry." I try to blink away, but my gaze swivels right back to her, a compass set to true north.

"It's almost like you want to kiss me, Zenzero." She bites her lip, her eyes locked on my mouth, too.

I just stare at her, like an idiot. Pazza drops her slimy ball right on my foot, headbutts me, and barks. But I'm oblivious. All I see is Frankie; Frankie, who's staring back at me, and it's like free-falling through time and space, lost in the vortex of her gaze.

It happens in slow motion, Frankie pressing on tiptoe, her fingers wrapping around my arms to brace herself. I suck in a breath as sparks shoot across my skin, and she leans into me. Her curves press against every hard plane of my body, her grip tightens. Before I know what's happening—

The sweetest lips brush mine. Her mouth is full and soft as it tastes my bottom lip and sucks gently. My inhale is shaky, my exhale a groan of relief. She slides her hands over my shoulders, up my neck, and weaves her fingers into my hair. Her touch is gentle but determined, warm and tender, as she presses faint kisses to the corners of my mouth.

I wrap an arm around her waist and tug her closer. Oh, God, her body. Long, strong, lean around her ribs, where I hold her, but soft where her breasts rub against my chest, where her hips curve into mine. Cupping her neck, I knead the tense muscles at the base of her skull. Frankie moans against my mouth, her lips parting, and the sound, I swear, it shakes the earth beneath my feet. I slide my other hand lower down her back and tuck her close, settling it at the tender curve of her spine.

How something I've dreamed of can so wildly exceed my imagination, I'll never know. I thought I knew what I could expect, how sweet she'd taste, how warm and soft her lips would be. But my dreams are nothing to reality.

Her tongue teases mine—slow, steady swirls that coax mine to find hers. I tilt her head in my grip, slant my mouth to deepen the kiss. As I rock her against me, tangling my tongue with hers, the kiss becomes as rhythmic as the waves behind us. Slide, tease, retreat.

"Oh shit." She pulls away breathlessly, shaking hands covering her mouth. "Okay. Wow. Just . . . wow. Okay. Yep, I kissed you. I shouldn't have done that. Pazza!"

Pazza scrambles toward us across the sand as reality hits me. Frankie kissed me. *She* kissed *me*.

She likes you! At least enough to kiss you.

"Ren, I'm sorry," she mutters, rubbing her forehead.

"Frankie, please don't apologi—"

"My yoga trainer's coming early in the morning, if that's still okay?"

Cheeks bright red, eyes down on the sand. Clearly, she wants to move on, which I have no idea what to make of. "Of course . . . What time? I'll join you."

That seems to break her from the depths of her embarrassment. She rears back like I've surprised her and raises her eyebrows. "This isn't that newbie warm-up 'yoga' that the team does with Lars."

"I'm aware, Francesca."

"Don't 'Francesca' me, Søren." Her features are guarded as she backs away slowly. "Eight o'clock."

I can't help but smile at her. "I'll be there. Good night, Frankie."

She doesn't answer, only spins slowly toward the house. I stare after her, watching Frankie's form grow smaller as she walks carefully up the steps and goes inside, Pazza trotting alongside her.

She kissed me. She *kissed* me. And I kissed her back.

I pull out my phone and open the brothers' group text. They're not going to believe this.

———

I wake up tired, aching, and frustrated after a night of too little sleep and too many dreams involving Frankie and her maddeningly soft lips. Rolling over, I rub my eyes and look at the clock. I have to be reading it wrong. That, or I slept through my alarm.

The faint din of a voice other than Frankie's, followed by her laugh, confirms the latter.

"Barnacles!"

I brush my teeth while hopping into sweats and tugging on a T-shirt. Quickly, I run my hands through my hair, smooth down my beard so it doesn't look too crazy, and jog down to my training room.

At the threshold, I freeze. There's a *man*. A man with very little attachment to clothing or, apparently, to having his hands for much longer. He's shirtless, wearing only bike shorts, gripping Frankie's hips while he stands right behind her in a highly suggestive position. It takes every feminist, evolved, twenty-first-century corner of me not to growl and throw him against the wall.

Caveman moment conquered, I stroll in. "Good morning. Sorry I'm late."

Frankie peers up from downward dog. "Good morning, Søren. This is Fabrizio."

"Fabi, you can call me." He extends his hand. I take it and indulge in squeezing a little harder than strictly necessary. Fabrizio doesn't seem to feel it, because he simply drops his hand back to Frankie's hip once I let go and focuses his gaze firmly on her beautiful backside.

She's wearing black leggings with a sheer panel zigzagging all the way up to her hip bone. Her toenails are painted black just like her fingernails, and her tank top is black and cropped, hugging her ribs. So much golden skin, so many muscles and perfect Frankie curves.

"Well then," Fabrizio says. "Søren—"

"Ren," I correct him, strolling to the other side of the room and circling my arms, softly twisting my torso, waking up my body.

He bends his head in apology. "*Scusa*. Frankie called you that, I just assumed."

"It's okay. She does it to tease me."

Frankie glances up at Fabrizio and says something to him in Italian. He laughs and his hands slide down her thighs, grasping her kneecaps. He's bent and practically using her backside as his pillow.

"So, Fabrizio," I manage between clenched teeth. "How long have you been teaching Frankie?"

He smiles. I swear he knows he's taunting me. As he stands, he sets a hand low on Frankie's back and smooths it over her spine.

"Three years," he says on a grin. "Now, why don't we start with something basic to see where you are in your practice, Ren?"

Moving to the front of the room, Fabrizio starts a sun salutation. While I only practice basic yoga with our team's nutritionist and wellness coach, Lars, I'm familiar enough to follow Fabrizio's sequences, and I do them with ease.

I can feel Frankie's eyes on me, but every time I glance her way, she's watching Fabrizio, chatting with him in Italian, then translating what I'm suspicious is only part of it for me. After what feels like a bajillion *chaturangas*, then warrior variations that remind me how damn tight my groin is, her instructor straightens and eyes me up.

"Ren, you are modest, my friend." Fabrizio turns to Frankie. "He is good. You two do some poses together, *si*?"

"Um." Frankie glances up from child's pose, her cheeks pink.

I roll onto my back and grin at her, feeling mildly vindictive about the half-naked, handsy Italian yoga instructor. Couldn't be some crunchy, maternal type. No. Had to be a guy who looks like he's a cover model on some cologne ad and who speaks her language. Literally.

It might be nice to see her squirm a bit. "What do you say, Frankie? Let's do it."

Frankie glares at me. Clenching her jaw, she turns and grimaces at Fabi. "Fine."

"*Eccellente!*" He claps his hands.

Frankie's scowling at me but I just give her a wider grin. There's my grump I love to needle with a smile.

"Camel pose. *Ustrasana*," he says. Frankie and I kneel at his direction, knees touching. Then, gripping each other's forearms, we lean up and away into the pose. Our groins fuse with the position—my pelvis pressed into the soft hollow between her hips. Frankie's breath hitches as I bite my cheek to stifle a groan. This is torture. I was half-mast when I woke up, but now there's nothing remotely "half" about what's inside my sweatpants.

"Breathe into the pose. Hearts open, chests to the sky," Fabrizio says, before he steps away for his water.

All I can feel is Frankie. The warmth of her thighs and the welcoming give between her hip bones that my aching body fits perfectly. She shifts, a deliberate movement. A decadent swirl of her hips.

Sweet Jesus.

I try picturing that one time I walked in on Freya and Aiden making out when they were first dating—like *really* making out—because there is nothing more revolting than seeing your sister with her tongue down a guy's throat, but not even that quells the heat surging through me. I'm a slave to the pound of my pulse, the urgent need to be closer to Frankie, deep inside her, connected.

"Francesca," I warn.

She cracks open one eye and smirks at me. "You got yourself into this mess, Søren. Before you accepted a couple's pose you might have considered we'd be pretzel-ing each other's intimate bits."

I hiss when she does another shimmy. That's it.

Gripping her forearms, I tilt my pelvis even deeper, sliding myself against the warmth between her thighs. Her eyes widen as she makes a tiny muffled noise.

"How ya doing, there, *fresterska*?"

"What did you call me?" she squeaks.

"You're not the only one who speaks another language." I roll my hips against hers and feel her nails dig into my forearm.

"Good." Fabrizio comes back. "You have beautiful energy together."

This guy's senses must be dulled by all the patchouli he's bathed in. There's nothing beautiful about this. It's pure, sexual, vindictive frustration.

"Now we end with one more pose that brings you together," he says.

After releasing each other's arms, we follow his direction to spin away and sit, back to back.

My rotation involves a subtle adjustment in my sweatpants after that camel-posing nonsense.

"Spinal twist." Fabrizio leans over us, drawing us upright until our backs are flush against each other's. I feel Frankie's vertebrae, the poke of her shoulder blades, and catch the faintest wisp of her orchid perfume mingled with tantalizing sweat. "Now, both to your right. Your hand to the other's leg, and lean into it, lengthening your spine."

Frankie's hand sits high and firm across my thigh. Mine grips above her knee, since my lumbar isn't quite as flexible. It's quiet but for our breathing.

"*Ujjayi* breath," he says softly. "In through your nose, and out, like the waves beyond us."

Our deep breaths sync, the rise and fall of our backs in tandem.

"At last." Fabi sighs happily. "Peace is restored."

THIRTEEN

Frankie

Playlist: "The Calculation," Regina Spektor

"So." Ren slides the milk my way along with a small crock of sugar. "Fabrizio, eh?"

I dump a heaping spoonful of sugar into my mug and stir, glowering at Ren. The empty ache between my thighs is entirely his fault. I haven't been this sexually frustrated since I hit puberty. I know I shouldn't have kissed him last night. I let my heart get carried away by his swoony sweetness, and I kissed him for it.

But I expressed regret. I made it clear it was an oopsie.

Why, then, did he have to get all flirtatious and corner us into doing tantric yoga this morning? Now I have to suffer his absurdly sexual presence all day, walking around with the lady version of blue balls. Just fucking great.

I take a slow breath that does nothing to cool me off, then sip my coffee. "I chose Fabi because I get to keep up on my Italian *and* stay limber."

Ren mutters something into his coffee.

"What?" I ask.

"Nothing." He sets down his mug and gives me a look I can't read. "Want some breakfast?"

"What's on the menu?"

Ren backtracks to the fridge. I make a valiant but largely unsuccessful attempt not to stare at all the muscles made obvious by his sweat-soaked shirt stuck to his body. "Egg whites. Berries. Turkey bacon."

"Yuck."

He grins over his shoulder. "Welcome to hockey season diet, Francesca."

"Don't you need carbs? Little bit of fat? You burn insane calories playing."

"I do." He closes the fridge door with his hip, arms brimming with ingredients. "But they have to be the right ones. I make smoothies for that."

Dumping his armful on the counter, he then begins chopping veggies. "I promise, it's a surprisingly good omelet. I'll add some cheese for you. We won't tell Lars."

I nab a freshly chopped piece of green pepper and crunch on it. Lars is the team dietician and wellness coach. "He'd kill me if he knew how I was influencing you. What do you think Lars eats? Besides wheatgrass smoothies. I think he has one percent body fat."

"No clue. But I'd bet the minivan he hasn't had a burger in a decade." Ren tosses the onions and peppers into a pan that holds the tiniest drop of olive oil known to man. "It would explain why he's so grumpy all the time."

"Now, let's not judge the grumps of the world. We have our reasons."

Ren glances up and sets down his knife. "You're not grumpy, Frankie. You're just . . ."

I bite back a smile and steal a piece of cheddar. "I'm grumpy."

"You're *serious*."

"You're sweet, Zenzero. But I'm grumpy. It's in everyone's best interest. Keeps the boys in line and afraid of my hexes."

Ren grins to himself while he lets the omelet bubble in the pan and blends us a berry smoothie. We eat quickly and in quiet, stealing spare glances while Pazza weaves between us, scarfing down whatever we drop.

When I take my last bite, Ren asks, "So. What's the verdict on the egg-white omelet?"

I drop my fork and pat my belly. "Delicious. Saved by the cheddar."

"Yeah." He sweeps up my plate and stacks it onto his. "The cheese makes it edible. Otherwise it really does taste like cardboard."

Sliding off my barstool, I take the last sip of my smoothie and set down the glass. "Thanks again for breakfast, Zenzero. Leave those dishes and I can do them after my shower?" My body's stiff. I need a hot shower before I try to do something as dexterous as dishes this early. If I tried now, I'd end up dropping and cracking everything I tried to hold.

He waves his hand. "Takes two seconds. And you're my guest."

"Well, then at least let me whip up something good for breakfast tomorrow. I make a mean microwaved breakfast sandwich."

With his laugh still echoing in the kitchen, I head for my guest room and hit the shower. I turn the water hot, letting it soothe my joints, which limbered up at yoga but then slowly stiffened as my body cooled. Once I'm out of the shower, I wrap myself in a towel, then throw my hair up in another towel to make a turban. I do my routine—moisturizer, under-eye concealer, a little loose powder so I'm not shiny. Gabby used to try to cover me in makeup, but any more than this and I feel like I'm wearing a mask.

I wear enough masks as it is.

I'm just capping my vanilla lip balm when I hear Ren's front door open and shut. Pazza's in my room and starts barking like crazy. Unease prickles my skin.

"Ren?" I call.

No answer. Pulling open the bathroom door, I call Ren's name again. Nothing.

Except for a faint rustling noise in the kitchen. Now I'm more curious than anything. Is Ren out of the shower already? Maybe he grabbed the newspaper. That would be why I heard the front door. It's not like people break into multimillion-dollar beach-front homes, slam the door behind them, and raid the kitchen.

Burglars raided your *pantry.*

Shit. They did, didn't they?

I have an overactive imagination. It's fed my anxiety for many years now, but with counseling, I've learned to coach it, to help myself focus on rational explanations and calm the nervous, irrational beast inside. And, ya know, weed helps. But there's no weed in my system currently, only logical thought telling me everything is most likely fine.

Slowly, I walk toward the kitchen. When I clear the hallway and have a good view, no one's there. But then I realize the refrigerator's open.

Suddenly, a man pops up. I let out a bloodcurdling scream and stumble back into the hallway wall.

"Frankie!" Ren yells from deep in the house. I hear a door banging open, the pound of his footsteps.

The man grins at me as he shuts the fridge with his butt and shines an apple on his shirt.

Which makes him seem much less threatening. Unless he's one of those smiling serial killers. Who eats a healthy snack first.

My terror starts to fade when I realize I recognize his eyes. They're Ren's eyes. Ren's cheekbones, his long nose, without the bump from being broken. This must be—

"Frankie." Ren collides with me, pulls me against his body, and spins so I'm shielded from the man. Glancing up, he locks eyes with the guy and mutters something that sounds remarkably close to *fustilarian.*

Exhaling heavily, Ren peers down at me. "Okay. You're okay."

A gentle hug and I'm pulled closer. "It's just my brother. Are you all right?"

I nod. "I'm sorry I freaked. I heard someone come in, and I called you, and you didn't answer, so I went to see who it was, and he just popped up like a jack-in-the-box from the refrigerator, and I lost it."

His brother leans a hip against the counter. Crunching on the apple, he speaks around his bite. "Ren seems to have lost his manners—but then again, I'd be a little addled, too, if I had someone like you in my arms with only a towel between us."

Ren and I gulp simultaneously. I realize now that he's bare-chested, a towel slung low on his hips. Mine is knotted above my breasts, but all our movements have loosened it considerably.

"I'm Viggo," he says.

Ren doesn't seem to care about an introduction. "What are you doing here?" he asks sharply. Viggo smiles and swallows his bite. "I brought the baked goods for your next club meeting."

"Baked goods?" I ask.

"Yes, ma'am," Viggo says, "I'm a self-taught pastry chef."

"He's also enrolled in carpentry school," Ren adds, "learning everything there is to know about bikes, and has taken up the fiddle. He has issues with commitment—"

"Attention," Viggo corrects him on a wide grin and a wink.

Ren sighs heavily, and his hand skates over my back as he stares at his brother. I don't even think he realizes he's doing it, soothing me with his touch. "Baking is one of his many hobbies that I made the mistake of supporting." Ren glares at him. "You know damn well it's not tonight. I have a play-off game. Not that any of the Bergmans can be bothered with hockey."

Shrugging, Viggo crunches his apple. "Oops."

Suddenly, I feel fabric shifting. A squeak sneaks out of me as the towel slips past my breasts.

"Ren!" I yelp.

He spins so his back is to Viggo again. I'm shielded with the towel pinned between us. "I've got you. Your virtue's preserved."

I snort in laughter. "My virtue. I lost my *virtue* in tenth grade, Zenzero." A blush heats his cheeks. "But thank you. I didn't want your brother seeing me naked."

At the worst possible time, my hip gives out, and I wobble in his arms. Ren catches me, then tugs me closer, but not before the towel slips lower and now—

Ren's eyes widen. My bare breasts smash against his chest. And for the second, but definitely most prominent, time, I'm feeling . . . "Ren," I whisper hoarsely. "Is that your—"

"Yes."

"Poking my—"

"Yes." He clears his throat. "And he's very sorry for being so assertive."

I felt the promising outline of it during yoga this morning, but now it's confirmed. The man is *ginormous*.

"It's okay," I tell him, trying to be calm about this. "It's . . . it's just a bodily response. It's not your fault, but holy shit—"

"You okay over there?" Viggo calls. Another crunch of his apple.

"When I'm out of this pickle," Ren mutters, "I'm going to ram one of those apples straight down his throat." He glances down at me. "I am so sorry about this."

"I'm the one who's sorry. It's all me and my bum leg's fault—"

"No, it's not, Frankie." He gives me a gentle squeeze that I think is supposed to reassure me but ends up just pressing all our nakedness together. I'm trying not to respond myself, but my nipples are rocks against his chest, my throat and cheeks burning with a flush. A warm, needy ache between my legs makes me feel even more unsteady.

"I have a plan," Ren says. "I'll just walk you backward, down the hall, and then you'll be out of Viggo's sightline. I'll close my eyes and you can get to your room in privacy."

"Okay." I nod. "Good idea."

Slowly, we start walking in step toward my room. Ren moves steadily, leading with a nudge of his knees that I follow as I take careful steps backward.

He peers down at me, trying very valiantly not to look below my chin, at my bare breasts pressed against his chest. It's his crowning feat of chivalry. I, on the other hand, I'm shameless. I can't stop fixating on how my nipples tighten, how they scrape across the soft dusting of hairs on his solid chest. I feel the hard planes of his pecs, the heat of his skin.

"It's like we're dancing." I stare up at him, trying to distract myself. "I bet you're a good dancer."

Ren grins. "Why do you think that?"

"How you're moving now. How graceful you are on the ice."

His grin broadens. "Thanks, Frankie."

"You're wel—"

We freeze as Ren's towel loosens between us. Before either of us can reach and save it, the towel drifts down, followed by mine, fluttering past our thighs.

Ren curses under his breath, holding me even closer, trying to pin the fabric somewhere around our knees.

I stare at him, wide-eyed with shock. "Did you just say *carbuncles*?"

"No." He grimaces. "Maybe—"

Before Ren can say another word, I gasp as our towels drop completely. We're naked, front to front. Ren opens his mouth as if to say something, when a low whistle interrupts him.

"Man, brother," Viggo says around a bite of apple. "I need whatever workout you're doing. Those. Glutes."

Ren's eyes drift shut. I've seen that look only after Maddox does something particularly asinine. That's Ren's "Give me grace, Jesus, I'm trying not to beat the shit out of somebody" face. "Get. Out. Viggo."

Peering past Ren's shoulder, I see Viggo smirk. "I kinda want to stick around and see how this plays out."

"Frankie," Ren says, deathly quiet.

"Hmm?"

"I'm going to pick you up but hold you close so he can't see you. I'll keep my eyes straight ahead and then set you in your room."

I nod. "Okay. Good plan."

"And then once I set you down, I'm going to murder my brother."

———

I usually hover in the corner with the other in-house PR and media folks during press conferences. Press conferences aren't my responsibility, but they affect my work. To do my job well, I need to keep track of everything that's going on with the team, so watching press conferences unfold live is imperative.

Rob, Ren, Tyler, and Coach sit up at the table, cameras flashing on them. They're all in their suits, but unlike Rob and Tyler, Ren's hair isn't wet and curled up at the edge of his collar like normal. His cheeks aren't flushed from the cold air and sixty minutes of hockey. He wasn't allowed to play again with his concussion and his healing shoulder, which doesn't seem to bother him much now, but Amy said shouldn't weather contact sports yet.

"Why is Ren up there?" I ask Nicole, our press coordinator, out of the side of my mouth.

She glances over at me, arms folded across her chest. "Why wouldn't he be? He's alternate captain. He's also a media darling. They love him."

"He didn't play."

"And he'll be explaining how soon that's going to change."

Rob finishes answering a question when one of the guys in the bullpen calls out, "Ren, there are multiple photos circulating from yesterday and today showing you alone with the team's social media coordinator, Frankie Zeferino. Can you speak to the rumors that you two are together?"

The world freezes with a resounding record scratch. Well, that's what happens inside my head.

Ren's usually a pro at press conferences, but this is new territory for him. Ren never gets photographed with a woman, never gets asked about evidence of a love interest, because there have never been any. I've seen Ren blush a lot the last couple of days. I've seen him trip over his words and scramble for the right thing to say. I'm prepared for this to turn astronomically bad.

But instead Ren blinks those pale cat eyes and leans on his elbows, close to the microphone. "Who I do or don't spend time with outside the rink has nothing to do with my professional performance, which is the focus of this press conference. While we're on that subject, I'll be returning for Thursday's game. Next."

He points and takes another question, moving on effortlessly. Hot. Damn.

"He's so good," Nicole mutters. She smiles over at me. "You two, huh?"

"Oh, no, it's not—"

"I'm teasing. Darlene told me you're just staying with him. I'm sorry about your house being broken into."

I exhale. I hate those kinds of *teases*. I never know someone's kidding until they enlighten me. My heart's pounding, adrenaline making my hands shake. "Thanks. It wasn't too bad, all things considered."

Turning back to Ren, I let my focus on him steady my breathing. I feel pride watching him, how capably and calmly he handles himself. Always the gentle smile, always polite to the reporters, who, to their credit, are pretty polite to him. Everybody loves Ren.

It's only when the cameras are packed away, chairs scraping as reporters stand, that I process the fact that Ren defused the hell out of that question.

But he also didn't answer it.

Our guys are filing out, back toward the bowels of the stadium, where Coach will finish up his postgame talk and send everyone out to celebrate our narrow win. I scramble as fast as I can, weaving through the sea of reporters.

Once I'm past them, so I don't draw undue attention, I hiss-whisper Ren's name.

He glances over his shoulder and stops, his smile widening as he sees me. "Francesca."

"Don't 'Francesca' me." I poke his stomach and swear under my breath. I think I just broke my finger on his abs. "You did *not* handle that properly."

He tips his head, a frown tightening his features. Ren gently takes me by the elbow, coaxing me to walk with him. There's a wall of people waiting behind us, so I let him pull me along.

"Mind telling me," he says quietly, "how you would have had me handle it?"

I make an awkward, baffled noise in the back of my throat. I'm so flustered I can't even find words.

"You taught me that denying something is the surest way to guarantee people think you're hiding something. I dismissed it without negating it. Just like you've always said to."

"*Rennnn*," I groan. This was a time to shut it down. Denial. Short and sweet.

He frowns down at me and pauses, bringing me gently to the side of the hallway. "What did I get wrong? How can I fix it?"

An odd lump of emotion forms in my throat. Ren's saying what I've wondered so many times in my social life. My empathy for his confusion cuts my frustration in half.

"I would have preferred you to say, 'Frankie Zeferino and I are not together. We're colleagues, and I was giving her a ride to work. That's it.'"

Ren stares at me for a long moment, then nods. "Okay. I'm sorry. I can go find Mitch and tell him."

"It's your call. It's your public life."

He narrows his eyes. "It's *your* life, too, Frankie. I don't want something being said about you that you don't want."

At some point in our discussion, while trying to stay out of people's way as they passed, I got myself rather smashed to his front. Now the hallway's quiet, leaving only the two of us and the heat pouring off of his suit, his clean, spicy scent. Warmth runs through every part of me that's touching him and jolts me with awareness. I take a step back.

"It's okay, Zenzero. Maybe . . . maybe you did it right. Time will tell."

"Either way, I'll find Mitch. Tell him what you said."

I grasp his arm. "Ren, wait."

He really doesn't mind that people would think we're dating? Even when he's saving his heart for this woman? I'm so confused. But as is always the case for me after a long day out in the over-stimulating, socially draining world, I'm too tired to try to figure this out anymore. I just know that what's done is done today, and him backtracking to find Mitch will only heighten Mitch's suspicions. That guy's a nosy motherfucker.

"It's fine," I tell Ren, releasing his arm. "I promise. I overreacted."

"Okay. Tell me if you change your mind, though." His eyes search mine as his smile returns. "You've got a hangry look brewing. Let's get a burger in you."

I open my mouth to disagree with him, but then my stomach rumbles. "I hate when you're right."

Ren laughs, and the sound follows me all the way to the restaurant.

FOURTEEN

Ren

Playlist: "Mama, You Been on My Mind," Jeff Buckley

"Oh my God," she groans. Standing in my kitchen, Frankie rips open a bag of root beer gummies and snaps apart one of the little sticky bottles with her teeth. I ordered a huge box of them after I learned they're her weakness, figuring I'd surprise her with them at work. Seeing as they were delivered here first, that plan went south when she recognized the box. "Where did you *get* these?" she asks.

"Same place as you, I'd imagine. The corporate beast that is Amazon."

"Third-party seller?"

I pop one in my mouth and chew. "Yep."

"Extortionist, soulless bastards," she mutters.

My belly laugh echoes in the kitchen as I pour the kettle for two cups of tea. "Some things are worth the cost."

"I swear, when I'm in law school, I'm going to look into what I can do about that. It's bullshit. I need these things. And it's like they know. They *know* they can get me to pay fifteen dollars a bag."

Holding her tea and mine, I use my elbow to slide open the door. Pazza squeezes through the moment she can and bounds down to the sand.

Following her, Frankie crosses the threshold next and watches her pup fly toward the ocean. Steadily, she walks toward the water, then lowers herself carefully onto the blanket I laid out, its corners tucked into the packed sand. When I catch up to her, she's sitting with her knees drawn up, staring out at the water.

My chest squeezes, impossibly tight. Seeing Frankie in sweats and a messy bun on her head, looking so at home here, is a bittersweet moment. I want it to last, but I know soon she'll be gone, with no guarantee that I'll have time like this with her ever again.

"Pazza's in for a rude awakening," she says, lighting up a joint and exhaling slowly, "when she's back to living in my little bungalow, no exciting trips to Aunt Lo's or this swanky spot."

I settle onto the blanket next to her, still holding our teas. "Why won't she go to Lorena's anymore?"

Or spend time here?

Because she *doesn't plan to spend time here, idiot. Pretty clear, if she's saying that.*

Frankie gently extracts her thermos from my grip. "Well, with law school, I'll have a better routine, no overnights or days away. No need to stay at Lo's." She shrugs.

For a while, we sit in silence, staring at the ocean, watching the moon paint the water silvery white. Pazza digs in the sand, rolls and snuffles and bounds away, returning obediently when I whistle and call her back. After long, peaceful minutes, the delicate weight of Frankie's hand jars me, pulling my attention from the shore.

She stares at her fingers sliding over my hand. Her brow furrows, and she pulls her hand away. "Tell me about the real Ren."

I peer over at her. "What do you mean?"

"The one hiding behind all that happy-go-lucky shit. The one we sort of danced around discussing after yoga."

I drop back onto the blanket and stare up at the stars. "Oh. That one. Well . . ."

As if she read my mind, Frankie holds out the joint in front of me. I stare at it, then extract it carefully from her grip. Over half the team smokes weed, for lots of reasons—pain relief, reducing anxiety, recreation. I've just been so uptight since the moment I signed, I never even considered it. But the thought of being a smidge more relaxed as I talk to Frankie, less stuck in my noisy thoughts, sounds pretty appealing.

After taking a small hit, I exhale slowly and battle the desperate need to cough. Frankie grins down at me. "I've corrupted you."

I laugh before it turns into a hacking cough. It doesn't take long, under a minute maybe, before a quiet heaviness settles in my limbs. My mind is stunningly clear. "Wow. I regret not trying cannabis sooner."

She belly laughs and ruffles my hair. "Welcome to the dark side, Zenzero."

I meet her eyes and smile, searching her face. "You said you want the real Ren. Is this quid pro quo? Does this mean I know the real Frankie?"

Her smile falters, even as her finger twines a lock of my hair around its tip, a steady, soothing motion. "Yes, I think so. More than most people do, at least." She nudges me. "Quit deflecting."

Turning my head, I watch the constellations. "The real Ren is still a bit of an unsure misfit."

"Why?"

I shrug and lift my hand, signaling I want another hit. "Who knows." Carefully, I take another small drag on the joint and hand it back to her, speaking through my exhale. "I was awkward when I was younger. Then we moved when I was in high school, so I had to start all over again, trying to find a few friends. I never found my stride."

"Until hockey?"

I smile up at the stars. "Yeah. I'm happy on the ice. And I actually get along with the guys. They like my weirdness. I don't know, I feel accepted, I suppose."

"That's important," she says quietly. "I have that with Annie and Lo. I'd be miserable without them."

I turn my head and stare up at her. "What about your family?"

Frankie shrugs. "Eh. I love my sister, Gabby, but she was a real asshole when we were younger. I was her baby sister having all these meltdowns and issues, and she felt ignored. We're mostly past that, but we're also really different people with a country between us. With Ma, I'm a walking time bomb, and every step I take is one closer to falling apart. Nonna's cool about the arthritis, but she doesn't get autism. I drive her nuts with my lack of a filter. I used to embarrass her at church and in her social circle. The Catholic Church and I don't get along too well, and it's, like, her life."

"What about your dad?"

She stares down at the sand, dragging her finger slowly across its surface. "He died when I was twelve. It's part of why I make my mom so anxious. She never got over losing him. He was a firefighter, and when he died on the job, it just deepened her anxiety about her family's well-being, if that makes sense."

Carefully, I press my hand to hers, my knuckles sliding against hers. "I'm sorry."

Slowly, her fingers dance with mine. "That's all right. I'll always miss him, but the pain dulls after a while." She sighs, stubs out the last of the joint, and sets it next to her tea. "So, tell me about Shakespeare Club."

I tip my head, confused by her changing directions. "What about it?"

"What you like about it. Why you still participate." She sips her tea and stares at the ocean.

"Well, it started in high school, a couple of nerds like me who loved reading and performing these words from a time when language *meant* something—when you didn't just throw words at each other, or, I don't know, maybe you did, but at least you had to get creative about it."

"Thus, the oaths."

My cheeks heat. I'm not embarrassed per se, but I wasn't doing it with the awareness that anyone was listening. "You noticed that."

She grins and sets down her tea. "I think my favorite to date is *boil-brained codpiece.*"

"It gets the job done. I don't like swearing at people, particularly in public. Maybe it sounds extreme, but I feel the weight of every little fan who watches me, whose parents read what I say in print. I—I guess I want to respect that. Still, at some point, you have to let off some steam, you know?"

She nods. "Shakespeare Club keeps it fresh in your mind. Anyone I know a part of this motley crew?"

I prop up on my elbows and take a long drink of tea, avoiding her eyes. "I can't tell. It's a secret."

When I glance up, there's a twinkle in her eye, a small smile tugging at her lips. "And how does one gain access to this exclusive gathering?"

"Well, first they have to be invited by a member. Then they have to recite their favorite lines of Shakespeare."

"Sounds kinda easy."

"Oh, there's more to it. Membership is contingent upon authenticity, upon words spoken from the heart. They have to say it like they mean it, like it matters to them."

"Why?" Frankie asks.

"That's how you keep it safe. If someone were to join and bring a dismissive attitude, it would ruin everything."

"Well, maybe I'll have to brush up on the Bard, then."

I whip my head sharply to meet her eyes. "Y-you'd want to come?"

"Someday, maybe. Sounds like a good time. Plus, I imagine you're very compelling, reciting Shakespeare. I have to see it."

My cheeks heat further. "I'm not sure about that, Frankie."

"Why not?"

"Because . . ." *Then you'd see me in all my nerdiness. My absolute oddball dorkdom.* "I'm self-conscious," I say defensively.

She rolls her eyes. "Ren, let me tell you something. Any person who ever saw you having a fucking ball being a theater geek and gave you shit for it, they weren't worth your time. My therapist says, show people who you really are, and you get the absolute thrill of knowing they love you for *you.* That's why the friends I do have aren't many, but they know and love the real me."

You know the real me, her eyes seem to say as she peers down at me.

My banged-up shoulder twinges from leaning on my elbow, and I drop down onto the blanket, as stunned by her words as I am by the pain lancing through my body. Frankie slides her hand up my arm, to my shoulder. When she rubs it, kneading the tender spots with her fingers, a groan rumbles out of me.

"Feel good?" she asks quietly.

"Uh-huh." My limbs are heavy, my thoughts calm. I feel like putty in her hands.

"Good. Now let's hear why you're hiding in that nice-guy shell."

"I feel like I'm being interrogated."

She grins. "I'm taking advantage of your relaxed state. You're so damn chipper." Her finger pokes my cheek, where a dimple is visible when I don't have the beard. "I need the dirt, Zenzero."

I give her a teasing glare that melts when she goes back to rubbing my shoulder. "The dirt is I was a late bloomer. Then when I got to college and kind of filled out, found my stride with hockey, people started treating me differently. And I didn't know what to do with that. I was the same person I'd always been, but now that I looked a certain way and had met with some socially constructed measure of success, I was suddenly supposed to *feel* different?"

Her fingers still for a moment, then gently resume. "Go on."

"That's really all there is to it. I just found my place with my Shakespeare geeks, playing hockey, and I guess I'm still trying to figure out how to be *me* and belong to both of those worlds. This 'nice-guy front' you speak of is what trying to hedge my bets looks like."

"Have you had a relationship that made you feel like you could be all of those things?"

"No."

"Bad relationships?"

"I never had a serious relationship, bad or good."

"Ah," she says. "So hookups. Yeah, those are over before you even get to know each other."

I stare at the night sky, bracing myself for her reaction when I say it. "No hookups, either."

Her fingers still. She drops her hand. "Holy shit, Ren. You're a *virgin*?"

Turning, I face her. "Yes."

"You're messing with me." She smacks my chest. "This isn't funny."

"Frankie, I'm not messing with you."

"You're twenty-five. Smart. Handsome. Like soaked-panties, sexually deviant handsome—"

"I'm sorry, I'm *what*?"

"Just. Forget I said that." Shaking her head, she blinks at me in disbelief. "I'm having a really hard time processing this."

"It's the truth."

"Wow."

I try to meet her eyes, but they dance away, to my mouth, my body, before they meet my gaze again. "You can ask me why."

"Why?" she yells, throwing up her hands in disbelief. "I mean, holy hell, Ren."

"I never wanted it with the women I met." I shrug. "I mean, my body obviously did. Plenty of times, but I just . . . I'd get to making out with some girl at a party, at her dorm, and, yes, I learned my way around a woman's body, but I still felt awkward. It didn't feel right."

"Until the mystery lady."

I glance up at her and feel my heart slam against my ribs. "Until her."

"How is she different?" Frankie asks.

My eyes search hers. "I'm not exactly sure. At least, I'm not sure what it was at first. Now that I know her better, I think we just connect well. Similar humor, maybe some similar soft spots. A lot of physical chemistry, at least on my side of things. And . . . she's the first person who I ever felt right around. Like I'm not a walking contradiction who'll never belong anywhere, but someone who actually makes a bit of sense. Like I don't have to choose between these different parts of myself."

"She sounds like the best kind of person, then," Frankie says quietly.

I smile up at her and tell her the absolute truth. "She is."

FIFTEEN

Ren

Playlist: "Everything I Am Is Yours," Villagers

That talk on the beach unlocked something inside me. I've always been attracted to Frankie, enjoyed her humor and wisecracks, how she hides her big heart beneath that grumpy front, but up until now it was fractured in fragmented, inadequate moments of time. Now, a few unbroken days and hours with her feel like a bittersweet gift—a window into what's possible, but still a mirage, a fantasy held just out of reach.

Even on the road, proximity to her is a new kind of torture. One game down in Minnesota, I've spent forty-eight hours sharing meals with her, meetings, interviews, photos. Stealing only fleeting glances, the barest touch and conversation.

And slowly, I've been unraveling.

I steal a glance at her. Catch how her skin glows gold under the lights, and those black dress pants hug her round backside, mold to her long legs. She's beautifully tall. Tall enough that when I hold her close, I don't have to bend in half or crouch down. When she kissed me on the beach, it felt like we were meant to do that. We fit. Perfectly.

Frankie spins her cane and yell-dictates to her phone, her face painted with a persistent scowl. It makes me want to chuck her cell over my shoulder and kiss her until that wide smile and one deep dimple transform her face to pure joy.

But I can't. I have to watch her bullshit with the guys, get into it with Rob about *The Office*, trip Kris when he pranks her by pretending that he accidentally tweeted a nude selfie. Frankie isn't mine. She's the team's. Or, really, we're *hers*. She has all of us wrapped around her finger.

Because she has our backs, keeps us in check, shows us how to handle the trolls and how not to go crazy dealing with social media.

And she's always there, steady and loyal. I'm going to miss spending practically every day with her once the season ends. Worse, after this season, when she's on to law school, if she doesn't want what I want, if there's nowhere for us to go from here, and I have to say goodbye, I'm going to be devastated.

Just that thought spikes my blood pressure. I glance away from her and distract myself with fixing my skate laces, ensuring they're tied tight. Now's not the time to get emotional and frustrated. Now's the time to focus on the game, on the moment right in front of me.

Don't worry about tomorrow. Tomorrow will worry for itself, my dad's always told me. But then again, he has the life he wants—a wife he loves, the brood of kids he dreamed of, a family of his own. Easy for him to say. What's there to worry about when everything's going your way?

When the team coordinators round us up and send us through the tunnel, my body's loose and warm, my shoulder wrapped for stability underneath my pads. It barely twinges with pain when I rotate my arm fully, and I haven't had a headache in seventy-two hours. Last game, I was finally cleared to play, but Coach only let me out for half the number of shifts he normally would.

I grumbled about it, and he told me to talk to Amy. Amy told me I was lucky I'd been allowed on the ice at all. So I shut my mouth, then nearly pulled a muscle grinning so wide when Coach told me today that I'd been cleared for full-time play.

On Minnesota ice, the energy's palpable, intense with the hunger to prove ourselves in enemy territory. We scraped by with a 3–2 win two nights ago, but it was messy and scrappy. We didn't play our game, and tonight's the night to reclaim our style of play, not to sink to theirs.

The guys are quiet as we skate around, doing warm-ups, everyone getting into their mindset for the game. When I steal a glance at her again, Frankie's still nose-deep in her phone, muttering to herself. Her hair drops in a sheet of near black down her shoulder and I squeeze my hand inside my glove, feeling the reflexive need to smooth it back.

It's a cruel irony that my two most important personal interests are at odds with each other: winning the Stanley Cup and winning Frankie's heart. The longer the play-offs run, the longer I have to wait to pursue her. Normally I find irony amusing.

Not this time.

Someone yells about an incoming puck, jarring me from my thoughts.

Focus, Ren. Deal with the here and now.

I catch it and pick up my speed as I skate around, flicking the puck up on my stick, spinning, faking, losing myself to muscle memory.

The din of voices echoes in the rink, but my hearing narrows to the soothing sounds of smooth, wet ice, the scrape of my skates as I spin and travel backward, my mind quieting, my body centering. Breathing deeply, I soak up that frosty bite in the air, a bursting cool that fills my lungs.

Pure tranquility.

Until I look up and lock eyes with Frankie. Her face is tight, strained in a way I haven't seen before. She looks worried and nervous. Skating her way, I stop near the bench. One hand's worth of fingers are tangled in her necklace, the other holding her phone, white-knuckled by her side.

"What's wrong?" I ask.

She swallows as her eyes dance between mine. "Nothing."

"Obviously it's not nothing. You look anxious."

Her hand drops from her necklace. "I'd like to formally request you not get beaned tonight. That's all."

I frown, turning only long enough to slap the puck away, returning it to Kris across the ice.

Then I spin back around. "I always try not to, Frankie."

"Didn't stop you from getting pancaked to the plexi last time we were here," she grumbles.

A small grin pulls at my mouth. "Francesca." I lean in. "Are you worrying about me?"

"No." She wrinkles her nose and flicks her hair behind her shoulder. "And scoot back. You stink like a sweaty hockey player."

"I am a sweaty hockey player, Francesca. I'd think you'd be used to the smell by now."

She closes her eyes like she's searching for serenity and coming up short. "I'm just reminding you, it's in everyone's interest here that you play it safe."

My stomach tightens with a surge of nervous happiness. Frankie cares enough about me to be worried I'm going to get hurt. Enough to scowl at me from across the ice and offhandedly warn me to take it easy.

Kris sends the puck back my way. I flick it up onto my stick and juggle it. "Don't worry, *älskade*. I'll be careful."

Her frown deepens. "Of course you speak one of the few European languages I have no familiarity with. That word at yoga. Now this. I don't like this recent development of second-language use, Søren."

"Hmm." Smacking the puck toward François, who was not remotely anticipating my shot on him, I earn one of his colorful French oaths. "This coming from the woman who was talking smack in Italian behind my back during yoga with Fabi. Pretty hypocritical."

"That—" She huffs. "Fine. Fair. But just so you know, I can still look up what you said."

I grin and start to skate away. "Good luck. Swedish is not phonetic."

Before she can give me further hell about it, I circle the net, power across the ice, and let my mind settle. But my heart won't stop galloping at breakneck speed.

———

Third period, tied 1–1. Thanks to a few games off, my legs are still fresh, my lungs easily pulling air. I crouch low for the face-off and win the puck, passing it to Rob and soaring up the ice into the attacking zone. I've had my eye on Number 27, the one who hit me late and dirty into the boards last time we were here. When I played the other night, he and I only had one shift that overlapped because I played so little, but tonight's another matter.

He's up my ass. Constantly.

So far, I've been able to stay clear of his dirtiest attempts, which seems to infuriate him. He's not the first defender to be perturbed by my agility on ice, given my size. He's also not the first defender to target me like his sole mission is brutalizing my body. Every team we play, I'm a target. I'm our leading scorer, and I'm good at avoiding scrapes, winning the puck, catalyzing offense. I defy physics, and it shocks and then quickly pisses off my opponents.

To be fair, it shocked me at first, too. But now I understand it's my strength, this intuition I have, the way I sense incoming hits and slip away, my body's ability to hold peripheral awareness of so much, then sneak myself and the puck right where we need to go. I couldn't explain *how* I do it if I wanted to—it's just something my brain-body connection implicitly knows.

That said, while I'm adept at dodging disasters, evading and putting up with Number 27 is getting old. Countless hooks, pokes, and slashes, slapping his stick into my skates, hoping to trip me. He's tried and missed smashing me into the boards more times than I can count. And unlike past times when I've weathered his and other defenders' abuse with stoic detachment, simmering frustration has been building to an angry boil inside me. I don't know why what I typically ignore and let roll off my back is irking me so relentlessly tonight. Why my hands itch to do damage, my fists twitch to draw blood. All I know is, they do.

Maybe you're hitting your limit, Bergman. We all have them.

Fair point, subconscious. I've spent three years in this league being squeaky-clean. Backing away from fights, playing a fair game, never taking the bait. I do every PR stunt they ask of me, show up for every magazine cover and interview the league wants. And the whole time I've smiled, kept myself out of trouble, and not asked for a damn thing except a beautiful game to play and my peaceful home to rest in when I'm not on the ice.

But most of all I've waited. And waited. And *waited* for Frankie. And now I've had to survive living with her, seeing shower water dripping down her chest, watching her eat my omelets with sleepy eyes and gorgeous bed head, sharing sunsets on the beach with her and her fluffy dog, which I miss already. And I still can't have her. I can't tell Frankie what she means to me or touch her how I'm dying to.

I feel like Mom's pressure cooker the time she forgot about her rice and the lid exploded, showering the room. A mess of suppressed, unmet need, blowing its top.

As 27 knocks my skates again, I spin, slam a shoulder into him, and barrel on with the puck toward the goal. My entire focus narrows on the net. I fly up the ice, deking, weaving, knowing my footwork's faster than the defender can keep up with, knowing this goal is *mine*.

I dump it off to Tyler, speeding past the Wild's last man back, and pick up the puck when Tyler fakes and flicks it to me. As I bear down on the goalie, the puck glued to my stick, then pull back to shoot, my foot gives out from under me thanks to Number 27's stick, which hooks my skate and trips me.

I'm falling, heading straight for a face-plant, but somehow, I still manage to get my shot off.

My gaze follows the puck waffling through the air, dipping low. Just as I crash to the ice, it sneaks past the goalie's pads and lands with a *thwack*, safe inside the net.

Goooooaaaaallll!

"You lucky bastard!" Tyler yells, hoisting me up. "Three minutes left, and you pulled that off!"

Rob's lit up with pride, smacking my helmet and bumping my chest like always. "That was amazing."

When I skate by, 27 shoves me. I freeze, hold his eyes, then begin to skate past, but he puts up his arm again and shoves me once more.

"That's it," Tyler snaps, yanking off a glove. "He's so fucking overdue—"

Rob stills Tyler's hand. "Ren can fight his own battles. And if he doesn't want to, they're not yours."

Number 27 spits out his mouth guard and grins nastily, revealing four missing teeth. "He's too pussy to fight his own battles. Is he your bitch, Johnson? Gotta protect your—"

Tyler launches at him, but I manage to get in between them. "He's not worth it," I tell Tyler, shoving his glove into his stomach and spinning him away. "Get out of here. Cool off."

I glare over my shoulder at the guy, straighten my helmet, then turn and start to skate away.

"*Mammering rough-hewn eunuch,*" I mutter.

Rob snorts in hysterical laughter, skating next to me.

"What did you fucking call me?" 27 yells, shoving me from behind. The ref skates in, turning 27 away.

Tyler howls in laughter as I grab his arm and drag him with me, skating toward the boards to switch for the next shift. All we have to do is keep the lead I just bought us for the next three minutes and avoid a penalty. Then we win the series and advance to the next round of the play-offs.

Rob skates past me, still struggling to contain his laughter. "Best thing I've ever heard on the ice."

I grin, spinning my mouth guard around, feeling the relief of another goal and telling off that jerk. I'm almost to the boards when I lock eyes with Frankie, who's scowling again. Dropping my mouth guard, I give her a bright smile. Suddenly her eyes widen, her hands waving in alarm. I turn to look over my shoulder and spin deftly, just in time to slip 27's right hook. Hurtling past me, he flies into the boards and crumples to the ice.

When I turn back, Frankie's eyes are wide, her mouth open.

"See," I tell her, swinging over the boards and onto the bench. "Told you I'd be careful."

SIXTEEN

Frankie

Playlist: "lovely," Billie Eilish, Khalid

After the game, Ren begged off dinner with the team. Rob implied it was because of a massive headache, but I have a suspicion Ren's absence has a lot more to do with what happened when 27 launched himself at Ren and ate ice instead of landing a blow.

I shouldn't be doing this, but I am. I walk the soft, carpeted hallway of the hotel, straight toward Ren's room. He's always booked right by me, and it's maddening. Every time I hear him turn on the shower, opening and shutting his hotel dresser drawers—because Ren's that guy who unpacks his suitcase tidily for a two-night stay— I have to try not to picture him walking around his room, gloriously naked, with that Viking sledgehammer between his legs, which I'm now shockingly acquainted with after the yoga and shower-towel debacles.

Knocking softly, I wait. Ren opens the door and squints at me. He's holding a massive ice pack to his head and looks unsteady on his feet.

"How was I supposed to know the guy only has one nut?" Ren mutters.

I shrug. "You couldn't have known. Just a bad coincidence. Not like he didn't deserve it, though."

Turning, Ren leaves the door open and backtracks to his bed, dropping on it with a groan. "It was just an off-the-cuff Renaissance swear. Just a bunch of old words thrown together."

"One of which was *eunuch*," I say pointedly.

Ren lifts his palm like, *so what?* "I've cursed hockey players using worse Shakespeare than that for ten years now, and never once has it created a problem." Ren sighs, sounding exhausted. "I have to get my frustration off my chest somehow. I don't fight. I don't take the bait. *I* don't say nasty things about their mother or call them homophobic slurs. Elizabethan oaths are how I hold on to a little shred of dignity."

Now, that's something you don't hear every day. I have the ridiculous urge to squish his cheeks together and kiss Ren breathless for the adorable things that fall out of that mouth. Instead, I settle for shutting the door behind me and carefully lowering myself to the edge of his bed.

"Well." I pat his hand. "I can tell you feel bad about calling a guy with one nut a *eunuch*, but he's an *asshole* guy with one nut. He was coming after you, bullying you, Ren. You just stuck up for yourself, and you didn't even mean to land such a pointed blow."

Ren shifts the ice pack on his forehead and doesn't say anything.

"Can I ask you something?"

He pivots his head on the pillow and meets my eyes. "Yes."

"What made you decide to play a professional sport that is arguably the most tolerant—celebratory, even—of hostility and aggression, when you're clearly a nonviolent person?"

"There's so much more to the game than that," he says, almost as if to himself. "I love the beauty of it. Grace and coordination, the team effort of hockey. I just choose not to embrace its most vicious aspects."

"And you feel like you stooped to his level tonight."

"I didn't mean to," he says quietly. "I was relieved he didn't smash my face, *again*, but I felt awful when I watched him slam into the boards, then fall on the ice. I know he brought it on himself, I understand that in some sense of karmic justice he deserved that, but . . ."

Ren sighs heavily, eyes closed. "I don't know. It was like high school all over again. I felt weirdly vindicated and guilty. Does that make sense?"

I nod. "Yes. I get why you needed to skip dinner."

"Oh, I was coming to dinner. I'm starving. I wasn't *that* torn up about it. But then I started this headache."

"Have you been getting headaches a lot?"

He swallows and presses the ice pack harder onto his forehead. "They started a few weeks ago. Amy says it's what sometimes happens after a couple concussions. So, nice life development."

I steal the moment to stare at him. Tousled hair, haphazard waves of russet and gold. Full soft lips half-hidden beneath his beard. Stupidly, I lean in and push back a piece of hair stuck to his forehead.

His eyes drift open, pale as ice and just as capable of freezing me. "Why are you here?" he whispers.

Voices echo in the hallway, muffled, rooms away from us. I hear myself breathing, rough and rapid. "I'm not sure. I was . . . I guess I was worried about you."

His gaze holds mine, like he's trying to puzzle me out. I only hope he can't. Scrunching his eyes shut, he tugs the ice pack over them. "Sorry. Light hurts."

His free hand fists by his side. I watch his jaw tic. He's hurting. And as weird or maybe even wrong as it sounds, I feel relieved that I'm not the only one. That Ren might seem like his life is a breeze, but he's as much a slave to the fallible human body as I am. He knows what it is to hurt, to be debilitated by pain.

Slowly, carefully, I set my hand on top of his fist. "Relax," I say quietly. "Tensing up makes pain worse."

He sucks in a breath when I slide my hand over his knuckles, gently prying open his grip. I pick up his hand and start a firm massage, running my thumb along his Mount of Venus, up through the webbings between his fingers.

Ren groans. "God, that feels good."

"Good."

I tell myself to breathe, even as heat simmers beneath my skin and every hair on my arms stands up. It's probably reading *Sense and Sensibility* for book club this month, but what is it that's so sensual about the simple touching of hands? How can sharing the barest contact feel so intimate?

After a few minutes, I gently set his hand on the bed. Before I can pull it away, he slides his palm against mine, how our mouths and bodies move in my daydreams. Soft, slow. Hot. Close.

Our fingers lock, and I don't know who did it first, only that it happened.

"'If I profane with my unworthiest hand this holy shrine,'" he whispers, eyes still shut, "'the gentle sin is this: My lips, two blushing pilgrims, ready stand to smooth that rough touch with a tender kiss.'"

I swallow nervously. "*Romeo and Juliet*."

"Ten points for Slytherin. Ten more if you can tell me what Romeo's saying."

I grin at him. Ren would know what house of Hogwarts I'm in, not that I'm terribly hard to peg. "That Juliet's hand is a place Romeo feels unworthy of, too pure for him to touch. Which is clearly just a pickup line, considering he admits he shouldn't hold her hand and offers to make it up to her by kissing her."

Ren's hand squeezes mine. "And how does Juliet feel about that?"

Breath leaves me, short and fast. My heart's pounding, emotion knotting in my throat. "I don't know."

"Yes you do. You have an incredible memory. It's like you see something once and you can recall it."

I don't exactly have a photographic memory, but I do have a damn good one.

"You knew that line from *Hamlet*," he presses. "Every Shakespeare play about a king." God, he's such a dork. So kissable.

But I can't do it. Not when he's a *virgin*, for Christ's sake, someone waiting faithfully for a woman to love and cherish and give everything to. He and I are literally on opposite ends of the spectrum. I have no business kissing him.

Newsflash: you already have.

Okay, I have no business kissing him *anymore*.

I stare at our hands, tangled together. "'Palm to palm is holy palmers' kiss.'"

"Mm-hmm," he says blearily, his grip slackening in mine. "'Let lips do what hands do.'"

Bringing our hands right over his heart, he knots our fingers tighter and sighs. "'They pray.'"

His breathing steadies. His face grows slack. And I let myself steal the faintest touch of his face. I smooth his beard, whisper my knuckles against his cheek, up to his temple.

"What are you doing to me, Ren?" I whisper. "What am I going to do?"

His hand twitches in mine, but his features are smooth; he is clearly deep in sleep. I stay, holding his hand, smoothing his hair. Longer than I should.

Much longer.

———

This is why I've spent the past four years of my life locked down. Because when I keep my heart and feelings and body closed off, I don't find myself waking up nauseously emotional, horny to the point of distraction, or horribly slept. I don't do stupid things like sit with a ginger giant for an hour, until my eyes droop and my joints start screaming for their own bed to sleep in. I don't have dreams that I can't remember except for what they made me feel. Hot. Lonely. Hungry.

It's all Ren's fault.

I'm sore and tired as we stumble off the bus back in LA. My little Civic flashes her lights as I unlock her from across the parking lot and hoist my carry-on bag higher up my shoulder.

"Frankie." Ren jogs toward me, hauling all his shit. Really, when is the guy going to let the minions be minions for him?

"Yes?" My stomach tightens, seeing him run my way. We spent the day tacitly avoiding each other. Or maybe I avoided him.

Okay, I avoided him. Because this is what my stomach did every time I looked at him. And what was there to say? *Hey, I don't know what's going on with me, but I'm having lots of feelings for you, which revolve around fascination, desire, and bone-chilling fear.* I'm an unfiltered person, but even I know that would be too much.

I want to kiss Ren and push him away. I want a bath and a bike ride. I need a night alone and a weekend with my friends.

I'm coming unhinged.

He catches up to me. "Can I follow you to your place?"

"You want to *follow* me?"

His cheeks turn red. "That came out wrong. I wanted to come *with* you but drive my own car, and let you drive yours. Because it's your first time going back to your place since . . . everything happened. I was going to offer to just do a walk-through, make sure you feel safe."

Buh-bye, somersaults. Now my stomach's graduated to back handsprings. I grip my cane so hard my knuckles ache. "Well, that's really thoughtful of you. But I was going to pick up Pazza first from

Lorena. Echo Park's even more out of your way. That'll make for a late night."

"I figured you'd want to go get Pazza," he says without missing a beat. "It'll help you feel safer to have her there. And no, I don't mind the drive. I need some quiet in the car after days with the hooligans, anyway."

He takes a step closer. "Please, Frankie? It'll give me peace of mind, too."

His hair rustles in the wind, unruly and backlit by the glow of the practice facility. Those wintry eyes sparkle beneath long sable lashes tipped with auburn. How do you say no to someone as beautiful as Ren Bergman?

Especially when he's even more beautiful on the inside.

I don't know. He's got a heart of gold but buns of steel. It's a toss-up which is better.

"Okay," I say on a sigh.

His hand reaches and squeezes mine, then gently releases it before I even process what he's done. My palm burns from that fleeting contact, as last night's touch rushes to the forefront of my memory.

Without a word, he slips my bag off my shoulder and soldiers ahead of me.

Dragging my feet the whole way to my car, I follow Ren, who holds open my door, merrily sets my bag in the trunk, then doubletaps it like some chipper bellhop.

He rushes over to his van, which is parked right next to my car, and waves me to go first. I decide to turn on my audiobook, since book club meets soon, and I am way behind on *Sense and Sensibility*.

It's not my favorite Austen. There's something about the story that makes me sad as I read it. Their father's death and the grief it brings the Dashwood women. How unfair it is, estates being entailed away from a man's own daughters to their male cousin. Marianne's immature romanticism, the way she so easily overlooks Colonel Brandon's kindness to her and falls for that asshole Willoughby.

Then there's poor Elinor. Just day after day, hiding her heart for Edward, because she's mindful of what it could cost her and her family if she expressed affection for a man whose feelings she's unsure of. She's so dutiful. So patient. She deals with a low-functioning mother, a sister who's doing everything Elinor isn't—throwing caution to the wind, madly chasing her impulses—all while mothering the youngest daughter, Margaret. Her existence feels so heavy that *I'm* tired of duty dragging Elinor down.

"Sense will always have attractions for me," the narrator reads.

"Damn straight." That I can empathize with. Because being sensible keeps you safe.

My fingers tightly grip my steering wheel, and I'm grinding my teeth so hard my jaw aches. I have to get my head on straight. Yes, it's true I find Ren attractive. Yes, I have a tender spot for the six-foot-three cinnamon roll. Yes, he's a fantastic kisser, especially for a virgin, which leads me back to a not-infrequent thought lately that a primal part of me wishes I got to be his first.

Because someone like him deserves the best first time, and while I'm not saying I'm some sex prodigy, I think I could please him. I know I sure as hell would enjoy trying. Teasing, adoring, and savoring this romantic, kind, gentlemanly, nerdy, hotter-than-sin—

Shit, I need to stop.

I tune back into the audiobook, willing myself to focus on the story, but Elinor and her damn restraint when it comes to Edward just heaps annoyance on annoyance as I drive, until I'm idling in front of Lorena's apartment building, yelling, "Just fucking tell him you love him already!"

Ren taps my window, and I startle so violently, I nearly shit myself. Once I can breathe again, I press the button until the window is lowered.

He leans his arms on the ledge and smiles, glancing from my dashboard with the pictured audiobook title to me. "Never seen Austen incense a person like that."

I turn off the engine and nudge open the door, making him take a step back. "Clearly, you haven't read *Sense and* fucking *Sensibility.*"

"Huh." He shuts the door behind me, following as I step onto the curb. "I didn't know the title included such profanity. Must be the unabridged version."

"It doesn't," I grumble. "But it should."

Ren presses the buzzer for Lo's unit, and the fact that he knows which one it is after only being here once before, when I was a shell-shocked mess, crying for my dog, just twists the knife deeper in my ice block of a heart.

"I actually haven't read that one," he says while we wait. "But you've piqued my interest now."

Before I can tell him to lay off my book club, Lo buzzes us in.

Lorena's in a certain state of undress that indicates she and Mia were having the cozy times, so I keep my pickup of Pazza quick. I get her into my car, then drive us home, Ren behind me the whole drive from Echo Park to Hawthorne.

When I pull up to the house, my heart starts pounding. My palms get sweaty. Pazza whines from her seat, and I pet her head, staring at my bungalow rental. The place I would normally be so glad to see looks sinister and unwelcoming. No lights on inside. A new handle and lock that I don't recognize mounted on the door, meant for the new, unfamiliar key I hold in my hand. It doesn't feel like coming home.

Sighing, I open my car door, but Ren's there already, opening it for me, grabbing my bag from the trunk, petting Pazza when she dashes over to him, like this is all just par for the course.

When I get to the door, my hands are shaking. I drop my keys, and Ren bends, scooping them up for me.

He holds them, his hand open, but his eyes connect with mine. "Do you want me to?"

I nod.

Quickly, Ren slips the key into the lock, lets himself in, and immediately flicks on the lights.

It helps a little. My misty-gray walls, fresh white trim painted everywhere. The cozy oatmeal-colored couch I've snuggled many nights on, decorated with Hogwarts-themed pillows and throw blankets.

Closing the door behind me, Ren turns the bolt and the sound makes me jump. His hand rests warm and steady on my shoulder. One solid squeeze, then he lets go. "You're safe, Frankie. Your landlord did a good job."

I nod again, worrying my lip between my teeth.

"Want me to take a walk around upstairs?" he asks.

"Yes, please."

Without another word, Ren heads up my stairs, two at a time, silent as a big cat, his large hand wrapped around the banister.

Pazza trots into the kitchen, sniffing around, nudging her bowl.

"I know," I tell her. "I'm coming."

Feeding her calms me a little bit. I'm a creature of habit, and this is our routine when I pick her up from Lo's. We come inside, I feed her dinner, then we head out to my tiny patch of backyard and she snuffles around, then does her business. After that, we curl up on the couch and read. Well, I read. Pazza lies on top of me and vies for my attention.

I hear Ren's footsteps roaming upstairs. Opening and closing closet doors. My shower curtain being snapped back, then straightened.

A smile tugs at my mouth as I open the container of dog food Lo made for Pazza and drop it into her bowl. He's upstairs, checking every nook and cranny.

As stupid as it is to get all feely about it, I do. I stand in my kitchen, savoring the sounds of care, because soon they'll be gone. I'll be back to being alone.

You like being alone.

Pazza whines, bumping my hand with her head. "We'll be fine," I whisper to her.

On a snort, she pulls back and shakes her coat, those pale gold eyes boring into me. *Sure, Mom*, they say. *Keep telling yourself that.*

SEVENTEEN

Frankie

Playlist: "Sirens," Cher Lloyd

"Frankie?" Ren calls from the steps. When he stops at the bottom of them, I stare at him, his tall frame filling the entranceway.

"Hi."

Super eloquent, Francesca, the little devil on my shoulder whispers.

I'm not trying to be eloquent, devil side. I'm trying not to rip off his clothes.

Ren smiles as a stray wave of hair flops across his forehead. Pushing it back absently, he strolls into the kitchen. "I did a thorough search. And trust me, with extensive experience in obscure and wildly unsafe hiding places, thanks to too many long Washington winters cooped up with bored, hyper siblings, I can assure you that your house is completely unoccupied, but for you and me."

Pazza barks at him and cocks her head.

He grins down at her, scratching her ear when she trots his way and drops to her haunches at his feet. "And Pazza, of course."

I stare at him as my heart bangs against my ribs, an inmate shaking its prison bars.

Let me out. Please. Just this once.

Drawing in a jagged breath, I spin away and beeline it for the back door. As I throw open the door, I whistle and snap my fingers in signal to Pazza. She bolts past me, jumping immediately at some insect that dances across the grass.

My throat tightens as I hug my arms around my middle. I hear the quiet rustle of Ren's steps, smell that clean, spicy scent that warms his skin.

His hand gently grips my elbow. "Are you okay?"

I nod without meeting his eyes, feigning concentration on Pazza. "I'm fine. I just needed some fresh air. Thank you for checking the house for me."

He steps closer. "I was happy to do it, Frankie."

My pulse thunders in my ears. It feels like my heart's rattling my ribs loose, it's pounding so violently inside my chest. If he touches me any further, I won't be strong enough to resist Ren anymore. I'll throw myself at him, beg him to give me everything for just a little while. To give me *for now* until he can have *forever* with her.

Her.

God, my blood boils, and a kick of anger surges through my veins. I hate her. I'm wildly jealous of this woman, who I can only assume is entirely, completely worthy of him. And I know, I *trust* that she is, because I trust Ren. He's measured and thoughtful. He has his head screwed on straight. He values the right things.

She's probably an understated beauty, because Ren's too wholesome to need a knockout—he only asks for beauty from within. She's one of those rescue-shelter volunteers who bakes perfectly circular chocolate chip cookies and makes friends with all the grandmas on the block. She wants three kids—two boys and a girl—and she loves to scrapbook. She also reads those criminally sex-free romances and is the least erotically adventurous woman on the planet—

Whoa, there, Francesca. Getting a little nasty, aren't we?

Well, yes. My thoughts have turned uncharitable. That's my jealousy talking. That's my covetous envy. A fierce possessiveness for someone I have no right to. An unwarranted, unfair animosity toward a woman I should be happy for.

"I want to apologize, Frankie. About last night."

I spin, tugged out of my thoughts. "What?"

Ren frowns up at me from his crouched position, petting Pazza. "I don't remember everything, because that headache was . . . unearthly painful, and I'd taken one of the pills for it that Amy prescribed me, but I have a vague memory of being very into hand-holding."

Heat rushes through me as I bite my lip. God, you'd think we'd made out, the way thinking of it affects me. "You were."

He grimaces. "It was unprofessional of me. I'm sorry." His face transforms to a wide smile as Pazza licks his face, perching her muddy paws on his knees.

"Pazza, down." My voice is sharp, and she drops immediately, jogging over to me. Ren slowly stands with a look of wariness on his face. "What's the matter?"

"Nothing. Just Pazza. Sh-she'll ruin your slacks." I point at the grass and mud staining his knees.

He smiles and shrugs. "I don't care, Frankie. I can do my laundry. I'm a spot-treating wizard, actually."

"Of course you are." I can't get a stain out of my clothes to save my life.

Why do all these little things about him add up to something so perfectly right to me? Why does he have to be so wonderful?

Why do I have to be so fucked up?

"Frankie." Ren closes the distance between us, sending the heat of his body pouring over me. "Why do I feel like you're avoiding the topic?"

"What topic?"

He lifts his eyebrows. "Of last night."

"Oh. Well. I mean, you weren't yourself." I wave a hand, taking a step back. The breeze sends his warm spiciness my way. He smells too tempting. "Non compos mentis and all. It's fine."

The line etched between his brows deepens. "Why do you seem upset, then? Tell me what's wrong, please, Frankie." Ren's eyes search mine.

"I can't."

I can't feel this way about you. I can't want you. I can't do this.

Something in his face changes as his gaze dances over my features, like he's read my mind.

"Can I ask you something?" he says softly.

No.

Nothing good's going to come of it, I can feel it already. He misinterprets my silence as assent.

"Was there . . ." Ren swallows, raking a hand through his hair. "What did you say last night when I was falling asleep? It's on the edge of my memory. But I can't recall it."

My heart thunders. Shit. *Shit.* "Um . . . nothing. I-it was nothing."

His eyes search mine. "Is it *nothing* because you didn't mean it? Or is it *nothing* because you're not sure you want me to have heard it, if I did hear it, that is?"

Roaring fills my ears. I lick my lips, clasp my shaking hands together. "I'm not sure," I whisper.

Ren steps closer. I search his eyes in confusion. If he heard me, if he knows I'm torn up over him, what then?

Holding my eyes, he brushes the back of his hand against mine, sending a bolt of electricity surging through my body. "There's something that I think I should tell you," he says quietly.

I stare at Ren, fear of the unknown gnawing inside me. I tug my lip between my teeth and bite until I taste the warm, coppery tang of blood.

"Frankie." His voice is urgent. He sweeps his thumb over my lip and tugs it free. The pad of his thumb presses my bite. His eyes hold mine, searching for answers I don't have. "You hurt yourself."

I pull away, but he steps with me, fluidly, intuitively, just like the

Great Naked Towel Tango. I take a final step back, until I'm flush against the house's stucco. It pricks my skin, a welcome discomfort. Just the tiniest pain compared to what's shearing through me.

He heard my confession. He knows I've caught feelings for him. And now he's going to graciously, gently break my fledgling heart. I know it already.

"Are you okay?" he whispers.

"Not particularly." I wipe my nose with the back of my hand, then sink my fingers into my fidget necklace. I spin the time turner, slip my thumb through the Quidditch goal. "I don't handle stressful situations well. I get anxious. Overwrought. Histrionic. It's very Victorian."

Ren stares at me, a series of emotions flying over his face before I have the faintest chance of identifying even one of them. "Now I know you're upset, Frankie. You're making bad, self-deprecating jokes."

I scowl at him. He stares down at me, his eyes pale and mysterious as the moon behind him.

I glance away. I can't handle the intensity of his gaze. I stare at his dress shoes, planted wide in the grass. The long line of his legs. Up his solid torso to the hollow of his throat. I close my eyes and remember what he looks like beneath that crisp dress shirt. He has one of those bodies that could be carved in granite. Power wrapped in beauty.

I want Ren so badly. I want him as much as I want to run away *from* him as fast as I can. Because I haven't wanted to let someone in in a long, long time. It's terrifying as ever. And it hurts even worse, now that I know rejection is coming before I even asked for a chance.

"Frankie." The plea in his voice draws my gaze. I couldn't look away if I wanted to. "After I say what I'm about to, I want to hear your honest feelings on it, but . . . not now, if that's all right. I was hoping you'll give it a bit of time to sink in first."

I wrinkle my nose. "That's not generally how I work, Zenzero. I don't have tons of filter between this and this." I point from my temple to my lips.

"One of the many things I like about you." He grins. "But I think what I have to say might leave you a bit . . . shocked. It will at least buy me the few precious seconds it will take to walk through your house and get in the van. And I'm going to do that. Because I am a coward."

I swallow in nervousness, clenching my hands into fists, as an odd current of fear and unease rolls through me. "You're about the least cowardly person I've ever met, but okay."

Ren exhales heavily. "So. Once I say it, I'm going to leave. And when you're ready—*if* you're ready—tell me, and we'll talk." He glances up to the night sky, like he's searching the stars for something mere earth can't give him. But then his gaze drops once more to me, a tender smile warming his face.

"First. I never wanted to keep this from you, but I—I didn't know what else to do but stay quiet when it was impossible. And then, when I knew you were leaving, I wanted to wait until you left the team, but I don't know what happened, except on the beach, last night, something feels like it's changed, and now I can't. I can't contain this anymore. It needs to be said.

"I want you to know, if you never want to hear about this again, I will respect that. I won't make it uncomfortable. I'll be professional at work and leave you alone. Okay?"

Is this how you let someone down easy? Seems like an odd way to do it. I search his eyes.

"Ren, I'm so confused."

He makes a sound of unease and rubs his forehead. "Yeah, I'm realizing that. Which . . . I don't know if that makes this easier or harder, but here goes."

Standing tall, throwing his shoulders back, he huffs a breath and stares intensely down at the ground. Until, finally, he peers up at me through thick lashes and holds my eyes. "The woman I've been waiting for . . ."

My stomach drops. That's how he's going to do it. Tell me about her, and like a bucket of ice water, douse every spark of lust between us.

I feel sick with sadness already, knowing that once I know who she is, this tiny moment I had with him—stolen kisses, heated glances, the soft whispers of tangled fingers, palm to palm—has to end. Because I am many things—obsessive, fastidious, blunt, and short-tempered—but one thing I am not, and never will be, is the other woman.

"That woman, Frankie," he says. "It's you."

It's you.

Two words. Missiles, tearing through my heart, landing on an earth-rattling *boom.*

Ren's right. I'm speechless. And long before I once again locate my body in time and space, Ren's gone from my yard, leaving me blinking rapidly into the middle distance while my brain tries to process the words it just heard.

It's. You.

Wandering shakily into the house, I slowly sink to the ground as my breath comes short and quick.

Countless moments with Ren flash through my mind, painted in a new, weighted, gloriously terrifying light.

I'm the one he's been waiting for.

I'm the one he's wanted.

My throat is bone-dry. I grab the counter and hoist myself upright, fumbling for a glass from the cabinet, filling it with filtered water, and draining it. Setting down the tumbler, I'm met with my reflection in the window above the sink. I hold her gaze, staring at her shocked features.

She's never felt so many conflicting emotions at once, and it shows on her face. Hope. Terror. Joy.

It's been so long since I embraced the part of myself that aches to come to life when Ren's near. The one that laughs and jokes, that hugs hard and kisses deeply. The one that cries at sappy movies and throws open her heart for those she loves. The one that believes someone could love her without one day resenting her, without seeing her laundry list of needs and hurdles as burdens but rather as beautiful parts of what make her *her*.

Because *I* know that having arthritis, being autistic, does not make me less whole or human. It doesn't make me wrong or broken. It makes some things in my life more challenging in ways, yes, and maybe I don't represent the "norm," but I can be someone who surmounts obstacles without it meaning there's something fundamentally lacking in my makeup.

Problem is, that truth has been harder to hold on to when I let people in. Because then my sensory limits, my unexpected emotions, my easily tired body, my unfiltered mouth, are part of the package deal with me, and apparently, they wear out their welcome. Everyone—my family and childhood friends, my one college boyfriend—*everyone*, except for Annie and Lo, whom I have loved and let in, has ultimately come to resent me.

So, when I moved away and started my life fresh, I told myself I simply wouldn't love or be loved that way, not anymore. Because each time I let someone in and they show me I'm not worth the work, it's become more painful, more difficult to bounce back.

"What are you going to do?" I ask my reflection.

For so long, my way of life has worked for me. It's comforted me to guard my emotions, be sensible with my heart, practical with my actions, controlled and ordered. Being safe allowed me to move beyond the pain of my past.

Silence fills my home. A weighty emptiness spills into its corners, as stark and illuminating as the moon outside. An uncomfortable question burrows deep in my chest and pricks my heart.

What if the life I've built, the one that was supposed to free me, has turned into a prison after all?

EIGHTEEN

Ren

Playlist: "Saturday Sun," Vance Joy

I woke up convinced last night was a dream. But then I rolled out of bed and passed my laundry hamper on the way to the bathroom, freezing as I noticed muddy paw prints and grass stains coloring the knees of my suit pants. And it all came rushing back.

Forcefully.

I told her. I really told her. I listened to an overwhelming intuition, an undeniable voice inside my head, telling me I should.

Because despite my brain-bruised fog the other night, I knew I remembered that I didn't just hold Frankie's hand; Frankie held it back as she whispered something that I couldn't remember but whose *sound* I remember. She sounded sad. Hopeful. Tender.

Knowing that she'd kissed me, the way we talked on the beach, the care in her touch in the hotel. Then everything she said that night over takeout—my brothers said if that wasn't a woman who has feelings for you, they didn't know what was.

I couldn't stand the thought that Frankie might feel something for me and be in any doubt that I felt the exact same for her, too. The deception's benefits no longer outweighed its risks.

So I told her that I wanted her. That I've *wanted* her. For years. Her eyes widened. And stupidly, I stood there for five eternal seconds, hoping maybe she'd leap into my arms, laugh wildly as we kissed under the stars.

Instead she blinked. And swallowed. Slowly.

So I left and hyperventilated while I drove home. Then I took enough Zzzquil to fell a horse and end the misery of consciousness for a few hours.

Now, as I walk into the practice facility, my stomach's in knots. I barely managed a protein bar for breakfast and forwent my normal iced coffee because my heart's flying just fine on its own without the help of caffeine. As I stroll into the practice facility, I have to take deep, slow breaths so that I don't break out into a panicked sweat.

"Morning, toots." Mildred smiles over her half-moon glasses from the practice facility's front desk.

"Morning, Millie." I set a piping-hot to-go cup on her desk ledge. "The usual."

She snatches up her coffee, popping off the lid and taking a long, savoring whiff. "Ah, that's the stuff. How much do I owe ya?"

"You always ask that, and I always tell you the same thing." Double-tapping her desk, I start walking away.

Millie grins. "You're a good egg, Ren."

Before I can answer her, a new voice cuts across the space. "Zenzero."

I spin around.

Frankie.

How is she lovelier every time I see her? What is it about her practice-day outfits—slouchy hoodies and fitted joggers, the long trail of her dark ponytail—that gets to me? Is it that when she's dressed this way, I imagine I'm seeing her soft side, the tender, walls-down woman I've glimpsed so rarely beneath that power-suit, buttoned-up front?

"Hi," I whisper.

She smiles, and it hits me square in the chest. Her smiles are few and far between. Each one's a victory.

"Hi," she says quietly.

Swallowing thickly, I scrub the back of my neck. It's so silent in the entranceway, you can hear the faint echo of the guys' voices all the way down at the other end of the building.

Clearing her throat behind a fist, Frankie walks closer to me. "I was wondering if you were free to get lunch after dry-land and ice time this morning?"

My stomach clenches. I search her eyes, but they're unreadable. Is this lunch to let me down easy? Or . . . could it possibly be to tell me what I've spent years hoping I'd hear? *I want you, too.*

"Sure," I finally manage. "Name the place."

"I'm not picky. You choose."

A wistful sigh interrupts us. We both turn and look at its source.

Millie blinks innocently behind her glasses. "Don't mind me. Just isn't every day you see young love—"

"Oh, we're not—"

"It's not that—"

Frankie's and my words tumble over each other. We stop at the same time, a mirror of blushing cheeks.

"Right," Frankie says quietly, tucking her hair behind her ear. "Lunch."

She walks past me, leaving me alone with Millie, who's suddenly very absorbed in something on the computer screen.

"Mildred."

She squints at the screen, avoiding my gaze. "Yes, dear. How can I help you?"

I lean my elbows on the desk ledge, lowering my face until she's forced to meet my eyes. I know they freak some people out, especially when I don't blink. They're Mom's eyes. Pale and silvery. They're an unexpected pairing with my hair. A little unnatural. A lot intimidating.

Millie looks me in the eye and swallows with a loud gulp. "I'll mind my own beeswax from now on."

"Excellent." Pushing off the desk, I call over my shoulder. "No more meddling, Mildred. Not with dropping confidential club activities, check-engine lights or spark plugs, or hotel room arrangements, or you're walking your way to the next club meeting."

She cackles. "We both know you're too much of a softie to ever follow through on a hard-hearted threat like that, but nice try, toots."

She's right. And sometimes I wish I wasn't so damn predictable.

"What are you getting?" Frankie stares at her menu, biting her lip. "Too many choices."

I glance up from my phone, where a meme that Andy was delighted to notify me went viral plays on a loop in my messages: me eating ice, right as I get my shot off. The goal I scored when 27 tripped me. It has Frankie written all over it. She makes these from time to time, and they always take off.

"Francesca."

"Hmm?" She finally glances up. "What? I'm trying to decide between burgers here, Bergman. Heh. Get it? *Burg*ers. *Berg*man."

I flip my phone around so she can see the meme.

She has the courtesy to blush, the tips of her ears turning bright pink. "Oh, that little old thing."

"Oh, Frankie. There is nothing little or old about this. In fact, it's quite fresh and large. So much so, one might call it *viral*."

"Give me that," she mutters. Snatching the phone out of my hand, Frankie spins it in her grip.

"Can't be that bad . . ." Color drains from her face. "Okay. It's that bad."

I bite my lip, trying not to give away that I really don't care.

Actually, I find it funny. Frankie didn't just loop my epic biff; she added a tiny gif of an umpire and the words scrolling across the screen as he gives the signal: *SAFE!*

It's clever. I get why everyone loves it. I look just like a baseball player sliding into home plate. Except I scored a goal to win a play-off series. And hockey's about eight hundred times more interesting and challenging than baseball. But I digress.

Frankie swallows thickly, her fingers drumming on the table. "Ren, I'm sorry, I never—"

I set a hand over her fidgeting fingers. My thumb gentles her palm, hidden beneath my hand, so no one can see the intimacy of that gesture. "I don't care. I was just giving you a hard time."

When she blinks up at me, her lashes are wet. "I feel *terrible*. You said you were a huge nerdsmobile in school, which I can only assume means you got made fun of *a lot*—"

"I mean, not a *lot*—"

"And here I am, making something that got a laugh at your expense—"

"Frankie." I squeeze her hand gently, somewhat stunned by the emotionality of her response. The Frankie I know would have rolled her eyes and told me "tough nuggets."

"I seriously don't care. I have a pretty nice life. If a few social media ploys happen to involve laughing at me, my love of the game and the lifestyle it affords me more than make up for it."

Finally, Frankie seems to relax. Her color comes back a bit in her cheeks, and her shoulders drop. "Okay."

"Good." I let go of her hand. Taking a drink of water, I grin at her over my glass. "Plus, I did score to win the series. I mean, that fall was practically heroic."

Her lips twitch. "Heroic. Yeah."

I break and laugh, lifting my hoodie to cover my mouth. Frankie's face breaks into a wide grin that she covers with her hand.

But not fast enough. For just a split second, I catch that bright, unbridled Frankie smile. And it's worth every horrible meme at my expense that she could ever devise.

As our laughter dies away, I notice there are a few people staring at me—*us*—all of whom are not so covertly taking video or snapping photos.

Which reminds me of something. "Francesca."

She lowers the menu. "Søren."

I drop my voice and lean in. "I hope I'm not insulting your intelligence when I ask this, but you did consider that we'd be photographed, right?"

"Yep." She lifts her menu and goes back to reading.

The waiter comes by, filling our waters. When he walks away, Frankie watches until he's a decent distance from us, then lowers her menu.

"What are a few more photos of us over lunch?" she says, sipping her water. "Whether it's the truth or not, it's what people think. Even *Darlene* bought it."

"She what?"

"This morning she texted me to ask, telling me I could be honest with her, and I wouldn't get in trouble. Apparently, she thought, especially after the press conference answer you gave, that you and I *were* a thing." Frankie snorts, then takes a sip of her water. "She said it seemed likely from the photo. Hilarious, right?"

Her words cut brutally. There's my answer, quick and painfully swift. God, the disappointment.

Frankie frowns as she takes me in. "What?"

I rub over my heart instinctively. It does nothing to quell the ache in my chest.

"Ren. Talk to me. Remember, I can't . . . I am even *worse* than the average human at intuiting. But the nice thing about me compared to most people is that I have no problem being told how and when I get it wrong." She leans in, sliding her hand toward me, halting halfway across the table. "Please."

I meet her hand so that our fingertips touch. "You just said the thought of us being in a relationship is laughable."

"I didn't say that," she says gently. "I said that deducing from a *photo* that we're in a relationship is hilarious. Darlene of all people should know better than to assume that much from a paparazzi shot." She tips her head, her eyes dancing over my face. "You thought I was saying I found the idea of *us* hilarious."

I slide my fingers farther across the table, until they're woven with hers. "Yes."

She squeezes my hand in her grip, making me glance up. "But that isn't what I said. And if ever you meet someone who means literally what she says, it's me, Zenzero."

"I understand. That makes sense." I'm weathering a boomerang of emotions, but I try to smile and show her I believe her. Because I do.

With a final squeeze, she withdraws her hand. "So. In the spirit of that, I'm going to be direct—"

The waiter shows up again. Worst possible timing. *Ever.*

I'm left hanging, the future of my love life discarded to place a lunch order. It's not entirely surprising. Food is serious business to Frankie. Turning, she tells him what she wants, snaps her menu shut, and sets it in his arms. I order, too, and we both watch him until he's gone, leaving us alone in our secluded corner of the restaurant.

"You were saying?" I offer. Trying desperately not to sound . . . well, desperate.

"Right. I have some questions and concerns. First, what do you want from someone when it comes to having feelings for them?"

"Well, I'm not talking about *someone*, Frankie. I'm talking about you."

She bites her lip. "Yes. That."

"That?"

"Just—" She waves her hand impatiently. "Talk. Elaborate."

"Well, if you felt how I felt, I'd want to date. We could keep it between us until you were comfortable telling other people, given work."

She nods thoughtfully, her fingers tangling in her necklace. "Ren, I'm attracted to you. I care about you, respect the hell out of you—" Frankie narrows her eyes. "What are you grinning about?"

Hearing her say it, I'm euphoric. I feel how absurdly wide my smile is, so I set a hand over it and shrug.

"But here's the deal. I haven't wanted a relationship in years."

"Years?"

"Stop repeating me. Yes, years. I've avoided it like the plague."

"Why?" I ask.

She puffs air out of her cheeks and drums her fingers on the table. "Historically, in relationships, people's patience wears thin with me and my circumstances. I've noticed I'm happier, that my self-esteem and well-being are better, when I'm alone. So, I've sort of released the idea of being a white-picket-fence and two-point-five-kids person."

"Well, that's fine. I want my house on the beach, which you like; a dog, which you have; and five kids, which—"

"*Five?*" Frankie's eyes widen comically. "Jesus, Bergman. My yaya hurts just thinking about it."

"Your *yaya?*"

"I told you, stop repeating me." Shutting her eyes, she breathes deeply and says on her exhale, "I got sidetracked."

"That's my fault." When she opens her eyes, I try to meet them. "Can I ask you something?"

She nods.

"Have you ever felt like *I* treat you that way?"

"No," she says immediately.

My heart does a celebratory somersault.

"But . . ." Frankie spins her necklace and watches me carefully. "We haven't been in a relationship."

"But I've wanted to be."

Her fingers pause. A blush pinks her cheeks. "It's not the same."

"You're right. So let me promise you, here and now, that I will never view you as a burden or a problem to be surmounted. You're a *person*, Frankie, one that I'm wild about. And any hardships, anything difficult in your life, well, I'll just be grateful that I get to be with you as you weather it."

"Until it gets old," she says flatly. "Everyone starts out talking like you, Ren."

I try not to let it hurt. I have to remind myself that her doubt and distrust aren't about *me*. They're about her past and how it hurt *her*. For someone whose thinking is as analytical and pattern oriented as Frankie's, the past is the best predictor of the future.

"Okay," I concede. "I know that it might be hard to trust me, that I will *never* see you that way. I understand it might require time to experience that. So, if you're willing to give me a chance to earn your trust in that capacity, I'll be content. We can go slow, take our time. The only thing I ask for is exclusivity."

She balks. "Of course I'd be exclusive." Reaching, she smacks my arm. "What kind of asshole do you think I am?"

"Well, I don't know what the kids are doing these days."

"The *kids*? Ren, I'm older than you."

"By a whopping one year."

She rolls her eyes.

"I just . . ." I sigh. "I just need faithfulness. That's it."

Frankie snatches a roll from the bread basket, rips it open, and smashes some butter into it, entirely focused on her task while she mutters under her breath.

"What are you grumbling to yourself?" I ask her.

Frankie gives me a withering stare and says around a bite of bread, "As if I'd want anyone else if I had you."

Affection unfurls inside me as her words settle, warm and deep in my heart. "That's a very nice thing to say, Francesca. And you *do* have me."

The way she looks at me, her fear and vulnerability gut-wrenchingly close to the surface, is like a blow to the chest. As is so often the case with Frankie—and I've noticed this with my sister Ziggy, too— her mind sees the world incisively, with a raw analysis that most of us avoid. Frankie cuts straight to the heart of love's vulnerability. And while most of us like to comfort ourselves with the delusion that love is bliss, it's not called *falling* in love for nothing. We love, entranced by the breathtaking view, and we fall, not knowing where we'll land.

Our food is set before us, plates turned to an exact angle for best presentation. Waters filled.

Then we're alone again.

Frankie stares at her food and sighs.

"Hey." I touch her gently, slipping her hand inside mine. "How are you feeling about all of this?"

She meets my eyes. "After last night, when you told me, then you left . . . I thought about if I could do this, if I wanted it." Her eyes soften, and her shoulders round, like she wants to curl in on herself. "And all I could think about was how much I missed you. I wished I was with you. So that's why I'm here, because right now, I can at least tell you, with complete sincerity, that I want to be with you, and I feel like I'll want to be with you more and more. But I also have to be honest, Ren. This is scary."

"How can I make it less so?"

She smiles softly. "Be honest with me. Be honest with yourself. When it gets to be too much, tell me."

"It won't, Frankie." I squeeze her hand. "I'll show you that."

"Well, that's that, then. But until we're out of the play-offs or we win the Cup, we act like we always have at work—completely professional. As long as the season runs, no matter what we do personally off-hours, nothing changes in how I treat you in front of others."

"What about if someone finds out while you're still with the team? Do you want to wait until after the season?"

Please say no. Pleeeease say no.

"Hell no," she says, waving a hand. "We'll be professional at work, and if anyone guesses why I'm spending time with you outside of it, it's not like I risk losing my job for it anymore. I'm leaving the team. It's no one's goddamn business what we do. I mean . . . does that work for you?"

I smile at her. "Absolutely."

"Good." Frankie smiles to herself and cuts into her meal. She's quiet as she works her way through her food, and just as I'm starting to worry about the silence, about the places her thoughts have taken her, I'm stopped by the gentle press of her foot next to mine beneath the table.

The tiniest gesture.

But it feels impossibly significant.

NINETEEN

Frankie

Playlist: "Crush," Tessa Violet

I don't know why I play footsie with him under the table. I don't know why it feels so relieving to confess that I feel vulnerable, that the prospect of intimacy terrifies me, because one day he could do what others have done before and hurt me.

What I *do* know is that as we eat and I replay his response in my memory, my heart beats calm and steady, an unfamiliar warmth centering beneath my ribs, radiating to tender, forgotten corners of my body.

I know that sunlight on Ren's hair shines like a weathered copper penny, that some fragile bud of happiness blossoms inside me as we eat in comfortable quiet. He's willing to prove his trustworthiness when he shouldn't have to, and I wish I didn't need that from him. I wish I didn't see people as guilty until proven innocent. But the past has been a harsh teacher, and its lesson isn't easily forgotten—I don't get hurt when I adopt a self-protective outlook.

"So." Setting down his fork, Ren leans back and lounges in his seat, hands behind his head.

"So." I slurp the last of my root beer, then frown down at it. When I glance up, he's smiling at me. "What?"

He shakes his head. "What do you plan to do between the season ending and starting law school?"

"Well, not too much. Study, read, catch up on sleep. Maybe get a hip replacement."

He drops his hands, his eyes widening. "Frankie, you didn't tell me your hip was that bad—"

"Easy, Ren. It was a joke. A bad one, obviously."

Ren scrubs his face, then rakes his fingers through his hair. "Okay, I'll catch up. Autoimmune diseases and major surgeries are fair game for humor."

"It's not major surgery. The new technique is minimally invasive. And yeah, I have a sense of humor about my medical dossier. You know the saying, 'If you don't laugh, you'll cry.' So, I crack jokes."

Our waiter comes by with a fresh root beer. "Oh." I glance up at him and smile. "Thanks."

He turns beet red. "S-sure, miss."

Spinning away, he's gone before I can say anything else, like "Can I see the dessert menu?" What? I have a sweet tooth.

Ren clears his throat, prompting me to turn back to face him. His eyes dance over my face. "I had no idea that was all it took to earn that kind of smile from you."

I wrinkle my nose. "What?"

"Root beer. And here I thought it was the gummies."

"You got those for *me*?"

Ren tips his head. "Of course, Frankie. I knew you liked them."

"Oh." I fiddle with my fork. "I thought you just liked them after trying them at my house."

A beat of silence holds between us. He leans in and wipes my lip clean.

"Ketchup," he says quietly. Then he sticks his thumb in his mouth and licks it clean with a *pop*.

Preschool Jesus with a Carpentry Awl, my wires are crossing. And as he leans close, he hits me with his spicy, clean scent. I stare into his kind eyes, absorbing his sheer size and proximity. I decide Ren is living temptation. I want under him. Yesterday.

I can't meet his eyes for long. They see too much; they travel too far under my skin and stir up feelings that make me shiver and gulp for air. That gently smiling mouth says he can go slow. Those pale cat eyes say, *I want you for dinner.*

"Frankie," he says.

"Hmm?"

"Will you come over tomorrow night?"

"Yes," I blurt.

And I may literally jump you when I arrive.

"Good." Lifting a hand, he signals the waiter. "Because I miss Pazza."

"Hey. A girl likes to know she's wanted for more than her adorable dog."

He smiles. It's a new smile. A secret smile. "Then let me reassure you. I want you for much more than that."

Gulp.

"But as I said, there's no rush or pressure," he continues. "On either of us. Physically. Emotionally. We'll go slow, just spend time together."

"Oh, I feel zero pressure. Going slow isn't necessary." And I swear to whoever is the patron saint of sexual satisfaction—trust me, there is one, Catholics have patron saints for *everything*—if that man doesn't seduce me the moment that I walk into his house tomorrow, I'm going to lose my mind.

"Great. You can come over tomorrow night. I can cook, and we can just relax."

Cook and relax. That sounds promising. Like Ren's version of Netflix and chill.

"That works. But let it be known, I'm going to expect you to pay visits to my humble bungalow, too. I like my hobbit hole."

"Sure. I'll spend time at the bungalow. Only thing I'm not sure about is overnights. I need a king-sized bed. I don't fit on those queens."

"I—what?" I stumble over my train of thought. Sex is one thing. Sleepovers are another.

Sleepovers mean cuddles and bonding. Intimacy I haven't accessed for years except for when I let Pazza smoosh me with her "hugs" on the sofa and I feel the ridiculous amount of love you can harbor for an animal creature.

"So, uh—" I clear my throat behind a fist, trying to look not entirely freaked out. "You're planning on overnights?"

Deep breath, Francesca. One step at a time.

Ren pins me with his cat eyes. "You've seen me work every moment I have under the lights, Francesca. I plan on being similarly dedicated when the lights are out."

Holy soaked panties.

He looks up at the waiter when he arrives at our table. "Can we have the dessert menu? Thanks."

"You're getting dessert?" I croak. I chug some root beer and try to snap out of the sex haze. "What's Lars going to say? He'll smell those simple carbohydrates on your breath. Then it's game over."

Ren grins. "Not for me. I know enough by now to understand that if I'm eating with you, dessert's in order."

"You're buttering me up."

"Hardly. I'm just trying to put a smile on that lovely face with the help of a little culinary indulgence."

I level him with a sharp look. "Don't count on too many smiles. I think I've hit my quota for today."

His grin deepens as sunlight spills through the restaurant. "Yes, ma'am."

Taryn, our water aerobics instructor, whips her body through the pool, her limbs knifing fluidly as if water's viscosity is just an urban legend rather than indisputable physics. "Let's go, ladies! You're pussing out on me."

To my left, Annie snorts. "I don't think she should be saying that."

"Nope," I pant. God, these treading-water segments. "That's asking to get sued."

"You're quiet tonight, Frankie. What's up?"

I shake my head. "Just winded."

"Which wouldn't be a problem if you came to water aerobics with any kind of regularity."

"Eat me, Annabelle. I have a demanding job. And not all of us have fifty pounds of pregnancy buoying us up in the water."

Annie gasps, then slaps the water toward me. "How dare you! This is stamina that I've built. And while my excess fat stores and uterine fluids are less dense than water—"

"Stop." I almost gag. "And never say 'uterine fluids' ever again."

She rolls her eyes. "My point is, I'm kicking this treading-water challenge's behind because I'm in shape, not because of the baby."

"Okay, Annabelle."

"Francesca, I swear—"

Taryn clears her throat. Loudly. "Do you two mind?"

We smile sheepishly and say in tandem, "Sorry."

Once Taryn's attention is directed at the seniors using those flotation devices that I'd give my left tit for right now, Annie glances over at me. "Something's up with you. I want to hear about it."

Dammit, *why* must I be so transparent? Ma's always said I wear my moods on my face, which brings us to another benefit of scowling—it hides everything else that you're feeling.

Ever since lunch, my gears have been spinning, my brain won't shut up. My anxiety's roaring at full throttle, and if I could wring my hands without drowning right now, I would.

I'm not good at transitions and changes. I'm terrible at facing newness. I'm worse at anticipating everything that could go wrong. This threshold I'm about to cross with Ren typifies all of that. Thus, the freak-out.

"I had a long day," I tell her. "You know how I get. I zone out when I'm wiped."

"Hmm." She sniffs. "And here I thought it would be a good idea to go get shakes and fries after we finished class—"

"Okay! I mean, I could carb up after this."

She narrows her eyes. "*And* tell me what's going on while you're at it."

After another twenty minutes of water aerobics hell and a quick shower to rinse off the chlorine, Annie and I drive to our nearby go-to dive diner. Once we have our goodies, we settle into a corner booth.

Sitting with a sigh, Annie lifts her legs, propping her feet on my side of the booth. "Do you mind?"

I gently pat her swollen ankles. "Of course not. So. How's the lab?" I ask, struggling with the ketchup bottle.

Giving up, I hand it to her. She pops off the lid and hands it back to me. "Exciting. Challenging. But it's also the same frustrating bullshit as always. Lots of mansplaining. Trying to get myself heard and respected. Pregnancy requiring special considerations in the lab for my safety hasn't helped, either. I swear, if I were a guy, I would *not* be having this hard of a time getting funding."

On a sigh, she sweeps up her milkshake and takes a long drink. "I hope I have a boy so I can raise him to be feminist as fuck. Another man in this world who values women as he should, who supports their equal abilities."

A weird twinge in my chest makes me set down my handful of fries. Ever since Annie told me she was pregnant, the far-off idea of children has hovered closer in my mind—how scary it would be to love this tiny helpless creature, but how incredible it would be to see them grow up and become the kind of wonderful human that Annie and Tim's baby will be. Ren and his talk today about a houseful in that beautiful beach pad, driving his dad-van, it's pressing in on me—one moment a claustrophobic fear, the next a dizzying hope.

"Frankie?"

"Sorry." I shake my head and snap out of it. "I'm with you. And I think you'll raise a great little feminist."

"How are things at work?" she asks. "And what's got you so distracted?"

"You know how I get during play-offs. It's this crazy duality of hype and burnout. We want to win, but we're all sick of each other. We're tired, the guys are nursing banged-up bodies, and we're all wiped from traveling for games. Same shit as this time last year and the year before that."

"Is that really all?" She reaches for my hand and pats it. "We can talk about him now. We've passed the Bechdel test."

"The what?"

Annie frowns at me. "Frankie."

"What? I don't know what you're talking about."

"All the TV you've watched, all the books you've read, and you don't know the metric for ensuring film and fiction don't just portray women only gathered to talk about men?"

"Uh. No. Guess I missed that in my quest for ultimate dorkdom."

She throws a fry at me. "Anyway. We've passed it. Caught up plenty about everything else in life. So, talk about him already."

"Who?"

Annie rolls her eyes as she slurps her milkshake. "Ren, you goober. He told you how he feels about you, didn't he?"

I gape at her. "What? *How* did you—"

"I didn't," she says, hands raised. "It was just a hunch. His attraction seemed pretty clear."

"Not to me!"

"Well, I know. As you've said yourself, men's interest is not something you pick up on. From the first time I met him, I swear, just the way he looked at you as you introduced us—*swoon*. But when he joined us for lunch? Confirmed it."

"Well, how nice to know that everyone else had it figured out except for me." I throw my napkin on the table and flop back against the booth. Sometimes the areas in life to which I seem so utterly blind and clueless are honestly humiliating.

"Hey, I'm sorry, I didn't mean it to upset you." Annie sighs. "Frankie, we both know that even if you did know, you didn't *want* to know. You didn't want to see it. Because you're hell-bent on spinsterhood."

"Annabelle. If you weren't *heavy with child*, this *spinster* would be giving your *breeches* an epic wedgie."

"Women didn't wear breeches back then, Francesca."

The bell dings as the diner's door opens, making me casually glance over my shoulder. The floor drops out from underneath me. Ren walks in. With a woman.

"Kill me now." I sink into the booth, feeling a cold sweat break out across my skin.

"What?" Annie perks up, like a little baby bird peering out from the nest. "What?"

"Jesus, Annie," I hiss. "I'm trying to *hide*, not draw attention to us."

Her eyes widen. "Oh, well, hello, handsome. Oof, there is something about him. Gingers don't even normally do it for me, but your man is—"

"He's *not* my man." I groan. I can't believe Ren is here. With a tall, willowy woman who has gorgeous dark red hair and wide green eyes.

Why would he be here with a woman when we just talked eight hours ago about trying to be together? There has to be a rational explanation, but hell if I can think of one. It's too much for my brain.

Pulling his ball cap lower, Ren sets his hand on the young woman's back and gently guides her in front of him while they're led by the hostess to be seated. His eyes dance across the space as he notices people looking at him, talking to themselves. I turn around and dive deeper into the booth.

"Who's that with him?" Annie asks.

"I don't know." I have no idea what to make of what I'm seeing, except that Ren's standing side by side with a woman who's as striking as he is and who most likely doesn't have a mountain of personal issues.

Unlike me. The fries and milkshake curdle in my stomach. This is what jealousy feels like. I hate it.

Annie sighs. "You're being ridiculous, hiding like that. It's pointless. He's going to see you. It's not like this is a big diner."

"Whyyy," I whine. "Why didn't we go to In-N-Out?"

"Because Betty's Diner makes the best fries. There was never a question of going anywhere else."

I groan as I rub my forehead. "My shit luck."

"Stop being such a Moaning Myrtle. Oh, I think he just saw me." Annie glances down at me and smiles, her cheeks pink. "Okay. I'm playing it cool. It's just hottie-pants Ren—"

"Hottie-pants Ren?"

She shushes me. "I'd sit up if I were you. You're going to look like a weirdo, slumped over in the booth when he comes over and says hi."

I'm just straightening when I see Ren walking my way, icy eyes sparkling from beneath the shadow of his baseball cap.

Ren. Ball cap. Beard.

Guh.

Someone in a nearby booth lifts their phone, and he deftly switches sides so the woman he's with is shielded from the shameless oglers.

Who is she?

"I'm okay," I mutter under my breath. "I'm okay."

"Just breathe, Frankie," Annie says quietly.

"Frankie." Ren smiles down at me, then glances over to Annie. "Hey, Annie. How are you?"

Annie smiles up at him, turns bright pink, and bats her eyelashes. "Um, yes."

I roll my eyes. "Hey, Ren."

Ren turns slightly, wrapping his arm around the woman's back, setting his hand on her shoulder.

Bile crawls up my throat. Painful, sharp stabs of jealousy. What is going on?

"Zigs, this is Frankie and her friend Annie."

The woman extends her hand first to Annie, who's closer, and next to me, bringing her features near enough to inspect. Of course. Startlingly young. Tall. Milky skin, vivid green eyes, rich red hair that's so long, it's almost to her hips. Her clothes don't fit her well — baggy sweatpants and an oversized, stained sweatshirt. Still, there's something familiar and appealing to me about her appearance.

"Wow," she says, eyes wide. "I'm finally meeting Frankie. Ren talks about you constantly."

My belly flip-flops, and I can't help but grin. Ren turns bright red and grimaces. She notices and stares at him.

"What?" Genuine confusion laces her voice as she glances from him to me. "You do."

"Yes," he says on a sigh. "You're right."

Pink stains her cheeks as she glances at the floor. "Sorry."

"You're good, Zigs. It's okay," he tells her quietly.

Something about her embarrassment, that moment of realizing her slip, reverberates with familiarity. I've done it so many times—said what everyone else is thinking but which is apparently catastrophic for adults to admit. I'll never get it, and try as I might to learn the pattern of what's said and what's not, I can't. Meaning, sometimes I fuck up. I've been in her shoes.

There's something familiar, too, about the wide-open curiosity in her eyes when we shook hands, her concerted effort to observe the niceties of an introduction but the eagerness to return to the sanctity of her own body and thoughts.

It all clicks into place. This is—

"You're his *sister*," I say in shock. "You're—"

"Yes, this is Ziggy," Ren says quickly, locking eyes with me. "My little sister."

Something passes between us. He's trying to tell me something with his eyes, but I'm the world's worst candidate for that. So, to play it safe, I keep my mouth shut and gather my thoughts for a moment.

I smile up at her, feeling an odd kinship with this young woman who, even after just a few moments of knowing her, I recognize so much of myself in. This has to be the sister he told me about. The one who's on the spectrum, too.

"Well, then," I say to her. "My turn to say Ren talks about you lots, too. And it's nice to finally put a face to the name."

She blinks at me, then away, on a reluctant smile.

Suddenly someone from a nearby booth wanders our way, hovering right near Ren. I see Ren's open expression shutter, his polite smile take over as he turns, shielding Ziggy behind his body.

"Sorry to bug you . . ." the guy says.

Why do people say sorry when they're doing something and they're going to keep doing it? Either demonstrate genuine remorse and stop doing it, or just own that you're being an invasive prick, bugging a professional hockey player for a signature at nine thirty on a weeknight, when he's just out for a quiet bite to eat.

"What's up, man?" Ren says.

"Just wondering if—"

I lift my cane, arced over my head like a wand, and say, "*Sectumsempra!*"

"Jesus!" The guy stumbles back, knocking into a chair and running back to his booth. I give him a death glare until he sinks out of sight.

Ziggy slaps a hand over her mouth, making her voice come out muffled. "That was awesome."

Ren peers down at me. "Little aggressive of a curse, right out of the gate, don't you think, Francesca?"

Annie shakes her head. "You don't know the half of it. When she and Tim get drunk, she calls *Imperio* and he follows her orders. It's like sick, twisted, Pottermore charades."

If she weren't three hundred weeks pregnant, I'd kick her under the table. "That's private, Annabelle." She waves me off. "Well, now that we lost the fan, why don't you join us?" Annie says to Ren.

Ziggy opens her mouth, but before she can answer, Ren squeezes her shoulder gently. "That's okay. We wouldn't want to encroach on your catch-up," he says. "And I haven't seen this one in a while. She's overdue for a big brother inquisition."

Ziggy rolls her eyes. It makes me smile. And it also makes my heart flip-flop that Ren's protecting time with his sister.

"Hang in there," I tell her. "As the baby of the family with a bossy older sibling, you have my sympathy."

"Hey." Ren shoves me gently, and I milk it, flopping over to the bench. "Shit, Frankie." He wraps his arms around my shoulder, hoists me upright. "I'm so sorry, I'm—"

His features change when he sees I'm trying not to laugh and realizes I'm fine. He narrows his eyes. "That's a dirty move."

"I thought it was pretty funny," Ziggy says dryly.

"Yes, well." Ren straightens and gives me a half-hearted glare. "We'll leave you to it." Turning to my friend, he smiles much wider. "Annie, good to see you." Back to me with a skunk face. "See you at work tomorrow, Francesca."

I stick my tongue out at him. "Søren."

Ziggy sucks in a breath, glancing between us. "She calls you *Søren*? Holy—"

"Come on." Ren takes her by the elbow. "We're leaving. Bye!"

Annie grins, watching them walk to their booth. Ren drops onto the bench facing me and lands me with a piercing stare. Slowly a grin warms his face like he can't help it.

"Oh, Frankie," Annie says wistfully. "You are in trouble."

I sigh as I feel myself smiling back. "Don't I know it."

TWENTY

Frankie

Playlist: "Work," Charlotte Day Wilson

I lift my hand to knock on Ren's door, but it swings open before I can.

My fist drops lamely to my side. Jesus Tossing Tables in the Temple, Ren's wearing joggers.

Fitted, dark gray joggers. And a white long-sleeved shirt, pushed up his forearms.

"Francesca." He steps back, holding the door open wider. Pazza bounds in and jumps up, setting her paws on his stomach.

"Pazza, down!" I poke her butt with my cane and push the door shut behind me.

When I look back, Ren's eyes are on me, a small smile warming his face. "I don't mind when she jumps. It's nice that *someone* looks happy to see me."

I tip my head.

Ren sighs. "That was a hint. About you."

"I don't speak *hints*." I walk by him, dropping my bag and leaning my cane on the wall so I can reach to take off my shoes. "Say it or don't—ack!"

Warm, solid arms sweep me off my feet. Three long Ren-strides, then I'm set gently on the kitchen island, Ren's hands splayed on either side of me. His mouth whispers over my cheek, his lips teasing their way to the shell of my ear. "There's no pressure. You just have to be a *little* happy you're here."

"I'm very happy," I say breathlessly. My hands slide up his arms and rest on his rounded shoulders, sending air rushing out of him. Ren's warmth presses closer between my legs. Gently, his hands span my waist and draw me nearer. Soft, nuzzling kisses down my neck light a solar flare deep inside.

"Good," he whispers. One last, firm kiss to the base of my throat before he pulls away. "I'm happy you're here, too."

Carefully, he lifts me off the island and begins to step back, but I launch myself at him, wrapping my arms tight around his broad chest. "I'm sorry that I was frowning when you opened the door. It surprised me. When I'm startled, I frown. Always have. But I am happy to see you, okay?"

"Oh. I understand what you mean. I'm sorry I gave you a hard time about it."

"That's okay," I say quietly.

His arms engulf my body and hold me close. Lips to my hair, my temple, he takes a long slow breath, then presses his mouth to my forehead. "You smell so good."

A smile against his chest. "So do you."

That makes him laugh. "Glad to hear it."

"Spicy." I stick my nose straight into his shirt and inhale. "Man soap."

Another kiss warms my face. "Orchids. Night air."

Tugging my arms tighter around him, I press my stomach into his hips and bite my lip. Ren is hard and thick inside his sweatpants, and all I can think about is the exquisite weight of him over me, inside me.

"Frankie," he says, a pained hitch to his voice. "I, uh . . . The oven's about to go off."

Groaning, I drop my forehead to his chest. "Why are we eating again?"

"Because I want a happy Frankie, and Frankie's happiest when she's well fed."

"I'll be very happy if you and I end up in that big Ren-sized bed." I blink up at him, trying to smile.

He frowns down at me. "You feeling okay?"

"Yes." I drop my arms and walk past him, grabbing my cane. "I just can't make myself smile any more than you can start a hockey brawl."

"Hey, now." He walks deeper into the kitchen. "Don't bust me for my nonviolence."

"I would never."

Ren stands with his back to me, stirring something that smells fan-fucking-tastic—aromatic and gamey, some kind of stew.

As my eyes drag up his body, my opinion on the injustice of life is cemented. Why do men look like such sexy beasts in loungewear? Ren's wearing sweatpants that hug his big hockey butt and cling to the long, powerful muscles of his legs. His shirt tapers to his waist and shows off his cut biceps and shoulders. He might as well be naked—no, it's actually *more* sensual because he *isn't* naked. It's the most frustratingly sexual thing I've seen.

Ever.

"Frankie."

"Hmm?" I blink away guiltily from staring at his ass.

"I like your butt, too."

Lifting my cane, I poke the butt in question. "Men have been objectifying women for millennia. Simply doing my part to settle the score."

Ren laughs and reaches an arm toward me. I slip inside it and lean against his chest, getting an up-close look at the goodness on the stove.

"Well, yum. What is it?"

He grins down at me and runs his hand along my arm, as if to make sure I'm warm. Like he doesn't understand that he's a human furnace, radiating comforting heat. "*Kalops*," he says.

"*Kalops*."

"Yep." With a kiss to the top of my head, he taps the spoon free of liquid and sets it aside. "Swedish beef stew. My mom's recipe."

"Why haven't I ever met your mom? Or your dad, for that matter?"

Ren's eyes shutter, and he glances away, turning toward a pot of boiling potatoes. "Dad's an oncologist with too many balls in the air. Mom's been pretty busy with Ziggy since I signed. She's had a tough time the past few years, and Mom doesn't like to leave her alone. Ziggy was . . . in a dangerous place for a while. I don't think my mom's gotten over that."

"Why couldn't she just bring Ziggy to a game?"

Ren sighs. "You met her, Frankie. Going to an obscure diner is about as much of the outside world as she can manage right now. A cacophonous space like the arena would literally cause a meltdown."

I know he's not throwing around the term *meltdown*, either. One of the things I admire about Ren is that he chooses his words wisely, that he believes in the power and responsibility of language.

People use the term *meltdown* cavalierly, but in reference to autism, it's a very specific thing. When faced with sensory overload, meltdowns sometimes look like an adult having a tantrum or catatonically shutting down. It's the body and mind doing whatever they can to put the overwhelming input to a stop—an emotional surge protector, the mental switch when an overflow of information trips the mind's circuit breaker. Meltdown is a survival instinct.

"Well, I get it," I tell him. "You know I wear earplugs during games." My hip twinges with discomfort and wobbles a little. Before I take a spill and make Ren crap his pants with worry, I grab one of the stools from his kitchen island and ease myself onto it. "Still, it has to bum you out that your parents don't come."

I do a tally of the family whom I *have* observed at Ren's games. Freya, the eldest, who came with some hunk with Caribbean blue eyes and black hair—Aiden, I think was his name. Ryder and Willa of course—they've come the most. Then the older brother, Axel, who came alone and looked like he'd swallowed something sour. We didn't meet. I just saw him from a distance when he awkwardly hugged Ren, then took off. What about the other ones? "You have a bajillion siblings. One of them couldn't hang with Ziggy so your parents can attend a game?"

No answer.

"Do your brothers and sisters know why your jersey number is seven?"

His whole body stiffens. I watch his throat work as he swallows. "I just like the number seven."

"Bullshit, Zenzero. It's for your family. Seven siblings, isn't it?"

Who barely come to his games. In what world does being a professional hockey player make you the black sheep of the family?

As if he's followed my train of thought, he shrugs, opening the oven and peering in. A burst of cinnamon and sugar wafts from behind the oven door, but before I can glimpse what's in there, he snaps it shut. "The Bergmans aren't a hockey family."

"You're *Swedish*, for Christ's sake. Northern Europeans invented hockey."

"Nova Scotians, sweet pea."

I choke on nothing particular except the absurdity of what just came out of his mouth. "I'm sorry, *what* did you just call me?"

Ren grins as he turns off the heat underneath the stew and covers it with a lid. "I need an endearment for you. I'm trying them out."

"Um. How about *Frankie*? That'll do fine."

"Pff." Ren closes the distance between us, standing inside my legs. Those warm, calloused hands slip around my neck and delve into my hair, massaging aching muscles. "You call me sweet things."

I groan as he hits a tender spot. It makes my eyes fall shut. "The Italian word for a root vegetable. And a thinly veiled reference to a brutal, pillaging Viking. Not exactly amorous."

"They don't have to be amorous," he says quietly. "They just have to be mine, for you . . . turtledove."

"Nope."

"Huckleberry."

"Hell no."

"Lambkin."

I crack an eye open and give him a look. "You're hopeless."

"We both knew that." He presses a long kiss to my forehead again. "You're in my kitchen," he whispers, tipping my head up to meet his eyes. "Pinch me."

I grab a nice little bit of skin at his side. Just skin, because there sure as shit isn't any fat on his torso.

"Ow! Frankie, I was being figurative."

Oops. "Sorry. I'm a literal gal, Zenzero." I grab his hips and pull him closer. "Let me kiss it better."

Sliding my hands under his shirt, I shiver with the delight of my palms running over that taut warm skin, the ridges of his stomach.

A low, strangled noise rumbles out of his throat. "Frankie—"

"Shh. I won't go too far."

I spot the tiny red mark where I pinched. Leaning toward him, I press my lips to his stomach, then slowly trail my way to just above his hip. It feels much sexier than seems logical. I mean, it's his stomach. I'm kissing a boo-boo.

But then his fingers slip through my hair, and helplessly, he tips his hips forward.

"Careful, you'll poke my eye out with that thing." I kiss his stomach again and palm the formidable outline of his erection straining those sinful sweatpants.

On a groan, he pulls away and bends over, hands on his knees as he takes long, slow breaths. Just like after sprints on the ice. It's oddly satisfying to see I've affected him that much. "You're dangerous, Francesca."

I smile down at him and pat his back. "'Bout time you figured that out."

Belly full of Ren's killer cooking, we're settled on Ren's couch watching *Sense and Sensibility*. Hugh Grant stands across the screen from Emma Thompson, both of them dressed in Austenian clothes. Hugh, as Edward Ferrars, is trying to talk to Emma Thompson, playing Elinor, of course. But he's just awkward as hell. I can't think of anyone who has cornered the market on adorably awkward better than old-school Hugh Grant.

Then again, Ren's pretty good at working the adorable angle, too.

Ren shifts slightly, sliding his fingers through mine again and squeezing gently. Never enough to hurt my fingers. Which is good, because they're throbbing just fine on their own.

I've tried to ignore for the past two days that my normal baseline discomfort has ratcheted up to nagging pain and stiffness. I shouldn't be flaring. The biologics and low-dose corticosteroids I take generally work well. If a flare's coming, I'm going to be pissed. Unfortunately, there's really nothing I can do except wait and see. And burrow deeper into Ren's arms as I yawn.

My eyes keep drooping, not because I'm bored. The movie's *gorgeous*. It has my attention.

I'm enjoying comparing what I'm reading for book club to the film and noticing the liberties they've taken. But the truth is the team's schedule gets to me. And trekking all day through various degrees of pain and discomfort, not to mention the mental work of keeping up with a demanding job and all the socializing, wears me out.

Then there's being tucked inside Ren's arms. His legs, too. It's so cozy, I can't help but feel sleepy, lounging on his massive sofa in the living room. Dove gray. Soft linen. Plush yet firm. The solid wall of his chest heats my back, and the heft of his arms around me is more soothing than my weighted blanket.

Soft lips press to my temple. "Still awake, sugar lump?"

I half-heartedly jab him with my elbow.

"That answers that," he groans.

"You know what you can call me?" I glance up as he leans over me and we brush noses.

He kisses the tip of mine. "What?"

"Grumpapotamus."

He frowns. "I don't like calling you any iteration of *grumpy*." Smoothing my hair back from my face, he stares down at me. "You're not grumpy. You're just . . ."

"Grumpy. We've discussed this. Best not to dispute it. Better to ask *why*?"

He sighs. "Okay. Why?"

I slide my hand along his thigh and watch his jaw tic. "Because I want to turn off the movie. And stop playing spoons."

A slow grin warms his face. "You don't like cuddling?"

"I mean, I do. You're a top-notch cuddler."

He dips his head in a bow. "Thank you."

"I just want more."

Ren unthreads his fingers from my hand and cradles my jaw in his grasp, his thumb scraping across my lips. "We'll get there, Frankie. I want more, too," he whispers, before his mouth sweeps softly over mine. He nudges my lips open, teases the tip of his tongue against mine.

I wrap an arm around his neck and slide my fingers through his hair. It's silky yet thick, and he sighs into my mouth when I scrape my nails along his scalp. Ren wraps an arm around my waist while one hand cups my face, his thumb gentling the dimple in my cheek. His touch is restrained tenderness. But his kiss is pure hunger.

Sparks skitter across my skin and heat pours through my veins as a sweet ache settles between my thighs. I've made out a good bit in my day, and up until now I would have said it was a pretty fine history of tongue tangles and handsy gropes. But as our kiss deepens and my body warms under his touch, I'm confronted with a new understanding of the past. Nothing I've done prepared me. *Nothing* compares to this.

Ren pulls back and grins, his gaze not leaving my lips. I'm waiting. For hands to slide down my waist, to shuck my leggings and rub me to a rough, powerful orgasm, but instead, I feel warm fingers, calloused and rough, weaving through mine again.

A shuddering sigh leaves me. I'm painfully aroused. Perplexed and in awe that someone who's waited this long seems determined to wait longer.

Ren brings my hand to his mouth and presses hot, slow, open-mouthed kisses to my palm, then the tip of every finger. I'm practically panting, arching toward him as his mouth drifts to the tender inside of my wrist. His tongue swirls in slow, steady circles that aren't hard to imagine teasing somewhere else that longs for touch.

Exhaling slowly, Ren plants one last kiss to my wrist, then lowers it. I stare at him in obvious confusion, my hair mussed from his fingers, my lips parted.

A dry laugh jumps out of him, before he stifles it. "Come on, honey bun. Time for bed."

I gape at him as he stands and holds out a hand for me. "Are you shitting me?"

"Okay, so 'honey bun' was weak, I'll give you that."

"Not *that*."

He frowns before recognition dissolves the crease between his brows. "Oh. *Going to bed*. No. It's late. Why wouldn't we go to bed?"

"Well, uh." I gesture to the massive hard-on that's at my eye level, about to bust his sweatpants. "I'd say we have a good eight inches of reason right there."

Sighing, he tries and completely fails to adjust himself. A hard-on like that isn't going anywhere. "It's fine."

"Whatever you say." Taking his hand, I leverage myself up with a bit more effort than normal, straightening slowly and assessing him for any signs of fussing or pity. But he just watches me intently, observing, absorbing. Nothing more.

"*You* might be fine," I tell him. "But if you thought a hangry Frankie was scary, you're looking at a sexually frustrated Frankie. Brace yourself."

Stepping close, Ren wraps his arms around my back and pulls me close. "I said let's go to *bed*, Francesca, not to *sleep*."

With a quick kiss to the tip of my nose, he spins away, going through what I already know after a few nights staying with him is his nightly routine of locking up. Double-checking the security system and locks. Making sure the outdoor motion-sensor lights are on.

Pazza snuffles awake from her position near the door, where she's been snoring. Ren sweeps up my cane, then sets it by my side.

While I stand dumbstruck, wondering how a virgin got so damn good at the game of seduction.

TWENTY-ONE

Ren

Playlist: "Toothpaste Kisses," The Maccabees

After I locked up last night, we brushed teeth side by side at the twin sinks in my bathroom, Frankie scowling around toothpaste suds and the hum of her electric brush, me grinning at her reflection in the mirror. Before I had her over last night, as I cooked and tidied up and changed the sheets on the bed, I had a long think about what Frankie told me at lunch the day prior. How scary this was for her, to open up and try being together.

The only thing I have on my side, I realized, is time. Time to show her I can take it slow, build trust and comfort. Time to show her I don't find a single thing about how she ticks or what she needs to be intrusive or inconvenient or anything else the people from her past made her feel.

So, when she came over, I held her hand instead of slipping it inside those tight black leggings, much as I wanted to. I swirled my tongue over the silky skin of her wrist, rather than the silky skin between her thighs.

What I failed to anticipate was exactly *how* cranky it would make her to go slow. So, making an adjustment, I figured I'd tuck her in, touch and kiss her, give her an orgasm, and put a smile on her face. After brushing teeth, I kissed her thoroughly to try to erase that pout darkening her features. It seemed to work somewhat, because she wandered out of the bathroom without any cranking, straight toward my bed, where she dropped with a groaning flop.

But by the time I showered off, used the bathroom, and came out, she was snoring softly, tucked inside the blankets, her dark hair a splash of ink against paper-white sheets.

Slipping into bed, I thanked God for my memory foam mattress, which absorbs motion and didn't even shift her body in the least as I settled in next to her before I turned off the light. And then I curled around Francesca Zeferino, kissed her cheek as I breathed her in, and fell asleep.

Her soft moan is the first thing I hear. Then birds chirping outside. I blink awake to sunlight bathing her in its glow and lift my head enough to get a good look at her. Frankie's eyes are scrunched shut, her jaw tight. I can't tell if she's dreaming or just pissed that she's partially awake.

Glancing over my shoulder, I read my clock. It's only a few minutes until my alarm goes off, so I silence it before it starts playing banjo music and makes the little ray of sunshine in my arms likely to commit murder.

Another quiet groan leaves her. Carefully, I prop myself up on my elbow, searching her for the reason she sounds so uncomfortable.

She has arthritis, bud. Of course she's uncomfortable, especially in the morning.

Not that Frankie needs to know, but once I realized what she was dealing with, I did my homework on RA. I know the cost of sleep. Lying still settles inflammation in your joints and stiffens them. It's unavoidable.

But why is she *hurting*? Aren't her meds supposed to manage that? A fierce surge of worry and protectiveness blasts through me. I want to wrap her up and kiss it all better. I want to take everything inside her that hurts and put it in my body. I'm big. Solid. Someone like me should have this, not someone like Frankie. It's unfair. Patently unfair.

"Think any louder," she grumbles, "and you'll wake me up."

I smile, gently sliding my hand down her arm and back up as I press a kiss to the crook of her neck. "*Morrn, morrn, min solstråle.*"

"Calling me names again."

I huff a laugh. "I just said, 'Good morning, my sunshine.'"

"Sunshine or not, nothing good about mornings." On a long groan, she rolls slowly from her stomach to her back, her face pinched. "At least not for me."

"Frankie, what's wrong?"

She sighs. "Mornings are the worst. And you don't have a heated mattress pad. Which is basically the only thing that helps."

Relief soars through me. "Actually, I do." Leaning past her, careful not to press on her body, I flip the switch for my heated mattress pad. It was one of my first purchases when I signed with the team, to combat the muscle soreness and body aches from playing a whole new level of hockey, a good chunk of change for the promise that it's up to temp in less than thirty seconds.

"You do?" Her big hazel eyes widen. A long happy sigh leaves her as warmth floods the surface of my bed. "You do."

I stare down at her, taking in her face, still soft with drowsiness, a pillow wrinkle slashed across her cheek. Her hair's uncharacteristically frizzy, and her lips look extra full, pursed in sleepiness.

"You're staring at me," she whispers.

I nod, bend, and press a kiss to her jaw, then her neck. Everything about her is smooth and soft, so impossibly tempting.

This is why I put on fresh sweatpants when I got into bed last night—I'm so hard, the brush of the sheets, the weight of the blanket over us, is nearly excruciating. I want so badly to spread her thighs, grasp her hips, and sink inside her—to feel Frankie's body tight around mine, to move with her and hear her cry out, but now's not the time. Not yet.

You say that a lot, Bergman. Not now. Not yet.

Tell me about it. Or rather, tell it to my tortured morning wood.

"I'll be back," I whisper against her neck.

Throwing off the sheets, I jump out of bed and pull on a shirt. Another noise coming from Frankie makes me spin around, shirt halfway down my chest. "What is it?"

She frowns at me. "I wouldn't have minded my coffee delivered by a shirtless Søren, that's all I'm saying."

I tug down my shirt the rest of the way. "I'm feeling rather objectified right now, Francesca. Now, I planned on bringing a breakfast snack and some coffee. Need anything else?"

She shakes her head. "Besides your nakedness? Nope."

Pazza's been lying dutifully at the foot of the bed, but she bolts upright when I open the bedroom door. There's a happiness to the pound of her paws, her nails clattering on the hardwood floors, that makes me smile. I pull open the sliding door, watch her run across the deck, down the steps, and to the sand, where she promptly pees on the row of fescue that partially shields my property from the shore. She runs a bit farther off, sprinting across the hard sand, terrorizing a seagull.

When I whistle, she comes running back up the deck, pausing long enough for me to hose down her legs and towel her off.

"Breakfast, pup."

She jogs over to her bowl of food that Frankie packed, while I make Frankie's coffee how I know she likes it and warm two of the cinnamon rolls that I baked.

It's domestic. And peaceful. Letting out the dog, making coffees while Frankie rests in bed and has some time to get comfortable for her day.

Don't get ahead of yourself. She said she's nervous to do this. She said she'll try. That's it.

Worry tightens my stomach. While I value Frankie's honesty, her forthright communication style, which seems to go hand in hand with autism, being so keenly aware of her apprehension about a relationship is nerve-wracking. I'm mildly terrified Frankie's going to break my heart before she even realizes it's hers to shatter.

Pazza whines up at me and cocks her head. If dogs smile, this one just did.

Sweeping up the tray of goods, I stroll down the hall, shoulder open the door, and nearly drop everything. Frankie's sitting up in bed in nothing but one of my V-neck undershirts. On me, it's snug, fitted enough to be invisible beneath the tailored dress shirts I have to wear before and after every game. But on Frankie, it drapes.

Torturously.

The V neckline knifes down her chest, exposing her collarbones and the line of her sternum, the shadow curving between her full breasts. Dark nipples poke sharply against the fabric. Staring at them, my mouth waters.

"See?" she says, clearly fishing for some positive feedback. "Look at me. Vertical." With a few rotations of her wrists, she sweeps up her arms, like an actress prepared to receive applause. "I even got up and peed. Splashed my face off. Changed into something comfy. Aren't you proud?"

I gulp.

She grins, seeing where my eyes have snagged. "Thought you might like that."

"*Like* is an interesting choice of word." I cross the room, set the tray between us on the bed, and hand Frankie her coffee.

After taking a long sip, she sighs contentedly.

"Hardly seems fair," I say, trying to keep my eyes on the cinnamon roll I'm cutting into quarters but largely finding my gaze drawn over and over to her breasts. "I wouldn't look nearly as good in one of your shirts."

She smiles. "The heating pad helps my joints, but it makes me sweat like a prostitute in church. None of my shirts felt good when I put them on. Too scratchy. Too hot. I just needed something big and soft and nice smelling."

I pop a bite of cinnamon roll in my mouth and graze the back of my hand against her nipple, pebbled sharply through the material. "Glad you found one."

"Hope you don't mind," she says. A subtle shiver rolls through her as my finger dips into the valley between her breasts and teases the other nipple just the same way. "I riffled through your drawers and found it."

My head snaps up. "You went through my drawers?"

"Mm-hmm," she says before taking a bite of cinnamon bun and chewing. "Who knew Søren Bergman color-codes his underwear, socks, shirts—"

I kiss her, if for no other reason than to stop her teasing. And while I know nobody likes morning breath, now we both taste like cinnamon and coffee.

When I pull away, her eyes are hazy, and she has icing on her lip. I lick it away and feel her breath hitch. "I like things tidy," I say quietly. "Helps me find them more easily."

Her smile is slow but warm, and when she lifts a hand and brushes the hair off my forehead, I want to drop to my knees.

"Hi," she whispers.

"Hi," I whisper against her lips. I kiss her again, then sit back and lean against the headboard, like her. We eat in quiet, but it's comfortable. Easy and peaceful.

Until Frankie finishes her cinnamon roll and licks the tips of her fingers. Not that I've been anything less than hard for the past twelve hours, thanks to Frankie's proximity, but now my cock throbs as a furious ache builds in my groin.

Frankie *tsk*s and sets down her coffee. "Can't have that, Zen-zero."

I glance up from my coffee. "Can't have wha— Jesus!"

Her hand slides over my joggers, right between my legs, and I nearly scald us, violently sloshing my coffee as I throw it down on the nightstand. I want to stop her, but if I do, I'm pretty sure I'll keel over from the blood rushing to every inch of me that Frankie's palming with expert strokes.

"F-Frankie, you don't have to—"

"Søren Bergman, unless you're about to go into cardiac arrest or the house is on fire, shut up and let me make you come."

I grunt as she releases me and then slides her hand beneath the elastic of my sweats. Turning toward her, I set the tray off the bed and drag Frankie down, flat on the mattress. My mouth clamps over her nipple, as I suck hard through the cotton of her T-shirt. With new wetness, her nipple's evident, a dark berry color I want to lick and bite and tease for hours. Cupping her full breasts, I groan appreciatively.

When I drag my teeth gently over one wet, stiff peak, her fingers delve into my hair. She gasps and arches into me. "Holy shit, Ren."

Working her nipple with my mouth, I slip my hand down her stomach and curve it over the wet heat seeping through her panties. Just a faint slide of my finger and her thighs clamp on my touch.

"Oh. Don't stop doing that," she pants. Her fingers tighten in my hair, holding me close. Her hips tilt upward.

I grin in satisfaction, until I feel her palm gliding over my boxer briefs, her grip hugging the length of me, up and down. "Frankie."

It's all I can say, all I can see and feel. Her lips press to my hair as I suck and tease her nipples, as I gently rub her through her panties, quick, tight circles. Frankie's hand works me, sure and fast, sending dizzying heat and a furious ache for release surging down my spine. The need to thrust, to drive and pound, takes over. I press my hips harder into her grip, feeling the warning of release building, hot and powerful.

"Ren," she whispers.

I lift my head long enough to meet her lips, to kiss her as she cries against my mouth and comes in soft, beautiful waves against my hand.

I want to savor it—the hazy satisfaction in her eyes, the way she smiles wider than I've ever seen her—but her hand is temptation itself, and I'm scrambling at the edge.

Holding my eyes, she bites my lip, dragging it between her teeth. The pain of it trips the wire that sends me soaring. On a grunt of pure bliss, I come, while Frankie's hand works me in gentle rubs that stretch out my orgasm.

After a long, silent moment, I flop back on the bed and pull her carefully with me, holding her head to my chest but distanced from the hot spill all over my stomach. With one firm kiss to the top of her hair, I sigh heavily.

"Ren?" she says quietly.

I peer down at her. "Yes?"

"I'm feeling a little worried."

I grasp her chin, tilting her head so she'll look at me. "Why?" Her face is tight, anxiety clear in her features. "What is it?"

She reaches and kisses me. "Because if it's that great when our clothes are on, what the hell's going to happen when they all come off?"

Searching her eyes, I try to see why the promise of something so good scares her so much. But I come up short. There's no answer, other than the fact that all of this is new and unnerving for Frankie, as it is—albeit in different ways—for me. There's nothing to be done or dismissed about that. Just space to be made. Time and patience.

With a kiss to her forehead, I rest my head on hers, allowing quiet to be answer enough. For now.

TWENTY-TWO

Frankie

Playlist: "Somewhere Over The Rainbow,"
Leanne & Naara

At some point recently, my life became an Austen novel. As if the book itself might be capable of some kind of sexually repressing black magic, I'm tempted to throw *Sense and Sensibility* out the window and hope it sends Ren bounding into my room to make an honest woman out of me.

It's been beautiful, glorious, dizzying torture. Days of cuddling and finger tangling and making out and dry humping, and Holy Saint Francis of Assisi and His Furry Animal Friends, I need Ren to use that big old stick God gave him and score with me already.

I bypass two of the guys in the hallway, breezing into the training room. I need to find Ren, because it's four o'clock. Which is when my plan of action kicks in.

I'm not the world's best at lying on the spot, but I am damn good at premeditated subterfuge. In precisely three minutes my stomach will start to hurt. I'll let Ren know I'm going home for the night, that I'll miss the game.

Darlene's in on my plan and made sure one of the PR interns is prepared to at least keep up with Twitter and Instagram during the game, so we're covered on that front. It'll only be the second game I've ever missed. The first I missed was because I got a horrible chest cold—thank you very much, immunosuppressant medications—and finally had to admit defeat, laid up on the couch and yelling hoarsely at the TV while Pazza's head swiveled furiously between the hockey game and me.

"Seen Ren?" I ask Lin.

He shakes his head as John tapes his ankle for him.

"Schar? Have you seen Bergman?"

Kris glances up from heel stretches. "Negative, Frankie."

Muttering under my breath, I storm out of the training room and roam the halls, my ears attuned, hoping I catch the warm, low tenor of Ren's voice.

I'm supposed to be at Ren's childhood home in exactly one hour, and with the bitch that is LA traffic, I want to leave plenty of time for me to get there and for his parents to make it to the arena. Because Ren Bergman was not playing another professional game without his parents being there, complex family dynamics or not. Plus, it gave me a perfect opportunity to hang out with Ziggy. He talks to her on the phone every day, and a few days ago—sue me— I eavesdropped. Ren caught me, those cat eyes crinkling as he grinned, and the scary connection between that expression and my libido was reinforced, because I nearly came on the spot. *Want to say hi, Francesca?* he said.

I abhor phone calls, but I have some pride. I took that phone from him, and don't ya know, chatting with Ziggy was weirdly okay. After that, I felt like we had enough foundation for me to act on my idea.

Lost in thought, I slam right into a familiar chest. Warm, spicy, solid. I have to fist my free hand to not grab him by the shirt and kiss him.

"Francesca."

I smack his stomach. "That's Frankie to you, Zenzero."

"Whatever you say, ladybird."

My eyes roll so hard it hurts. "Hopeless."

Gently, Ren grasps my arm and steers us to the side of the

hallway as Andy and Tyler walk by. I usually don't sense when people are coming or going around me if my focus is otherwise occupied. I'm that person who'll stand in the middle of the hallway, gabbing, oblivious to blocking your way.

"Everything okay?" Ren asks quietly.

Clearing my throat, I set my hand on my stomach. "Actually, no."

The look of sheer panic that immediately tightens his face makes sympathy rush through me.

I bring my hand to his chest, an intuitive gesture of reassurance, but then I pull it back when I remember where we are. "I'm okay overall, but my stomach—it's *no bueno.*"

He tips his head. "Your stomach? Did you eat something bad? Do you have a virus?"

"Ren. Relax." The fact is that twinging cramps have been bugging me since last night, sharp and persistent. I've also been an achy, creaky mess for the past week, too. I'm due to start my period, so it's not entirely surprising. It makes it much less difficult to feign discomfort. Because I *am* uncomfortable, just nothing that would normally keep me from working. When you live with chronic pain, you get used to living through it. You just do life, until you collapse. Then you pick yourself up, change around the meds, and try again.

"It's . . . lady stuff," I tell him.

He visibly relaxes. "Oh. Okay. You know, I'm not delicate, Frankie. You can say you have cramps and you're getting your period."

I smile at Ren, delighted by his attitude and somewhat surprised. It's a natural bodily function. I don't see why we have to wrap it up in euphemisms. But long ago, I learned that's what's expected, especially from men. It's nice to know that with him, I don't have to play that game.

"Okay. Yeah. I have horrible cramps, so bad that I'm nauseous.

I'm heading home." Holding his eyes for a brief moment, I slip my fingers inside his, careful that it's hidden from anyone's view in the hallway. "Good luck tonight. Hat trick or bust, Bergman."

He grins. "As always, I can only promise my best."

Isn't that true. It's all anyone can do. And so few of us are comfortable admitting that. When I release his hand and start to turn away, Ren calls my name.

"Yes?"

Stepping closer, he drops his voice. "Can I come over tonight?"

"I mean . . . like I said, I might be out of commission."

"I know that. I just want to stay with you."

My heart does a pirouette inside my chest. "Oh. Well, sure. But let's be real. My bed sucks compared to yours. How about I'll meet you at your place after the game?"

Ren opens his mouth to speak, pauses, and smiles politely at one of the team coordinators as she passes. When she's gone, his eyes return to me. "Just go there now. Use the soaker tub in my room, relax. Okay?"

"Okay." We hold eyes, and Ren's jaw tics. I know he wants to hug. Kiss. He has this habit of swaying me in his arms when we hug that's not only dreamy but soothing. "Bye," I whisper.

He squeezes my hand, then releases it. And I walk away with a sinking feeling that grows with each step. I don't like leaving him without kissing him goodbye.

Who the hell are *you?*

Good question. Something's shifting inside me, a mere week into this little experiment. One in which I'm prying open the iron-clad doors of my heart and letting someone in. Something inside me doesn't just want to creak those doors open oh-so-slightly. It wants to fling them wide open in welcome. It wants to trust love and tell the universe, *Do your worst.*

Because there's no arguing, eventually the universe will.

Okay. So, meeting Ren's parents in person was a shit ton more stressful than I thought. I felt like some sneaky teenager who'd almost been caught making out in the basement. They don't know I've savored their son's breathtaking body with desire guiding my hands. They don't know that he makes his mother's cinnamon roll recipe for me and kisses my forehead every morning when he hands me my coffee. They don't know that I've laced profanity with his name so many times as he made me come apart.

And if I have my druthers, they never will.

I also felt a tad awkward, first because I snuck Ziggy's number from Ren's phone, texted her, and asked her if she was okay with my idea—which I simply presented as an opportunity to get her parents out of her hair and talk, girl to girl. While the idea was born out of wanting to get Ren's parents to a damn game already, fact is, I *do* want to be a friend to Ziggy, to give her some encouragement I could have used when I was first diagnosed. I'm reaching out not only because of this heart-spinning feeling I have for Ren, but also out of genuine concern for Ziggy and a wish to know her better.

So, then came calling Mrs. Bergman, explaining I was a good friend of Ren's who knew Ziggy and wanted to offer to hang out with her as another woman on the spectrum, have a heart-to-heart. I told her Ren wasn't in on this—that I wanted to surprise him with their presence. After which Mrs. Bergman sounded pretty wary. I asked her to use Willa and Ryder as a character reference and call me back.

She called me not even ten minutes later, sounding a lot nicer than before. See, Willa and I *are* friends. So there.

When I got to Ren's beautiful childhood home—sprawling calm, a sea of creamy white walls and natural wood, it was surreal to put a face to his mother's voice, to see Ren's eyes and cheekbones in her features. Then greeting his dad with that booming voice and wide smile that I knew instantly he'd given Ren, along with his wavy, copper-penny hair, and broad, powerful build. I was so nervous, my palms were slick with sweat, and my heart was banging against my ribs.

But once they left, most of my anxiety left with them, leaving just enough nervousness about doing right by Ziggy as I try to reach out to her.

She stares at the TV, watching the hockey game. The second I glance at the screen, I can pinpoint Ren. Taller than everyone, swooping around the goal. A lick of russet curling from under his helmet.

"One day I want to be able to go," she says quietly. "I can tell he's sad I never come. That I make it pretty much impossible for Mom and Dad to go."

I don't say anything right away. I don't know all of what happened, except that Ren said Ziggy was in a dangerous place at some point. Seems best to simply give her space to talk and process, especially when I don't know the particulars.

I don't touch Ziggy, either, or even sit terribly close. I can tell she doesn't like it. Since the moment I walked in, she's kept at least six feet between us. Her parents didn't hug her goodbye, either. Just kissed her forehead and left.

So, instead, I'm curled two spots away in a corner of a sofa that's so capacious, it makes Ren's look like a pin cushion. Nestled under blankets, I stare at the TV for the most part, crunching on popcorn and cursing these cramps.

"What do you feel keeps you from going?" I finally ask her.

She laughs emptily. "All of it. The crowds. The noise. The lights. Even the drive there. Traffic makes me claustrophobic. I hate just *sitting* there. I jumped out of the car and walked the final quarter mile the last time we were stuck in gridlock on the 405. Mom freaked."

That makes me snort a laugh. "Eh. I don't blame you."

Ziggy glances my way, her sharp green eyes, which I now recognize are twins of Ryder's, spearing me. "How do you do it?" she asks.

I raise my eyebrows. *I* told Mrs. Bergman I'm on the spectrum. But I haven't told Ziggy.

Because *she* hasn't told *me*. And I don't want to pressure her. "Do what?"

"You're autistic," she says matter-of-factly. "Like me."

"Did Ren tell you?"

She nods. "Just like he told you about me."

Touché.

Staring at her hands, she mutters, "He said you're someone I could talk to if I wanted."

"Well," I say on a groan, as I shift on the couch and try to buy myself some comfort. "He's right. I am. So, do you?"

Ziggy glances up, staring at the TV again. "I don't know. Sometimes I think so. Other times, I don't think I want to know."

"Don't want to know what?"

She shrugs. "The hard parts. The stuff that doesn't get better. The past few years have sucked. I can't imagine anticipating anything more challenging than this."

Setting the bowl of popcorn between us, I peer at her. She's rail thin. Curled up into herself.

If she's anything like I was at that age, she doesn't eat regularly, and she's chronically under-slept and anxious. Which has me deeply curious about what kind of support she's getting. "Are you in therapy?"

"Talk therapy," she says flatly. "I find it occasionally helpful. Mostly exhausting."

"Other than talk therapy, are you in occupational therapy? Have you learned about sensory diets?"

She scrunches her nose. "Occupational therapy, no. But the guy mentioned it in talk therapy, maybe? I don't remember. I zone out a lot when I go. I do it to please Mom and Dad. Because they're worried about me."

"Well, maybe he's working you toward OT. That's where you learn about how to take care of the stuff that's hard to explain and draining to talk about. For example, sensory diets. Just like a dietician helps you figure out what your nutritional needs are, sensory diets are tailored for each individual person to keep your brain and body balanced and as peaceful as possible, at least until the outside world throws it all up in the air."

Ziggy turns so that she's angled slightly toward me. "What do you mean?"

I lift my fidget necklace. "I'm a fidgeter, always have been. My mom said she could have sworn I was going to get an ADHD diagnosis when she took me for my comprehensive eval. But here we are. I'm autistic. And I need sensory input to feel settled and calm. So, I sit on a big exercise ball—that way I can bounce and swivel and sway. I have a necklace that people don't think twice about me playing with, and with it I can stim when I need to, without it drawing particular attention to me. I do yoga every morning and swim to burn energy, any activity that doesn't hurt my joints."

I flip the hem of my dress slacks. "French seams. No itchiness. Tag-less shirts." I drum my fingers, wracking my brain. "What else . . . Oh yeah. I usually wind down the day under a weighted blanket and my dog on top. But I'm sensory *seeking*, so maybe you wouldn't like that. You seem sensory—"

"Avoidant," she finishes, staring down at her ripped-up cuticles and biting a nail. "Yes and no. It just needs to not catch me off guard, but I like hugs. From the right people. At the right time. I'm not a robot."

"I didn't say you were. But I understand feeling defensive about it. It's a stereotype of autistics, that we're these cold, emotionless shells, which isn't true. We just feel differently. And often the case is that we actually feel *so* much, we have to compartmentalize it, funnel it into coping mechanisms that make it manageable."

She sucks in a shaky breath. "You're the first person who gets that."

I try to sift through her meaning, which isn't easy for me. I have a hunch she's not just referring to fidget necklaces or how much talk therapy sucks when you're tired of talking. I have a growing suspicion no one has really touched Ziggy since she had her breakdown and got diagnosed. I mean, I saw Ren hold her shoulder, gently touch her back, but has someone hugged her? Held her? Helped her contextualize these big, overwhelming, scary feelings and challenges, so she knows that they don't have to consume her, that they don't make her inhuman or broken, but that instead they prove her resilience, her capacity to heal and grow?

Loving touch reminds us of our humanity. Most everyone needs it, in some shape or form or timeframe. Sometimes, all we have to do is ask.

"When's the last time someone hugged you, Ziggy?"

A tear slips down her cheek. Shit. I made Ren's baby sister cry. He's going to disown me and stop giving me great orgasms and never again make me Swedish food—

Chill, Francesca. Focus on Ziggy.

Another tear spills over, and she blinks it away, staring at her hands in her lap.

"Ziggy," I ask her quietly, "would it be okay if *I* hugged you right now?"

A small, eternal silence hangs in the room as tears spill faster and faster down her cheeks. I witness the weight of her grief, which I entirely recognize, and it clutches my chest in memory, twists my heart.

Ziggy wipes her nose with her sleeve, then nods, two slow dips of her chin.

Carefully, I set the popcorn aside and scoot closer to her on the couch, holding my arms open. I let Ziggy come to me. Because I know, from the way her brother opens his arms and lets me choose how and when I fall into them, what a world of difference it makes when someone doesn't just tolerate you for where you are but *embraces* you for it.

Slowly, like a sapling cut and felled, she drops toward me, until her forehead lands on my shoulder, her cheeks wet with tears. The sobs start quietly. But they don't stay that way. They build, a wave of buried emotion, finally surfacing. Pain. Confusion. Hopelessness. I feel them seeping out of her. I feel their echoes in my memory. Tears stain my cheeks as I carefully wrap an arm around her, rubbing her back in steady figure eights.

"You're going to be okay, Ziggy. And while it might not be as soon as you'd like, you're going to figure this out. You're going to be happy again one day, I promise."

Her sobs grow sharper, and suddenly she clutches her arms fiercely around me, a vise grip of bird bones and tenacity. "God, I hope so."

"You will," I whisper, laying my cheek to the top of her head. "I promise. And I don't say that lightly. I *promise*, okay?"

I sway her in my arms until her cries grow quiet. As I gently release her, she sits up, palming her eyes, and gives me a tentative, watery smile.

Handing her the box of tissues, I join her in blowing noses and wiping eyes. Our eyes puffy from tears, we both seem lighter, steadier, and between us feels like clarity to the air after an earth-shaking storm. I reach for my bag and pull out my laptop.

"What are you doing?" Ziggy asks quietly.

I smile as I flip up the screen and power it on. "You and I are getting on my favorite sites for sensory doodads and comfy clothes. My kind of shopping—straight from the couch. Sound good?"

Her face brightens. Carefully, she scoots across the couch until she's nestled close. When Ziggy glances at me, her bright green eyes glitter with something I haven't seen in them before. Something small and fragile, but unquestionably *there*.

Hope.

TWENTY-THREE

Frankie

Playlist: "Close To You," Rihanna

"Love nugget?"

Ren's voice reverberates through the house, echoing in his bathroom, where I'm soaking in a tub that was clearly made for a giant. A gentle, ginger giant whom I've missed unreasonably much all evening.

His parents got back to their house first but said Ren was on his way to have a quick visit with Ziggy, so I bolted, picked up Pazza from my place, and drew myself a bubble bath.

"In here, stud muffin," I call.

His laugh is low and quiet, but it still carries through the house. Long, solid strides grow louder, until the bathroom door creaks open and dress shoes clack on the room's polished tiles.

"Stud muffin," he says, a hand over his eyes. "I can get down with that."

Shifting in the water, I make sure the essential bits are covered in bubbles. I'm suddenly, bizarrely self-conscious. Maybe it's because I feel shaky, a little unsure. Maybe Ren will be glad about what I did with Ziggy and his parents.

And maybe not.

"My virtue is preserved," I tell him. "You may uncover your eyes."

Dropping his hand, Ren smiles at me, sending air rushing from my lungs.

I haven't seen this smile before. It's deeper. More complex. That's the only way I can think to describe it. He drops gently onto the edge of the tub and plays with a strand of my hair that came loose from the messy bun piled on my head.

"Hi." I glance up at him, fighting the nervous urge to hold my breath and vanish underwater.

He's just so beautiful to me. And yes, in part, that's because Ren is objectively handsome, but there's much more to it. There's the kindness in his eyes, the readiness of his smile, yet the feeling that some smiles of his are special, some are just for me.

His dress shirt's a crisp white, which somehow works against his fair skin and the faintest whisper of freckles along his chest and neck. His wavy hair's disheveled from a quick postgame shower, his beard quickly combed but in need of a real trim, which it won't get, of course, until after play-offs.

I feel an odd tightening in my stomach, a need to throw myself into his arms, as he smiles over at me in his suit and loosened tie, with nothing between him and my nakedness but a tub of water and rapidly dissolving bubbles.

"Only two goals tonight, Mr. Bergman." I *tsk* in mock disapproval. "I expected better."

"Apologies," he says dryly. "Frankie." Releasing my hair, Ren slips his hand behind my neck, massaging gently. "Thank you for what you did tonight."

"Oh . . . Um. Sure."

I blush in embarrassment. I want to dissolve. Let the lukewarm water take me.

I've never handled thanks well. It makes me feel put on the spot, topped off with a splash of imposter syndrome. Wouldn't anyone do what I did when the opportunity presented itself? Being thanked for doing the decent thing feels weird.

As if he's read my mind, Ren shakes his head slowly. Leaning in, he kisses me with absolute tenderness, as his thumb slides maddeningly along my neck.

When he pulls away, his eyes are on my mouth. He leans in and steals one more kiss before straightening. "I've been told in no uncertain terms that you're to come to Ziggy's family birthday party, and if I don't bring you, I'm not welcome."

A genuine laugh jumps out of me. "She's a good one, Ren."

He nods, his face sobering. His hand moves down my neck to my shoulder, his fingers tracing droplets of water slipping down my skin. "Yeah, she is."

"She'll be okay. We talked about a lot tonight. I just don't think your parents—no offense to them—or the counselor are coming at it the best way. They're still approaching her therapy from her breaking point. But the root of Ziggy's breakdown wasn't depression or anxiety. Those were her symptoms. She got depressed and anxious because she was burned out. Now what needs to happen is being *proactive*, not reactive."

Ren tips his head. "Go on."

"Basically, she needs help learning her sensory thresholds, her needs for comfort, routine, social environments. She needs an eating schedule—I shit you not, I had one for a while in high school because I forgot so often—and she needs to be homeschooled if she wants, just to get a break from people until her battery is recharged.

"Oh, and we ordered her some clothes that will fit her, too." I raise my eyebrows. "Honestly, she's six feet tall, with this long, pretty body, and she was wearing boy clothes. I mean, I asked her what she wanted to wear—didn't want to make any assumptions—and

she said the reason she wore her brothers' hand-me-downs was because they were the only comfortable clothing she could find, but
she wants to dress differently. She just didn't think she could feel
comfy and look how she wanted. I reassured her that both were
possible, as I am evidence."

Ren laughs, and his eyes dance. "You always look beautiful,
Frankie."

"Thank you. So, we ordered some size small extra-long leggings
from this place that makes them so soft, with no itchy seams. A
bunch of tag-less long- and short-sleeved, one hundred percent cotton tops. Soft hoodies, a fidget necklace like mine, and she also
wanted to try some stim—*mmph!*"

His lips are on me again, but this time his hands are clasping
my face, his tongue sweeping against mine, his mouth hungry.

"I cannot express how grateful I am to you," he whispers against
my lips. "And I want to hear a lot more tomorrow. But I don't
want to talk about my baby sister anymore, not tonight. You're naked, in my tub, and if I don't touch you *now*, I'm going to lose my
mind."

Heat rushes through me. My breasts tighten, and a fierce ache
builds between my legs. "Then touch me."

Ren keeps kissing me, but his hands are busy, furiously working the sleeves of his dress shirt open, then cuffed up his arms, before his hand dives in the water and finds my clit like a homing
beacon.

"Jesus, Ren." I lift a hand from the water to brace myself on the
tub's ledge as he kisses me, his mouth patient but urging.

Open. More. Harder.

I scrape his lip between my teeth, flick my tongue teasingly, and
earn his quiet growl. His fingers slide over me steadily, a whispering
touch that works me to a frenzied, desperate need. Drifting his

mouth down my jaw, to the delicate space behind my ear, he swipes his tongue across my skin and blows cool air.

A shiver wracks me. "Ren," I whisper.

"Hmm?"

"I want—" I'm cut off, gasping as he curls one finger inside me and rubs my G-spot with the kind of dedicated accuracy that betrays his profession. Target. Aim. Score.

My first wave of release blindsides me, jarring me up in the water. I grip the tub's edge so hard my hand aches, but Ren doesn't stop.

"Another," he whispers, followed by a hot, tangling kiss as teeth and tongue battle for control.

"I c-can't." I've never orgasmed back to back. *Multiples.* When they were first just hookup buddies, Lorena condescendingly bragged about Mia giving multiples *alllll* the time. While Annie and I pouted in the corner that the doofuses we'd been stuck with couldn't seem to string a decent orgasm together for us if their lives depended on it.

Well, not until Tim, for Annie.

Not until Ren, for me, apparently—"Oh, *God*," I yell.

Ren swipes away the last of the bubbles covering my breasts and drags his tongue over each pebbled tip. Time becomes fuzzy. Seconds become minutes stacked on minutes without the slightest sense of their passing. If it takes forever, I have no clue, and Ren doesn't seem to care. I'm blissfully mindless of the construct of time, and Ren's unfazed by the steady work of his touch, each hungry kiss grounding me to the present, cherishing me.

He's doing something different with his fingers, and it is magic.

"I'm gonna co—" I cry out and turn toward him, throwing my arm around his neck because I can't do this alone. I can't feel this much as I soar over the edge from new heights. Weightless, breathless, satisfied.

"Beautiful," he mutters, warm and soft against my neck. "So beautiful." Gentle kisses chase gentler words.

My tongue's thick, my body heavy and loose. Who needs pot when you have orgasms? "*Urgubuh,*" I mutter.

He smooths away hair that's stuck to my face. "Is that right?"

"Sorcery," I wheeze, chest heaving as I drop back into the water.

Ren laughs while he stands and reaches for a towel from the towel warmer. As soon as I see that hot fluffy cotton waiting for me, I realize my lips must be nearly blue. I'm shivering.

Holding the towel, Ren averts his gaze as I step out of the tub, into the warmth waiting in his arms. Wrapping my body tight in the towel, he smiles down at me. "Afraid I'm capable of no such wizardry, Francesca. Just good old-fashioned muggle labor."

I point to the legitimate situation in his pants. "Care to explain the wand, then?"

He rolls his eyes. "Honestly. That's the best you can come up with?"

"Nine to fourteen inches!" I say indignantly. Ren bends, then begins gently drying my legs and feet with another warm towel. "That's impressive length. If you read *Harry Potter* with any kind of dedication, you'd know me calling your penis a wand is the world's best compliment to a man."

He lifts an eyebrow from his crouched place at my feet, looking thoroughly unimpressed. But when I open my mouth to argue the point, he's somehow already upright, kissing me before I can say another word.

"Did you and Ziggy eat?" he asks, bending to scoop up his suit jacket and my pile of discarded clothes. I absolutely stare at his butt.

"Yep. We ordered pizza—*owww.*" A hard, painful cramp clenches my belly, followed by the familiar warmth of blood trickling down my thigh. "Fucking hell."

Ren's hands are on my shoulders, his head bent as he tries to meet my eyes. "What's wrong?"

He freezes as he notices the blood. He blanches. "Oh God, Frankie. Did I hurt you?"

"No, Ren! You didn't do anything wrong." I sigh. Thank God for bathwater. Because talk about a close call. "It's my fucking womanly curse."

His entire body relaxes. Relief washes over his face and he rubs my arms gently. "I'm sorry you're hurting. Do you have stuff here? Do you need me to run out?"

I stare up at him, feeling a wave of irrational emotion pricking my eyes. "I forgot. I picked up Pazza, and I was in a rush . . ."

To get here as soon as possible and be naked in the tub when you came home, hoping I could seduce you.

Yeah. I keep that thought to myself.

He squeezes my shoulders gently. "What brand?"

I blink at him. Guys aren't supposed to be *this* chill about periods, are they? Especially after such a narrow escape. But Ren's not just any guy, is he?

"Um," I say unhelpfully.

"Here." He gently sweeps me up in his arms, carrying me into his room.

"Ren!" I squeak as he hoists me higher in his arms. "It's a period, not consumption."

"I know, it's just easier. Because I know you're going to fight me about—"

"Not in your bed. I'll make your mattress look like a crime scene!"

Flipping back the sheet, Ren lays me down and strides over to a closet, where he quickly retrieves two thick beach towels. With military precision, he folds them crisply in half, stacks them on top of each other, and shoves them under me, wrapped like a burrito in my bath towel.

Retrieving my phone and water bottle from the other side of the room, then extracting one of his undershirts from the dresser, Ren sets everything next to me on the bed.

"There," he says.

I scowl up at him. He smiles.

Patting his pockets, Ren checks for his wallet and phone, pulls out his keys. With one last kiss to my cheek, he turns away and strolls out of the room, looking all sexy hockey player in his after-game suit.

"Just text me brand and size. And get comfy!" he yells from the hallway. "You're allowed out to grab a bag of root beer gummies, but I swear if you're anywhere other than in my bed when I get back, Francesca, you'll be in big trouble."

I want to tell him where he can shove his high-handed directives, but don't you know, instead I find myself silently, happily snuggled in his bed, a sunshine grin warming my face.

Not that I'm surprised by my shit luck, but I *would* get my period right when it seemed like Ren was going to quit torturing me and finally let me get under him. Another week—because my periods are assholes—of cruel celibacy. Okay, maybe not *celibacy*. He made me come last night just from teasing my nipples while doing this thing with a vibrator—

"Frankie?"

I jerk from my seat in the car. "Huh?"

Ren's mouth tips in a grin but his eyes stay pinned on the road. "You didn't hear a word I just said, did you?"

"Nope. Sorry." I take a slow, calming breath. "Didn't mean to zone out. I was daydreaming."

He squeezes my leg gently. "You don't need to be sorry. I didn't know your thoughts were elsewhere."

"*Elsewhere* makes me sound very philosophical, when really I was just picturing new variations on mutual non-penetrative pleasure, and how much I really want you to bend me over the sofa, then—"

"Frankie." Ren's voice is strangled. "I'm going to be walking into practice with a . . ." He gestures to his groin and a pronounced erection.

"I'm sorry." I bang my head on the headrest and sigh. "I'm just frustrated. I hate periods."

"I said I didn't—"

"No." I lift a silencing hand. "Absolutely not. No way are you losing your V-card to me while I'm riding the crimson tide. Noooope."

"It's not like I'll be swapping tales with the guys over a pint. It'll be private to you and me. I don't care."

"*I* care."

Ren sighs. "Clearly. And here we are—you, a fresh level of ornery, and me, so freaking hard I'll be lucky if I can skate straight."

"Aw. Dumpling. Are we having our first fight?"

Before he can sass me back, a sports car cuts us off, exploiting the safe following distance Ren's afforded the car in front of us.

Ren has to hit the brakes hard. His hand instinctively spans my chest, holding me back as his eyes fly to the rearview mirror, rightfully anticipating a possible rear-end collision, which we somehow avoid.

Adrenaline pounds through my body. I exhale in relief and glance down at Ren's arm, still protectively stretched across me. Tears blur my vision. I'm holding my breath. It flashes through my mind that if I'd been with my family, with my friends from college, it would have been a whole smothering to-do. Worries about whiplash. Demands for X-rays.

Please don't do it. Please don't—

Abruptly, Ren's arm leaves my body, and with a slam of his fist, he nails the horn. Jabbing a bunch of buttons until his window lowers, Ren yells at the douchebag Boxster in front of us, "*Swag-bellied miscreant!*"

I bite my cheek. Bringing my hand to the base of Ren's neck, I slip my fingers through the shaggy upturn of his thick hair, hoping to soothe him a little.

Ren jerks a sharp glance at me. "Are you okay?"

I nod.

"Nothing hurts?" he presses.

I shake my head. And wait with bated breath for what comes next.

"Okay." He exhales heavily, scrubbing his face. Turning, he cups my cheeks and kisses me.

His hands start traveling my body, like he doesn't believe me. "You sure nothing hurts?"

"I'm okay, Ren." Gently, I scrape my nails through the scruff of his beard and kiss him back. "Trust me?"

He nods. "Okay. We're all right." A car horn sounds behind us. Ren's gaze swivels to the rearview mirror with a ferocious glare. Bright morning sun beats down on him, making his hair glow fiery red. And by Jesus Skipping through the Resurrection Garden, Ren *scowls*.

Everything inside me turns inferno hot. Not-smiling Søren Bergman is nothing short of magnificent.

"You're awfully handsome when you're angry, sweet cheeks."

He narrows those cat eyes on me. "Why are *you* the one using infuriating pet names and smiling," he grits out, "and *I'm* the one cursing at strangers while gnashing my teeth to dust?"

*Because we're both so sexually frustrated thanks to the worst tim-
ing ever that we're about to explode?*

"Because the world is a cruel place, and Los Angeles drivers
suck." I smile and point ahead. "Eyes on the road, love button.
Traffic's moving."

TWENTY-FOUR

Frankie

Playlist: "And the Birds Sing," Tyrone Wells

"She's so tiny," I whisper. Naomi Grace Churchill was born yesterday afternoon. She's my goddaughter and I might be mildly obsessed.

"And you're hogging her," Lo gripes.

Mia elbows her. "Chill out. Let her get her fix. Frankie obviously has baby fever."

My head snaps up and my eyes find Ren instinctively. He leans against the wall, arms folded across his soft gray T-shirt. Old jeans hug his long legs. Ball cap pulled low. Not a soul recognized him when we came to the hospital. Or if they did, they were nice enough to leave him be.

The corner of his mouth lifts as his cat eyes crinkle, startlingly pale in the shadow of his cap's brim. But he doesn't say a word.

Annie smiles at me. "You do look good with a baby, Frankie."

"That's why you had her for me," I tell her. Naomi holds my pinky with her fist. Her skin is flower-petal soft.

"Oh, is that what I did?" Annie says dryly. "And here I thought she was for Tim and me."

"Nope. I'm taking her home."

Tim laughs. "How about you take her home at night. We've barely slept at all."

Lorena's practically baring her teeth at me.

"Ugh, fine," I grumble. "Take her from me. We should get going anyway."

"Where are you headed?" Lo takes her carefully from me, cradling Naomi in her arms and swaying instinctively. If I have baby fever, Lo's having a baby febrile seizure.

"Don't drool on her. Ren's sister's birthday party."

"Aw, that's nice!" Annie winks at me, then directs herself to Ren. "So, Ren, you're bringing Frankie to a *family* event—"

"Annabelle," I warn.

Ren smiles at me, then turns and looks at Annie. "I am. She gets to meet everyone today. Thoughts and prayers appreciated. I'm one of seven, so it can be a bit much."

"Ah," Lo says. "So that's why Frankie's been sitting here, looking like she's about to poop herself."

"You know, guys . . ." I stand slowly from the recliner next to Annie. "I'd say I hate to leave, but I'm a shit liar, so to everyone except Naomi, who's never said a snarky word, I say, smell ya later."

I give Annie a gentle hug first, then make the rounds until we're at the door. "Wait!" Annie calls.

Ren and I freeze, then turn around. "What is it?" I ask her.

Tim smiles sheepishly. "My grandma has the kind of crush on Ren that you probably never want to know about and she's sick with a cold, so she can't come to the hospital to meet the baby. I thought it might make her decade if we got a picture of him holding Naomi and sent it to her."

I'm about to be all no-BS-Frankie and decline for Ren—because shouldn't a guy just get to be a man sometimes, rather than a jersey?—but Ren simply shrugs and comes forward.

"I don't mind. Sure."

Annie looks at me and mouths, *Sorry.*

I point to Ren and shrug. If he doesn't care, I don't. I simply feel protective of him. He's always smiling, always being nice, always signing things. I want him to say no when he wants to. And when he's having a hard time, I'm happy to step in, as an expert.

"Let me wash my hands real quick." Ren uses soap and water at the sink, eyes on his task. I watch him, stupidly enjoying how his hair kicks out around his ball cap, his scruffy play-off beard, the purse of his lips as he concentrates.

Staring at him, I feel all warm and fuzzy. That big L-word bangs around my head, and I practically smother it.

Too soon. Not yet. Slow down.

"Here." Ren takes Naomi gently from Lorena, capably spinning her to nestle inside his forearm.

Jesus Walking on the Water. I've seen Ren hold babies before, but not . . . "*My* baby," I mutter.

"She's not your baby." Lo swats my butt playfully. "She's mine."

"She's *our* baby," Annie says diplomatically.

Tim gets the camera close and catches the exact moment Naomi's eyes blink open and then widen as she sees Ren. "All right," Tim says. "Got it!"

I step closer and set my head on Ren's bicep. It's like a pillow. If a pillow was solid muscle carved out of stone. Still, he smells spicy and clean, like the soap he used while showering this morning. I brushed my teeth extra long so I could watch the top half of his body not hidden by the steam, muscles bunching and flexing as he washed himself.

"She likes him," Mia says smugly. "And look at his face. Ren's got baby fever, too."

I roll my eyes. But when I look back at him, Ren's gaze meets mine, the smallest smile tipping his lips.

A smile that's not bright as sunbeams or wide as the ocean. Not the smile for fans or grandmas or passersby. A small, knowing smile.

For me.

———

"Okay." Ren parks the van and blows air from his cheeks in a slow, steady stream. "I'm not going to lie, my family's weird and overwhelming. I'm one of the rowdy ones, and *I* still find us too intense sometimes. So, if you just need somewhere quiet to slip away to, I'll show you my old room, and you can take whatever time you need. That's the nice thing about my family, they won't be remotely insulted if you tell them to their face that you need a break from them. Willa's done it dozens of times—"

I clasp his hand, curling my fingers around his. "It's okay, Ren. I know I can tell you if it's too much. I'm sure everything will be fine."

Ren laughs uneasily. "Yeah. Right. Okay."

"Hey." Cupping his face in my hands, I give him a slow, thorough kiss. When we break apart, he sighs, dropping his forehead to mine.

"Thanks," he whispers. "I needed that."

I reach for one more kiss. "Me too."

Rounding the car, he opens my door as always, then offers his arm.

There's a slight hill from where he parked, and he's glaring at it. "They should have left me a space up front."

"Why?"

Ren throws up a hand. "For you. So that you don't have to walk all this way. Here, I'll carry you—"

"Okay, Zenzero. Time-out."

Ren spins, hands on his hips, and if he weren't so preciously worked up, I'd find it a very intimidating stance.

"You don't scare me with that Big Red gun show, so just relax."

He drops his arms. "I want this to be nice for you." He gestures to the house again. "And we're starting it off with a quarter-mile walk to the house. You put on a tough show, Frankie, but I know walking on stuff like this hurts you. And you're hurting right now."

"Eh. I have the Elder Wand, and I'll grab your arm if I'm about to biff it. Okay?"

He sighs. "Fine."

I take his arm to placate him. Immediately, he squeezes it to his side.

Ren tugs his ball cap lower and scratches his neck. "It'll be fine," he says, as if to himself.

I smile up at him. "Exactly."

The walk isn't terrible, but Ren's not wrong. My hip would have been happier without having gone that far on uneven ground. Ren doesn't knock, doesn't hesitate, just throws open the front door of the house and yells something in Swedish that I don't understand.

A chorus of the same phrase echoes back, making me startle.

He grins down at me. "I told you we're weird."

"You're here! Finally. You're late." Ren's mom strides toward me, hugging me hard.

"Oh—" I start to say, but Ren cuts in.

"Mom, I told you I had a practice." He catches my eye and sighs. I was forewarned that his mother is brutally blunt. I reassured him blunt is the last thing that's going to bother me. "Hey," he says to his mom. "Easy on her."

Elin's hands loosen. "Right. Sorry! I hug hard. But you—" She clasps my shoulders lightly, pinning me with the same wintry eyes she gave her son. "I must be gentle with you."

Ren massages the bridge of his nose.

"Thank you for having me, Mrs. Bergman—"

"Oh, just Elin. Please," she says on a bright smile.

I tap Ren's stomach. "You have my purse."

"Ah. Right." Sliding my bag off his other arm, he hands it to me.

I have to set it down so I can grip the straps, pull them open, and extract the wine I brought. Straightening, I swallow a groan of discomfort in my back and hand her the bottle. "Thank you."

"How kind." Elin takes it, gives me a smile, and then slinks her arm in mine. "You take *my* arm now, Frankie."

My eyes travel to the wide-open room. The massive, rough-hewn dining table. Clean lines, the expansive kitchen, and then to the right, the comically big sectional sofa. Noise centers in the kitchen filled entirely with women, bringing me to a nervous stop.

Elin glances over at me. "We don't normally divide like this, but they all just finished a football game, and while the women were ready for a cocktail, the men didn't want to stop playing. Why don't you join us? We're just making drinks now."

I smile nervously at Ren over my shoulder. Ren smiles softly back.

"Frankie!" Willa jumps up from her stool and gives me a hug. "You just missed a massacre. We kicked their butts, didn't we?"

"Yes, we did," Ziggy says, a soft smile brightening her face. She opens her arms first, so I know it's okay for me to step into them.

"Happy birthday, Ziggy," I whisper. As I step back, I set a wrapped package in her hands.

"What is it?" she asks.

"Open it."

Ziggy drops it on the counter, tears off the paper. She squeals. "It just came out! Mom, Frankie got me book six! Oh my gosh."

When we last talked, Ziggy told me about this fantasy romance series she was tearing through, so I got her the next in the series, which just came out last week. Jumping up and down, she lunges herself at me and hugs me hard. "Thank you so much."

I hug her back. "You're welcome, Ziggy."

Sighing happily, she clutches it to her chest. "Oh! And did you see I'm wearing the clothes we ordered? Just changed into them from my soccer stuff."

I give her a once-over. Black leggings that fit down to her ankles. An emerald-green T-shirt that matches her eyes. "You look great, Ziggy."

She blushes bright pink. "Thanks. It's so comfy."

"Good." I squeeze her arm gently before turning to Freya, whom I've only met once before.

She's almost her mother's copy. Sharp, striking features. Pale eyes, wavy white-blond hair worn just past her chin.

"Hi." I offer my hand. "I'm Frankie."

"I remember," she says. "Freya." Her voice is smoky, and while I can't read her expression, her voice seems tinged with sadness. She shakes my hand gently, not squeezing, which isn't surprising. She's a physical therapist, Ren said. She'd know to take it easy. "It's nice to finally meet you, not just wave hi in the stadium."

"Arena," Ziggy corrects.

Freya waves it off. "Whatever. We're a soccer family." She smiles at me. "Ren's said such great things about you for so long."

I catch his eye and watch him turn bright red. "Oh?"

She cocks a blond eyebrow. "I mean, he's been crazy about you for—"

Ren cuts her off with a hug, muffling her against his chest before he sets her at arm's length.

"Freya Linn. You've been wimping out on me."

She thumps his stomach with a loose fist, but it just bounces off his abs. She shakes out her hand. "Am not."

Ren smiles at me, hooking an arm around Freya's neck, pulling her in and giving her a noogie. She twists his nipple, which makes him yelp and spin away.

"*Strumpet*," he calls her.

She lunges for his nipple again, but he's too fast. Setting his hands gently on Ziggy's shoulders, he stands behind her. "The birthday girl is base. No more nipples."

This is the real Ren. The one I'm seeing a little bit more of each day I'm with him. Playful, dorky, a smidge antagonistic, still a bit bashful. My smile's so wide my cheeks hurt, watching him among his family.

"Happy birthday, Zigs." Ren hugs her from behind and kisses the top of Ziggy's head, slipping a card into her hand.

She tears it open, reads it, folding what looks like a gift card tight in her grip. When she glances up at him, she's teary-eyed. She hugs him for a long moment, and he hugs her back.

Ziggy turns to face us all and wipes her nose. "Ren got me a gift card big enough to get the cleats I wanted," she says quietly.

Elin smiles over at Ren and shakes her head. "The money Americans spend on shoes—"

"They're not *shoes*," Ziggy says defensively. "They're cleats, and they mean so much to me. Thank you, Ren." She hugs him again. When she turns back from hugging him, she smiles at me, stacking the gift card on top of the book I got her. "I'm glad you brought Frankie," she says.

Ren grins at me over Ziggy's head. "I'm glad I brought Frankie, too."

My cheeks heat. Ren's looking at me how he looked at me when he stepped past me then into the shower this morning, and it's revving my engine in ways that aren't acceptable for family gatherings.

"So." I turn toward Freya. "What's this challenge he's talking about?"

"Freya and I are doing a squat challenge," Ren answers. "But she's failed to report her reps for the past week." He points to

Freya's long, muscular legs sticking out of ripped-up denim shorts. "Clearly, she's slacking."

Freya narrows her eyes at him from the other side of the kitchen island. "I'm not slacking." Inverting a giant bottle of wine into a tall glass pitcher, she steals a piece of fruit from the pile that Elin's chopping next to her. "I've just been a little busy with work, lifting and moving the human body all day. I could squat-press *you*, Ren."

Ren lets out a low whistle. "Challenge accepted."

Elin smiles to herself. "Do you have siblings, Frankie?"

"An older sister."

"Ah," Elin says, peering up at me. "You're close, then."

"No, not really. I mean, we love each other, but there's an age gap and a country between us."

"Hmm." Elin glances down at her task. I feel like I just failed a test or something.

Willa leans in and whispers, "Don't worry, she's just curious. There's no right or wrong answer. Trust me. If I got folded into this family, anyone can." Pulling out a stool at the island, Willa pats it. "Come on, sit."

Ren opens his mouth, probably to tell her they kill my hips, but I talk before he can. "Ren, why don't you go say hi to the guys? I'll hang here for a little, then wander out and visit with them. Gives me some time to settle in."

Ren seems torn, his eyes dancing between the women like he doesn't quite trust them.

Suddenly he points a finger at Freya, then to his mother. "You two. No embarrassing stories from the early years. Frankie's seen me make a fool out of myself enough."

Freya rolls her eyes. "Why are men *so* fragile? We have other things to talk about besides the time you pooped in Grandpa's hat after it had fallen off the coatrack and landed upside down."

"I was *potty training*!" Ren yells. "It looked exactly like the kid-die toilet upstairs."

Elin throws her head back in laughter. "Oh. That one gets me. Every time."

Ziggy glances up from her phone. "Best part of that story is, nobody noticed until Grandpa put his hat on his head."

Willa blasts a laugh next to me. But my eyes stay locked on Ren, who stands flushed and embarrassed from ten feet away. "Søren—"

The room goes silent.

"*What* did you just call him?" Freya says.

Ren smiles at me, ignoring her. "Yes, Francesca."

"I did almost the same thing."

Ziggy drops her phone on the counter. "You did?"

"Mm-hmm." Extending my hand, I wait for Ren to come within reach. When he does, I wrap my arm around his warm, solid back. "Except I was at Mass, and I figured the baptismal font seemed as good a place as any to take a pee."

Willa slaps the counter and laughs. "You didn't."

"Oh, I did." I slide my hand along Ren's back and rub gently between his shoulders, meeting his eyes.

See? You're not alone. So long as I'm here.

I wish he could read my mind, could hear what I want him to know.

And the funniest thing happens. It's as if he does just that. Because he leans in, with a soft kiss to that tender place behind my ear, and whispers, "Thank you."

No sooner does Ren make for the sliding glass door leading out to their deck than a tall blonde throws it open and bumps into him. Tugging the door shut behind her, she greets everyone happily. Golden hair cut blunt to her shoulders. Sparkly eyes that dance between green and blue, land and sea.

She is sunshine incarnate.

And when she looks up at Ren, I want to summon lightning and smite her.

He gives her a hug hello and quickly steps back. Standing next to each other, they could not be more perfect-looking. A very odd, terrible feeling settles in my stomach.

That's the kind of person I used to picture Ren with. An effortless social butterfly—emotionally nimble, expertly gregarious, who passes out smiles like a pageant queen at the parade.

She even looks like him somehow. Statuesque and tall. Strong features, wide smile, alluring body.

"Well?" She elbows him in the ribs. "Can I finally meet her?"

Willa clears her throat. "Since you were *my* friend first, Rooster, I'd like to do the honors. Rooney, this is Frankie. Ren's lady love."

So *this* is Rooney, Willa's best friend from college.

Rooney walks away from Ren, leans in, and gives me a gentle hug. "So good to finally meet you."

When she straightens and winks at me, it's as blindingly unnerving as staring into the sun. But maybe I'm just that unused to people as pathologically cheery as Rooney. She puts Ren's temperament to shame.

"You too," I manage.

Freya stirs whatever alcohol is in the pitcher. I watch it swirl obediently in the wake of a long wooden spoon. Fruit. Booze.

Sangria.

Oh thank God. I need a vat of it. This is so many people in one place, including a woman who in this moment of insecure weakness only reminds me of all the ways I feel inadequate. "Get out of here, Ren," Freya says on a wave, as she takes an experimental taste from the pitcher. "And if you see my husband being sporty outside, tell him I hope he trips." Elin smacks Freya's butt and mutters something in Swedish.

"Not touching that one." Ren waves and slides open the door.
"Come out soon, okay?" he says to me.

I nod. "I will."

Very soon, if I have anything to say about it.

Rooney plops down next to me, reaches for a carrot, and swipes
it through a bowl of hummus.

Crunching, she looks me over. "You are *hot*."

Willa sighs. "Is there no faithfulness anymore?"

Rooney blows her a kiss. "You were my first, honey. But you
chose Ryder over me. It's time for me to move on."

I stare between them. "You two . . . were . . . together?"

"They don't speak our language, Frankie," Ziggy says, swiping
through her phone. I think she's reading. At her own birthday
party. Smart girl.

"What do you mean?" I ask.

Ziggy glances up. "It's all one big joke. If you take any of it
literally—which is how you and I tend to take everything—it's
very confusing."

Rooney smiles sheepishly. "Sorry. It's a bad habit. I'm an only
child who grew up watching a lot of *Gilmore Girls* with no one to
be the Rory to my Lorelai."

"But that would make you her *mom*," I say confusedly.

Ziggy lifts a hand. "My point is made."

Willa gently pats my arm. "What Rooney means is she likes to
talk. A lot. And I do, too. We talk back and forth, mostly about
nothing, but it's all wrapped up in love. Make sense?"

Not really.

I never talk unless I have something meaningful to say, and
then I have *lots* to say. Talking for talking's sake is exhausting.

Ziggy grins at me as if she just thought the same thing, then
goes back to her phone.

A shadow graces the patio doorway, and in steps the oldest Bergman brother, Axel. He's taller than Ren and lean, like he runs marathons. Long, wiry muscles. Ramrod-straight posture.

He's very handsome, if not a little intimidating, with his severe expression. Ryder's and Ziggy's grass-green eyes. Tousled chocolate hair like Viggo's.

He freezes when he sees all of us. "Why is everyone staring at me?"

Rooney mutters under her breath, "Because who the hell *wouldn't* stare at him?"

Willa snorts. Axel narrows his eyes at her.

"No one's staring, Ax," Freya says, pouring more wine into the pitcher. "You just walked in. People tend to look at a person when they enter a room."

Axel sees me, but his expression doesn't change. An odd prick at the back of my neck makes me sit straighter.

"You're Frankie," he says. There's very little inflection in his voice. Because faces confuse me, I rely on tone of voice to intuit subtext. I get nothing from this neutral delivery.

"I am. You're Axel." I offer my hand. "Good to meet you."

Striding my way, Axel takes my hand, squeezes it. "You too." When he notices Rooney, he does a double take. "Your hair's shorter."

She grins. "Yeah. I chopped it. What do you think?"

He stares at her, wetting his bottom lip with his tongue. "You changed it."

Her smile falters. "You don't like it?"

"Change makes Ax spiral," Freya says, stirring the sangria. "He nearly disowned me when I got the pixie cut a few years back."

Axel stares at Rooney still. "I think . . . I need to get used to it. In my head you have long hair."

"Well, at least I'm in your head," Rooney tells him. Her smile's back, and it is formidable.

Clearing his throat, Ax backs away. "Bathroom," he says.

Three long strides, and he's gone. The kitchen goes unnaturally quiet. And a furious blush stains Rooney's cheek.

TWENTY-FIVE

Frankie

Playlist: "Mushaboom," Feist

Willa leans and watches Axel's departure until a door beyond my view clicks shut. Snapping back, she lobs a block of cheese at Rooney. It bounces off her forehead. "You are *shameless* with him."

Rooney picks up the cheese and pops it in her mouth. "He's such a hunk. I can't help it."

Elin grins to herself as she rinses off her hands. Freya sets a glass of sangria in front of me, and I nod in thanks. I don't really know what to say, so I sip my drink instead.

"Rooney always goes for the broody types," Willa says.

"I *used* to," Rooney corrects her. "I've sworn off men."

Every woman in the room except me erupts in laughter.

"I have!" she says. "They're all horrible. Except Ax. He's different."

"He is, is he?" Willa says, wiggling her eyebrows.

"How long have you, uh . . ." I clear my throat, trying to be conversational with her. "Sworn off men?"

"Let me think." Rooney taps her chin and stares at the ceiling. "Five weeks. It's been brutal. But I ordered a dildo, which should be here any day, so things are looking up."

Willa snorts into her sangria. Elin seems unfazed, and Freya just chuckles under her breath.

Ziggy's reading and misses it entirely.

When someone drops that kind of truth in a group setting, they're on my good side forever. "Cheers to that." I lift my glass. Rooney clinks her glass to mine, and when she smiles at me, I actually find myself smiling back.

Conversation takes off without my help after that, though I find my moments to chime in here and there. After not too long, there's only one glass of sangria in my system, but I'm flushed and relaxed, slightly buzzed, which is when I feel like I have a tiny glimpse of what it's like to be a socially fluent human. To flow with conversation and enjoy it, instead of following it like a tennis match, trying desperately to keep track of who served and whose turn it is to volley back.

But I'm also warm, and a little agitated, which I've learned by now means I need fresh air and a few moments of quiet. Excusing myself, I step out onto the back deck and nearly collide with Ren's father.

"Shit!" I yelp. "I mean, shoot. I mean—"

His laugh is so like Ren's that it makes me do a double take. "Frankie. I'm no saint. You can curse around me." Steadying me, he neatly steps to the side. His hand gestures toward a chair for me to sit in.

"Oh. Um. Okay." Awkwardly, I plop into the chair, picking up a place mat off of the outdoor table and fanning myself. "Sorry, again, Dr. B." It's what I heard both Willa and Rooney call him, so it seems like the way to go. "I wasn't looking where I was going."

He waves his hand, groaning softly as he drops into a chair across from me. "You mind if I join you? Those beasts I raised down there wore me out."

"Be my guest," I tell him.

"Thank you."

I smile, watching all five of the Bergman brothers volleying a soccer ball, trying to keep it in the air. Viggo chests it, then cracks a shot into the nearby net, before the only brother I don't recognize, and by process of elimination is Oliver, jogs off to scoop it up. My gaze sweeps past the lawn beyond us, sprawling and flat, nestled among blossoms and a grove of trees a ways off. Dusk is my favorite time of day, when the sky glows peach and violet and the air turns cool.

When I glance back over, I freeze. Dr. B's pant leg has lifted enough to reveal a titanium rod in place of an ankle. I stare in complete shock.

On a quiet groan, he massages the muscles right above his knee, staring out into the yard at his sons, a soft smile warming his face. When he glances my way, he pauses. His gaze travels my expression. "He didn't tell you?"

I shake my head.

"My military souvenir," he says while patting his thigh. "Gets sore after a long day and trying to keep up with them. I'm sorry if it upset—"

"No," I blurt.

My heart's pounding. Why wouldn't Ren tell me? All my hemming and hawing about my challenges' potential pitfalls in a relationship and he never thought it would help for me to know he grew up seeing that kind of love firsthand?

See? Fulfilling interabled coupledom is *possible*, the little Lorena on my shoulder gloats. I'm tempted to flick her off her perch, if she weren't a figment of my imagination and it wouldn't completely disconcert Ren's dad.

"Please don't apologize," I finally manage hoarsely, bringing a hand to my throat and rubbing uneasily.

Dr. B grins at me, and it's another dead ringer for Ren. "If it makes you feel any better, you're not the first person I've surprised. I think sometimes my kids forget it's not normal to everyone else. It's all they've ever known."

"How was that? Being in a rigorous profession, married, having kids, with . . ."

"With a physical limitation?" He glances out to the field and sighs. "Hard sometimes. Discouraging others. Always healing."

"Why? Why 'healing'?"

Dr. B drums his fingers on the arms of his chair. "Well . . . when it happened, Freya was a toddler, Elin was pregnant with Axel. I was devastated. I thought I'd never be able to give my wife and children what they needed. Not as I'd envisioned, at least. I'd never be able to practice medicine again how I'd hoped. I felt like my life was over.

"But then Axel was born, and I held him, those eyes just like mine staring up at me, and something clicked. I realized he loved me. Already, he loved me, just how I was. I'd made him with his mother, and he was my flesh and blood and not having most of my leg didn't change that. Finally, I understood my life wasn't over, only my *idea* of my life was.

"That's when I fully released my old expectations, how I thought my life should be, and instead loved my life for what it was: a gift. A heart beating in my chest. Breath in my lungs. A wife and children who loved me as I was."

My eyes blur with tears. I dab my face as they spill down my cheeks. "That's very . . . encouraging," I whisper. "Thank you for telling me."

He nods, holding my eyes for a long moment before our gazes shift together, toward the field again. Dabbing my eyes, I search the grass until I see Ren's in goal. Right as Oliver takes a penalty shot, he dives, completely missing. All five brothers fall into various postures and volumes of hilarity, and Dr. B laughs, watching them. As if he knows I'm watching him, Ren glances up as he stands and catches my eye. His laugh dies away as our eyes lock. My heart skips inside my chest.

Suddenly, the door slides open again, and Ziggy bounds out, practically throwing herself at her dad and landing in his lap. He catches her with an *oof* before she kisses his cheek and wraps her arms around his neck. I'm relieved to see their easy affection. It means that her parents have stopped keeping so much distance between them and Ziggy, that she feels more comfortable with physical closeness again.

"Hi, Ziggy Stardust," he whispers, wrapping his arms around her.

"Hi, Daddy." Ziggy glances over at me and repositions herself on his lap, like it isn't comical someone so grown and long limbed is draped over her dad. It's sweet and innocent and entirely Ziggy. She's still a girl in a lot of ways. Very much how I was as a teen.

Dr. B rests his cheek on her head and sighs, his eyes crinkling happily. "You know who Ren's named after?" he asks me.

I nod. "Kierkegaard."

"That's right. I was reading his *Works of Love* toward the end of Elin's pregnancy with him. I'd read aloud to her while she soaked in the tub, after I'd put Freya and Axel to bed. It just fit. The name, his philosophy . . ."

"I'm not familiar with Kierkegaard in any detail," I tell him honestly.

Dr. B glances up at the fading daylight and smiles. "'To dare is to lose one's footing momentarily. Not to dare is to lose oneself.'"

"The other one, Daddy," Ziggy says quietly.

He kisses her forehead. "'The most common form of despair is not being who you are.'"

Ziggy smiles. "That's my favorite."

"And *my* favorite," Dr. B says, as he shifts Ziggy on his lap, "is—"

A new voice breaks in. I glance over my shoulder to see Ren smiling down at me, hands in his pockets. "'To cheat oneself out of love,'" he says, "'is the most terrible deception; it is an eternal loss for which there is no reparation.'"

My throat's dry as a desert. I lick my lips and feel myself melting in the heat of his stare. "That's a good one."

Ren nods. "Yes, it is."

"Frankie!" a voice yells from below.

I turn and lean against the deck rail, squinting to find who said it. "Yes?"

Viggo waves. "Come down here. I need a partner."

I glance across the field. They're setting up . . . badminton? Oliver and Axel stretch the net with Ryder's help. I don't see Freya's husband, Aiden, anywhere. When I glance up at Ren, I see he's glaring down at Viggo, his jaw tight.

As I stand, I shuffle out from between the table and chair and salute Dr. B and Ziggy both. "It was good talking to you. But now it's time to go get my ass handed to me at badminton."

Dr. B grins and pats Ziggy's back, his eyes holding mine. "Go on and show 'em how it's done."

Peering up at Ren, I smile. Hands on his hips. A flush in his cheeks. Angry Big Red stance. I thread my arm around his waist and smile up at him.

Ren frowns as I hold on to him while we walk down the deck stairs to the back lawn. "I told Viggo croquet would be better," he grumbles.

"Maybe. But I think I can hold my own in a corner of the net. We'll divvy up the area, and I'll stick to mine." I pat his cheek. "Remember. Give me a chance. Don't assume I can't."

"I'm trying. I'm . . . ." He sighs. "Can I be honest?"

"Always. Please."

"Okay." He rakes a hand through his hair and tugs roughly. "I'm worried you'll get hurt. Not because I think you're incapable or that badminton is beyond you—truly, I don't—but look at us—" He gestures to his brothers, all of whom are over six feet and pushing two hundred pounds.

"Well, that's a fair point. But it's not a contact sport."

"*Everything* is a contact sport in the Bergman household."

I laugh. "It's okay. I'll be careful."

Ren wraps an arm around my shoulders and kisses my hair. My head rests on his shoulder in a way that I can see behind his back, where Oliver is stealthily creeping toward him. I've seen that stance. That's an "I'm about to depants a guy" stance.

Shoving myself around Ren so that he's shielded behind me, I lift my cane and point it at Oliver.

Ren's younger brother grins, frozen to the spot. "Foiled by Bellatrix. What's she gonna do?"

"I might be Slytherin," I tell him. "But I'm no Death Eater."

Ryder glances between us. "What the hell is this? Did I just fall into a ninth circle of nerd hell?"

Ren shoves him. "Lay off. She's protecting me."

Oliver grins, feinting to the right. I arc my cane and yell, "*Stupefy!*"

He freezes perfectly, mouth agape, mid-crouch.

"That all you got?" Viggo calls.

Lifting my cane higher, I touch the tip to Oliver's chest. "*Locomotor Mortis.*"

Trying not to smile, Oliver snaps up, legs locked together, and topples over onto the grass. A burst of applause sounds from the deck, where Ziggy, Dr. B., and now Willa, Rooney, and Elin stand.

"Woo-hoo, Frankie!" Willa hollers.

Before I can respond, I'm tucked tight inside Ren's arms, a soft kiss pressed to my cheek. "You saved me," he whispers.

I grin up at him and steal a kiss. "I did, didn't I?"

TWENTY-SIX

Ren

Playlist: "Close," Nick Jonas, Tove Lo

"What's up with Frankie?" Andy asks. "She's been extra moody this week. And I didn't even see her leave tonight." Yanking his jersey over his head, he throws it down, shaking sweat off like a wet dog. I sit on the bench and stare at my locker. Dazed.

Come home hungry.

That's what her text says. The moment the buzzer went off and the game ended, with a narrow win on our part, Frankie dissolved into the flood of staff and personnel while some PR intern handled wrap-up and quick interviews, obviously covering for her. As soon as I could, I strode into the locker room and riffled through my bag until I found my phone. Because I knew she wouldn't leave like that without an explanation.

Come home hungry.

I swallow nervously. There are a couple ways to interpret that message. One of which sends lust slamming through my system.

A shove to the shoulder makes me glance up.

Andy's still there. "What's that again?" I ask him dazedly.

"I said—" He shoves me once more, and this time I shove him

back, sending him stumbling into his locker. "What's up with Frankie?"

I pull off my helmet and drop it, dragging my fingers through my hair. "Stomach was bugging her again," I lie off-the-cuff.

"Well, at least it's not that nasty shit Maddox brought around."

Maddox is out with bronchitis. After he hacked a lung around us all the past week at practice.

Around *Frankie*. I fist my hands and try to exhale slowly. If she gets sick from his carelessness . . .

Andy scrunches his nose. "It's just weird. Frankie's such a hard-ass. Sick or not, she's always here. You think she's okay?"

Patting his arm, I give him a distracted smile. "I think she'll be fine."

"Hey." Kris walks up to me. "You seen Frankie? It's weird without her."

Andy rolls his eyes. "Dude. He just said she's got a stomach-ache. Listen, would you?"

While those two devolve to bickering, I tune them out, strip quickly, and grab a towel. When I walk by and hear their ongoing conversation, I can't help but think how right Kris is, how weird it is without her being here. How unprepared everyone will be when we're without her for good.

As I step into the shower, water running over me, I feel the press of anxiety in my chest. Fear that I won't always have her, tenuous hope that no matter where life takes her next, I'll be by her side because we've built something solid and long-lasting between us—

There's something solid and long-lasting between you two, all right.

I glance down at my hard-on. There he is. Jutting straight out and miserably unfulfilled, which is pretty much how it's been most of the past few weeks. Just thinking about Frankie makes me ache, always has. But recently, the torture's been all the greater, with the time we've been spending together, surrounding me with her night air and orchid scent, feeling the silk of her hair brush my cheek when she nestles into me, wrapping my arms around her in bed and tucking her soft body against my hard one.

Emphasis on hard.

My cock twitches angrily at the memory of the way she arches into my touch when she comes, how her full backside nestles against me when she's ready to fall asleep.

Groaning, I slap the tiles and turn the water ice cold, shivering while I quickly wash myself. It works. I get my body under control but still my mind wanders to Frankie. Biting her lip while she thinks. Stepping inside my arms, letting me sway and kiss her. Tangled in bed, exploring, learning each other's bodies through clothes and stolen touches beneath them.

Snapping the towel off the hook and wrapping it around my waist, I wander over to my locker. No need to change in the shower area now that I know Frankie won't be here.

Yes, my modesty on that front was entirely for her. Because I held out hope that if I could avoid her seeing me and my dangly bits, I wouldn't simply be one of the guys who couldn't be bothered to cover himself up when she was milling around. Just like her body was and is still largely a mystery to me, I wanted mine to be a mystery to her, too.

Come home hungry.

It has to mean for more than a late dinner. My stomach tightens with nerves. I pull out my phone, swipe it open, and type.

Yes, ma'am.

When I shut the front door, air rushes out of me. Frankie stands at the stove, wineglass in hand, swaying to music playing from her phone. A slow, sensual rhythm making the tiniest pair of pajama shorts flutter as she moves. A tissue-thin top drapes off her shoulder, and her hair's piled on top of her head, faint wisps of chocolate ribbons caressing her neck.

Glancing over her shoulder, she smiles as she sets down her wine. "Welcome back."

I close the distance between us, slide my hands around her ribs, and tug her against me. I kiss her, suck at her bottom lip, tease her tongue.

"Ren," she says breathlessly. "Everything okay?"

Shaking my head, I kiss her neck, drag her lobe between my teeth, making her jolt, then melt in my arms. "I missed you," I whisper.

Her laugh is soft and breathy. "It's been an hour."

I cup her face, angling it so I can kiss every point I want to. "No, it hasn't," I mutter. "It's been years."

Frankie stills, tipping her head and bringing a hand to my cheek. Her eyes search mine.

"What's wrong, Ren?" she asks quietly.

I pull back enough to hold her gaze, my thumb sliding over her dimple. "Just something one of the guys said. It made me nervous. Sad."

"What is it?"

"When you leave," I whisper. "I'll miss you."

Her face softens. "Oh, Ren. I'll miss you, too. But . . ." Blinking away, she smooths back my hair. "I mean, assuming we'll still be together. I'm hoping, that is—"

I kiss her. "Frankie," I whisper against her lips. "God, I'll do anything. . . ." There's the truth, strong and steady as my heart beating inside my chest.

I love you.

I always have. I've loved her since the moment I saw her. Somehow, inexplicably, it's true.

I kiss her again, tangling tongues, holding her hips against mine, showing her how badly I need her. "Do you know how long I've wanted you?" I say against her neck, dragging my tongue over her collarbone.

She sighs. "Me, too." Her hands come to my tie, struggling with the knot. I yank it loose, then attack the buttons of my shirt. Frankie grabs my buckle, tugging it so hard, she loses her balance and nearly bumps into the stove. I catch her by the elbow and wrap an arm around her to keep her steady.

"Shit," she mutters, staring at the meal she was cooking.

I reach past her, flicking off burners. "Later."

She nods, leaning up, kissing me, arms around my neck.

I scoop her up and wrap her legs around my waist. "Does that hurt?" I ask against her mouth.

"No," she whispers, dropping her head, stretching her neck for me to kiss.

I groan when she reaches between us and palms me over my suit pants. "You're done?" I ask.

She nods furiously. "Today. Thank God."

Setting her on the kitchen counter, I press her back, then kiss my way down her stomach. I shuck her shorts, dragging them off of her legs and tossing them aside.

"What are you—Oh *God*," she gasps, her arms dropping softly onto the cold granite.

"You said come home hungry." I kiss her stomach, swirl my tongue lower and lower. "And I'm more than happy to follow orders."

My hands part her, as finally, *finally* I see her close, breathe her in. Velvet soft skin, dark curls that I run my fingers through. Exploring the delicate skin of her stomach, I reach farther and cup her breast. "Look at you. Perfect."

She arches into my touch as I tease her nipple and press slow, wet, open-mouthed kisses on the inside of her thigh. "Ren, you don't have to—"

"Don't bother finishing that sentence, Frankie. I'll die if I don't do this."

She laughs breathily. "So dramatic—" A gasp leaps out of her as I bend and sweep my tongue where she's warm and wet, decadently soft. My thumb teases her clit with faint, featherlight touches, while I taste her and spear her with my tongue.

Faint, steady cries leave her. Her fingers delve into my hair, but there's no tug, no push, no direction. She's hesitating.

"Are you holding back on me, Francesca?"

Breath rushes out of her. "N-no."

"You're taking what you want?"

She nods, but it's slow. Tentative.

I yank her hips to the edge of the counter, cupping her bottom as I drop to my knees and swing each of her legs over my shoulders. "No, you're not."

Frankie cries out, a broken sob as I lock my mouth over her and take her with my tongue. One finger curled deep inside her, where she's softer, tender, so impossibly wet. Then two. I want her ready. I don't want it to hurt when I'm inside her. I only want pleasure for Frankie, no more pain. No more than she already has in her life.

She's sweet as honey, warm silk. I nuzzle, nibble, and finally lower my lips to her tiny, swollen clit, and gently suck—

"Yes!" she slaps the counter, canting her hips up into my face.

I pull back long enough to bite her thigh tenderly, chasing it with a kiss. "Tell me what you want."

"I—" She cries out again as I flick her clit with my finger. "I want it harder. Rough."

"You want to fuck my face."

"Jesus," she moans. "You would be the unexpected king of dirty talk."

"Tell me."

"I want to fuck your face!" she yells.

Grinning up at her, I lower my mouth, so my breath whispers over where she's glistening wet and flushed. "Then do it."

When I tongue her again, hold her close, she grinds up, wild, reckless, riding my mouth, fisting my hair, guiding me until she explodes on a hoarse scream.

Her thighs tighten around my shoulders. She cries out again, and this time a rough sob follows. Soft, pulsing waves against my lips. A rush of sweet release hits my tongue and I groan, palming myself reflexively. I almost come from just tasting her.

She's panting, wracked with shivers as I stand, then sweep her into my arms and stroll down the hallway. Once in the bedroom, I slowly lower her down my body, clenching my teeth when she slides against my groin.

Frankie stares up at me, her hands resting on my chest. Time slows, the only sounds the distant roar of the ocean, the steady rhythm of our breaths. Carefully, she runs her fingers beneath my suit jacket and slips it off. Tugging it off my arms, she tosses it on the nearby chair. I stare at her as I yank off my tie and make quick work of the rest of my buttons. Frankie rushes me, shoving off the fabric, tugging at my undershirt.

When I'm shirtless, she presses a hot kiss to my chest, scrapes her teeth over my nipple.

"God." I fist her hair, holding her close.

Frankie pushes away and I tackle her shirt, dragging it over her head. A moan tears out of my chest as I see her. So beautiful. More breathtaking than I could have ever imagined. I stare down at her as my heart pounds. Soft breasts, her nipples taut. Long muscles, a maddening slope to her hips. Golden skin. I run my hands up and down her waist and sigh. She's so soft.

"You're beautiful, Frankie. So impossibly beautiful."

She smiles and presses up on tiptoes, giving me a long, slow kiss. "Take off your clothes," she whispers, her hand dropping to my buckle again. "I want to see you."

I shuck my pants and boxer briefs, sweep her up again and carry her to the bed. After laying her down, carefully, I stand over her.

She bites her lip as her eyes trail my body. "Søren. You are magnificent."

Her thighs rub together as she stares at me. I pull her legs apart and fist myself, a long tug of my cock that draws a rough groan from me as I stare at her. A fierce, primal force drives me to touch myself while I look at the most intimate part of her.

"This is what you do to me, Frankie. You've done it for years. Made me so hard, I ache."

"Well, that sounds fair," she says dazedly. She stares at my length as I pump it, her eyes wide, lips parted. "Seeing as I've been nothing but despicably wet around you for too damn long. Do you know how uncomfortable drenched panties are, Ren?"

A growl rolls out of me. Dropping over her, I slip an arm under her back and drag her up the bed with me, settling between her thighs. "Confession."

Her hands slide up my arms and cradle my head. "I'm listening."

"I'm terrified this is going to be a disaster."

She laughs and kisses me. "That's impossible. It's you and me. We'll talk. Show each other what we need."

I bend, kiss her, lost for words. My heart thunders in my chest, anxiety pinching my shoulders. As if she intuits that, Frankie's hands glide along my back and gently massage my shoulders.

"Look at me," she whispers. She smooths my hair off my face and smiles up at me. "Trust me?"

I nod.

"Good. I trust you, too."

Frankie and I have talked about birth control. Clean bills of health. How we both really want nothing between us. Meaning there's nothing stopping us from finally being connected as close as two people physically can be.

Taking each of her hands in mine, I drag them up over her head. It sends her breasts high, shows the curve of her ribs, the hollow between her hips that's ready for me. I rest myself against her, holding her eyes.

Slowly, robbed of breath, I ease inside her, just a few inches, and stop. Frankie pants for air, her eyes scrunched shut. It's unlike anything I've ever known. Warm, tight, intricately smooth yet somehow not.

"Are you all right?" I whisper.

She nods furiously. Then shakes her head. "You're huge. It's like a Mack truck trying to take a back alley."

I laugh into her neck. "I'm sorry. I'll go slow. I want to make it good for you," I whisper.

She kisses me gently. "I'm not worried about that," she whispers back.

"Good. That makes one of us."

A laugh bursts out of her, and I have to clench my jaw because of how it makes her body flex around mine. "Just give me like . . . five hours to get adjusted," she mutters.

"I'll be lucky if I last five minutes, Frankie."

"Go slow while you can, okay?" she whispers. "It's better that way. Gentler. Like this."

At her cue, I loosen my grip and free her hands. Gripping my backside, she guides me with her as she leans her hips back, then rocks up. Air rushes out of me.

"God, you feel incredible." I set my mouth over hers, kissing, tasting, sharing breath as I follow her rhythm and my body's instinct. I pull away and moan helplessly as I ease in again.

Holding my weight on my elbows on either side of her face, I kiss her neck, her jaw, her lips, finally sinking so far inside her, I feel where I can't go any farther.

Frankie gasps. I pull back reflexively, but she stops me, panting for air. "It's okay. Don't stop, okay?"

My body's begging to thrust and pound and take. It's too harsh, too much. "I don't want to hurt you."

"You won't," she says gently, her hands drifting to my backside again, guiding me, pulling me to her. "I promise you won't."

Waves of muscles tighten around my cock. A sigh falls out of me as I draw back, then press into her, sure and slow. I feel sparks soar up my legs, a fierce need to move guiding me.

"Again," she whispers. "Again."

Our moans echo in each other's mouths as I thrust into her, as Frankie hugs me tight. Her hips roll in rhythm with mine, first slow, then urgently. Faster.

"Faster, Ren," she rasps. "Faster."

The last thread of my hesitation snaps, unleashing a torrent of need. I find her clit with my thumb and circle it steadily in time with each drive into her. Fast. Deliberate. The slap of skin on skin, the quiet rhythm of her cries. More waves, fluttering and faint, teasing spasms along my length as our bodies move together.

I'm so close already, I have to stop. One more stroke, and I'll be done for. Seating myself inside her, I kiss Frankie's breasts, suck her nipples roughly. My body trembles as I hold back.

"Ren, it's okay," she says gently. "It's okay for you to come. You already made me—"

"No," I mutter against her skin. "I want to feel you come with me. I want to feel you come all over my cock. I *need* it, Frankie."

Her body tightens around me. "I do, too," she says softly.

"Then let me do this." I flick her clit, suck her nipples, and slowly rock inside her. "Yes," she chants quietly. Her hands search my body as she writhes beneath me. "I'm coming," she mumbles. "I'm coming. Oh my God—"

She shakes beneath me as the grip of her body tightens sharply along my length. I want to hold still and savor every expression as she comes undone, but I can't. I have to move. It's an unrelenting demand, a consuming need to move furiously inside her, until lightning snaps up my spine, and I thrust into her with a final roar.

I spill so long that stars dance at the corners of my vision, before finally I can tug in air. A shiver wracks her body as I press gentle kisses to her throat, her jaw.

Dropping against Frankie, I turn her with me, so she's tucked into my side, her bad hip up off the mattress and splayed carefully across me. My hands dance over her skin, my lips travel her cheeks, until finally our mouths find each other's, hands gentle faces, and we sigh, a long, satisfied exhale.

Frankie blinks open her eyes and smiles up at me on a happy sigh. "Told you we had nothing to worry about."

TWENTY-SEVEN

Frankie

Playlist: "Cinnamon Girl," Lana Del Rey

Ren tosses aside the washcloth he used gently between my legs, along his length. Falling back on the bed, tugging me close, he stares up at the ceiling, moonlight casting his hair a cool tarnished copper. His skin is pale as moonbeams, his gaze an icy winter sky. Tight, powerful muscles bunch in his arms as he wraps me in his embrace. I touch him everywhere I can, running my hands along long muscle, firm skin, the sharp indent where his hip meets his backside.

"Wow." With a thick swallow, he turns and glances at me. "Was that . . . okay for you?"

I laugh and press a kiss to his neck. "So much more. So much more than okay. It was *wow*." Interlacing my fingers with his, I kiss his hand. "What about you?"

He shakes his head from side to side. "There's nothing . . . Nothing comes close to what I just felt with you." Pressing his lips to my forehead, he hugs me close, then glances down at me, breathless, eyes glowing.

Smiling, he smooths my hair off of my forehead. "You're incredible," he says quietly.

I run my hand along his chest and place a kiss at his heart. "So are you."

Hooking my leg higher over him, I drift my hand across the

Chloe Liese

terrain of his body, tracing the planes of muscle and bone. I kiss him as I run my hand down his stomach, touching him gently. Even relieved of an erection, he's thick and heavy.

And I'm already aching for more.

With each touch, I watch him harden. It makes me feel delirious, learning this new part of Ren—his desire, his wants, every idiosyncrasy of his pleasure.

He throws his head back when I slide my grip lower, my fingers wandering to cup him, exploring velvet-soft skin, hard muscles. His abs ripple, and his grip tightens on my shoulder.

"Oh, hell," he mutters. His hips falter as he presses into my grip. Slowly, I ease my way over his body, kissing down his ribs, the narrow line of hair pointing to his erection.

"Frankie, you don't have to—"

"I want to," I whisper. I want to taste him. I want to bring him pleasure for pleasure's sake.

And it'll be the first time he's let me do this.

Ren groans and rolls his hips as I take a soft, teasing lick. He reaches for my waist and spins me so he can reach between my thighs. Rubbing my clit with his thumb, he curls two fingers inside me.

A rough cry rips out of me before I grip the root of his cock and take him deep into my mouth. My legs shake as he strokes my G-spot, works my clit. Ren breathes unsteadily, his free hand delicately cupping my head, his fingers knotting in my hair.

"Oh God, Frankie. Your mouth. Jesus."

I moan with pleasure, watching him fall apart under my touch, locking eyes with those pale irises that widen as his hips falter.

"Close," he whispers, warning me, trying to pull away. I shake my head, hold him tight in my grip.

Stay. I want this.

My orgasm begins at the heart of me, radiating out. Ren feels it, his eyes widening, then growing hazy as he thrusts into my mouth. Air rushes out of me as I fly over the edge, as light dances behind my eyelids. With a pained shout, Ren arches his back, pouring in hot, long pulses down my throat. His breath is rough and erratic. I slowly release him with one final kiss to the tip and smile up at him.

With no preamble, he reaches for me and pulls me flush over his body. After long, quiet moments, he presses cool lips along my neck, up to my mouth with a heavy, satisfied exhale.

"Well, Zenzero," I say happily against his neck. "Not that I'm surprised, but your Rookie of the Year, MVP status remains unchallenged."

A laugh rumbles out of him as he meets my lips for a tender kiss. "I feel like this is all we should be doing. Like I want to quit my job and spend the rest of my life doing this with you."

"Guess what?" I whisper.

"What?"

"That's what off-season's for."

A warm, mischievous smile brightens his face. "And there goes all incentive to win the series."

I used to find the morning after I slept with someone cringey. Mostly because it was always a mistake. It was never my intent to stay over, to be small spoon, a man's muscly arm my pillow as I slept. But as with everything when it comes to Ren, each morning since our first night has proved deliciously different.

I woke up to a hand slipping between my legs. Hot, warm kisses painting my neck. Another time, gently laid on my back. Others, turned on my stomach. Always a warm mattress beneath me, gentle hands massaging my stiff joints. An eager, already expert mouth and fingers and body spiraling me to glorious orgasms, sending light exploding beneath my eyelids just like the sun cresting the horizon.

That's the first—and my favorite—part of our routine. The second is a morning walk, at least while the weather is warm enough.

I stroll along the sand, watching the ocean breeze whip Ren's hair into a mad fury of sunrise-copper waves. I hold his arm to steady myself, and I feel my body loosen, my joints open with each step across firm, cool sand.

"I was out cold last night when you came home," I tell him.

Ren glances down at me and smiles. "Oh, I know. I heard you snoring the moment I came in."

I glare at him. "I'm congested." His face tightens in concern. "Allergies, Zenzero."

"Hmm." He glances away.

"How was Shakespeare Club?"

I almost died of the cuteness last night. I got my quiet night, curled up on the couch with Pazza, but first I got a goodbye from the sweetest dork that lives. There he was, a well-loved mass-market of *As You Like It* shoved in his back jeans pocket, massive tray of baked goods from Viggo tucked in his arms. And a secretive, delighted glint in his eye that I'd never seen before.

As if the universe is set to prove me wrong, Ren peers down at me, cat eyes crinkled with that same conspiratorial sparkle. Leaning to press a soft kiss to my temple, he murmurs, "It was fun." The words buzz softly against my hair before he straightens and glances ahead.

Pazza tears off after a gull, barking madly, and when it soars into the sky, she drops glumly to her haunches.

Watching her, I'm distracted from where I step, so when I hit a dip in the sand, my leg buckles, pitching me toward the water. Just before I anticipate an icy wake-up swim, I'm yanked back, a warm hand wrapped around my waist and hoisting me upright.

"*Oof.*" I bump into Ren's chest, my hands reflexively fisting his shirt. Embarrassment heats my cheeks, and rather than meet his eye, I rest my head on his chest, listening to the steady rhythm of his heart.

He presses a kiss to the top of my head. "You okay?"

I nod, but a stupid tear rolls down my cheek. It's the first time I've tripped like that in front of him, and it feels exposing. Indecently vulnerable.

Holding me close, he wraps both arms around me tight. Like he knows I need a minute.

"I'm tough," I whisper.

He nods. "I know you are."

"I can take care of myself."

"You have," he says. "You still do. You always will. I've just joined in, too. Now we take care of each other."

I hiccup a stifled cry and press my forehead to his sternum. His chin fits exactly over my head. I feel his Adam's apple as he swallows.

"Frankie?" he says quietly.

On a sniffle, I say, "Hmm?"

Sliding one hand from my back, slowly down my arm, he holds out my hand and interlaces our fingers. "Dance with me?"

I rear back enough to meet his eyes. He's grinning, but there's a blush on his cheeks. A look, I'm starting to learn, that he wears when he's nervous. "Okay?"

Tucking me close in his grasp, Ren brings our joined hands to his chest. As he sways us, he hums softly in my ear. It's warm and low. No melody I recognize, but it doesn't matter. It's beautiful all the same.

"You got ahead of me," he says quietly. "Trying to do a dip before I've even asked you to dance."

Fresh tears spill down my cheeks. "Søren."

"Yes, Francesca."

A long, silent moment holds between us as an unfamiliar force churns from the core of my body. A powerful, surging, unstoppable *something*, it roars through my chest, tearing through my heart. A lock slipping into place, it settles with a small, quiet, irrevocable *click*.

The door of my heart swings open, and out tumbles the most terrifying handful of words.

Inside me, the irrefutable truth that clatters into place.

I love Ren.

That knowledge makes me feel free, weightless, as if Ren let go of me right now, I'd catch on the sea breeze and float serenely to the sky.

"What is it, buttercup?"

I turn my head enough to playfully sink my teeth into his pec. "You've got me all tied up. No nicknames when I can't defend myself."

He smiles down at me, slowing our dance until we're still but for the wind that swirls around us, whipping our hair and clothes.

Ren dips his head and kisses me. A soft, searing sweep of his lips. Gentle and cherishing.

"I love you, Frankie." Those wintry eyes search mine as he holds me close. "I've loved you for a long time. And I know maybe that's not how you feel, and that's okay. But I needed you to know. This. You and me . . ." He sweeps back the hair tangling across my face. "It means everything to me."

I nod, trying to swallow the lump of emotion in my throat. But all I can manage, as I cling to this man, is the faintest, tear-choked "Me too."

Three subsequent games. One more at home, two in Denver. Zero wins. Lots of great sex. Lots of cuddles and talks, sneaking into hotel rooms and lounging on the couch. But the team's mood is somber, and mine's not much better.

There's a tickle in my throat, an ache settled in my joints. My body's warm and slow. I'm either preparing for the flare of the year or I'm coming down with something. Which I'll be damned if I tell Ren about.

Sitting on the deck, Ren rubs his forehead as he reads the sports page on his phone. His brow is knitted, his jaw tight. And for some reason I feel responsible.

"What if I jinxed you?"

Ren glances up from his phone. "What?"

"Since we started sleeping together, you've lost three in a row."

Ren chuckles to himself and takes a sip of coffee. But when he sees my face, he sets down his cup with a clunk and leans in. "You're serious? Practical, rational Frankie is blaming her sex life for a team that's just not having its best play-offs."

I shrug and bite into my bagel. "I don't know. I mean, you guys suck. *Bad.*"

"Gee. Thanks."

Setting my hand on his massive thigh, I squeeze affectionately and glance out to the sand, where Pazza bolts toward the water, barking at the waves.

"Not you, specifically, Zenzero," I say quietly, pulling out a tissue and blowing my nose. Ren and Rob are basically the only thing holding the team together. Maddox is still out sick—not that he was playing spectacularly—but he took down a few other key players, too, with whatever contagion gave him a lung infection.

Ren glances over at me, rests a hand to my forehead, then cheek. "You started sniffling in your sleep last night. You haven't stopped this morning."

"I'm fine." I brush his hand away lightly and sip my coffee. "Seasonal allergies."

He makes a noncommittal noise. Turning slightly to face me, Ren sets one leg on his knee and rests an arm along the back of my chair. His hand slides around my neck and massages.

I hiss at the pain-pleasure of his touch. I ache everywhere, and while I don't have a fever, I'm thinking it's only a matter of time. Not that Ren knows that. Because if he did, he'd tuck me in and insist on staying home and taking care of me. That's not happening, not when tomorrow's game five of the series, and if he doesn't show to practice today or the game tomorrow night, Coach will disown him, *and* they'll definitely lose.

When Ren slides his thumb up my neck toward the tender base of my skull, I almost cry uncle and confess how shitty I feel, but for once, my mother's number lighting up my phone to FaceTime is a welcome interruption.

"Gotta take this," I mutter, leaning out of his grip.

Ren makes no move to leave.

I lift my phone and raise my eyebrows. "You mind?"

He smiles, settling back into his chair with his coffee. "Not at all. Please take it. I'd like to meet her."

Sputtering, I nearly drop my phone. "I. What? Ren—"

"You're going to miss her call, snickerdoodle."

I roll my eyes and swipe to answer her. "Hi, Ma." Ren's mouth quirks. I smack his chest. "My New York comes out when I talk to her. Don't you dare make fun of me."

"Love bug, I would never."

I practically growl at him.

"Frankie?" my mom yells. She's staring down her nose through her glasses, walking through the kitchen.

"Ma. Sit down. You make me nauseous moving around like that."

"Nice to talk to you, too," she says. "Glad you're alive. It's been a while."

Ren lifts an eyebrow in censure. I stick my tongue out at him.

"Don't stick your tongue out at me, young lady—"

"Ma, it wasn't for you. It was for him."

"Oooh," she croons. "A man? Finally. I told Gabby I thought you were going for that friend of yours with all the fancy piercings, but she told me you don't bark up that tree."

"Gabby would be correct. Besides, Lorena's way out of my league." Sighing, I swivel the phone so the camera faces Ren. "Ma, this is Ren Bergman. Ren, this is my mom, Maria Zeferino."

He waves hi and her jaw drops. "Jesus," my mom whispers. Ren glances nervously from me back to her.

I lean toward him and grin. "Where do you think I got my love of gingers, Zenzero?"

Ren turns a brilliant red. Clearing his throat, he smiles at her. "Nice to meet you, Mrs. Zeferino. Frankie's said wonderful things about you."

Like hell I have. I dig my heel into his bare foot, but he doesn't seem to care.

Ma cocks an eyebrow. "Nice to meet you, Ren. But I doubt that highly. I drive her crazy. It's why she moved a country away from me."

I roll my eyes, bringing the phone back to facing only me. "I moved cross-country for a kick-ass job and mellow weather."

She waves her hand. "How's your health?"

"It's fine," I say through gritted teeth.

"You exercising? Taking your meds? Getting your bloodwork and X-rays—"

"Ma. I said it's fine."

She squints at me. "You look thin. And your nose is red. Are you sick?"

Ren makes a disapproving noise. "See?" he whispers. "I told you."

I glare at him. "And I told you," I hiss back, "that I don't need another fussy mother. So, back off, Ren."

He sits straight, eyes narrowed. On an abrupt stand, he sweeps up his coffee and goes inside.

Guilt settles in my stomach. I shouldn't have snapped at him, but damn, is it aggravating to be talked to so paternalistically. I'm a grown woman. It's my body to manage.

Or mismanage.

And tough shit. I warned him this would be an issue, that it was a sensitive and unwavering boundary for me.

As I hear him through the open screen door, banging around in the kitchen and muttering to himself, my stomach tightens in unease; weight presses on my chest that no deep breathing resolves. I'm definitely getting sick. Just with what, I'm not sure.

Tell him. Trust him.

I can't. Because I can't trust him to be objective. He'll toss aside his responsibilities and then down that terrible resentment road we'll go. I'll drag him, he'll go along happily . . . until he's miserable, and I'm left with someone who has to choose between me and a fulfilling life. I won't. Fucking. Do it.

"You done?" Ma says.

My head snaps down as I peer at my phone. "Sorry. My mind wandered."

"Tell me where it went." She leans in and sets her cheek in one hand. "I've got all day."

Searching her eyes, I bite my lip in hesitation. I love my mother. And before I was always a checklist of health issues, I felt like we were close. Has time whittled away that barrier between us? Can I open up to her and unburden myself?

Her eyes are like mine, and they brighten as she smiles. "I know I can be overbearing," she says. "But I called because I miss just talking. That's all. I trust you to take care of yourself, okay?"

Oh, the guilt.

"I won't nag or poke you about anything health related," she says. "I promise. I'll just listen. And we can talk about other stuff."

With a glance over my shoulder, I see Ren wandering the kitchen, presumably cooking breakfast. Regret tugs at my heart. I just pushed him away. I've become a bit of an expert at that, haven't I? As if I need further proof, I peer at my mother, the woman who loves me imperfectly, but loves me nonetheless. Who after our mutual hurts and blunders, I've slowly, systematically withdrawn from.

Leaning close to her image on my phone, I clear my throat, searching Ma's eyes, the ones she gave me. "I miss you," I tell her unsteadily.

Her gaze softens behind her glasses. She sniffles. "I miss you, too, honey. But you look like sunshine and seventy degrees almost year-round suits you. So that makes missing you a little easier, knowing you're happy where you are. You are happy, right?"

I nod. "Yeah, I am." Glancing over my shoulder, I see Ren, at the window, eyes down. As if he senses me watching him, he glances up. Our eyes lock. I offer him a tentative, apologetic smile. He gives me one back, then turns and disappears deeper into the kitchen.

"I feel like I'm seeing something I shouldn't," Ma says wryly.

Breaking my distraction, I refocus on her. "Sorry. I snapped at him, and I wanted him to know I was sorry. And . . ." I sigh. "I feel like I owe you a sorry, too. I've been distant. Gabby nags me every time we talk to just have it all out with you, but I never know where to begin, Ma."

She nods. "I know, honey. I feel the same way. But maybe we can just talk for now, then work our way toward the hard stuff eventually, huh?"

"Okay," I say tentatively. "Well, what do you want to talk about?"

Ma settles into her chair and sweeps up her coffee. "That hunk of redhead love you were all cozy with when I called."

I scowl at her.

"Now, don't deny you've got yourself a big hot cup of ginger tea." She wiggles her eyebrows. "And while you're at it, spill."

TWENTY-EIGHT

Ren

Playlist: "Let's See What The Night Can Do,"
Jason Mraz

"I'm sorry again about this morning," Frankie says quietly.

I switch lanes and smile over at her when it's safe to. "It's okay, Frankie. I get why you were upset. I channeled my inner dad on you a bit."

Her hand plays idly with my hair at the nape of my neck. She has these little ways that she touches me—twirling my hair around her fingers, sliding my palm against hers in a steady rhythm—that make me feel like she's wrapped me into her sensory habits, her need to move and touch, and I can't find a word to explain how much that means to me. Emotion hitches in my throat as she leans and presses a kiss to my neck.

"Zenzero," she says against my skin. "Why won't you tell me where we're going?"

Because it's expensive, and after googling the restaurant, you'll veto it.

My grip tightens on the steering wheel as her hand drifts up my thigh. Dangerously high.

"Hey. No seductive interrogation tactics while I'm driving."

She laughs and nips my neck.

"It's nothing revolutionary," I manage, willing myself to stay focused on the road. "Only somewhere to eat that's completely private, so nobody will bug us and there'll be no bad press before you quit the team."

Frankie sits back suddenly and lets loose a harsh, wet cough. Tugging her sweater tighter around her, she stares out the window and idly rubs her throat. Seasonal allergies, my ass. She's coming down with something, probably that crud Maddox spread around the team, and she's hell-bent on denying it.

"Someplace private to eat is not very specific," she says. "Am I dressed up enough for it?"

I glance over at her, then back to the road. Beneath her gray sweater she wears a black maxi-dress that pops against her skin. The neckline of her dress scoops over her breasts, revealing mouth-watering cleavage that her fidget necklace barely hides. Evening sunlight dances off of her collarbones, the tip of her nose, and brings out the flecks of bronze in her hazel irises.

"You're perfect," I tell her.

Snorting, she laughs. "I'm far from perfect, but if you mean I'm appropriately dressed, then I'll take it."

As I turn into the private valet parking entrance, Frankie sets a hand on my thigh again, her voice softer. "But while we're on the subject, you look pretty perfect yourself, Zenzero."

I glance down. I'm wearing charcoal gray slacks and a white dress shirt, sleeves cuffed, no tie. "You dressed me."

"I did. I have excellent taste. And my muse is very handsome. Inspiration wasn't hard to come by."

I smile as I turn off the engine. "Thank you, honey cakes."

"They get worse and worse," Frankie mutters. She cranes forward, glancing up at the building's brick facade. "What *is* this place?"

"A well-kept secret."

She turns and gives me a narrow-eyed frown. "This better not be some practical joke of a surprise party. I hate surprises."

"I know you do, Frankie. It's just you and me."

Finally.

After a quick elevator ride, we're led to our table overlooking the water. Frankie settles into her seat, peering about analytically as I scooch in her chair. "This place feels expensive, Søren."

"Francesca. Please don't do this."

She raises her eyebrows. "Don't do what?"

"Give me hell for taking you somewhere half-decent and private to eat." I drop into my chair and open my menu. "We cook virtually every night. Chinese is the rare splurge. I can spring for a meal out."

She mumbles under her breath, lifts her menu, and opens it.

Peering around, I take in the space, then Frankie, who glances away from her menu and stares out at the water, a private smile tilting her lips. It's exactly what I wanted, what I thought Frankie would want. The ocean behind us. Seclusion. Heat lamps so she doesn't get cold. And her favorite kind of food.

She returns to the menu, promptly drops it, and stares at me, slack-jawed. "It's all burgers."

"That's the idea."

"It's like you're trying to get laid or something, Zenzero."

I smile as she bites her lip and tries not to smile back at me.

Suddenly, her face turns to a frown. "We need to talk about something," she says seriously.

My heart leaps off a cliff and free-falls into panic. "Oh? What's that?" Worst-case-scenario thoughts blitz my mind with stunning clarity.

She's not satisfied.

This isn't working for her.

She wants to be just friends.

"I don't know your middle name." Her frown deepens. "And I

realized it's one of those details you're supposed to know when you're serious about someone. I feel like I failed because I didn't ask you that. That and a few other things."

No longer plummeting to its doom, my heart flips and lands in a pool of sweet relief. I drop my head on a rough exhale.

Frankie doesn't notice. "I realized in the shower earlier," she continues, "I've shared more life with you, had more sex with you than anyone else, talked about worldviews and politics, but I don't know your middle name. I know you want to stay with the team for as long as you can, that you want to miss the woods as much as you love the ocean, that you want a piano in your house, but I don't know your middle name. And I should. Am I making any sense?"

Finally, my body's calmed from the free fall my heart just took, and I glance up, meeting her eyes.

"What is it?" she asks, looking at me in confusion.

"Oh, I just catastrophized. I thought you were breaking up with me for a minute."

Her mouth drops. She blinks rapidly, and then she bursts into laughter. Hysterical, *loud* laughter. "How?" she says between fits of laughter. "How could you think that?"

"I don't actually find the internal panic I just went through *that* funny, Frankie."

She sobers. "I'm sorry. It isn't funny, you're right. It's just that, Ren . . . I'm happy with you. *So* happy." Her features grow guarded. "Are *you* happy?" she asks quietly.

I slide my hand into hers and tangle our fingers. "Far beyond happy, Frankie. I'm over the moon. Every day."

A small, pleased smile warms her face. "Good." After a beat of silence, she pulls away and takes a sip of her water. "All right, fill in the gaps for me, then. Middle name. Cough it up."

"Isak. Yours is Chiara."

"How did you . . . ?" She gives me a look. "You totally scoped out my ID, didn't you?"

I smooth my napkin, straighten my knife. A man needs a little dignity in life.

Taking my nonanswer for the answer that it is, she moves on. "Do you really want five kids?"

Glancing up, I meet her eyes, trying to trace the route of our conversation, which isn't always clear when Frankie and I talk. She doesn't do all the pit stops and detours that "typical" dialogue takes. Sometimes I need a minute to catch up, but I find it wildly refreshing to speak so directly with her.

"It's a ballpark," I tell her. "I'm open to discussion. You?"

"A couple at least."

I stare at her, finding it easy to picture her as a mom, and a good one, at that. Playful, empathic, affectionate. I can see her sitting near the water in a comfy beach chair, reading a book with a baby sleeping on her chest. That picture, that moment in my mind's eye, it's something I want with a physical hunger.

Frankie smiles and slips her legs between mine under the table. "I think you like me, Zenzero, conversational speed bumps and all."

God, if she only knew how much. "I more than like you, pumpkin patch. I love you, exactly as you are."

She smiles and peers down at her menu again. "That's the disturbing thing."

After we order, we watch the sun set, and I smile as she moans and sighs over a gourmet burger. When the server clears our plates and leaves a dessert menu, Frankie picks the chocolatiest confection, then sits back with a sigh in her chair. The sea breeze sweeps her hair up and drags dark strands across her face. Frankie deftly tugs them back and glances at me, catching me staring at her.

"Hi," she says quietly.

I grin and stretch my legs farther beneath the table, tangling with hers. "Hi."

"This has been really nice, Ren. Thank you."

"Good." I lift my water in a toast to her. I'm not touching alcohol, not when I'll be driving her home. "Congratulations on law school, sugarplum."

Her lips twitch as she lifts her root beer. "Thanks, pudding pop."

The waiter clears his throat, looking like he might have gotten more than he bargained for when he took this exclusive two-top. Frankie glances away, hiding her smile by sipping her drink.

Accepting the check, I pull out my wallet and hand him my card. "Thanks."

The best kind of server, our waiter simply sets the dessert right in front of Frankie, slips one candle in it, which he lights, then silently disappears.

"Huh." Frankie reaches for something on the middle of the table. "What's this?"

I watch her pick up the fortune cookie paper as if it's in slow motion. It must have fallen out of my wallet. I didn't mean for her to see that. Not yet.

Faster than you'd think, she snatches it up and spins the worn paper between her fingers. But I'm fast, too, and my hand clamps over it.

Her eyes narrow at me. "What?"

"It's . . . private."

"A private fortune?" She tries to pull her hand away, but my grip is solid. "What's the big deal?"

"Please, Frankie. It's a souvenir of sorts. It's special to me."

She frowns. "Why won't you let me read it?"

The lightbulb goes on over her head. Her eyes widen. "Souvenir?

Is this from that night? When you came over and ate all my Chinese?"

"Excuse me. We split that food fair and square, Miss Revisionist History. In fact, I think you stole one of my wontons, maybe even two."

Wrangling the paper out of her grip, which I feel a little bad for—late in the day, Frankie's hands get stiff and, in her words, "sloppy"—I flip open my wallet and slide it back inside.

I'm saving that fortune paper for a day in the future. One involving a sparkly ring and me hiving with anxiety.

Giving me a scowl, Frankie lifts a fork to dig into her cake, then pauses as she sees the solitary candle. Her face blanks. "Why the candle? It's not my birthday," she says.

"I told him we were celebrating you. I think he misunderstood."

Frankie peers at the flame as if it holds a secret. "What do I do?"

I rub my knee against hers, knowing touch is sometimes all she needs for a little reassurance.

"It might not be your birthday, Frankie. But you can always make a wish."

She glances up at me and holds my gaze. The sunset blazes in her eyes, sets her skin on fire. I soak in every detail I can when she closes her eyes and blows out the tiny flame with one powerful breath.

As smoke curls in the air, my heart says its own wish, too.

———

Once we park in my garage and get inside, Pazza's thrilled to see us. Frankie doesn't even scold her when she jumps up and tries to lick me. She's far away, her brow furrowed. Gears turning.

Following Pazza out onto the deck, Frankie watches her run

down to the sand and wander the shore, sniffing and digging. I'm right behind her, plugging my phone into the speakers.

Frankie turns and glances up at me, then at the speakers. "What's with the music?"

I bow, straighten, and offer my hand. "Madam. May I have this dance?"

The line between her brows vanishes as she belly laughs. "You were totally born in the wrong century." Stepping closer, she fists my shirt, yanking me close. I cup her face, leaning to kiss her. "Wait." Frankie sets her hand on my chest.

I pull back. "What?"

"You shouldn't kiss me—" She pauses, biting her lip.

"Last I checked, allergies aren't contagious, Francesca."

"Don't 'Francesca' me, Søren," she grumbles. After a beat of silence, she meets my eyes. "Okay, I might have a small cold, all right? Now, please, *please* don't go nursemaid on me. This is what I meant that day when we got lunch. When this all started, Ren."

I hold her eyes, then press a kiss to her cheek. Closer to the corner of her mouth.

"Ren—"

"If I don't have whatever this sickness is by now, I'm not getting it, Frankie. Just let me kiss you." I sweep my lips over hers, a faint teasing touch as my thumbs gentle her cheeks. She tastes sweet like chocolate, and her lips are decadently soft.

As I deepen the kiss, the breeze wraps around us, a blanket of sea air and the faint wisp of flowers. Frankie drapes her arms around my neck and leans in.

"You have my heart, Søren Bergman," she whispers against my neck. "Please, please be careful with it."

I wrap my arms tight around her, swaying her with me.

"Always." Pressing a soft kiss to the corner of her mouth, I slide my grip down to her waist, my other hand tangling with hers. "Same goes for you, Francesca. Or else I'll be reduced to writing maudlin amateur poetry."

She sets her head on my shoulder and sighs happily as I lead us in a slow sway across the deck. "Such a good dancer," she mutters. "You're annoyingly good at everything you do."

"Well, not everything. I can't do a backbend to save my life. I'm horrible at long division. And I'm still learning how to be good at something else."

Frankie peers up at me. "Like what?"

I snort softly, feeling a blush creep up my cheeks. "You're going to make me say it?"

"Ohhhh." She waves a hand. "No worries there. You're the best lover I've ever had, Zenzero. Hands down."

My heart twists. Not out of an ego boost, but because I tell myself it has much more to do with what Frankie *feels* when we're together. In her heart, not just in her body. That for her, as it is for me, it's not just sex. It's making love.

"I'm sorry if I haven't told you," she whispers. "It's not for lack of me thinking it. A lot. Frequently."

I press a soft kiss to her lips.

Her eyes meet mine, and she stares at me curiously. "You know how you told me to get into Shakespeare Club, you have to recite verses that mean something to you?"

"Mm-hmm."

"If I were standing at the entrance for your meeting, determining whether or not *you* got in, what would you say to me?"

The wind sends a swirl of dark hair across her face. I slip it safely behind her ear, tracing my fingers down the shell of her ear, the smooth line of her neck. "Francesca, are you trying to say you'd like to be wooed?"

She smiles up at me. "I was attempting to be coy. How'd I do?"

"Nailed it." I pull her closer, feeling her heart beat hard against my chest. "Let's see. Ah, just the thing."

Clearing my throat, I search her eyes. "'Doubt thou the stars are fire, doubt that the sun doth move, doubt truth to be a liar, but never doubt I love.'" I peer down at her, giving her a soft kiss. "How's that?"

Frankie's smile deepens as she kisses me back. I hold her close in my arms under the night sky's canopy of fiery stars.

TWENTY-NINE

Frankie

Playlist: "My Body Is a Cage," Arcade Fire

There's a restless energy among the team. Ren's features are un-characteristically tight, like he's only half-present, distracted with worry. Worry that I hope isn't directed at me. Even though I'm a fair candidate for it. I feel like shit stuck to the bottom of a beat-up sneaker.

I went to bed last night feeling under the weather and woke up knowing I was heading straight for the eye of the storm. My chest is heavy. I keep stifling a wet cough in the crook of my arm. And when I used the restroom just ten minutes ago, my pee was dark, my skin sallow as I stared at my reflection over the sink. I know I need to drink water, but I can barely get it past my throat.

Worst part is, I'm not even the saddest-looking one in the room. Andy's quiet—which he never is—Tyler's cranky, Lin's heart's not in it. Rob's got a scowl going, which my memory has filed away under the label "I had a fight with the wifey," and if François were any more stressed, I'd slip him one of my emergency Ativan.

Like always, the team's gathered in a warehouse corner of the arena, where trucks back in with all kinds of stock you wouldn't think is necessary but is apparently vital to running a sports rink. It's where the guys do their usual soccer ritual that's just supposed to keep them limber, connected, and distracted before they suit up for the game.

Their version of soccer isn't a game, per se. It's just the guys in their warm-ups, circled around, volleying the ball. The sole aim of the exercise is to not let the soccer ball hit the ground. It makes you careful with your touches, aware of your teammates. It's a smart pregame activity.

They're just sucking at it.

Ren stands on the opposite side of the room, amid the circle, a head taller than either guy flanking him, hands on his hips. He's staring at me, clearly lost in thought. I tip my head and jerk my chin. *Pay attention.*

When Kris drops the ball, Ren finally blinks and breaks away from watching me.

Rob sighs and scoops up the ball. "Again."

"Why?" Tyler says. "We're losing tonight, at which point the play-offs are over, and you know it."

Ren drops his hands and gestures to Rob. Rob volleys it to him. As Ren chests it, then easily uses his thigh to send it back to Rob, he yells, "*Scapegrace!*"

Rob's eyes narrow as the ball sails his way, but when he heads it toward Lin, a grin lights his face as he hollers, "*Rapscallion!*"

Half of the guys' gazes swivel over their shoulders to me. I studiously focus on my phone so they don't feel intruded on. I'm having a hard time focusing my eyes, and out of my peripheral vision, I can see them all passing some kind of inscrutable look among themselves, like they've been caught doing something they shouldn't.

I cough thickly into my arm as Lin says his word, so I miss it. But when François cracks it toward Andy, his bellowed oath echoes in the room: "*Base-court apple-john!*"

Lin snorts. Tyler doubles over in hysterics, and Andy flies toward the ball, saving it from touching the floor. Juggling it, he settles it on his foot, then stares at Kris, deadly serious. *"Mewling cut-purse."*

Laughter erupts in the room, the ball starts flying, not once touching the ground, as shoulders drop and frowns dissolve. I watch the ball travel in a psychedelic blur across the space as stars dance in the corner of my vision. The room's warmer, my labored breaths a refrain as it tilts and spins beneath me.

I take a step back and brace myself against the wall, rubbing a hand over my face. My hand comes away damp. I'm sweating. Clearing my throat, I try to take a slow breath, and squint, one-eyed, hoping it clears my vision.

For a moment, the world seems clear, and I can see how different the atmosphere is in the space now. As if a switch was flipped, the room's mood is shades brighter, like the sun bursting over land the moment it escapes a cloud.

The oaths just keep coming, their laughter swelling in volume and complexity like a swarm of bees. These guys either all picked up on Ren's cursing creativity over the past three years, or they've turned into giant Shakespeare dorks, too. Whatever the explanation, the effect is the same. Morale restored. Spirits lifted.

God, the brilliance. Ren did what he always has—brought the joy, made people feel better. And this is why he's instrumental to the team. This is why, as my legs buckle and I sink to the floor, I can only hope he's too busy to notice that not even his miraculous sunshine can save this little cloud from being swallowed up in the storm.

Without opening my eyes, I already know where I am. I know by the smell, the scratchy sheets, the threat of fluorescents nearby. Maybe a bathroom light left on, the door wedged open.

The fucking hospital.

When I take a jagged breath in, my lungs feel less soupy than they did, however long ago that was, when the warehouse went sideways and my legs turned to goo. I have no concept of time.

I can feel my hip throbbing like a son of a bitch. I lick my lips and am surprised to feel they aren't chapped. I feel the warmth of a calloused palm pressed to mine, long fingers wrapped possessively around my hand.

Ren.

My eyes blink open, slide right, toward the hand that he holds. I smile involuntarily at the sight of him, sleeping. Slouched low in those wildly uncomfortable hospital recliners, his mouth faintly open, smudges under his eyes.

I'm weak. I can feel that. My body feels heavy, and I already want to go back to sleep, but I want Ren to know I'm okay even more.

My nose itches. I scratch it and bump clumsily into an oxygen cannula. My hand aches where the hep-lock is taped on, where the needle sends God-knows-what into my system. Antibiotics.

Saline. Steroids. Pain relievers.

The prescription list is written in scraggly marker on the whiteboard at my feet. I can't read it for shit. I just know it's long. Ren shifts in the chair, stays asleep, and I watch him. I've watched him sleep before, and maybe that sounds weird. But sometimes I wake up before him and watch dawn paint his face, cast shadows over his cheekbones, his soft lips, that smooth brow, relaxed in sleep. His brow isn't smoothed now. It's furrowed. He's worried.

I try to squeeze his hand but can barely do it. Clearing my throat, I rasp, "Ren."

His eyes snap open, dart my way, then widen. Sitting upright, he stands and bends over me, cupping my face. "Hey," he says. His voice is unsteady. His eyes red-rimmed.

"I'm okay," I whisper.

He nods. Blinks, eyes wet with unshed tears. I try to lift my arms to wrap around him, offer him comfort, but they're too heavy.

My voice feels raw, but I clear my throat and croak out, "Come here, Zenzero."

A sound breaks from him as he leans closer, rests his head in the crook of my neck. I turn my head and kiss his temple. His arms slip carefully between me and the mattress. He sighs, slow and heavy. The sound of relief.

"Frankie." It's all he says, but I feel what he means, love and worry braided with my name.

When he pulls away, he sits and drags the chair closer. After smoothing back my hair, he slides the cannula back where it's supposed to hook around my ear.

"How long have I been out?" I whisper.

He focuses on my hair, his fingers making gentle work of its tangles. I'm sure I look like double-microwaved hell.

"Forty-eight hours."

I lift my eyebrows. "Impressive." Clearing my throat again, I grope for the button to raise myself up a bit. "How'd the game go?"

Ren drops his hand from my hair, squeezes my hand. "We lost."

"I'm sorry, Ren—"

"Good morning, sunshine!" Lorena stands, framed in the doorway, reading my thoughts, seeing the frustration, the embarrassment.

The helplessness.

Crossing to the other side of the bed, she smacks her lips to my forehead. "I won't even ask. I can tell you feel like shit."

Dropping to the foot of the bed, she starts massaging my legs. I groan because it feels amazing, and I also hate that the people who love me know me this well. I feel weak and needy.

"I heard you made quite the dramatic exit." She gives me a saucy grin.

I glare at her. "Why are you here again?"

Ren swallows his smile, hiding it behind a fist and clearing his throat.

"Because you have double-lung pneumonia," Lo says, "and you're one of mine. Because I love you, and when we're healing, we need all the love we can get."

Ren brings my hand to his cheek, kisses my palm, then sets it against his beard. Reflexively, I curl my fingers into the soft hairs, scrape my nails along his scruff.

Lo sighs. "Well, I'll leave you two lovebirds. I'm gonna go bug your nurse. Boss somebody around." Standing, she kisses me again on the forehead and pats my leg. "Welcome back, baby."

Ren watches her walk out, then gently stands and shuts the door behind her.

I stare at him as he moves, loving the way simple clothes drape beautifully on his body. Ball cap pulled low. Jeans that are dark and worn, a weathered blue T-shirt that brings out the ice in his eyes and the copper in his hair. When he sits, he strokes my cheek with the back of his knuckles.

I clear my throat roughly, then lick my lips. Ren reaches reflexively for the hospital tray and sweeps up a lip balm. Uncapping it, he swipes it over my mouth, then pops the cap back on.

"You did that?" I ask. My voice sounds watery.

"Pretty much the only thing I *could* do was make sure you didn't wake up with cracked lips." His smile is faint. "Frankie. Why didn't you tell me how bad you were feeling?"

I search his eyes. "I knew you'd worry. I didn't want to pull you away from the game, from the best chance of winning."

His eyes tighten at the corners. "So you decided you'd make that choice for me?"

Shifting in the bed, I try to buy my hip some relief. "I know you, Ren. This way, you got to play the game, and I got to have the peace of mind that I wasn't a roadblock. This is what I talked about when we agreed to give a relationship a chance. I don't want to be a point of resentment. I don't want my health stuff to prevent you from doing your work and being successful."

Ren just stares at me. "Frankie, you're more important than a hockey game. Unequivocally."

"Maybe one game. But this happens to me, Ren. I catch shit because my immune system hates me, and my meds don't help. Trust me, it won't be the last time. Down the line, you'll be glad that I keep this stuff to myself."

He shakes his head, blinking rapidly. "I . . . I'm . . . Are you *serious*?"

I frown at him. "Absolutely. Tell me how the hell you would have felt if you didn't play that game and they lost. If you sat next to me in the hospital, useless, while I slept in a drugged stupor with a perfectly curable issue, and you watched your team struggle and fail without you. In the back of your head you would have been wondering if you should have been there, if, with your help, they would have won, thinking 'if only Frankie hadn't gotten sick—'"

"That's the last thing I'd think."

I laugh bitterly, but it's complicated by a coughing jag. Ren pours a cup of water, plops a straw in it, and holds it to my mouth. I drink half of it and drop back on my pillow with a sigh.

His face is taut, his jaw clenched.

"Why are you angry?" I ask, confident I've read *this* emotion correctly.

He whips his head toward me, pinning me with those wintry eyes that feel particularly cold at the moment. "Because what you're saying is bullshit." The word snaps in the air. Swear words really do have more weight when a person uses them rarely.

He stares at me, unblinking. "I *was* here with you. I'm the one who had half an eye on you and caught you before you nearly cracked your head on the concrete. I'm the one who knew what to do. I'm the one who wouldn't let anything come between you and me until I knew that you were okay and that you were going to wake up."

I stare at him in disbelief. "You missed the game."

"Of course I missed the game, Frankie!" He sits back and stares at me, stunned. "How could you even—"

"I told you that's the *last* thing I ever wanted!" I yell hoarsely. "I didn't need you here, Ren."

He leans in, a breath away from me. "*I* needed to be here."

"Exactly. This is *your* trip. And every time you choose my health problems over your own life, it will be your trip, too. Then, when it builds up, when you make these choices, time and again, you'll resent *me* for it. If you didn't act like a lovesick idiot every time I got a cold—"

"Double. Lung. Pneumonia," he growls, ripping off his ball cap and slapping it onto the cart. "You were unconscious. Your oxygen saturation level was terrifying. This isn't a head cold, Francesca."

"You shouldn't have come." I drag myself up higher in the bed, trying to get some kind of ground over him. "You can't choose me and my health shit over your career and commitments. Eventually—"

Ren stands abruptly, sending the chair scraping across the room. Planting his hands on my hospital bed, he leans in, eyes locked on mine. "I will *always* choose you. And I will never resent you for it. That's what we agreed—that I would demonstrate what I just said with my actions. But apparently even *that's* impossible to trust. I have to be an asshole who leaves his critically ill girlfriend in the hospital to play a stupid hockey game to prove himself.

"Guess what, Frankie? I'm not that guy, and I never will be. If you can't trust me, after all that I've entrusted to *you*, showing you who I am and that I am a man of my word, then that really fucking hurts."

"You're making this about you," I counter. "You're letting emotion cloud your judgment. And this is how *I* will end up getting hurt. In the moment, you didn't want to feel guilty for not being with me. To avoid that, you stayed. But every time you do that, it'll feel a little bit less worth it. And every time, you will blame me a little bit more. Even though I'm telling you I don't need you here."

Ren pushes off the bed, pacing the room like a caged animal. Scraping his hands through his hair, he sweeps up his ball cap from the hospital cart and tugs it on, brim pulled low.

"I can't believe you're that cynical, Frankie. I can't believe you'd say that about me."

I stare up at him as hot tears spill from my eyes. "I'm not cynical. That's what happens, Ren."

"No, that's what *happened*. And it was wrong. But that wasn't me, Frankie. What about me? Don't I get a say in how this goes?"

His words land uncomfortably close to my heart.

Trust him. Believe him.

He takes one look at whatever face I'm making and sighs in defeat. "Because if not, how do I ever outstrip your past? No matter how much I reassure you that I will never resent you, that I will never consider you and my own happiness at odds, you don't believe me. I have to act how *you* think I should. I can't have my own needs in this relationship."

"That's not fair." My throat hurts from talking. I reach for the cup of water and Ren strides forward, helping me when I can't even hold up my arm long enough to get it.

I suck on the straw and peer at him as my eyes fill with fresh tears. Will he really always look at me like this, when I'm at my worst? Like he loves me, like my pain is as real to him as it is to me?

Like there's nowhere else that he'd rather be?

"How is that not fair?" he says quietly, setting down the cup.

"Ren, I'm just trying to say there's a compromise here. When I feel like this, you can take care of me in reasonable ways, but don't put your life on hold."

He shakes his head. "No. That's literally saying my love for you has to have conditions. I'm not okay with that. That's you trying to find a loophole so you don't have to trust me all the way."

I glare at him. "You're being so fucking condescending right now!"

"Frankie." Scrubbing his face, he sighs. "I understood becoming a couple to mean that, among other things, when either of us was hurting, we were no longer alone in that. So, I have a relationship to your pain. It's not mine, and I don't get to tell you what to do with it, but I get to choose to love you through it. And if and when you need care and comfort—which, like it or not, the past forty-eight hours, you did—I get to be the person who gives it to you. That's basically the *point* of a relationship. Isn't it?"

My jaw's tight. I feel pushed and cornered and talked down to, tired and sick and infuriatingly defeated. "Well, then we probably would have been better served discussing this philosophy of yours rather than middle names and numbers of kids over dinner. Because I'm not sure I agree with that."

His eyes narrow as he tips his head. "I was here because I *love* you. Partners who love each other are there for each other. You don't agree with that?"

Stubbornness draws the arrow. Wounded pride aims. Anger fires, fatally accurate. "I never said I loved you."

Ren opens his mouth, then freezes. Slowly he straightens and stares down at me. I can see his gears turning. It's playing with semantics. We both know I've meant it, even though I have yet to say those exact words.

His jaw tics. His eyes glisten as he stares at me. "What are you saying?"

It hurts like hell, looking at him. Knowing that I'm pushing away the best person I've ever had in my life, but that's the problem. I don't belong with someone as good as Ren. He's not detached enough, not selfish enough. His boundaries are too lax, his impulse for intimacy too quick.

The truth is there, like it's always been. Sunshine and storms share the sky, but never together. They brush, tangential, fleeting moments of breathtaking beauty—the burning, life-giving sun piercing through a blackened sky—until it's over so quick, it makes you wonder if it ever happened at all.

"I'm saying you should leave, Ren."

He rears back like I've struck him. Blinking, he glances away, then down to the ground. "You don't mean that, Frankie. You're angry. And while I disagree with you, you're allowed to be angry with me. But I'm not leaving."

I shut my eyes, press my back into the bed, and swallow my tears. "Yes, you are."

"Frankie—"

"Get *out*."

It's silent for a long moment. Nothing but ambient noises—doors open and shut, the beep of a machine. I keep my eyes closed, hold my breath, and pray for the torturous moment to end.

Suddenly his voice is near my ear. "I'll give you time. But I'm not walking away from this, not for good. You deserve better than that. And I do, too."

I bite my tongue, tears slipping down my cheeks. Finally, I feel his heat, that clean, spicy scent, drift away. Long strides fade from the room before the door clicks shut.

And then I fall apart.

Not a minute later, Lo reenters my room and looks straight

from my tearstained face to Ren's empty chair. "Okay. What level of self-sabotage did we just activate?"

I dab my eyes with one hand, and with the other, I lift a sparkly painted middle finger.

"Grumpy meets glitter," she says. "I like that."

"It's been that way forever."

"Just like your piss-poor attitude."

I slam a fist into the bed and glare at her. "I sent him packing. I can send you, too."

"Ooh." She fakes a shiver. "I'm scared."

I clench my jaw and shut my eyes again. Closing the door behind her, Lo takes her time walking over to me.

"Actually," she says, "*you're* the one who's scared." My hands twist the sheets as Lo drags Ren's chair next to the bed and plops down on it. "The question is, what exactly are you scared of?"

When I don't answer her, she wraps her hand around mine and leans in. "Relationships aren't perfect, Frankie. They're living, breathing things. They have growing pains. They have highs and lows. They take trust and forgiveness. They don't require perfection or flawlessness. They just require two people who want to love each other and keep learning the best way to do that."

I open my eyes and slant her a sharp look. "Who needs the Hallmark Channel when I have you and Ren?"

Lo searches my face. "Oh, honey." She sighs and thumbs away my tears. "That's what you're scared of, huh? Being loved by that big redhead teddy of a lover who worships the ground you walk on?"

I wipe a stray tear angrily from my cheek. "I kicked him out, Lo. What did I do?"

"You reacted badly to being loved well."

"I love him," I sob, covering my face. "And I just made him leave."

"I know, Frankie. And that is what we have to work on. Because Ren doesn't need that shit in his life, and neither do you." Lo gently squeezes my hand. "So, what's the therapist say? When you've talked to her about him?"

"Well . . ." I clear my throat. "I haven't actually—"

"Oh, woman." Lo releases my hand. "You haven't talked to her about him."

I shake my head.

"Because you knew what she was going to remind you about, and you're too scared to own the truth she would have dropped on you."

I nod.

"Which is?" Lo presses.

"That I deserve love for being exactly who I am," I admit miserably. "That the person worthy of my love will love all of me."

Exactly what my therapist has told me. Exactly what I told Ren that night on the beach. I'm damn good at giving advice and shit at taking it.

Lo sits back in her chair and throws her feet on the bed. "That's right. So you've got to make a decision. If you believe you're lovable, you have to believe there's someone out there up for loving you. Isn't that him?"

"Yes," I whisper as I wipe away tears.

"No, you will never know if he's going to hurt you, not definitively. Guess what, Frankie? *Nobody* knows if love's going to hurt them. You simply have to take a chance."

My breath comes fast and short. I fist the sheets, trying to breathe. God, I fucked this up. So badly. I'm still terrified and insecure and insanely vulnerable, but she's right. *I'm* right. If anyone is going to love me, if there's anyone I want to love and be worthy of loving, it's Ren. And when he showed me how much he felt that way about me, I pushed him away. Because this is frightening. Beautifully, vulnerably frightening.

I try to smile at her. "It'll be fine. I'm okay."

She cocks an eyebrow. "Really? 'Cause you look like you're try-ing not to shit yourself."

I groan. "You know I can't smile on command."

"So why try with me?"

"Smiling conveys all-right-ness. I'm trying to show you that I can handle this."

"Hey." Lo squeezes my hand. "Yes, you're going to be all right. And yes, you can handle this. But guess what?"

"What?"

She smiles. "You don't have to do it alone."

Three weeks. Lots of bickering with Lo, who just finally left my place a few days ago, when she was confident that I wasn't going to pass out in the shower or spiral into another fit of anxious sobbing. Five tele-therapy sessions with my counselor to actually talk through my hang-ups about having a relationship.

I'm not fixed. I'm not perfect. And I never will be. But I'm healthy enough to travel and ready to be brave. I can only hope Ren will find that's enough for him.

At the airport, I sit in the terminal, phone pinched between my ear and shoulder.

"So, listen," Willa says over the line. "Word is Aiden showed up at the Love Shack—"

"I'm sorry, what?"

"The Love Shack," she says simply. "Trust me. Once you get to the A-frame, it will all be very clear."

"I'll be lucky if Ren doesn't spin me around in the road and tell me to go right back where I came from."

Willa snort-laughs. "Please. He's going to lose his shit with happiness when he sees you. The person he's going to send packing is Aiden."

"Just don't pull away as soon as you drop me off."

"Of course I won't," she says. "But I'm telling you, you have nothing to worry about—"

The flight attendant announces early boarding over the speaker, cutting through our conversation. Signing off with Willa, I stand and grin at the grannies who eyeball my cane and mutter "faker," loud and clear.

Even when your illness isn't invisible, people can still be blind to it. But I'm done being embarrassed or humiliated or defensive. I'm being me. Because that's enough. And for the first time in too many years, I know that I'm loved for exactly who I am. The person who reminded me of that waits for me in a little cabin in the woods. I can only hope he'll forgive and love me still.

THIRTY

Ren

Playlist: "The Night We Met," Lord Huron

"Easy." Aiden drops the axe and wipes a hand across his sweaty forehead. "What did that log ever do to you?"

I glance up, meeting my brother-in-law's gaze. "Just staying busy."

Aiden rolls his eyes. "Could you be any more tortured?"

"I didn't ask you here, Aiden. It's my stretch at the cabin, *my* time here that you're crashing."

My parents own an A-frame in Washington State, which is where I spent a lot of my childhood, up to my sophomore year of high school. We moved to LA because Dad got a great offer at UCLA Medical, and while I enjoy Southern California, I like coming back to the Pacific Northwest. Bundling up, seeing my breath in the air when I wake up. Surrounded by evergreens and deep blue sky.

The siblings all get use of the cabin, but the older ones have to come during our scheduled time and do maintenance to keep that privilege. My time is usually midsummer since my work schedule is most flexible then, but Ryder swapped with me and gave me this stretch of late spring when I essentially begged him.

"Bit of a theme I'm bumping into lately," Aiden says roughly. "I'm unwanted here. As I'm also unwanted in my own home. The one I worked really damn hard to buy and fix up." Aiden lifts the axe and swings, splitting a log in two. "Thank you for reminding me. Not that you've asked why I'm here or what's wrong."

"You're right," I grunt, hauling an armful of wood over to the stack and dropping it. "I haven't."

"Which is very unlike you," Aiden calls.

"Guess I turned over a new leaf."

I swing and split another log, feeling the ache in my muscles, the burn in my back. All I've done is try to exhaust myself around here. Otherwise, I can't sleep to save my life.

Three weeks.

Three weeks and those two words are still ringing in my head. *Get out.*

After I got home, I beat the hell out of the punching bag, cried in the shower—yes, you heard me, I cried—and then I took advantage of Ryder's willingness to trade times at the cabin and came straight here. If I spent another moment in my house with Pazza's chew toy lying on the floor or Frankie's scent all over my sheets, I was going to lose my mind.

Aiden just showed his punk butt up here two days ago, looking disheveled and under-slept. I didn't ask him what was going on with Freya because I didn't want to know. I have enough of my own problems.

In the hospital, I told Frankie I'd give her time, that I wasn't walking away for good. I'm about at the end of my rope with that waiting, though. I promised myself after a month, she was going to hear from me, see my face, and have to talk this out.

"You surly is weird. When you scowl, you look like Axel." Aiden drops to the ground and leans against a massive hemlock, sipping from his water between pants for air. "Shit, when did I get out of shape?"

"Happens when you work all the time."

He levels me with a look. "So, you *do* know why I'm here."

I glance at him over my shoulder before I turn and swing, splitting another log. "I have no idea why you're here. I just know you're a workaholic." Aiden's a professor at UCLA. He's actually the one responsible for pairing up Willa and Ryder when they were both his students, largely against their will at first. "You teach, grade, lecture, guest panel, publish constantly. When would you have time for exercise? Or anything else, for that matter."

Aiden's jaw tics. He has near-black hair, a shade darker than Frankie's, and three days' worth of scruff, a sharp contrast to his blue eyes and the dark circles below them. He looks angry and exhausted.

Welcome to the club, Aiden.

"Freya kicked me out."

My head snaps up. "She kicked you *out*?"

He sighs, eyes shut, head against the tree. "Say it again. I love hearing it repeated."

"Aiden, I don't have the capacity for your sparkling sarcasm. I've got my own . . ." I exhale roughly, feeling a swell of emotion tighten my throat. "I'm dealing with my own stuff. Say what you need, but I can't be your cuddle buddy right now. Call Ryder or something."

Aiden chucks his water at the ground. "What, so he can drive here and beat the snot out of me for hurting his sister? No, thanks. You're the listener in the family."

I drop my axe to the ground with a thud. "You hurt Freya?"

Aiden lifts his hands and leans away. "Not physically. Jesus, Ren, what do you think of me?"

"Doesn't matter. Emotional wounds are just as painful, sometimes more so."

Scrambling to stand, Aiden locks eyes with me. "I didn't mean to hurt her, Ren. I don't even know when it happened. All I know is that I got off track with her at some point. I've been busy lately, a little distracted.

"I missed something, I'm not sure what, but she's angry with me. *Really* angry. I begged her to talk it through, told her I wanted to fix it, but she said . . ." He scrubs a hand over his face and looks toward the water nearby. "She said she needed time. That she doesn't know if it can be fixed."

When he glances over at me, his eyes are red-rimmed and bloodshot. He looks shattered. "I can't lose her."

"So don't. Go home and fight for her."

He laughs but it breaks with emotion. "How do you fight for someone who doesn't want to be fought for? How do you repair something that they say is irrevocably broken?"

"You show up and demonstrate hope. You show her that, yes, things break, and they'll never be what they were before, but when you piece them together, they can still be beautiful, only different."

Thunder rumbles in the distance, followed by a fat raindrop that lands on my cheek and slides down.

Aiden sighs. "She's never been like this. I've never seen her so bleak. That light that's always in Freya's eyes was gone."

"So go put it back." I shove a handful of wood in his arms. "Quit hiding here and go fight for what you promised to fight for. Love for a lifetime, thick or thin, sickness and health . . ."

God, the words just rip through me, like a hot knife. I kick a pile of wood and storm off. Aiden's wise enough to leave me alone. I hear him dump his armful and traipse back into the cabin. For his own good, I hope it's to pack up and go home.

Droplets of rain become a waterfall. The sky blackens, thunder booms, and though I'm under a canopy of trees, I flagrantly avoid caution and wander through them, scooping up twigs and smacking anything I can like I would line up pucks for drills.

It's not enough. Circling back to the clearing, I pick up the axe and go at the dead tree Aiden and I started on this afternoon. My hands throb with fresh blisters ripping open, but I don't care. Better to hurt on the surface than deep inside.

Thunk. Thunk. Thunk.

A grunt leaves me with each swing. Until I can't even hold an axe anymore, and it falls at my feet. I groan, pressing my forehead to the tree. *How* did I lose her? I did exactly what I promised her I wouldn't. I made a choice that made her feel like a problem I prioritized rather than the person I love.

And "therein," as Shakespeare says, "lies the rub." Because I will always choose her. I will show up for her and care for her, the same way she's shown up and cared for me—with tenderness and empathy—but until Frankie stops seeing herself as a burden, she'll always see my choices through that lens of obligation. Meaning all I can do is hope that with some time and perspective, she'll see things differently. Once again, I'm left waiting.

I've waited for her before. You'd think I'd be able to cope, but it's like slowly suffocating without her, aching to know how she is and what she wants and if there's a chance in hell she'll finally see herself through *my* eyes.

Helplessness and anger possess my body. A raging cry surges through me as I yell into the woods, and lightning cracks through the sky. I jump back instinctively as the world flashes blue-white, revealing the outline of a woman down the drive to the main road. A torturous ghost of a woman.

Long hair plastered to her face, a short walking stick. She glances up and I choke when I recognize them—gold-green eyes, sun and earth, glowing in the light of the storm.

My heart jumps in my chest. "Frankie?"

She smiles and lifts her hand in a wave.

I say her name again. And again. Then, I'm running toward her, sprinting down the muddy road, breath filling my lungs for the first time in weeks. Laughter taking over breath. She's here. She came.

I stop, toe-to-toe with her as she looks up at me, shivering. Clumped dark lashes. Two curtains of wet, dark hair framing her face. "H-hi," she says shakily.

I swallow as a tear slides down my face. "How did you get here?"

"By plane. Then Willa," she says simply.

I glance past her shoulders and see Willa and Ry's Subaru pull out from the main road, followed by a stream of staccato honks. Staring down at Frankie, I shake my head and blink. This can't be real.

"Ren," she whispers. Stepping close, she cups my cheek. I jolt at the touch, and my heart takes off inside my chest. "I'm so sorry. You loved me and I threw it in your face. It . . . it scared me, Zenzero. I'm not going to lie. No one's ever loved me with no reservations."

I stare at her as rain pours down, as a love whose magnitude and depth and strength I can barely fathom wraps around my heart and pulls me toward her.

Her eyes search mine. "What I said at the hospital, it wasn't true. I have—I *do*—" On a shaky exhale, she steps closer. "I love you, Ren."

"Frankie. I love you," I whisper, cupping her face, so close, so soft.

"Still?" she asks warily. "Even after the past few weeks?"

"Still. Always. I'd wait lifetimes for you, Frankie. You would *always* be worth it."

She peers up at me. "Ask me."

"Ask you what?" I say dazedly.

"'Membership is contingent upon authenticity,'" she repeats, just as I told her months ago. "'Upon words spoken from the heart.' Ask me what I'm prepared to say."

I shake my head. "Frankie, you don't have to—"

"This." She brings her hand to rest over my heart, her eyes searching mine. "I want in. Lifelong privileges, ideally, but I'll settle for a month-to-month trial membership if necessary."

"Frankie, you already have it."

"'Love is not love,'" she blurts, wiping rain from her eyes and blinking up at me. "'Which alters when it alteration finds, or bends with the remover to remove. O no! It is an ever-fixed mark that looks on tempests and is never shaken.'"

"It's cold, you're still—"

"Please, Ren, let me tell you. Let me say what you mean to me." She inhales roughly, then shouts through rain and thunder, a rush of wind through the trees,

> "'Love's not Time's fool, though rosy lips and
>   cheeks
> Within his bending sickle's compass come;
> Love alters not with his brief hours and
>   weeks,
> But bears it out even to the edge of doom.'"

I hold her close and kiss her, then pull back enough so I can stare into those wide, deep eyes. "I love you. I always have." Wind rushes through the trees, wraps around us, as I tuck her close, as I press a kiss to her lips and whisper, "It was always only *you*."

Her cry breaks against my kiss, as I sweep her up in my arms, shielding her the best I can from the rain. She shrieks with laughter, clutching her bag and cane tight against us, throwing her head back to the open sky. Tears of heartache become tears of joy, as the clouds break for the determined sun.

I kiss Frankie and taste hope.

THIRTY-ONE

Ren

Playlist: "Like I'm Gonna Lose You,"
Meghan Trainor, John Legend

I watch firelight play on her skin, a wash of sunset watercolors. Gold and bronze, ruby shadows beneath her chin, the swell of her bare breasts. Frankie, naked on a couch dragged in front of the fire, is a vision of sated beauty.

Leaning past her, I poke the fire and throw on another log. Her hand slides up my back and tangles in my hair.

"That was nice of Aiden to make himself scarce," she says.

I laugh dryly. "It was a *requirement* that Aiden make himself scarce."

Which he did. He took one look at me holding Frankie, both of us sopping wet from the rain, laughing and love drunk, hiked his bag onto his shoulder, and muttered something about the airport as he walked out. I heard the tires of his rental catch on the gravel, then the noise of an engine fading in the rain. Then I tore off her clothes, set Frankie in a hot shower, and got down on my knees to show her how much I missed her.

Frankie smiles up at me. "I feel bad, but it's best he's not here. You are a noisy lover, Mr. Bergman."

A blush heats my cheeks as I glare down at her playfully. "I think you mean *passionate*, Ms. Zeferino."

Her smile deepens, broken only briefly by a lingering cough that sounds much better than it did three weeks ago.

I slide my finger along her dimple. "This has tortured me many months, Francesca. Years, to be precise."

"My dimple?" She slaps a hand over her cheek and my finger, looking self-conscious. "It's weird I don't have two, isn't it? It always bugged me because my mind craves symmetry."

"That's why I like it. You were always so neat and exact. Then you had this lopsided dimple that I only saw when you gave a rare smile. Even if it's an imperfection, it's beautiful to me."

Her face falls. "Some imperfections aren't so beautiful, Ren."

"No. Perhaps not." I slip my fingers through her hair. "But if they're yours, I love them. And you love mine."

She grabs my wrist, stilling my hand. "I need to explain this. I need you to understand."

Smoothing her cheek with my fingers, even as she holds my wrist captive, I stare down at her. "I'm listening."

Frankie holds my eyes as often as she can, before they dance to my body, the fire, my mouth, my hair. "Something my therapist said to me a few weeks ago . . . I've spent a lot of time thinking about it."

I wait for her, listening in silence but for the snap and pop of the cured wood roaring in the fireplace.

"She said you can't believe someone's love for you until you think that you're worthy of it," she says quietly, staring at the fire. "You have to love yourself. And in that way, I think you are far ahead of me, Ren."

"How do you mean?"

She sighs. "Some days I do feel cynical. Other days I'm optimistic. I think that on hard days, when everything hurts and everything feels difficult, I don't find myself very lovable. And I know it's not *true* that I'm not allowed to struggle, that I'm not lovable when I do, but it feels . . . *real*."

I pull her close.

Frankie blinks up at me, breathtakingly lovely, lit by the fire, bare and rain washed, wary and hopeful. "Does that make sense?" she asks.

"I think so. I'm not saying it's the same, but it reminds me a bit of when I spiral into old places from the bullied years. Telling myself I don't fit, that I can't get it right, that I'm not good enough because I'm not a 'normal dude.'"

"What do you do when that happens?"

"Sometimes I call Ryder and just let him make me laugh. Other times, I reread a book that was the escape I needed at a critical moment in my past, that made me feel like I belonged. Most often, I just count down the minutes until I see you again. Because you, Frankie, have always made me happy. You have always made me feel like I'm exactly who I'm supposed to be, that it's good."

She sniffles. "How? I've always been so surly."

I laugh. "Maybe that was why. You were the nicest surly grump I'd ever met. You cared. You seemed like you at least picked up on those parts of me that I tried to minimize. Like the parts that I felt made me weird were actually the parts you liked best."

"Ren," she says, cupping my cheek. "You are weird." We both break down laughing as she strokes my beard and steals a kiss. "And so am I. But not everyone has to love us, just the people who matter. That's what I told you, but you *showed* me: be yourself, and let those who are lucky enough to love you, love you for who you are."

I wrap my arms around her, kiss her hair, her temple, her cheek. My lips find the corner of her mouth as she tips her head to meet my kiss. Slipping my hand around her back, I hold her close. "I love you." I tap her bum and squeeze. "So much."

She grins up at me. "And you love my butt."

"It's only fair. You love mine."

Sighing, she kisses me, nuzzles my nose. "This cabin's cozy. Let's move here."

"I don't think so. You'd never leave. You'd wall up the windows with books and make Uber Eats use a four-wheeler to bring us Chinese."

"That sounds like a brilliant existence."

I smile down at her. "Where you go, I'll go. I didn't take you for a drafty Pacific Northwest girl, but . . ."

As if only by the power of suggestion, she shivers, her nipples hardening in the cold. It makes parts of *me* harden, too. I stare at her, tenderly cupping her breasts.

"Excuse me. Eyes up, Zenzero."

I don't glance up. I kiss each nipple, swirl my tongue and lick until they're stiff peaks and her breath comes shorter, faster. "What?" I ask.

"I—" She sighs, pulling me over top of her, taking my aching hard-on in her grip, rolling her thumb over the exquisitely sensitive tip. "I forget. I was going to argue about something, but this is much more enjoyable."

"Frankie," I whisper. Easing inside her, I hold her close.

"Ren," she breathes against my skin.

My mouth finds hers, as I taste and savor and tease. As my hips roll, each stroke steady and reverent. My hands find the soft swell of her breasts, the velvet between her legs. My fingers sweep over her as her hands claim my shoulders, then neck, as she sighs, quiet cries that grow in desperation.

The room is a haze of firelight and candle glow. Smoky air and sweat and soft blankets tumbling to the floor. Her hands hold mine and tangle our fingers. Glorious, tortured need, sharp demand, course through my body.

I call her name, pressing my body deep inside her. Frankie

clasps me close and writhes beneath me, as the waves of her release catch me in their power and take me with them.

On a gasp for air, I turn her with me, our bodies close, our hearts closer. I kiss her hair, look into her eyes. And I stare at Frankie for long, quiet moments, memorizing firelight on her skin, the way flames dance in her eyes, which watch me intently.

I push up on my elbows, carefully separating myself from her. "I'll be right back."

"Where are you going?" Her hand trails down my chest. Her voice is tentative.

"You'll see." Giving her a kiss, I smile down at her. I was going to wait, but if this experience has taught me anything, it's that the only right time to tell someone what they mean to you is the moment you know it. No more waiting. No more partial truths.

I sit up and hurdle the sofa, strolling down the hall until I find my jeans in a pile near the bathroom. Yanking out my wallet, I extract the paper and toss my wallet aside.

Frankie watches me reenter the great room, arms behind her head, a wide smile on her face. "I think you should slow down probably," she says. "The floors seem slippery. You, rushing, naked, lit only by a fire . . . It seems dangerous."

I grin at her, freezing for just a moment to let her feast her eyes, before I run at the sofa, stopping myself enough to gently land back on the couch with a flop.

She sighs. "One day I'll turn you into an exhibitionist for me."

"Here." Pressing a kiss to her temple, I offer her the fortune cookie paper, pinched between two fingers. "You do the honors."

Frankie unfolds the paper, spins it around, and stares at it, then reads quietly, "'Your love is the one you look upon.' Oh, Ren," she whispers, throwing her arm around me and kissing my neck. "This is insanely sweet. And thank goodness you weren't 'looking upon' the wonton soup when you read it."

I laugh as I kiss her back. "I'm so glad it was you instead."

"You didn't really love me at first sight," she says skeptically. "That doesn't exist."

"I don't know, buttercup. You walked through the door on my first day, and my heart kicked in my chest. Knocked the wind right out of me."

"Hmm. Well, for my part, I realized I liked you when I bumped into that fabulous naked chest."

"Francesca." I growl softly against her neck and nip it.

"Okay. It was when you were doing shirtless push-ups."

Pressing her into the sofa and sliding down the blanket, I settle between her legs. "Gumdrop, you're taunting me."

"Doodlebug." Frankie slides her arms down my back. "I'm going to be real honest and confess the first thing I liked about you *was* your butt, but only because you'd passed me while my head was down, walking into the meeting room, so I only caught the back half of you." She gives the backside in question an affectionate squeeze.

"But then I walked in and saw this copper hair, those wintry eyes." She sighs. "And I thought, 'Well, damn. He's off-limits, Frankie. So *fuhgeddahoudit*.'

"Don't notice the way he listens attentively. Don't fall for how gentle he is, how hard he works. Don't feel yourself falling deeper when you see him demonstrate that strength lies not in an assertion of power but in acts of service. Don't love him when he reads children's books and tears up or holds your friend's baby like he was *made* to hold babies. Definitely don't give him your heart when he dances with you by the shore and makes you feel like you're light on your feet."

She smiles up from underneath me, her hands gentling my face. "Don't fall in love with him when he touches you. When he makes you feel from a place in your heart that you didn't know existed. All that ridiculous naysaying, and I still never stood a chance."

Her hand rests over my heart as I hold her eyes. "Francesca?"

"Yes, Søren."

"I love you. Always."

"Always," she whispers, and seals her words with a kiss.

Ren

Playlist: "Halo," Vitamin String Quartet

Three years later

In the past three years, Francesca Zeferino has developed the devastating habit of surprising me with unexpected, sweet, romantic gestures that have me falling even more in love with her, which just shouldn't be possible. I already love her more than I ever knew I could love someone, more than I ever thought possible. And yet, as we sit on a balmy August night in Griffith Park for a performance of Shakespeare's *Romeo and Juliet*, wearing ridiculous disguises, I know, somehow, I love her more than I ever have.

Riveted on the performance, Frankie holds my hand, fingers tangled tight, tighter than I ever grip hers, never wanting to cause her pain, to inadvertently squeeze too hard and hurt her tender joints with my big, rough hands. Wearing rose-tinted wire-rim glasses, a shoulder-length auburn wig beneath a garishly bright orange beanie that clashes spectacularly with the wig, she leans into me, head on my shoulder, gaze fixed on the stage.

I should be staring at the stage, too—it's the most intense, powerful moment of the play, when Juliet unearths from the sheath at Romeo's hip the dagger to end her life, having realized Romeo, her love, her husband, is dead, having killed himself because of a cruel twist of fate that kept him from learning Juliet wasn't actually dead, only faking her death so she could escape her life and they could be together, to live free of their families' disapproval, which has torn them apart.

Shakespeare's tragedies aren't my favorite, simply because I'm a sensitive soul, and sad endings cling to me, linger in my heart longer than I'd like. But Frankie surprised me with this—an early birthday present before the hockey season kicks off and Shakespeare in the Park summer performances come to an end. I couldn't say no.

I peer in concern at Frankie as she watches Juliet weeping, bringing the dagger to her heart. Eyes tight, a tear streaking down her cheek, Frankie sniffles, dabs her nose with the back of her free hand. My heart aches. I hate it when she cries. Gently, I reach for the tear sliding down to her jaw and thumb it away.

Frankie glances up at me, no disguise good enough to hide that gorgeous face I know so well. Wide, dramatic hazel eyes framed by thick, dark lashes. The lone, deep dimple in her left cheek that appears as her eyes search mine and a smile breaks across her face. I was already grateful for the dark brown shaggy wig I'm wearing, the matching fake goatee that feels funny against my freshly shaven face, and the black ball cap tugged low, granting me anonymity. But now I'm even more thankful for this disguise—it's made her smile, brought her joy when she was sad.

And now I'm smiling, too.

We must look like total weirdos, smiling wide at each other during the play's most heartbreaking moment, eyes crinkled as we try not to laugh at how ridiculous we both look, but, thanks to the very thing making us grin like goofballs, no one's looked at us twice, and they're not looking at us now. I've sat in the park and watched Shakespeare on a warm, breezy summer night with my girlfriend, hand in hand under the stars, just like I've wanted to, no prying eyes, no covert photos being taken, no fans apologizing while still asking for autographs or pictures with me.

First, her homemade pasta on the back deck; now, a beautiful night of Shakespeare in the Park, hand in hand, shoulder to shoulder, no practices, no publicity, not a damn thing on my to-do list but her. Now this—staring into her eyes, feeling how much she loves me, how much I love her.

It's been the perfect night. Right now, this moment, is perfect. Even if its backdrop is the bleak, heart-aching end of a tragedy.

For never was a story of more woe, than this of Juliet and her Romeo.

After the prince's line ends and his voice falls silent, applause erupts, lights on the stage in the park brighten, and the cast pours onto the stage and joins hands.

We stare at each other as the applause builds, no eyes on us, just how I want it. Our heads lean in, gazes locked. Frankie softly drags her knuckles along my jaw, her finger across my bottom lip. I cup her neck and bend closer, brush noses, before I press my mouth softly to hers.

God, kissing her. It's this intoxicating cocktail of familiar and comforting, fresh and captivating. My hand slides up her neck, my fingers seeking their place, tangled in her long, dark hair, but I'm met with the edges of her wig instead. A frustrated growl rumbles in my throat.

Frankie smiles against my kiss, then laughs softly, a puff of warm air gusting across my skin.

"What's so funny?" I ask.

Hand still cupping my face, she turns my head gently, then speaks against my ear, making me shiver. "The goatee. It feels weird." Another burst of soft laughter makes her breath dance over my skin, makes every hair on my body stand on end. Frankie didn't use to laugh often or smile much. I still feel a rush, a wild thrill, when, even indirectly, I elicit those responses from her.

Smiling, too, I clasp her jaw and turn her head, leaning in to whisper against her ear, "I have a beard most of the year, Francesca. How are you not used to that feeling?"

She shakes her head, pulling back to meet my gaze, smiling, her eyes bright as they search mine. "It's just different," she says. I read her lips, because her voice is almost inaudible in the noise of the audience's applause and the production's closing string music, which has a punk edge, a nod to the performance's anachronistic choices, seamlessly weaving old and new, Renaissance garb, architecture, and music, with modern-day parallels.

The crowd starts to disperse—blankets folded, chairs collapsed, bags slung on shoulders, grass brushed off knees. Conversation thickens the air as people talk and laugh, animated, charged by that infectious energy unique to watching live theater, to being a part of a singular, flesh-and-blood, unrepeatable performance, as paradoxically real as it is unreal.

The night feels magical, hazy at the edges, darkness deepening around us. I want to take that magic with us, the rest of the world to stay hazy and far away. I want to drive her home with the windows down and watch her hair whip in the wind, until where it ends and the summer night's darkness begins is indistinguishable. I want to lay her down and slide in deep and feel her, tight and hot around me, her fingers raking up my back. I want to hear that rough edge in her voice as I touch her, please her, in all the ways I've learned with only her, for only her.

Frankie arches an eyebrow and taps my cheekbone, which is hot with a blush. Her smile deepens. "You're thinking filthy thoughts, Søren Bergman. I can tell."

My eyes narrow playfully. I turn my face enough to plant a kiss in her palm. "Stop perceiving me."

She snorts a laugh. "Too late. Your face is bright red, naughty plans are written all over it. Not that I'm complaining. This was *my* plan from the start, to get in your pants. Butter you up with home-made Italian, take you to see Shakespeare, get you all horny-sad—"

"I'm not horny-sad!" I say indignantly.

Frankie's eyebrow arches higher. "You're a bad liar, Zenzero."

"Okay, I am a little horny-sad."

"See," she says, triumph and gloating rich in her voice. "I knew it, I knew—*oh*."

I feel my own gloating triumph as I press a kiss to her neck and her voice dies off. I smile against her skin, hearing her breath hitch, loving how sensitive she is there, loving that I *know* how sensitive she is there. "I am horny-sad. And I need you to make it better, Francesca. I like my happy endings, you know that."

"Oh, I'll give you a happy ending, all right," she says breathily, clasping my jaw, lifting my face, and kissing me deeply. Her hand slides up my thigh, higher, higher, and stops *just* south of where I'm already well on my way to being hard, so undone by her, the feel of her mouth on mine, the smoky timbre of her voice, her familiar flowery scent that seems even sultrier in the warmth of a summer night.

"Let's go, then," I mutter against her kiss, pulling away, starting to stand, but Frankie grips my hand hard, stopping me. I frown down at her, which isn't something I generally do, but right now she has me thoroughly confused. Why is she hitting the brakes?

Frankie's expression morphs from that confident, sexy flirtation she's always wielded effortlessly with me, ever since she finally said yes to dating me. Now she looks a bit unsteady, a little unsure, and uncharacteristically emotional.

I sink back down to our blanket. "What is it, gumdrop?"

Not even that earns a smile, not really. I get a sad little half grin tugging up at the left side of her mouth, revealing only a fleeting flash of her dimple.

"I just, uh . . ." She clears her throat and glances around, then back to me. "Just want to wait out the crowd, you know? I'm moving kinda slow today. Getting knocked around by a bunch of spry people my age makes me cranky when it's a slow day for me. I don't want to get grumpy."

I lean in, my heart tugging. I wrap her hand in mine. "I'll never let you get knocked around. You know that."

She bites her lip. Her eyes look a little wet, like she's about to cry. "Yeah." It comes out thin and hoarse. "I know, Zenzero. But some nights I don't want my boyfriend doubling as my bodyguard. I just want to hold your hand and have all your attention on me instead of focused on protecting me from people trying to knock my legs out from underneath me."

Frankie slides her hand against mine, palm to palm. Nostalgia washes over me, the memory of a night at a hotel while on the road during the season, when she checked up on me after I'd been hurt, when she comforted me, when she indulged my nerdy Shakespeare nonsense in my headachy, fuzzy state. In fact, it was this very play, *Romeo and Juliet*, that we talked about.

Palm to palm is holy palmers' kiss.

I stare at her hand, gliding my hand with hers. "Of course, I understand," I tell her, holding her eyes. "We'll wait to leave."

Her eyes search mine. "You don't mind?"

I smile, shaking my head, feeling love fill and spill through me, beyond me, so powerful, so real it's as if it saturates the air, wraps us up, as real as the warm breeze, the fireflies and starlight flickering around us. "I told you once, and I'll tell you again, Francesca, I'd wait lifetimes for you. You'd always be worth it."

She bites her lip. "You schmuck. You beautiful, perfect schmuck. You're stealing my thunder."

My brow wrinkles as I frown again in confusion. "What thunder?"

She wipes at the corner of her eye beneath the silly rose-colored glasses, then tugs them off, tossing them onto the blanket. There's no one left nearby now, just lingering techies breaking down parts of the set that I imagine need to be stored safely, crew members packing up equipment.

I watch her yank off the beanie next, then the wig, piled up beside the glasses.

I follow suit, gently peeling off the goatee, which has started to itch, the ball cap, and the wig, which has made my head sweat. I shake out my hair, raking my fingers through its strands, damp at the roots.

"Søren, please," Frankie says, gently swatting my wrist. "Not in public. You'll make the crew members faint with that kind of show."

I roll my eyes. "Nobody's as taken by my red hair as you are, Francesca. Particularly when it's sweaty."

She sighs. "You clearly haven't been on hockey TikTok, and that's for the best. Now, c'mon."

I gather our disguises and sweep them into the canvas bag we brought, where I stashed water bottles for us, Frankie's beloved root beer gummies, and a container of my favorite cookies Viggo bakes, *vaniljkakor*, Swedish vanilla thumbprint cookies with jam in the middle. Then I stand, slinging the bag onto my shoulder, offering Frankie my hand. She takes it, grips her cane in the other, and stands, too, leveraging the cane when she straightens.

Our eyes meet, and I frown at her in concern. She still looks like something's upsetting her, like something's wrong.

"Let me take you home," I tell her, gently guiding her hand with mine, toward where our car is parked in an accessible spot.

Frankie tugs back, shaking her head. "Not yet."

I turn, facing her fully. "Frankie, what's—"

"I want you to see the stage," she blurts. "Come on."

"I don't think we're allowed to just walk onto the stage—"

"Søren, please don't act like you aren't dying to poke around the set."

I blush. "I mean . . . I wouldn't exactly *mind*, but we'd need to ask permission. And I don't want to make you wait around while I dork out on a Shakespeare set."

She stands, hand wrapped around mine, and gives me a look so intense, so piercing. "That waiting-lifetimes thing," she says quietly, seriously. "It goes both ways. I would stand there and watch you nerd out on that stage, watch you, gleeful, giddy, dorky to your heart's content, as long as you wanted. So don't do that. Don't make this one-sided, understand?"

I swallow roughly. "Okay."

She nods. "Okay. Now, come on."

"Are you sure we can go up there?" I ask as we start in the direction of the stage, then up the stairs leading to it.

"Zenzero, of course we can. I told them we were coming and you'd want to look around. They were all about it. As a token of my thanks, I said we'd take a selfie of us on the stage, share how much we enjoyed the show. We'll post a few days from now so no one knows when we were here."

"Smart woman."

"It's like social media was my job for years or something," she quips dryly, cane tapping as she crosses the stage, peering up at the elaborate wires strung across the stage, bearing the bulbs they used to illuminate the show, to cast a romantic glow on the star-crossed lovers as they danced and kissed and fell in love, the fine netting that held flower petals until they drifted down over them as they promised themselves to each other in a church made of trees and starlight, hopes and dreams that would ultimately die with them.

For minutes, Frankie indulges me as I tentatively, then more confidently, explore the set, the beautiful blend of Renaissance architecture colored by modern murals, graffiti art, the stage floor painted to look like ancient cobblestones marred by modern detritus, flowers blooming up among the litter.

"Happy?" she asks.

I turn, smiling at her. "Very."

She smiles, too, but it's a little wobbly, a bit unsteady. "Good."

"Love button. What's wrong?" I take a step toward her, an instinct, concern drawing me nearer.

"Wait." She stares at me, gaze holding mine. "Actually, never mind. If you could come here, that would be wonderful."

Uneasy, worried, I cross the stage quickly toward her. "Frankie, what's wrong—"

"I know you don't love tragedies," she blurts, stopping me. A few feet remain between us, but slowly, she starts toward me, closing the distance. "I know they make you sad. And I never want you to be sad. But . . . it felt right. It felt like the right time."

"Right time for what?" I ask.

Suddenly the twinkly lights flicker on above us. I startle at that but don't glance away from her. I'm too focused on Frankie as she swallows roughly, first our fingers brushing, then her hand wrapping around mine. It's shaking.

Worry fills me. "Frankie—"

"Ren," she says, silencing me, her gaze piercing, unwavering, demanding my full attention. "I'm okay. I promise. I'm just . . . fucking loaded up with adrenaline. My hands are going to shake."

"Adrenaline? I don't understand."

"I brought you here," she says, her voice uneven, her hand clutching mine, "to see a love story that ends tragically because I think it's a damn important thing to remember, that it happens. That not all love stories end happily. We have to tear off the rose-colored glasses and see life for what it is—mercurial, unpredictable, sometimes violent and sad and bleak, nothing promised to us.

"Because happy endings don't always come our way, but when they do, we don't fuck around with them, don't take them for granted." Her hand clasps mine so tight, my knuckles knock together. "We grip those happy endings with two hands, and we don't let go. You, Ren . . . you're my happy ending."

My heart starts to pound. "You're mine."

"I know," she whispers, smiling despite the tears pooling in her eyes. "I know I am. Somehow, some way, I got lucky enough that you love me as much as I love you, that our love keeps getting bigger and richer and more beautiful."

I bite my cheek, trying damn hard not to lose it and burst into tears. Why is she saying this? What does this mean?

Frankie steps even closer, her eyes fastened on mine. "Somehow, Søren Isak Bergman, I love you more every day. I don't understand it, don't know how it's possible, but it is. 'My bounty is as boundless as the sea,'" she says quietly, her voice hoarse, rough at the edges as her gaze holds mine. "'My love as deep. The more I give to thee, the more I have, for both are infinite.'"

A tear spills down my cheek. She's just quoted Juliet's love profession to Romeo.

"I don't have to understand how much I love you to want to love you the rest of my life, Ren." Frankie glides her thumb across my left hand as she holds it, down my fourth finger. Her eyes never leave mine. "I want infinite time to infinitely love you, but all I get is this one life to do it, as best I can, and I want every second I've got. So . . . what I'm getting at, what I'm wondering is . . . if you'll marry me."

Air rushes out of me. "What?" I stare at her, blinking. I'm in shock. I can't believe what's happening. "You're . . ." I shake my head. "Frankie, I was going to take you to Italy, I was going to sweep you off your feet—"

"You've done enough of that," she mutters, fighting her own tears, stepping so close, our chests brush. "In multiple interpretations of that expression. Now it's my turn."

Her hand cups my cheek tenderly, her thumb sweeping over my skin. "Marry me, my sweet, hot-as-hell, tenderhearted, adorkable love," she whispers. "Please?"

I stare at her, nuzzling my cheek into my palm, fighting more tears. "There's nothing I want more."

A smile breaks across that serious, lovely face, warming her eyes. "Really?"

"You knucklehead," I say roughly, dragging her into my arms. She drops her cane with a clatter, throws her arms around my neck, and kisses me so deeply I can't breathe, can't think. All I can do is feel this—her body and mine, our hearts thundering against each other's chests. "You know you're all I've wanted for as long as I've known wanting," I tell her between kisses, between gasps of air. "You know my answer. It's been my answer since the moment I saw you."

Frankie pulls back and holds my eyes, sniffling, blinking away tears. "Still, Søren, a gal likes to hear those words for sure. Even if she's pretty damn hopeful she knows what that answer is."

I shake my head, stunned, giddy, delirious with joy. "My answer is—"

A flurry of flower petals bursts overhead and drifts down, like snow, like starlight. Pure magic.

Frankie lets out a crack of hoarse, smoky laughter.

A deep belly laugh rumbles out of me. "I'm going to hazard a guess that there might have been a late cue."

Frankie puffs air from her cheeks, blowing a petal off her mouth, brushing one away from my nose. "There might have been." Her smile softens, her head tips. "Now . . . before you were interrupted, you were saying?"

I cup her face and kiss her once, softly, slowly. "Yes," I whisper. "A thousand times, yes."

A quiet, happy hum fills her throat. "I like the sound of that word on your lips, Søren."

"Me too," I whisper, my hands sliding down her back. "Now, let's go home, Francesca. I like that word on your lips, too. Time to make you say it for hours."

Her eyebrows lift. A delighted, scandalized laugh jumps out. "Wowy. Hours, huh?"

I sweep her into my arms, bending, picking up her cane and giving it to her. I hitch my fiancée higher in my grip, walking us off the stage. "Hours, days, weeks, months, a lifetime, Francesca. That's a promise."

Frankie

Ren opens the door to the house, practically bouncing on his feet. His joy is infectious. Somehow, even though I'd swear I couldn't possibly be happier, knowing he said yes, knowing he's going to be *my husband*, I am happier, simply for basking in his happiness, his wide, beaming smile, those striking, sparkling pale eyes that meet mine as he shuts the door behind me, then gently presses me against it. Ren cups my neck, sinks his fingers into my hair.

"You asked me to marry you," he whispers.

I nod, smiling. "I did. And you said yes."

"Hell yes, I did."

"Søren." I *tsk*, swatting his big, beautiful ass before giving it an affectionate squeeze. "Listen to that language. I'm rubbing off on you."

He grins. "Don't worry. Those Shakespearean oaths aren't going anywhere."

"Better not be." I push him away gently. "Now, let me go and handle that pup, who's probably chewing her way out of her crate by now."

"Pazza!" he yells, eyes wide. "I have to tell her!"

I wrinkle my nose. "What?"

He's already jogging away, through the great room, down the hall to our bedroom, where we keep Pazza's crate. "Hark, what ho! Pazza, we've got news!"

I cackle a laugh. "You're such a dork!"

Pazza comes bounding down the hall with Ren, who's giving me a teasing glare. "I heard that."

I wrap my arms around him and kiss him, deep and slow. "You *are* a dork. Who I love so much. My big, gorgeous adorkable sweetheart."

"Mm-hmm," he mutters against our kiss, before pulling away, crouching to pet a panting, happy Pazza, who glances between us expectantly, tongue lolling out of her mouth. "Pazza, guess what?" he says.

Her tail thumps the ground as she sits and Ren cups her furry face, scratching behind her ears. "Mommy asked me to marry her, and I said yes!"

Pazza barks happily, putting her paws up on his shoulders before she licks his face.

"Pazza," I say sternly. "Down, you misbehaving canine."

Ren just smiles. "She's happy for us. She's allowed to jump this time."

I roll my eyes, but I'm smiling. Of course I'm smiling. I can't help it, watching them. "Come on," I tell them, snapping my fingers at Pazza, who spins and follows me obediently toward the sliding doors. Ren tugs them open, letting Pazza bound out across the deck, down to the sand to do her business, before she sprints back in, dancing around her little sand-catching mat to wipe her paws clean, like I've taught her.

"Now," I tell my dog—*our* dog—feeding her a treat after she's sat politely, waiting. "Time for you to go lie down. We'll be back. Eventually."

Ren raises his eyebrows. "Where are we going?"

"Upstairs."

He tips his head. "Upstairs?"

"Let's go." I take his hand, guiding Ren with me up the stairs to the second floor, through the sunroom where we often sit and read and cuddle, out onto the second-floor deck Ren's had fancied up as a luxurious, relaxing space for sunbathing privacy. Taking the remote with me that controls the tinted glass railing, I press the button that raises the railing until it's as tall as Ren, hiding us from the world, until all that surrounds us is smoky glass and a starlit sky.

Ren glances around, taking in the space. He watches me as I light the votives strewn across the deck tables and plant pedestals, covering everything except the wide central chaise lounge, which is long enough for Ren to stretch out on without his feet hanging off, backs that recline up and down with the tap of a button.

After I set down the lighter, I walk Ren toward the lounge, gently pushing until the backs of his knees hit it and he sinks down. He eases back on his hands, grinning up at me. "This is awfully romantic, doodlebug."

I shrug, my smile coy. "I figured a little romance couldn't hurt tonight."

His grin widens. "I very much agree."

I drop my cane against the side of the lounge, then reach for my white T-shirt, lifting it over my head. It falls to my side as I reach for my bra behind me, but Ren's there already, springing up, stepping close. His mouth presses to my neck, a soft, lingering kiss, a flick of his tongue. "Let me," he breathes against my skin.

My hands fall away. His fingers deftly unclasp my bra, and with both hands, he drags the sheer white fabric down my arms before he brings his hands back up, over my shoulders, to my neck. "God, you're beautiful," he whispers, hoarse, uneven. His hands are shaking.

I smile as I drift my hands up his torso, beneath his T-shirt, too. Ren raises his arms, letting me drag his pale blue tee over his head, off his body. I kiss his chest, right over his heart, and breathe him in—spicy and clean—the scent an instant aphrodisiac that makes me ache and want so fiercely, I have to swallow a moan as I press my bare chest to his.

Ren groans as I kiss him, as I wrap my arms around his broad, strong back and savor the firm, soft warmth of his skin. "You're beautiful, too," I whisper. "So beautiful."

He grins against my kiss. "I love when you say that."

"I know," I tell him quietly, undoing the button of his jeans, then his fly. He helps me work them off his hips, yanks them down with his briefs all at once. Then he grips the waistband of my black linen joggers, tugging them down alongside my underwear with swift efficiency. We tumble onto the lounge, naked, skin to skin, sighing at the pleasure of our bodies touching. Ren pulls me closer, his tongue sweeping my mouth as his hands squeeze my ass.

I cup his face, drag my fingers through his hair, open my mouth wider, taking our kiss deep, slowing it, savoring him, drinking in this moment.

"You want to marry me," he whispers.

"Course I do," I tell him. "You're all I want."

He sighs as I straddle him, rubbing myself, wet and aching,

against his hard cock, thick and hot beneath me. Ever considerate, always sweet, he reaches for a couple pillows on the lounge and wedges them beneath my knees.

I smile against tears, moving over him, working myself against him, watching his eyes grow hazy, his mouth lift in a sexy smile. "Like this, huh?" he asks.

"Definitely like this," Heat pools low in my belly as I feel him get even harder, as my clit throbs with each stroke of his cock's tip against it. "That is, if you're okay with it."

"Very, very okay," he says tightly as I trace his nipples with my fingertips, then gently rake my nails down his torso.

His hands drift up my waist, until he cups my breasts and caresses them—loving, tender touches, a delicious contrast to the sharp flicks of his thumbs over my nipples that make me gasp with pleasure.

"Please, Frankie," he says roughly as I move against him, bringing us both closer and closer. His hips nudge up beneath mine. "Let me be inside you."

I nod quickly, so close to coming already as I lift up my hips. Ren grips the base of his cock and guides himself inside me, throwing back his head as he first enters me, but it's only a second before he drops his head and his eyes find mine. He watches me, his hands on my hips as I work myself down on him, feeling so full, stretched, so blissfully connected to him.

"Ride me, Frankie," he says roughly. "Hard."

I bite my lip as I seat him fully inside me, a sweet aching heat pulsing through me as I watch him gasp, feel his grip tighten, then slide up to my waist. "Shit," he groans as I start to rock my hips. "Oh, shit, Frankie, this isn't going to last long."

"No," I pant, as I feel my release clambering at the edges of my body already, coursing deeper, straight to where we move together, where I feel every stroke of his cock inside me hitting that perfect place, deep—so deep. "No, it's not."

"I'll make it up to you," he groans. "Next round. It'll be hours. Days—"

I laugh. "Stop it. I love this, just how it is."

He laughs, too, but it breaks into another moan as I move faster. Ren sits up straight from where he's been reclining on the lounge, wraps his arms tight around me. Our noses brush, our mouths meet in a harsh, teeth-clacking kiss. Tongues chase and tease, mouths wet, panting breaths.

"Don't stop," he begs. "Oh God, don't stop—"

"Never," I whisper brokenly, clutching at his hair, his shoulders, hips grinding fast and hard with him. "I'll never stop."

A grunt leaves him, a jerk of his hips, as he tries to stave off release. He pins our hips together, rubbing my clit to his pelvis. I kiss him messily, wildly, panting against his mouth. "Ren," I plead, my eyes starting to fall shut. "Oh, fuck, Ren, that's it, just like that—" I tear open my eyes as the first wave of my release crashes through me. "Come on, baby," I tell him, "come with me."

Holding my eyes, watching me, Ren nudges his hips up, first a gentle thrust, one, then another, before he fucks up into me in earnest, a big, aching breath heaving from his chest as he calls my name, as he grips me fiercely. He pants, harsh and fast, his hands shaking, legs trembling beneath me as he clutches my body, as he shouts rough and loud and spills long, hot juts inside me.

I work him with my hips, give everything I can as he rocks into me again and again, his gaze never leaving mine.

Finally his eyes squeeze shut, and he sucks in a sharp, quick breath. His sign, like mine, that he can't take another second of it. I bring my body to a stop, breathing fast and shallow. He's breathing like that, too.

For a moment we lie collapsed onto each other, panting for air, wrapped by the sultry night breeze, the distant, incessant roar of the ocean, a blanket of stars canopied above us. Then, carefully, I lift my hips, savoring the pleasure-pain sound that rolls up Ren's throat as I ease my body from his and tumble beside him on the lounge.

Ren paws around clumsily for the remote, pushes the button that sends the back of the lounge reclining, drifting down until we lie flat, side by side, facing each other, wandering hands, a blanket tugged up, feet brushing as our legs tangle.

Ren brings a hand to my face and gently brushes away the fine hairs stuck to my sweaty, tearstained cheeks. "Thank you," he whispers.

I tip my head, searching his gaze. "For what?"

His smile is soft and tender, so perfectly him. "For giving me my happy ending."

I wiggle my eyebrows. "You're very welcome."

He swats my butt gently. "Not *that* happy ending, sweet pea, though it was fantastic."

"It was, Zenzero," I murmur, leaning in for a kiss. "It really was."

Ren kisses me back, then pulls away and strokes my cheek, his eyes holding mine. An even wider smile breaks across his face. "I get to tell *everyone* we're engaged. I get to buy you an outlandishly elegant ring. A rock the size of Texas."

I smack him on the shoulder. "Don't you dare."

"Oh, I dare, snickerdoodle, just try to stop me." He sighs happily, combing my hair with his fingers. "We get to tell my parents. My siblings. Your family. The team. Our friends. They'll all be so happy for us."

I smile. "Yeah, they will."

"What kind of wedding?" he asks as I tuck my head under his chin, cuddling close.

"On the beach," I say simply. "What do you think?"

The beach is our happiest place, a place with beautiful, rich memories not without their bitter fears and pains and heartaches, sweetened, softened by love.

He nods. I can hear the smile in his voice, its wistfulness. "The beach. Perfect."

"You're perfect," I mutter against his chest, before pressing a kiss there.

"Mmm, no," he says softly. "But I am perfect for you."

I smile. Because he's right. Neither of us is perfect. We're weird and odd and we carry our fair share of fears and worries and hang-ups. But we love each other. We see each other. We work hard to make each other feel understood and safe and adored.

"Everything about tonight was perfect," he says quietly, a finger beneath my chin, guiding my face up until my gaze finds his. "Dinner. Shakespeare under the stars. The twinkly lights, the flower petals, even if the cue was late. You made me love a play that's always broken my heart a little bit, that will never make me sad again because I'll always remember what came after I watched it with you. But most importantly . . ." He slides an arm beneath my neck, tucking me close, so close against him. "In a thousand tiny ways, you've shown me the past three years, Frankie, that nothing has to be perfect; that sad, hard moments will come, but what doesn't change is this—us, our love. Thank you. Thank you for loving me, for wanting me."

"You did it first," I whisper, blinking back tears. "Seems like the least I could do." I stroke his cheek and press a kiss to his lips. "I love you."

He smiles against our kiss and nuzzles my nose. "I love you. *We* love each other. We always will."

I nod, my arms tight around him. I hold him as close as I can, heart to heart. "Always."

ACKNOWLEDGMENTS

This book was a uniquely vulnerable story to write. When I first wrote and published it in 2020, I'd known for a while that I wanted to create a main character who was autistic, like me, but I was terrified to put so much of myself into someone on the page. I was terrified—very much like my autistic main character, Frankie—to be seen so deeply and risk rejection and hurt because of that. But, like Frankie, I ultimately realized that while avoiding risk protects me from potential pain, it also prevents me from potential joy.

I'm so glad that my courage won out, that I took this risk and wrote this story.

At the end of the day, Frankie is me in some ways, and in many others, she is not. She's an amalgamation of life experiences and autistic friends and the openheartedness of the autistic community. Special thanks to authenticity reader and fellow autistic, Katie, for her wise feedback; through that I truly believe Frankie, while not encapsulating the totality of autism (no single autistic person ever will!), does justice to the many spectrum girls and women who deserve to be authentically, positively represented. Ren, my sweet, adorable man, is in many ways an aspiration of what men can feel and be when they unpack toxic masculinity and lean into vulnerability. He's the gentlest, sweetest male character I've ever written, and his heart of gold is one of my greatest joys to have ever put to page. I hope he's brought you hope for what men and boys can feel and be, too, when they lean into the power of honoring their emotions and communicating that with those they love.

This story revels in hope for love that can love all of us. It's what we all deserve. It's the kind of love that, when we receive and give it, reshapes hearts and heals old wounds and makes us brave enough to love ourselves and others more openly, more vulnerably, more powerfully.

The Bergman Brothers series, continuing with this book, portrays a big messy family, found family, and friends—imperfect people trying exceptionally hard to love each other well. There are rough patches and plenty of struggles along the way, but ultimately, their love is accepting, affirming, and profoundly safe. Some might say this isn't very realistic. To which I say, I'd like it to be, and this is why I write. As Oscar Wilde said, "Life imitates Art far more than Art imitates Life." I believe stories affirming everyone's worthiness of love and belonging have life-changing power—to touch us, heal us, and deepen our empathy for ourselves and others. Stories have the power to reshape our hearts and minds, our relationships, and ultimately the world we live in.

I hope that, by now, as it has been for me, this Bergman world is a haven for you, reader, where these intimate relationships with oneself and others, platonic, familial, romantic, and beyond, affirm the hope for all of us—that we can be open-minded and open-hearted, curious and not judgmental; that we can welcome and embrace one another, just as we are, and become better, wiser, kinder, for having experienced all that is possible when we do.

Keep reading for a preview of
Freya and Aiden's story,

EVER AFTER ALWAYS

Aiden

Playlist: "Melody Noir," Patrick Watson

The day I met Freya Bergman, I knew I wanted to marry her.

Some mutual friends threw together a pickup soccer game one balmy summer Sunday and invited us both. I'd played in high school, kept up with a recreational soccer league while I went through undergrad. A poor PhD student by that point, I liked the game enough to value the opportunity for fun without a price tag. No awkward outings where I didn't buy an entrée because I'd just paid my rent and emptied my account, no well-meaning buddies insisting—to my humiliation—on treating me. Just a place and time where I could stand tall and feel like I was everyone's equal. A lazy morning under that bright California sun, juggling a ball, goofing off with friends.

But then *she* walked in and goofing off went out the window. Every man on that field froze, backs straight, eyes sharp, and all manner of stupidity vanished as quiet settled over the grass. My eyes scanned the field, then snagged on the tall blonde with a wavy ponytail, wintry blue eyes, and a confident grin tipping her rose-red lips. A shiver rolled down my spine as her cool gaze met mine and her smile vanished.

Then she glanced away.

And I swore to God I'd earn her eyes again if it was the last thing I did.

I watched her trying not to be flashy when she juggled the ball and messed with ridiculous moves that she nailed more than flubbed, how effortlessly she balanced skill and playfulness. I watched her, and all I wanted was closer. More. But when we broke into two sides, I realized with disappointment we'd been placed on separate teams. So I volunteered to defend her, with the arrogant hubris typical of twenty-something men, thinking a guy my size who could still put down some fast miles had a prayer of keeping up with a woman like her.

That was the last time I underestimated Freya.

I all but killed myself on the field, trying to track her fast feet, to anticipate her physicality, to find the same explosive speed when she flew up the sidelines, betraying a fitness I didn't quite match. I remember marveling at the power of her long, muscular legs, which made me daydream about them wrapped around my waist, proving her endurance in a much more enjoyable form of exercise. Already, I knew I wanted her. God, did I want her.

I *may* have been taking defense a bit more intensely than everyone else on that field. I *may* have stuck to her like glue. But Freya radiated the magnetism of someone who knew her worth, and in a flash of desperation, I realized I wanted her to see that I could be worthy, too, that I could keep pace and stick close and never tire of her raw, captivating energy.

In Freya's aura, I forgot every single thing weighing on my mind—money, a job, money, food, money, my mother, oh, and money of course, because there was never enough, and it was an ever-present shadow darkening moments that should be bright. Like the sun ripping a cold, solitary planet into orbit, Freya demanded my presence. *Here. Now.* Just a few dazzling minutes in her gravitational pull and that pervasive darkness dissolved, leaving only her. Beautiful. Bright. Dazzling. I was hooked.

So, in my young male brilliance, I decided to show her my interest by sinking my claws into her shirt, tracking her every move like a bloodhound, and doing anything I could to piss her off.

"God, you're annoying," she muttered. Faking right, she cut left past me and took off.

I caught up to her, set a hand on her waist as she shielded the ball and leaned her long body right against mine. Not romantic, but I remember exactly how it felt when her round ass nestled right in my groin. I felt like an animal, and that was *not* how I worked, at least not before Freya. But she felt right, she smelled right, she *was* right. It was simple as that.

"Don't you have someone else to bother?" she said, even as she glanced over her shoulder and those striking eyes said something entirely different. *Stay. Try. Prove me wrong.*

"Nah," I muttered, my grip tightening in every sense of the word, my desperation for her already too much. Grappling for possession, I met her move for move in a tangle of sweaty limbs and scrappy effort, until finally I won the ball for the briefest moment and did something very stupid. I taunted her.

"Besides," I said, as she came after me. "I'm having fun messing with you."

"Fun, eh?" Freya stole the ball off me too easily, pulled back, and cracked it so hard, straight at my face, she snapped my glasses clean in half.

As soon as I crumpled to the ground, she fell to her knees, brushing shards of the wreckage from my face.

"Shit!" Her hands shook, her finger tracing the bridge of my nose. "I'm *so* sorry. I have a short fuse, and it's like you're hardwired to push every button I have."

I grinned up at her, my eyes watering. "I knew we had a connection."

"I'm really sorry," she whispered, ignoring my line.

"You can make it up to me," I said, with as much Aiden Mac-Cormack panty-melting charm as I could muster. Which was . . . challenging, given I'd just taken a point-blank shot to the face and looked like hell, but if there's one thing I am, it's determined.

Freya knew exactly what I meant. Dropping back on her heels, she arched an eyebrow. "I'm not going on a date with you just to make up for accidentally busting your glasses."

"Um, you intentionally *pulverized* my glasses. And quite possibly my nose." I sat up slowly and leaned on my elbows as the breeze wafted her scent my way—fresh-cut grass and a tall, cool glass of lemonade. I wanted to breathe her in, to run my tongue over every drop of sweat beading her throat, then drag her soft bottom lip between my teeth—to taste her, sweet and tart.

"Just one small kiss." I tapped the bridge of my nose, then winced at the pain, where a bruised cut stung from the impact of my glasses. "Right here."

She palmed my forehead until I flopped back on the grass, then stepped right over me.

"I don't give out kisses, four-eyes," she said over her shoulder. "But I'll buy you an apology beer after this, then we'll see what I'm willing to part with."

To this day, Freya swears she was trying for the goal, which was, ya know, twenty yards to the right of my head, but we both know that's not what happened. The truth is, we both learned a lesson that day:

Aiden can only push so far.

Freya can only take so much.

Before something breaks.

Badly.

ONE

Freya

Playlist: "I Go Crazy," Orla Gartland

I used to sing all the time. In the shower. On road trips. Painting our house. Cooking with Aiden. Because I'm a feeler, and music is a language of emotion.

Then, one week ago, I crawled into bed alone *again*, curled up with my cats, Horseradish and Pickles, and realized I couldn't remember the last time I'd sung. And it just so happened to be when I realized that I was really fucking fed up with my husband. That I had been. For months.

So I kicked him out. And things may have devolved a bit since then.

Hiccupping, I stare at Aiden's closet.

"You still there?" My best friend Mai's voice echoes on speakerphone, where my cell rests on the bed.

"Yep." *Hiccup.* "Still drunkish. Sorry."

"Just no operating any heavy machinery, and you're doing fine."

I hiccup again. "I think there's something wrong with me. I'm so pissed at him that I've fantasized about sticking chocolate pudding in his business shoes—"

"What?" she yells. "Why would you do that?"

"He'd think it's cat shit. Pickles gets diarrhea when she eats my houseplants."

A pause. "You're disturbing sometimes."

"This is true." Coming from a family of seven children, I have some very creative ways to exact revenge. "I definitely have a few wires crossed. I'm thinking about resurrecting some of my most sinister pranks, *and* I'm so horny, I'm staring at his closet, huffing his scent."

Mai sighs sympathetically from my phone. "There's nothing wrong with you. You haven't had a lay in . . . how long, again?"

I grab the bottle of wine sitting on my dresser and take a long swig. "Nine weeks. Four days"—I squint one-eyed at the clock—"twenty-one hours."

She whistles. "Yeah. So, too long. You're sex starved. And just because you're hurt doesn't mean you can't still want him. Marriage is messier and much more complicated than anyone warned us. You can want to rip off his nuts and miss him so bad, it feels like you can't breathe."

Tears swim in my eyes. "I feel like I can't breathe."

"But you can," Mai says gently. "One breath at a time."

"Why don't they warn us?"

"What?"

"Why doesn't anyone tell you how hard marriage is going to be?"

Mai sighs heavily. "Because I'm not sure we'd do it if they did."

Stepping closer to the rack of Aiden's immaculate, wrinkle-free button-ups, I press my nose into the collar of his favorite one.

Winter-skies blue, Freya. The color of your eyes.

I feel a twisty blend of rage and longing as I breathe him in. Ocean water and mint, the warm, familiar scent of his body. I fist the fabric until it crumples and watch it relax when I let go, as if I never even touched it. That's how I feel about my husband lately. Like he walks around our house and I could be a ghost for all it matters. Or maybe he's the ghost.

Maybe we both are.

Slapping a palm on the closet door and slamming it shut, I hit the wine bottle again. One last gulp and it's gone. Freya: 1. Wine: 0.

"Take *that*, alcohol," I tell the bottle, setting it on my dresser with a hollow *thunk*.

"Is he still in Washington?" Mai asks, tiptoeing her way around my tipsy rambling.

I stare at his empty side of the bed. "Yep."

My husband is, at my request, one thousand miles north of me, licking his wounds with my brother and duly freaking out because I put my foot down and told him this shit would not stand. I'm home, with the cats, freaking out, too, because I miss my husband, because I want to throttle this imposter and demand the guy I married come back.

I want Aiden's ocean-blue eyes sparkling as they settle on me. I want his long, hard hugs and no-bullshit musings on life, the kind of pragmatism born of struggle and resilience. I want his tall frame pressing me against the shower tiles, his rough hands wandering my curves. I want his sighs and groans, his dirty talk filling my ears as he fills me with every inch of him.

Distracted with that vivid mental image, I stub my toe on the bedframe.

"Fuckety shit tits!" Flopping onto the mattress, I stare up at the ceiling and try not to cry.

"You okay?" Mai asks. "I mean, I know you're not. But . . . you know what I mean."

"Stubbed my toe," I squeak.

"Aw. Let it out, Frey. Let it *goooo*," she singsongs. "You are, according to my kids, Elsa, Queen of Arendelle, after all."

"But with hips," we say in unison.

I laugh through tears that I furiously wipe away. Crying isn't weak. I know this. Rationally. But I also know the world doesn't reward tears or see emotionality as strength. I'm an empowered, no-nonsense woman who feels *all* her feelings and battles the cultural pressure to contain them, to have my emotional shit in order. Even when all I want to do sometimes is indulge in a teary explosion of hugging my condiment-named cats while cry-singing along to my nineties emo playlist. For example. Like I might have been doing earlier. When I opened and started chugging the wine.

In a world that says feelings like mine are "too much," singing has always helped. In a houseful of mostly stoics who loved my big heart but handled their feelings so differently from me, singing was an outlet for all I felt and couldn't—or wouldn't—hide. That's why, last week, when I realized I'd stopped singing, I got scared. Because that's when I understood how numb I'd become, how dangerously deep I was burying my pain.

"Freya?" Mai says carefully.

"I'm okay," I tell her hoarsely. I wipe my eyes again. "Or . . . I will be. I just wish I knew what to do. Aiden said, whatever it was, he wanted to fix it, but how do you fix something when you don't even know what's broken? Or when it feels so broken you don't even recognize it anymore? How can he make that promise when he acts like he has no fucking clue why I'm feeling this way?"

Horseradish, ever the empath, senses my upset and jumps onto the bed, meowing loudly, then kneading my boob, which hurts. I shove him away gently, until he moves to my stomach, which feels better. I have cramps like a bitch. Pickles is slower on the uptick but finally jumps and joins her brother, then begins licking my face.

"I don't know, Frey," Mai says. "But what I do know is, you have to talk to him. I understand why you're hurt, why the last thing you want to do is be the initiator when he's been so withdrawn, but you're not going to get answers if you don't talk." She hesitates a beat, then says, "Marriage counseling would be wise to try. If you're willing… if you choose to. You'll have to decide if you want to, even if you think it's too far gone."

And that's when the tears come, no matter how fast I wipe them away. Because I don't know if I have anything left to choose with. I'm scared we *are* too far gone. Crying so hard my throat burns, I feel each jagged sob like it's breaking open my chest.

Because the past six months, I've witnessed the core of my marriage dissolving, and now I don't know how to build it back. Because at some point, critical damage is done, and there's no returning to what it was before. In the human body, it's called "irreversible atrophy." As a physical therapist, I'm no stranger to it, even though I fight it as much as I can, working my patients until they're sweating and crying and cussing me out.

It's not my favorite part of the job, when they hit their low point, shaking and exhausted and spent, but the truth is, that's good pain—pain that precedes healing. Otherwise, muscles that go unchallenged shrink, bones left untested become brittle. Use it or lose it. There are a thousand variations on the fundamental truth of Newton's third law: for every action there is an equal and opposite reaction. The less you demand of something, the less it gives back, the weaker it becomes, until one day it's a shadow of itself.

"I'm so tired of crying," I tell Mai through the lump in my throat.

"I know, Frey," she says softly.

"I'm so mad at him," I growl through the tears.

Six months of slow, silent decline. It wasn't one big, awful argument. It was a thousand quiet moments that added up until I realized I didn't recognize him or us or, shit, even me.

"You're allowed to be," Mai says. "You're hurting. And you stood up for yourself. That's important. That's big."

"I did. I stood up for myself." I wipe my nose. "And he acted like he had no goddamn clue what was wrong, like nothing was wrong."

"To be fair, a lot of guys are like this," Mai says. "I mean, Pete has gotten better at carrying more of the emotional load of our marriage, but it took time and *work*. You remember two years ago, when I kicked him out?"

"Uh. Yeah. He slept on my sofa."

"That's right. So you're not alone. Guys do this. They mess up, and they're usually clueless at first as to how. Most men aren't taught to introspect on relationships. They're taught to drag race for the girl, then once they have her, to hit cruise control. I mean, not *all* men. But enough of them that there's a precedent."

"Okay, fine, most of them don't tend to introspect. But when things deteriorate like this, how are they happy?"

"I can't say they're *happy*. Complacent, maybe?"

"Complacent," I say, tasting it sour on my tongue. "Fuck that."

"Oh, you know I agree."

There's no way Aiden's happy with this corpse of a marriage, is he? And *complacent*? That's the last word I'd ever use for my husband. Aiden's determined, driven, the most dedicated and hardworking person I've ever met. He doesn't settle for anything. So why would he settle in our marriage? What happened?

Is he content to come home, exchange the same seven lines about our day, shower separately, then go to bed, just to do it all over again? Is he fulfilled by a quick peck on the cheek, satisfied that we haven't had sex in months?

We used to have such fire for each other, such passion. And I know that dims with time, but we went from a blazing roar to a steady, warm glow. I loved that glow. I was happy with it. And then I realized one day it was gone. I was alone. And it was so, so cold.

"This sucks, Mai." I blow my nose and throw the tissue nowhere in particular. I almost wish Aiden were here to cringe at the mess I've turned the house into. I'd watch his left eye start twitching and derive perverse satisfaction from actually eliciting *some* kind of response from him. "This sucks so bad."

"I know, honey. I wish I could fix it. I'd do anything to fix it for you."

Fresh tears streak my cheeks. "I know."

The security system of our Culver City bungalow beeps, telling me someone entered and used the security code.

"Mai, I think he's home. I'm gonna go."

"Okay. Hang in there, Freya. Call anytime."

Sitting up, I dab my eyes. "I will. Thank you. Love you."

"Love you, too."

I tap the button to end our call just as the door shuts quietly. Horseradish and Pickles leap off of me, bounding out of the room and down the hall.

"Should have named them Benedict and Arnold," I mutter. "Traitors. I'm the one who feeds you!"

"Freya?" Aiden calls, followed by a *bang*, a *thud*, then a muttered string of curses. I think I left my sneakers right inside the door, which he must have tripped on.

Oops.

The door clicks behind him. "Freya?" he calls again. "It's me." His voice sounds hoarse.

I swallow a fresh stream of tears and try to wipe my face. After a week, you'd think I'd be ready by now, that I'd know what to say, or how to say it. But my pain feels . . . preverbal, tangled and sharp—a hot barbed-wire knot of emotions, shredding my chest.

Pushing off the mattress, I rush to the attached bathroom and splash my face, hoping a few handfuls of cold water will wash away evidence that I've been crying. Then I glance in the mirror and groan, seeing how I look. My eyes are red-rimmed, which makes my irises appear unnervingly pale. My nose is pink. And my forehead's splotchy. All signs I've had a good cry. Excellent.

Aiden's reflection joins mine in the mirror, and I freeze, like prey who senses the predator's about to pounce. He stands in the threshold of the bathroom, his ocean-blue eyes locked on my face. He has a week-old beard, brown-black like the rest of his hair, that makes him look like a stranger. He's never had facial hair beyond stubble, and I don't know if I like it or hate it. I don't know if I'm glad he's home or miserable.

Silence hangs between us, until a drop of water falls from the faucet with an echoing *plink!*

My gaze travels his body, broad and strong. It feels like that first glimpse of home after a vacation that went just a few days too long. I realize I missed him, that my impulse to turn and throw myself in his arms, to bury my nose in his neck and breathe him in, isn't entirely erased. It's subdued but not gone.

Maybe that's a good sign.

Maybe that scares the shit out of me.

Maybe I'm drunk.

God, my brain hurts. I'm so tired of thinking about this, I don't even know what to think about the fact that some part of me wants to be in Aiden's arms, for him to turn his head and kiss that spot behind my ear, then whisper my name as his hands span my waist. That I want that feeling of coming home, I want him to look into my eyes the way he used to, like he *sees* me, like he understands my heart.

"Y—" My voice cracks with phlegm and tears, before another hiccup sneaks out. I clear my throat. "You're back already."

"Sorry, I . . ." He frowns. "Are you drunk?"

I lift my chin. "Plausibly."

"Possibly, you mean?" His frown deepens. "Freya, are you okay?"

"Yep. Grand. I asked you to leave because I'm in seventh fucking heaven, Aiden."

His expression falters. He drops his bag to the floor, and I try not to watch his bicep bunch, the way his shirt hugs his round shoulder muscles. "I know it hasn't been very long. But the janitor kicked me out of my office."

"You were"—another hiccup wracks me—"sleeping in your office?"

"Frankie showed up at the cabin a few days ago. I wasn't sticking around while she and Ren . . ." He coughs behind a fist. "Made up."

My brother Ren—thirdborn after me, then Axel—has been at the family A-frame cabin in Washington State for a few weeks, nursing a broken heart. I figured if I sent Aiden there, too, they'd at least have some camaraderie. Ren's gentle and sensitive, and he was hurting over the breakup. Of course I'd hoped that Ren's ex, Frankie, would come around, that they would be able to reconcile. But until then, Aiden might be of some comfort to him.

Seems my hope for their happy ending wasn't for nothing, after all.

I smile faintly, picturing my brother's relief, even though in a small, sad corner of my heart, I'm jealous of him. That possibility feels so far for Aiden and me.

"I'm happy for them," I whisper. "That's great."

"Yeah." Aiden stares down at the floor. "I've never seen Ren smiling like that."

Which is saying something. All Ren does is smile. He's a ray of freaking sunshine.

"So," Aiden says. "I came back and made it work, sleeping on the couch in my office, using the gym showers, until the janitor

busted me and kicked me out because they're shampooing the car-
pets. I'm sorry. I'll do my best to give you space. When you're
ready . . . we can talk."

I sniffle, blinking away tears.

"I know you said you're not sure if this can be fixed, Freya,"
Aiden says quietly. "But I'm here to tell you I will do everything I
can to make it right. I promise you that."

Nodding, I glance down at the sink.

After a long silence, he says, "I'll sleep on the couch. Give you
space—"

"Don't." I wipe my nose, dab my eyes. "It's a big bed. We're tall
people, and neither of us is going to sleep well on a couch. Just . . .
sleep on your side, and I'll sleep on mine. We can both wear paja-
mas. We'll get some rest, and in the morning, we can figure out a
good sleeping situation for going forward. Maybe we can find a
cheap bed for the office."

I blink up and catch Aiden's reflection in the mirror, the emotion tightening his face. "Okay."

I leave the bathroom, rushing past him and biting my cheek as
his hand softly brushes my wrist. "Go ahead, have a real shower," I
tell him. "I'll give you some privacy."

I leave him alone in our bathroom, silence hanging between us.

———

Soooo, I might have neglected to grocery shop while Aiden was
gone. There's a head of cauliflower—*ew*—two eggs, and some ques-
tionable apples.

I know myself. I'm good and buzzed, and if I'm going to tiptoe
around my husband and try not to blow a fuse the rest of the evening, I need to eat. Taking down our list of takeout places stuck to
the fridge, I scour the names that are jumping around.

I squint until the letters settle down and decide pizza sounds good. Then again, Aiden's picky about when he wants pizza. I might want to scream-cry at him, but erasing the ritual of making sure he's up for ordering nauseates me. Or maybe that's the bottle of Cab Franc I had on an empty stomach.

Whatever. Doesn't matter. I can be pissed and still be civil. I can ask the guy if he wants a pizza without it signifying all is forgiven and forgotten.

I blame being tipsy and hungry, relying on muscle memory, for why I walk right into the bathroom without considering that my semi-estranged husband is much more than semi-naked in the shower. Just as I'm about to speak, I hear it—his soft, hungry growl. Every hair on my body stands on end.

He exhales roughly, and a quiet, broken sound punctuates his breath, like a cry he's trying to stifle. My heart trips in my chest as I peer around the corner, through the glass door of the shower, and freeze.

Aiden's long body. His back to me. The tight muscles of his ass flexing, the divot of his hips deep and shadowed, droplets of water sliding down. One hand splayed on the tiles while the other is hidden, his arm moving.

My cheeks flush as I realize he's masturbating, something I haven't seen Aiden do in years, when we used to be sexually playful and do fun things like get ourselves off while watching each other, seeing who could last the longest until we were jumping on the other and finishing how we really wanted: together, so deeply connected—

Another low growl punctures the quiet, another broken, swallowed sound, and then, "Freya," he whispers.

A flood of tears crests my eyes. My name on his lips echoes around us.

He calls my name quietly again and again, then drops his forehead to the tiles as he groans. His arm flies, the sound of his cock gliding through his hand faster, wetter.

My body responds obediently, remembering what it's like for every tender, sensitive corner to burn awake, for my hands to run down his back, then lower, to pull him close, as I beg him to give me everything.

Desire and resentment smash inside me, a head-on collision of oppositional emotions. He wants me so badly, he's fucking his hand to my name, but he hasn't even tried to make love to me in months? He wants to fix it, but it's on *me* to talk?

Aiden's movement falters. A deep, wounded growl leaves him as he lifts his hand and slams it against the wall.

"Fuck," he groans. Dropping his forehead to the tiles, he starts banging it rhythmically.

And then . . . the groans become steady, jagged, thick. A sound leaves him that I realize I've never heard. Aiden's . . . crying.

I must make some kind of sound, too, because Aiden's head lifts. He's heard me. Slowly, he glances over his shoulder and meets my gaze. His ocean-blue eyes are as red-rimmed as mine, his jaw hard through his dark beard. The shower's turned his hair black, clumped his long lashes. He looks at me in a way he hasn't in a very long time.

Our eyes hold, and somehow I know we're remembering the same thing. The last time we had sex. Here, in the shower. How it started wildly, like we were clawing, flailing for a grip on who we'd once been, doing just what we used to—playing. I rubbed myself to orgasm beneath the water, he worked himself roughly as I stared him down.

I remember how his eyes fluttered, his arm faltered, and his mouth fell open, as one last rush of air left him. How he spilled across the tiles as his eyes never left mine, like always. Then he dragged me out of the shower, dried me off, and knelt at my feet. I came against his mouth again and again. . . . And then we did it once more, so urgently, we never even got beneath the sheets, like a solar flare, burning out bright. Before it became bleak. And cold. An emptiness that much darker without the startling beauty that had just brightened it.

I wipe away my tears, shattering the moment. Aiden blinks away and steps farther under the water.

"I'm sorry," I mutter, staring at anything but his body. "I didn't mean—"

"It's all right, Freya," he says quietly, shampooing his hair. But I can tell he doesn't mean it. I embarrassed him. Invaded his privacy. Because I guess we need that now. Privacy.

I will my eyes not to stare at him. Not the part of him I know so intimately, not his long legs and powerful quads, whiter at the top, tan from mid-thigh down because the man's a lucky freak of nature who turns golden brown the moment summer comes but has the loveliest alabaster skin in winter. It's more difficult than it should be.

"I came in," I say, steadying my voice, "to ask if you want pizza. I was going to order some because I didn't get groceries."

"I'll go grocery shopping tomorrow."

"Okay. But for tonight, I need to eat, so I'm asking about pizza."

He rinses his hair. "Pizza's fine."

"Fine. Thanks."

I rush out of the bathroom, my heart pounding. And then I feel the salt in my wound—a deepening twinge of cramps that have wracked my stomach all day, the first signs of what I knew was coming but have been dreading all the same: another cycle and no baby. Another twenty-eight days gone with a husband who's barely acknowledged it the past six months since we decided that I'd stop taking the pill. No caring inquiries about how I've felt or if I'm late or what I need. Just another month with a husband who's home from work later and later, who's always on the phone and pauses his calls when I walk into the room. A husband I barely recognize.

I throw the takeout list back on the counter, dial for pizza, and open a fresh bottle of wine. After pouring a fat glass of red, I take a gulp. Then I take another and refill my glass. At this rate, I'll wake up with a nice wine hangover. Tomorrow's going to suck. But my husband came home.

It was going to suck, anyway.

Chloe Liese writes romances reflecting her belief that everyone deserves a love story. Her stories pack a punch of heat, heart, and humor and often feature characters who are neurodivergent, like herself. When not dreaming up her next book, Chloe spends her time wandering in nature, playing soccer, and most happily at home with her family and mischievous cats.

To sign up for Chloe's latest news, new releases, and special offers, please visit her website and subscribe.

VISIT CHLOE LIESE ONLINE

ChloeLiese.com

Chloe_Liese

Chloe_Liese

Chloe_Liese

ChloeLiese

Ready to find
your next great read?

Let us help.

Visit prh.com/nextread

Penguin
Random
House